Ghost Stories

Ghost Stories

CLASSIC TALES OF HORROR AND SUSPENSE

Edited by

LISA MORTON and
LESLIE S. KLINGER

PEGASUS BOOKS
NEW YORK LONDON

GHOST STORIES

Pegasus Books, Ltd.
148 W 37th Street, 13th Floor
New York, NY 10018

First Pegasus Books paperback edition October 2020
First Pegasus Books cloth edition April 2019

Interior design by Maria Fernandez

Library of Congress Cataloging-in-Publication Data is available.

ISBN: 978-1-64313-595-3

10 9 8 7 6 5 4

Printed in the United States of America
Distributed by Simon & Schuster
www.pegasusbooks.com

For our dear departed mentor and friend Rocky Wood,
whose spirit is in good company in these pages

CONTENTS

Introduction

by LISA MORTON
and LESLIE S. KLINGER

"What, after all, except for the fun of the shudder," she reflected,
"would he really care for any of their old ghosts?"
—Edith Wharton, in the short story "Afterward"*

"These things always give me an impression of truth."
—M. R. James, writing about ghost stories
in an 1891 letter to his parents

I n December of 1847, John D. Fox moved his family to a house in Hydesville, New York. Although the house had an odd reputation (the previous tenant had vacated because of mysterious sounds), it wasn't until March of the following year that the family's troubles began. Before long, daughters Kate and Margaret claimed to be communicating with the spirit of a peddler who had been murdered in the house. The communications took the form of rapping noises in answer to questions asked aloud.

---

* When this story first appeared in Century magazine, the quote referred to "the fun of the frisson," but Wharton changed it later in 1910 when it was reprinted in her collection *Tales of Men and Ghosts.*

The Fox sisters (along with a third sister, Leah, who acted as their manager) soon parlayed their rapping skills into celebrity. The young ladies held public séances, underwent "tests," and inspired copycat mediums around the world. By the time the Foxes were debunked, they'd helped to inspire a new religion, Spiritualism, which was popular in both America and Great Britain, that held as its central tenet that the spirits of the dead continued to exist on another plane and could be contacted by human mediums. The Spiritualist movement had no less a figure as its international spokesperson than Sir Arthur Conan Doyle, whose wife Jean was also a medium.

It's no coincidence that the ghost story experienced a rebirth of popularity at about the same time. Both Spiritualism and the acknowledged, fictitious ghost story evolved out of the Enlightenment of the eighteenth century. Prior to that time, ghosts had either been confined to dramatic presentation (going all the way back to the haunted house comedy *Mostellaria*, penned by the Roman playwright Plautus several centuries before the birth of Christ) or tales that were presented as true, including mythological epics like *Gilgamesh* and the *Iliad*.

The first major work of ghostly literature is usually considered to be Horace Walpole's *The Castle of Otranto*. Published in 1764, Walpole's work also inaugurated the Gothic novel, a genre that waxed and waned over the next fifty years. Ghosts were a key ingredient in the great Gothics, even when—as in the works of Ann Radcliffe, the undisputed queen of the Gothics—their manifestations were eventually revealed to be the work of deceitful mortals.

But perhaps the real precursor of the modern short ghost story was the ballad. Ballads were the preferred way of telling stories (at least in the British Isles) up until the nineteenth century, and many of them were ghost stories. Like "Sweet William's Ghost" (sometimes known under the alternate title "Clerk Saunders"), presented below, these ballads and their numerous regional variants still retain a surprising amount of pathos, eeriness, and even a touch of gruesomeness.

As the Enlightenment brought a new belief in reason to Europe, formerly popular superstitions were reconfigured as fairy tales, intended as simple morality tales mainly for children . . . but not always. While the Brothers Grimm were collecting orally-transmitted folktales, eventually published in

1812's *Kinder und Hausmärchen*, other German anthologists found success in updating these old stories for adults. Johann August Apel and Friedrich Laun produced not one, but a remarkable five volumes of their ghost story anthology *Gespensterbuch* between 1811 and 1815. These tales, which, like *The Castle of Otranto*, typically involved aristocratic families enduring melodramatic plot twists in isolated, haunted castles, were translated into French and English. Mary Shelley cited a volume of such stories as the inspiration for her to "think of a story," resulting in the creation of her immortal classic *Frankenstein.*

It wasn't until 1828 that what is generally considered the first modern ghost story appeared: Sir Walter Scott's "The Tapestried Chamber," included in this volume. Although Scott's tale kept certain tropes of the earlier works—the traveler who arrives in the isolated castle, for example—his tale is comparatively succinct and atmospheric, with chilling descriptions that would almost fit into any modern horror tale:

> Upon a face which wore the fixed features of a corpse, were imprinted the traces of the vilest and most hideous passions which had animated her while she lived.

Ghosts found a willing home in the New World, too. When Nathaniel Hawthorne, one of early America's finest writers, turned his attention to uncanny fiction, he finely portrayed a young country still trying to define itself. While his "Young Goodman Brown" exposed the hypocrisy of religious convictions with its tale of a journeyer who stumbles on a witches' sabbat, "The Gray Champion," below, became possibly the first political ghost story, offering up a patriotic defender of freedom (a theme that Arthur Machen would employ a century later in "The Bowmen," also below). A few decades later, the American creator of both the modern horror story—in all its psychological and bloody glory—and the detective story, Edgar Allan

---

* Shelley wrote in the introduction to the 1831 edition of *Frankenstein* that she sought to create "a story to rival those which had excited us to this task. One which would speak to the mysterious fears of our nature, and awaken thrilling horror—one to make the reader dread to look round, to curdle the blood, and quicken the beatings of the heart. If I did not accomplish these things, my ghost story would be unworthy of its name."

Poe, would create what might be the first major story of spirit possession, with the ravishingly romantic and disturbing "Ligeia," found below.

But it took the arrival of Spiritualism to really unleash the ghost story. By the 1870s, Spiritualism had millions of followers in both the United States and the British Isles, spurred on by the works of mystic philosophers like Emanuel Swedenborg, non-fiction books like Catherine Crowe's 1848 *The Night-side of Nature*, and devastating events like the American Civil War that left parents, spouses, and siblings bereft and grieving for lost loved ones. The rise of Spiritualism in the nineteenth century is often thought of as a reaction to the scientific materialism of the Enlightenment, and indeed, even the Spiritualists at the time acknowledged this. As Crowe put it:

> The contemptuous scepticism of the last age is yielding to a more humble spirit of enquiry; and there is a large class of persons amongst the most enlightened of the present, who are beginning to believe, that much which they had been taught to reject as fable, has been, in reality, ill-understood truth. *

Just as wealthy Victorians on both sides of the Atlantic were flocking to séances in hopes of seeing a table levitate or hearing a dead loved one miraculously channeled by an attractive young medium, so at home they consumed ghost stories in the pages of the magazines that had become popular thanks to new printing technologies. Many of the ghost stories in this volume reflected Spiritualist beliefs; in some ("Mrs. Zant and Ghost" by Wilkie Collins, for example), the true horror was a mortal antagonist, while in others (Elizabeth Stuart Phelps's "Since I Died," or Olivia Howard Dunbar's "The Shell of Sense"), the human inability to grasp the cosmos was a source of terror.

Not all of the late-nineteenth-century ghost stories were influenced by Spiritualism, however. The study of folklore was in vogue, thanks to efforts like *Chambers' Book of Days*; ghost stories were traditional Christmas entertainments (not on, as is now the case, Halloween!), and often played on folklore (Charlotte Riddell's marvelously entertaining "The Last of

---

* *The Night-Side of Nature, or Ghosts and Ghost-Seers* (1850).

Squire Ennismore") and urban legend (Dickens' "No. 1 Branch Line: The Signalman"), both reprinted here.

As the nineteenth century headed into the twentieth, Spiritualist mediums were continually debunked, leading to a serious decline in the belief, at least until the Great War again made families yearn to communicate with their dead. This led to authors seeking fresh ways to carry the ghost story forward. Instead of looking toward the past, some ghost stories included here (Ambrose Bierce's unsettling "An Inhabitant of Carcosa," and Frank Stockton's "The Philosophy of Relative Existences") turned to the future; some took a more literary approach (Edith Wharton's chilling "The Lady's Maid's Bell," and "The Real Right Thing," a literary ghost story about a literary ghost, by Henry James); and at least one (Mark Twain's deliciously over-the-top "A Ghost Story") parodied both the genre and the fervent true believer.

The stage was set for a true master of the ghost story, someone both well aware of its history and gifted with a genius for crafting the bone-chilling scene, to refine the essence of the ghost story. That person was M. R. James, whose 1904 collection *Ghost Stories of an Antiquary* became one of the most critically acclaimed and influential ghost story collections of all time. James's ghosts are not the typical flimsy, translucent phantoms of yore, but something altogether stranger and more frightening, as in this description from a vision the protagonist has in "Oh, Whistle and I'll Come to You, My Lad," also found in this volume:

> . . . but now there began to be seen, far up the shore, a little flicker of something light-coloured moving to and fro with great swiftness and irregularity. Rapidly growing larger, it, too, declared itself as a figure in pale, fluttering draperies, ill-defined. There was something about its motion which made Parkins very unwilling to see it at close quarters.

The final story chosen for this volume, Georgia Wood Pangborn's "The Substitute," is well-positioned to point the way for the future of weird fiction: its terrors are subtle and tragic, its prose beautifully rendered. If its overall effect is slightly more hopeful than many of the tales that preceded it, its hope stems from that "impression of truth" that M. R. James was right in suggesting was an essential element of the classic ghost story.

Why do we read ghost stories? To scare ourselves? To rehearse how we would deal with an actual ghost experience? To experience a catharsis of the emotions? To reinforce our desire to know that life does not end with the mortal body's termination? Probably all of the above—but for whatever reason, the ghost story has fascinated humankind since the dawn of time. What follows are, in our humble opinions, some of the very best. So—boo!

—*Lisa Morton*
—*Les Klinger*
Los Angeles, August 2018

Sweet William's Ghost

(A POPULAR BALLAD)

Long before ghosts began to materialize in novels and short stories, they were a popular subject in poetry. The first recorded mention of a ghost in literature is found in an Akkadian version of the epic poem "Gilgamesh, Enkidu and the Nether World" (from about 2000 B.C.E.), in which the hero's late best friend returns in spirit form to tell him about the woes of the afterlife. When eighteenth-century British folklorists began to transcribe local ballads, one of the most popular was "Sweet William's Ghost." Although the ballad has been recorded in many variants, in most it tells the tale of a lady, Margaret, who is visited by the ghost of her true love, usually called William but sometimes "Clark Sanders." He asks for a kiss, but warns her that the kiss would kill her (in one version he tells her that his mouth "has the smell now of the ground"). In some versions she asks William about Heaven and Hell (he tells her of suicides gathered around the Devil's knee); in one, she must release William from his earthly bonds by making a wand of birch and laying it on his breast. The ballad remains popular even in the twenty-first century, when it's still performed by folk musicians.

THERE came a ghost to Margret's door,
With many a grievous groan,
And ay he tirled at the pin,*
But answer made she none.

"Is that my father Philip,
Or is't my brother John?
Or is't my true-love, Willy,
From Scotland new come home?"

"'Tis not thy father Philip,
Nor yet thy brother John;
But 'tis thy true-love, Willy,
From Scotland new come home.

"O sweet Margret, O dear Margret,
I pray thee speak to me;
Give me my faith and troth,† Margret,
As I gave it to thee."

"Thy faith and troth thou's never get,
Nor yet will I thee lend,
Till that thou come within my bower,‡
And kiss my cheek and chin."

"If I should come within thy bower,
I am no earthly man;
And should I kiss thy rosy lips,
Thy days will not be lang.

---

* "tirled at the pin": used a doorknocker

† "troth": a promise

‡ "bower": a lady's boudoir in a medieval castle

"O sweet Margret, O dear Margret,
I pray thee speak to me;
Give me my faith and troth, Margret,
As I gave it to thee."

"Thy faith and troth thou's never get,
Nor yet will I thee lend,
Till you take me to yon kirk,*
And wed me with a ring."

"My bones are buried in yon kirk-yard,
Afar beyond the sea,
And it is but my spirit, Margret,
That's now speaking to thee."

She stretchd out her lilly-white hand,
And, for to do her best,
"Hae, there's your faith and troth, Willy,
God send your soul good rest."

Now she has kilted† her robes of green
A piece below her knee,
And a' the live-lang winter night
The dead corp‡ followed she.

"Is there any room at your head, Willy?
Or any room at your feet?
Or any room at your side, Willy,
Wherein that I may creep?"

---

* "kirk": church

† "kilted": tucked her dress up (so she could easily follow William)

‡ "corp": corpse

"There's no room at my head, Margret,
There's no room at my feet;
There's no room at my side, Margret,
My coffin's made so meet."*

Then up and crew the red, red cock,
And up then crew the gray:
"'Tis time, 'tis time, my dear Margret,
That you were going away."

No more the ghost to Margret said,
But, with a grievous groan,
Evanishd in a cloud of mist,
And left her all alone.

"O stay, my only true-love, stay,"
The constant Margret cry'd;
Wan grew her cheeks, she closd her een,†
Stretchd her soft limbs, and dy'd.

---

* "meet": made to precise measurements

† "een": eyes

The Family Portraits

by JOHANN AUGUST APEL [*]

Johann August Apel (1771–1816) was a German jurist and writer. His short story "Der Freischutz," about a marksman who shoots bullets freed from natural law by the Devil, was based on German folklore and appeared as the first story in an anthology of horror fiction edited by Apel and Friedrich Laun in 1811. The success of the story inspired Johan Friedrich Kind and Carl Maria von Weber to use it as the title and main theme of their popular opera Der Freischutz *(1821). Apel published a few other collections of tales, and two of his stories, including the following, appeared in a collection entitled* Fantasmagoriana. *The other, entitled "The Black Room," has sunk into obscurity, while this tale can claim to be the direct progenitor of the first modern myth,* Frankenstein.

'No longer shall you gaze on't; lest your fancy
May think anon, it moves. ———
The fixture of her eye has motion in't.'

—Winter's Tale

Night had insensibly superseded day, when Ferdinand's carriage continued its slow course through the forest; the postilion* uttering a thousand complaints on the badness of the roads, and Ferdinand employing the leisure which the tedious progress of his carriage allowed, with reflections to which the purpose of his journey gave rise.

As was usual with young men of rank, he had visited several universities; and after having travelled over the principal parts of Europe, he was now returning to his native country to take possession of the property of his father, who had died in his absence.

Ferdinand was an only son, and the last branch of the ancient family of Meltheim: it was on this account that his mother was the more anxious that he should form a brilliant alliance, to which both his birth and fortune entitled him; she frequently repeated that Clotilde of Hainthal was of all others the person she should be most rejoiced to have as a daughter-in-law, and should give to the world an heir to the name and estates of Meltheim. In the first instance, she merely named her amongst other distinguished females whom she recommended to her son's attention: but after a short period she spoke of none but her: and at length declared, rather positively, that all her happiness depended on the completion of this alliance, and hoped her son would approve her choice.

Ferdinand, however, never thought of this union but with regret; and the urgent remonstrances which his mother ceased not to make on the subject, only contributed to render Clotilde, who was an entire stranger to him, less amiable in his eyes: he determined at last to take a journey to the capital, whither Mr. Hainthal and his daughter were attracted by the carnival. He wished at least to know the lady, ere he consented to listen to his mother's entreaties; and secretly flattered himself that he should find some more cogent reasons for opposing this union than mere caprice, which was the appellation the old lady gave to his repugnance.

Whilst travelling in his carriage, as night approached, the solitary forest, his imagination drew a picture of his early life, which happy recollections rendered still happier. It seemed that the future presented no charms for him to equal the past; and the greater pleasure he took in retracing what

---

* The person who rides the front left-hand horse of a pair or more drawing a carriage.

no longer existed, the less wish he felt to bestow a thought on that futurity to which he seemed destined. Thus, notwithstanding the slowness with which his carriage proceeded over the rugged ground, he found that he was too rapidly approaching the termination of his journey.

The postilion at length began to console himself; for one half of the journey was accomplished, and the remainder presented only good roads: Ferdinand, however, gave orders to his groom to stop at the approaching village, determined to pass the night there.

The road through the village which led to the inn was bordered by gardens, and the sound of different musical instruments led Ferdinand to assume that the villagers were celebrating some rural fête. He already anticipated the pleasure of joining them, and hoped that this recreation would dissipate his melancholy thoughts. But on listening more attentively, he remarked that the music did not resemble that usually heard at inns; and the great light he perceived at the window of a pretty house from whence came the sounds that had arrested his attention, did not permit him to doubt that a more select party than are accustomed to reside in the country at that unfavourable season, were amusing themselves in performing a concert.

The carriage now stopped at the door of a small inn of mean appearance. Ferdinand, who counted on much inconvenience and few comforts, asked who was the lord of the village. They informed him that he occupied a château situated in an adjoining hamlet. Our traveller said no more, but was obliged to content himself with the best apartment the landlord could give him. To divert his thoughts, he determined to walk in the village, and directed his steps towards the spot where he had heard the music; to this the harmonious sounds readily guided him: he approached softly, and found himself close to the house where the concert was performing. A young girl, sitting at the door, was playing with a little dog, who began to bark. Ferdinand, drawn from his reverie by this singular accompaniment, begged the little girl to inform him who lived in that house. "It is my father," she replied, smiling; "come in, sir." And saying this, she slowly went up the steps.

Ferdinand hesitated for an instant whether to accept this unceremonious invitation. But the master of the house came down, saying to him in a friendly tone: "Our music, sir, has probably been the only attraction to this spot; no matter, it is the pastor's abode, and to it you are heartily welcome. My neighbours and I," continued he, whilst leading Ferdinand in, "meet alternately at each other's houses once a week, to form a little concert; and to-day it is my turn. Will you take a part in the performance, or only listen to it? Sit down in this apartment. Are you accustomed to hear better music than that performed simply by amateurs? or do you prefer an assemblage where they pass their time in conversation? If you like the latter, go into the adjoining room, where you will find my wife surrounded by a young circle: here is our musical party, there is their conversazióni." Saying this, he opened the door, made a gentle inclination of the head to Ferdinand, and seated himself before his desk. Our traveller would fain have made apologies; but the performers in an instant resumed the piece he had interrupted. At the same time the pastor's wife, a young and pretty woman, entreated Ferdinand, in the most gracious manner possible, entirely to follow his own inclinations, whether they led him to remain with the musicians, or to join the circle assembled in the other apartment. Ferdinand, after uttering some common-place terms of politeness, followed her into the adjoining room.

The chairs formed a semicircle round the sofa, and were occupied by several women and by some men. They all rose on Ferdinand's entering, and appeared a little disconcerted at the interruption. In the middle of the circle was a low chair, on which sat, with her back to the door, a young and sprightly female, who, seeing every one rise, changed her position, and at the sight of a stranger blushed and appeared embarrassed. Ferdinand entreated the company not to interrupt the conversation. They accordingly reseated themselves, and the mistress of the house invited the new guest to take a seat on the sofa by two elderly ladies, and drew her chair near him. "The music," she said to him, "drew you amongst us, and yet in this apartment we have none; I hear it nevertheless with pleasure myself: but I cannot participate in my husband's enthusiasm for simple quartetts and symphonies; several of my friends are of the same way of thinking with me, which is the reason that, while our husbands are occupied with their favourite science, we here enjoy social converse, which sometimes, however, becomes too loud for our virtuoso neighbours. To-day, I give a long-promised tea-drinking. Every one is to relate a story of ghosts, or something of a similar nature. You see that my auditors are more numerous than the band of musicians."

"Permit me, madam," replied Ferdinand, "to add to the number of your auditors; although I have not much talent in explaining the marvellous."

"That will not be any hinderance to you here," answered a very pretty brunette; "for it is agreed amongst us that no one shall search for any explanation, even though it bears the stamp of truth, as explanations would take away all pleasure from ghost stories."

"I shall benefit by your instructions," answered Ferdinand: "but without doubt I interrupt a very interesting recital;—dare I entreat—?"

The young lady with flaxen hair, who rose from the little seat, blushed anew; but the mistress of the house drew her by the arm, and laughing, conducted her to the middle of the circle. "Come, child," said she, "don't make any grimace; reseat yourself, and relate your story. This gentleman will also give us his."

"Do you promise to give us one, sir?" said the young lady to Ferdinand. He replied by a low bow. She then reseated herself in the place destined for the narrator, and thus began:

"One of my youthful friends, named Juliana, passed every summer with her family at her father's estate. The château was situated in a romantic country; high mountains formed a circle in the distance; forests of oak and fine groves surrounded it. It was an ancient edifice, and had descended through a long line of ancestry to Juliana's father; for which reason, instead of making any alterations, he was only anxious to preserve it in the same state they had left it to him.

"Among the number of antiquities most prized by him was the family picture gallery; a vaulted room, dark, high, and of the gothic architecture, where hung the portraits of his forefathers, as large as the natural size, covering the walls, which were blackened by age. Conformable to an immemorial custom, they ate in this room: and Juliana has often told me, that she could not overcome, especially at supper-time, a degree of fear and repugnance; and that she had frequently feigned indisposition, to avoid entering this formidable apartment. Among the portraits there was one of a female, who, it would seem, did not belong to the family; for Juliana's father could neither tell whom it represented, nor how it had become ranged amongst his ancestry: but as to all appearance it had retained its station for ages, my friend's father was unwilling to remove it.

"Juliana never looked at this portrait without an involuntary shuddering: and she has told me, that from her earliest infancy she has felt this secret terror, without being able to define the cause. Her father treated this sentiment as puerile, and compelled her sometimes to remain alone in that room. But as Juliana grew up, the terror this singular portrait occasioned, increased; and she frequently supplicated her father, with tears in her eyes, not to leave her alone in that apartment—'That portrait,' she would say, 'regards me not gloomily or terribly, but with looks full of a mild melancholy. It appears anxious to draw me to it, and as if the lips were about to open and speak to me.—That picture will certainly cause my death.'"

"Juliana's father at length relinquished all hope of conquering his daughter's fears. One night at supper, the terror she felt had thrown her into convulsions, for she fancied she saw the picture move its lips; and the physician enjoined her father in future to remove from her view all similar causes of fear. In consequence, the terrifying portrait was removed from the gallery, and it was placed over the door of an uninhabited room in the attic story.

"Juliana, after this removal, passed two years without experiencing any alarms. Her complexion resumed its brilliancy, which surprised every one; for her continual fears had rendered her pale and wan: but the portrait and the fears it produced had alike disappeared, and Juliana—"

"Well," cried the mistress of the house, smiling, when she perceived that the narrator appeared to hesitate, "confess it, my child; Juliana found an admirer of her beauty;—was it not so?"

"'Tis even so," resumed the young lady, blushing deeply; "she was affianced: and her intended husband coming to see her the day previous to that fixed on for her marriage, she conducted him over the château, and from the attic rooms was shewing him the beautiful prospect which extended to the distant mountains. On a sudden she found herself, without being aware of it, in the room where the unfortunate portrait was placed. And it

---

* Renowned British ghost hunter Peter Underwood (1923–2014) created a taxonomy of ghosts (it originally included eight types, although he later expanded it to ten), one of which is the haunted object. Haunted objects can include portraits, skulls, weapons, parts of structures, or—particularly in America—dolls.

was natural that a stranger, surprised at seeing it there alone, should ask who it represented. To look at it, recognise it, utter a piercing shriek, and run towards the door, were but the work of an instant with poor Juliana. But whether in effect owing to the violence with which she opened the door the picture was shaken, or whether the moment was arrived in which its baneful influence was to be exercised over Juliana, I know not; but at the moment this unfortunate girl was striving to get out of the room and avoid her destiny, the portrait fell; and Juliana, thrown down by her fears, and overpowered by the heavy weight of the picture, never rose more."—

A long silence followed this recital, which was only interrupted by the exclamations of surprise and interest excited for the unfortunate Juliana. Ferdinand alone appeared untouched by the general emotions. At length, one of the ladies sitting near him broke the silence by saying, "This story is literally true; I knew the family where the fatal portrait caused the death of a charming young girl: I have also seen the picture; it has, as the young lady truly observed, an indescribable air of goodness which penetrates the heart, so that I could not bear to look on it long; and yet, as you say, its look is so full of tender melancholy, that it appears that the eyes move and have life."

"In general," resumed the mistress of the house, at the same time shuddering, "I don't like portraits, and I would not have any in the rooms I occupy. They say that they become pale when the original expires; and the more faithful the likeness, the more they remind me of those waxen figures I cannot look at without aversion."

"That is the reason," replied the young person who had related the history, "that I prefer those portraits where the individual is represented occupied in some employment, as then the figure is entirely independent of those who look at it; whereas in a simple portrait the eyes are inanimately fixed on every thing that passes. Such portraits appear to me as contrary to the laws of illusion as painted statues."

"I participate in your opinion," replied Ferdinand; "for the remembrance of a terrible impression produced on my mind when young, by a portrait of that sort, will never be effaced."

"O! pray relate it to us," said the young lady with flaxen hair, who had not as yet quitted the low chair; "you are obliged according to promise to take my place." She instantly arose, and jokingly forced Ferdinand to change seats with her.

"This history," said he, "will resemble a little too much the one you have just related; permit me therefore—"

"That does not signify," resumed the mistress of the house, "one is never weary with recitals of this kind; and the greater repugnance I feel in looking at these horrible portraits, the greater is the pleasure I take in listening to histories of their eyes or feet being seen to move."

"But seriously," replied Ferdinand, who would fain have retracted his promise, "my history is too horrible for so fine an evening. I confess to you that I cannot think of it without shuddering, although several years have elapsed since it happened."

"So much the better, so much the better!" cried nearly all present; "how you excite our curiosity! and its having happened to yourself will afford double pleasure, as we cannot entertain any doubt of the fact."

"It did not happen personally to me," answered Ferdinand, who reflected that he had gone too far, "but to one of my friends, on whose word I have as firm a reliance as if I had been myself a witness to it."

They reiterated their entreaties; and Ferdinand began in these words:— "One day, when I was arguing with the friend of whom I am about to make mention, on apparitions and omens, he told me the following story:—

"'I had been invited,' said he, 'by one of my college companions, to pass my vacations with him at an estate of his father's. The spring was that year unusually late, owing to a long and severe winter, and appeared in consequence more gay and agreeable, which gave additional charms to our projected pleasures. We arrived at his father's in the pleasant month of April, animated by all the gaiety the season inspired.

"'As my companion and I were accustomed to live together at the university, he had recommended to his family, in his letters, so as to arrange matters that we might live together at his father's also: we in consequence occupied two adjoining room, from whence we enjoyed a view of the garden and a fine country, bounded in the distance by forests and vineyards. In a few days I found myself so completely at home in the house, and so familiarised with its inhabitants, that nobody, whether of the family or among the domesticks, made any difference between my friend and myself. His younger brothers, who were absent from me in the day, often passed the night in my room, or in that of their elder brother. Their sister, a charming girl about twelve years of age, lovely and blooming as a newly blown rose, gave me the appellation of brother, and fancied that under this title she was privileged to show me all her favourite haunts in the garden, to gratify my wishes at table, and to furnish my apartment with all that was requisite. Her cares and attention will never be effaced from my recollection; they will long outlive the scenes of horror that château never ceases to recall to my recollection. From the first of my arrival, I had remarked a huge portrait affixed to the wall of an antechamber through which I was obliged to pass to go to my room; but, too much occupied by the new objects which on all sides attracted my attention, I had not particularly examined it. Meanwhile I could not avoid observing that, though the two younger brothers of my friend were so much attached to me, that they would never permit me to go at night into my room without them, yet they always evinced an unaccountable dread in crossing the hall where this picture hung. They clung to me, and embraced me that I might take them in my arms; and whichever I was compelled to take by the hand, invariably covered his face, in order that he might not see the least trace of the portrait.

"'Being aware that the generality of children are afraid of colossal figures, or even of those of a natural height, I endeavoured to give my two young friends courage. However, on more attentively considering the portrait which caused them so much dread, I could not avoid feeling a degree of fear myself. The picture represented a knight in the costume of a very remote period; a full grey mantle descended from his shoulders to his knees; one of his feet placed in the foreground, appeared as if it was starting from the canvass; his countenance had an expression which petrified me with fear. I had never before seen any thing at all like it in nature. It was a frightful mixture of the stillness of death, with the remains of a violent and baneful passion, which not even death itself was able to overcome. One would have thought the artist had copied the terrible features of one risen from the grave, in order to paint this terrific portrait. I was seized with a terror little less than the children, whenever I wished to contemplate this picture. Its aspect was disagreeable to my friend, but did not cause him any terror: his sister was the only one who could look at this hideous figure with a smiling countenance; and said to me with a compassionate air, when I discovered my aversion to it, 'That man is not wicked, but he is certainly very unhappy.' My friend told me that the picture represented the founder of his race, and that his father attached uncommon value to it; it had, in all probability, hung there from time immemorial, and it would not be possible to remove it from this chamber without destroying the regularity of its appearance.

"'Meanwhile, the term of our vacation was speedily drawing to its close, and time insensibly wore away in the pleasures of the country. The old count, who remarked our reluctance to quit him, his amiable family, his château, and the fine country that surrounded it, applied himself with kind and unremitting care, to make the day preceding our departure a continual succession of rustic diversions: each succeeded the other without the slightest appearance of art; they seems of necessity to follow each other. The delight that illumined the eyes of my friend's sister when she perceived her father's satisfaction; the joy that was painted in Emily's countenance (which was the name of this charming girl) when she surprised even her father by her arrangements, which outstripped his projects, led me to discover the entire confidence that existed between the father and daughter, and the active part Emily had taken in directing the order which reigned in that day's festivities.

"'Night arrived; the company in the gardens dispersed; but my amiable companions never quitted my side. The two young boys skipped gaily before us, chasing the may-bug, and shaking the shrubs to make them come out. The dew arose, and aided by the light of the moon formed silver spangles on the flowers and grass. Emily hung on my arm; and an affectionate sister conducted me, as if to take leave, to all the groves and places I had been accustomed to visit with her, or with the family. On arriving at the door of the château, I was obliged to repeat the promise I had made to her father, of passing some weeks in the autumn with him. 'That season,' said she, 'is equally beautiful with the spring!' With what pleasure did I promise to decline all other engagements for this. Emily retired to her apartment, and, according to custom, I went up to mine, accompanied by my two little boys: they ran gaily up the stairs; and in crossing the range of apartments but faintly lighted, to my no small surprise their boisterous mirth was not interrupted by the terrible portrait.

"'For my own part, my head and heart were full of the intended journey, and of the agreeable manner in which my time had passed at the count's château. The images of those happy days crowded on my recollection; my imagination, at that time possessing all the vivacity of youth, was so much agitated, that I could not enjoy the sleep which already overpowered my friend. Emily's image, so interesting by her sprightly grace, by her pure affection for me, was present to my mind like an amiable phantom shining in beauty. I placed myself at the window, to take another look at the country I had so frequently ranged with her, and traced our steps again probably for the last time. I remembered each spot illumined by the pale light the moon afforded. The nightingale was singing in the groves where we had delighted to repose; the little river on which while gaily singing we often sailed, rolled murmuringly her silver waves.

"'Absorbed in a profound reverie, I mentally exclaimed: With the flowers of spring, this soft pure affection will probably fade; and as frequently the after seasons blight the blossoms and destroy the promised fruit, so possibly may the approaching autumn envelop in cold reserve that heart which, at the present moment, appears only to expand with mine!

"'Saddened by these reflections, I withdrew from the window, and overcome by a painful agitation I traversed the adjoining rooms; and on a sudden found myself before the portrait of my friend's ancestor. The moon's beams darted on it in the most singular manner possible, insomuch as to give the appearance of a horrible moving spectre; and the reflexion of the light gave to it the appearance of a real substance about to quit the darkness by which it was surrounded. The inanimation of its features appeared to give place to the most profound melancholy; the sad and glazed look of the eyes appeared the only hinderance to its uttering its grief.

"'My knees tremblingly knocked against each other, and with an unsteady step I regained my chamber: the window still remained open; I reseated myself at it, in order that the freshness of the night air, and the aspect of the beautiful surrounding country, might dissipate the terror I had experienced. My wandering eyes fixed on a long vista of ancient linden trees, which extended from my window to the ruins of an old tower, which had often been the scene of our pleasures and rural fêtes. The remembrance of the hideous portrait had vanished; when on a sudden there appeared to me a thick fog issuing from the ruined tower, which advancing through the vista of lindens came towards me.

"'I regarded this cloud with an anxious curiosity: it approached; but again it was concealed by the thickly-spreading branches of the trees.

"'On a sudden I perceived, in a spot of the avenue less dark than the rest, the same figure represented in the formidable picture, enveloped in the grey mantle I so well knew. It advanced towards the château, as if hesitating: no noise was heard of its footsteps on the pavement; it passed before my window without looking up, and gained a back door which led to the apartments in the colonnade of the château.

"'Seized with trembling apprehension, I darted towards my bed, and saw with pleasure that the two children were fast asleep on either side. The noise I made awoke them; they started, but in an instant were asleep again. The agitation I had endured took from me the power of sleep, and I turned to awake one of the children to talk with me: but no powers can depict the horrors I endured when I saw the frightful figure at the side of the child's bed.

"'I was petrified with horror, and dared neither move nor shut my eyes. I beheld the spectre stoop towards the child and softly kiss his forehead: he then went round the bed, and kissed the forehead of the other boy.*

"'I lost all recollection at that moment; and the following morning, when the children awoke me with their caresses, I was willing to consider the whole as a dream.

"'Meanwhile, the moment for our departure was at hand. We once again breakfasted all together in a grove of lilacs and flowers. "I advise you to take a little more care of yourself," said the old count in the midst of other conversation; "for I last night saw you walking rather late in the garden, in a dress ill suited to the damp air; and I was fearful such imprudence would expose you to cold and fever. Young people are apt to fancy they are invulnerable; but I repeat to you, Take advice from a friend."

---

* The "kiss of death" is a common theme in ghost stories (see, for example, the ballad "Sweet William's Ghost"), and may derive from the condemning kiss Judas gave to Christ.

""In truth," I answered, "I believe readily that I have been attacked by a violent fever, for never before was I so harassed by terrifying visions: I can now conceive how dreams afford to a heated imagination subjects for the most extraordinary stories of apparitions."

""What would you tell me?" demanded the count in a manner not wholly devoid of agitation. I related to him all that I had seen the preceding night; and to my great surprise he appeared to me in no way astonished, but extremely affected.

""You say," added he in a trembling voice, "that the phantom kissed the two children's foreheads?" I answered him, that it was even so. He then exclaimed, in accents of the deepest despair, "Oh heavens! they must then both die!""—

Till now the company had listened without the slightest noise or interruption to Ferdinand: but as he pronounced the last words, the greater part of the audience trembled; and the young lady who had previously occupied the chair on which he sat, uttered a piercing shriek.

"Imagine," continued Ferdinand, "how astonished my friend must have been at this unexpected exclamation. The vision of the night had caused him excess of agitation; but the melancholy voice of the count pierced his heart, and seemed to annihilate his being, by the terrifying conviction of the existence of the spiritual world, and the secret horrors with which this idea was accompanied. It was not then a dream, a chimera, the fruit of an over-heated imagination! but a mysterious and infallible messenger, which, dispatched from the world of spirits, had passed close to him, had placed itself by his couch, and by its fatal kiss had dropt the germ of death in the bosom of the two children.

"He vainly entreated the count to explain this extraordinary event. Equally fruitless were his son's endeavours to obtain from the count the developement of this mystery, which apparently concerned the whole family. 'You are as yet too young,' replied the count: 'too soon, alas! for your peace of mind, will you be informed of these terrible circumstances which you now think mysterious.'

"Just as they came to announce to my friend that all was ready, he recollected that during the recital the count had sent away Emily and her two younger brothers. Deeply agitated, he took leave of the count and the two young children who came towards him, and who would scarcely permit themselves to be separated from him. Emily, who had placed herself at a window, made a sign of adieu. Three days afterwards the young count received news of the death of his two younger brothers. They were both taken off in the same night.

"You see," continued Ferdinand, in a gayer tone, in order to counteract the impression of sadness and melancholy his story had produced on the company; "you see my history is very far from affording any natural explication of the wonders it contains; explanations which only tend to shock one's reason: it does not even make you entirely acquainted with the mysterious person, which one has a right to expect in all marvellous recitals. But I could learn nothing more; and the old count dying without revealing the mystery to his son, I see no other means of terminating the history of the portrait, which is undoubtedly by no means devoid of interest, than by inventing according to one's fancy a dénouement which shall explain all."

"That does not appear at all necessary to me," said a young man: "this history, like the one that preceded it, is in reality finished, and gives all the satisfaction one has any right to expect from recitals of this species."

"I should not agree with you," replied Ferdinand, "if I was capable of explaining the mysterious connection between the portrait and the death of the two children in the same night, or the terror of Juliana at sight of the other portrait, and her death, consequently caused by it. I am, however, not the less obliged to you for the entire satisfaction you evince."

"But," resumed the young man, "what benefit would your imagination receive, if the connections of which you speak were known to you?"

"Very great benefit, without doubt," replied Ferdinand; "for imagination requires the completion of the objects it represents, as much as the judgment requires correctness and accuracy in its ideas."

The mistress of the house, not being partial to these metaphysical disputes, took part with Ferdinand: "We ladies," said she, "are always curious; therefore don't wonder that we complain when a story has no termination. It appears to me like seeing the last scene of Mozart's Don Juan without having witnessed the preceding ones; and I am sure no one would be the better satisfied, although the last scene should possess infinite merit."

The young man remained silent, perhaps less through conviction than politeness. Several persons were preparing to retire; and Ferdinand, who had vainly searched for the young lady with flaxen hair, was already at the door, when an elderly gentleman, whom he remembered to have seen in the music-room, asked him whether the friend concerning whom he had related the story was not called Count Meltheim?

"That is his name," answered Ferdinand a little drily; "how did you guess it?—are you acquainted with his family?"

"You have advanced nothing but the simple truth," resumed the unknown. "where is the count at this moment?"

"He is on his travels," replied Ferdinand. "But I am astonished—"

"Do you correspond with him?" demanded the unknown.

"I do," answered Ferdinand. "But I don't understand—"

"Well then," continued the old man, "tell him that Emily still continues to think of him, and that he must return as speedily as possible, if he takes any interest in a secret that very particularly concerns her family."

On this the old man stepped into his carriage, and had vanished from Ferdinand's sight ere he had recovered from his surprise. He looked around him in vain for some one who might inform him of the name of the unknown: every one was gone; and he was on the point of risking being considered indiscreet, by asking for information of the pastor who had so courteously treated him, when they fastened the door of the house, and he was compelled to return in sadness to his inn, and leave his researches till the morning.

The frightful scenes of the night preceding Ferdinand's departure from the château of his friend's father, had tended to weaken the remembrance of Emily; and the distraction which his journey so immediately after had produced, had not contributed to recall it with any force: but all at once the recollection of Emily darted across his mind with fresh vigour, aided by the recital of the previous evening and the old man's conversation: it presented itself with greater vivacity and strength than at the period of its birth. Ferdinand now fancied that he could trace Emily in the pretty girl with flaxen hair. The more he reflected on her figure, her eyes, the sound of her voice, the grace with which she moved; the more striking the resemblance appeared to him. The piercing shriek that had escaped her, when he mentioned the old count's explication of the phantom's appearance; her sudden disappearance at the termination of the recital; her connection with Ferdinand's family, (for the young lady, in her history of Juliana, had recounted the fatal accident which actually befell Ferdinand's sister,) all gave a degree of certainty to his suppositions.

He passed the night in forming projects and plans, in resolving doubts and difficulties; and Ferdinand impatiently waited for the day which was to enlighten him. He went to the pastor's, whom he found in the midst of his quires of music; and by giving a natural turn to the conversation, he seized the opportunity of enquiring concerning the persons with whom he had passed the preceding evening.

He unfortunately, however, could not get satisfactory answers to his questions concerning the young lady with flaxen hair, and the mysterious old gentleman; for the pastor had been so absorbed in his music, that he had not paid attention to many persons who had visited him: and though Ferdinand in the most minute manner possible described their dress and other particulars, it was impossible to make the pastor comprehend the individuals whose names he was so anxious to learn. "It is unfortunate," said the pastor, "that my wife should be out; she would have given you all the information you desire. But according to your description, it strikes me the young person with flaxen hair must be Mademoiselle de Hainthal;—but—"

"Mademoiselle de Hainthal!" reiterated Ferdinand, somewhat abruptly.

"I think so," replied the clergyman. "Are you acquainted with the young lady?"

"I know her family," answered Ferdinand; "but from her features bearing so strong a resemblance to the family, I thought it might have been the young countess of Wartbourg, who was so much like her brother."

"That is very possible," said the pastor. "You knew then the unfortunate count Wartbourg?"

"Unfortunate!" exclaimed Ferdinand, greatly surprised.

"You don't then know any thing," continued the pastor, "of the deplorable event that has recently taken place at the château of Wartbourg? The young count, who had probably in his travels seen some beautifully laid-out gardens, was anxious to embellish the lovely country which surrounds his château; and as the ruins of an old tower seemed to be an obstacle to his plans, he ordered them to be pulled down. His gardener in vain represented to him, that seen from one of the wings of the château they represented, at the termination of a majestic and ancient avenue of linden trees, a magnificent coup d'oeil, and that they would also give a more romantic appearance to the new parts they were about to form. An old servant, grown grey in the service of his forefathers, supplicated him with tears in his eyes to spare the venerable remains of past ages. They even told him of an ancient tradition, preserved in the neighbourhood, which declared, that the existence of the house of Wartbourg was by supernatural means linked with the preservation of that tower.

"The count, who was a well-informed man, paid no attention to these sayings; indeed they possibly made him the more firmly adhere to his resolution. The workmen were put to their task: the walls, which were constructed of huge masses of rock, for a long while resisted the united efforts of tools and gunpowder; the architect of this place appeared to have built it for eternity.

"At length perseverance and labour brought it down. A piece of the rock separating from the rest, precipitated itself into an opening which had been concealed for ages by rubbish and loose sticks, and fell into a deep cavern. An immense subterranean vault was discovered by the rays of the setting sun, supported by enormous pillars:—but ere they proceeded in their researches, they went to inform the young count of the discovery they had made.

"He came; and being curious to see this dark abode, descended into it with two servants. The first thing they discovered were chains covered with rust, which being fixed in the rock, plainly shewed the use formerly of the cavern. On another side was a corpse, dressed in female attire of centuries past, which had surprisingly resisted the ravages of time: close to it was extended a human skeleton almost destroyed.

"The two servants related that the young count, on seeing the body, cried in an accent of extreme horror, 'Great God! it is she then whose portrait killed my intended wife.' Saying which, he fell senseless by the body. The shake which his fall occasioned reduced the skeleton to dust.

"They bore the count to his château, where the care of the physicians restored him to life; but he did not recover his senses. It is probable that this tragical event was caused by the confined and unwholesome air of the cavern. A very few days after, the count died in a state of total derangement.

"It is singular enough, that the termination of his life should coincide with the destruction of the ruined tower, and there no longer exists any male branch of that family. The deeds relative to the succession, ratified and sealed by the emperor Otho,* are still amongst the archives of his house. Their contents have as yet only been transmitted verbally from father to son, as an hereditary secret, which will now, however, be made known. It is also true, that the affianced bride of the count was killed by the portrait's falling on her."

"I yesterday heard that fatal history recited by the lady with flaxen hair," replied Ferdinand.

"It is very possible that young person is the countess Emily," replied the pastor; "for she was the bosom-friend of the unfortunate bride."

"Does not then the countess Emily live at the castle of Wartbourg?" asked Ferdinand.

"Since her brother's death," answered the clergyman, "she lived with a relation of her mother's at the château of Libinfelt, a short distance from hence. For as they yet know not with certainty to whom the castle of Wartbourg will belong, she prudently lives retired."

Ferdinand had learnt sufficient to make him abandon the projected journey to the capital. He thanked the pastor for the instructions he had given him, and was conducted to the château where Emily now resided.

It was still broad day when he arrived. The whole journey he was thinking of the amiable figure which he had recognised too late the preceding evening. He recalled to his idea her every word, the sound of her voice, her actions; and what his memory failed to represent, his imagination depicted with all the vivacity of youth, and all the fire of rekindled affection. He already addressed secret reproaches to Emily for not recognising him; as if he had himself remembered her; and in order to ascertain whether his features were entirely effaced from the recollection of her whom he

---

* The author seems to have confused Otho, who was a Roman emperor whose reign lasted for three months in 69 A.D., with Otto I and II, who reigned over the Holy Roman Empire for most of the tenth century.

adored, he caused himself to be announced as a stranger, who was anxious to see her on family matters.

While waiting impatiently in the room into which they had conducted him, he discovered among the portraits with which it was decorated, that of the young lady whose features had the over-night charmed him anew: he was contemplating it with rapture when the door opened and Emily entered. She instantly recognised Ferdinand; and in the sweetest accents accosted him as the friend of her youth.

Surprise rendered Ferdinand incapable of answering suitably to so gracious a reception: it was not the charming person with flaxen hair; it was not a figure corresponding with his imagination, which at this moment presented itself to his view. But it was Emily, shining in every possible beauty, far beyond what Ferdinand had expected: he recollected notwithstanding each feature which had already charmed him, but now clothed in every perfection which nature bestows on her most favoured objects. Ferdinand was lost in thought for some moments: he dared not make mention of his love, and still less did he dare speak of the portrait, and the other wonders of the castle of Wartbourg. Emily spoke only of the happiness she had experienced in her earlier days, and slightly mentioned her brother's death.

As the evening advanced, the young female with flaxen hair came in with the old stranger. Emily presented them both to Ferdinand, as the baron of Hainthal and his daughter Clotilde. They remembered instantly the stranger whom they had seen the preceding evening. Clotilde rallied him on his wish to be incognito; and he found himself on a sudden, by a short train of natural events, in the company of the person whom his mother intended for his wife; the object of his affection whom he had just discovered; and the interesting stranger who had promised him an explanation relative to the mysterious portraits.

Their society was soon augmented by the mistress of the château, in whom Ferdinand recognised one of those who sat by his side the preceding evening. In consideration for Emily, they omitted all the subjects most interesting to Ferdinand; but after supper the baron drew nearer to him.

"I doubt not," said he to him, "that you are anxious to have some light thrown on events, of which, according to your recital last night, you were a spectator. I knew you from the first; and I knew also, that the story you related as of a friend, was your own history. I cannot, however, inform you of more than I know: but that will perhaps be sufficient to save Emily, for whom I feel the affection of a daughter, from chagrin and uneasiness; and from your recital of last evening, I perceive you take a lively interest concerning her."

"Preserve Emily from uneasiness," replied Ferdinand with warmth; "explain yourself: what is there I ought to do?"

"We cannot," answered the baron, "converse here with propriety; tomorrow morning I will come and see you in your apartment."

Ferdinand asked him for an audience that night; but the baron was inflexible. "It is not my wish," said he, "to work upon your imagination by any marvellous recital, but to converse with you on the very important concerns of two distinguished families. For which reason, I think the freshness of morning will be better suited to lessen the horror that my recital must cause you: therefore, if not inconvenient to you, I wish you to attend me at an early hour in the morning: I am fond of rising with the sun; and yet I have never found the time till mid-day too long for arranging my affairs," added he, smiling, and turning half round towards the rest of the party, as if speaking on indifferent topics.

Ferdinand passed a night of agitation, thinking of the conference he was to have with the baron; who was at his window at dawn of day. "You know," said the baron, "that I married the old count of Wartbourg's sister; which alliance was less the cause, than the consequence, of our intimate friendship. We reciprocally communicated our most secret thoughts, and the one never undertook any thing, without the other taking an equal interest with himself in his projects. The count had, however, one secret from me, of which I should never have come at the knowledge but for an accident.

"On a sudden, a report was spread about, that the phantom of the Nun's rock had been seen, which was the name given by the peasantry to the old ruined tower which you knew. Persons of sense only laughed at the report: I was anxious the following night to unmask this spectre, and I already anticipated my triumph: but to my no small surprise, the count endeavoured to dissuade me from the attempt; and the more I persisted, the more serious his arguments became; and at length he conjured me in the name of friendship to relinquish the design.

"His gravity of manner excited my attention; I asked him several questions; I even regarded his fears in the light of disease, and urged him to take suitable remedies: but he answered me with an air of chagrin, 'Brother, you know my sincerity towards you; but this is a secret sacred to my family. My son can alone be informed of it, and that only on my death-bed. Therefore ask me no more questions.'

"I held my peace; but I secretly collected all the traditions known amongst the peasantry. The most generally believed one was, that the phantom of the Nun's rock was seen when any one of the count's family were about to die; and in effect, in a few days after the count's youngest son expired. The count seemed to apprehend it: he gave the strictest possible charge to the nurse to take care of him; and under pretext of feeling indisposed himself, sent for two physicians to the castle: but these extreme precautions were precisely the cause of the child's death; for the nurse passing over the stones near the ruins, in her extreme care took the child in her arms to carry him, and her foot slipping, she fell, and in her fall wounded the child so much, that he expired on the spot. She said she fancied that she saw the child extended, bleeding in the midst of the stones; that her fright had made her fall with her face on the earth; and that when she came to herself, the child was absolutely lying weltering in his blood, precisely on the same spot where she had seen his ghost.

"I will not tire you with a relation of all the sayings uttered by an illiterate woman to explain the cause of the vision, for under similar accidents invention far outstrips reality. I could not expect to gain much more satisfactory information from the family records; for the principal documents were preserved in an iron chest, the key of which was never out of the possession of the owner of the castle. I however discovered, by the genealogical register and other similar papers, that this family had never had collateral male branches; but further than this, my researches could not discover.

"At length, on my friend's death-bed I obtained some information, which, however, was far from being satisfactory. You remember, that while the son was on his travels, the father was attacked by the complaint which carried him off so suddenly. The evening previous to his decease, he sent for me express, dismissed all those who were with him, and turning towards me, said: 'I am aware that my end is fast approaching, and am the first of my family that has been carried off without communicating to his son the secret on which the safety of our house depends. Swear to me to reveal it only to my son, and I shall die contented.'

"In the names of friendship and honour, I promised what he exacted of me, and he thus began:

"'The origin of my race, as you know, is not to be traced. Ditmar, the first of my ancestry mentioned in the written records, accompanied the emperor Otho to Italy. His history is also very obscure. He had an enemy called count Bruno, whose only son he killed in revenge, according to ancient tradition, and then kept the father confined till his death in that tower, whose ruins, situated in the Nun's rock, still defy the hand of time. That portrait which hangs alone in the state-chamber, is Ditmar's; and if the traditions of the family are to be believed, it was painted by the Dead. In fact, it is almost impossible to believe that any human being could have contemplated sufficiently long to paint the portrait, the outline of features so hideous. My forefathers have frequently tried to plaster over this redoubtable figure; but in the night, the colours came through the plaster, and re-appeared as distinctly as before; and often in the night, this Ditmar has been seen wandering abroad dressed in the garb represented in the picture; and by kissing the descendants of the family, has doomed them to death. Three of my children have received this fatal kiss. It is said, a monk imposed on him this penance in expiation of his crimes. But he cannot destroy all the children of his race: for so long as the ruins of the old tower shall remain, and whilst one stone shall remain on another, so long shall the count de Wartbourg's family exist; and so long shall the spirit of Ditmar wander on earth, and devote to death the branches of his house, without being able to annihilate the trunk. His race will never be extinct; and his punishment will only cease when the ruins of the tower are entirely dispersed. He brought up, with a truly paternal care, the daughter of his enemy, and wedded her to a rich and powerful knight; but notwithstanding this, the monk never remitted his penance. Ditmar, however, foreseeing that one day or other his race would perish, was certainly anxious ere then, to prepare for an event on which his deliverance depended; and accordingly made a relative disposition of his hereditary property, in case of his family becoming extinct. The act which contained his will, was ratified by the emperor Otho: as yet it has not been opened, and nobody knows its contents. It is kept in the secret archives of our house.'

"The speaking thus much was a great effort to my friend. He required a little rest, but was shortly after incapable of articulating a single word. I performed the commission with which he charged me to his son."

"And he did, notwithstanding—" replied Ferdinand.

"Even so," answered the baron: "but judge more favourably of your excellent friend. I have often seen him alone in the great state-chamber, with eyes fixed on this horrible portrait: he would then go into the other rooms, where the portraits of his ancestors were ranged for several successive generations; and after contemplating them with visible internal emotion, would return to that of the founder of his house. Broken sentences, and frequent soliloquies, which I overheard by accident, did not leave me a shadow of doubt, but that he was the first of his race who had magnanimity of soul sufficient to resolve on liberating the spirit of Ditmar from its penance, and of sacrificing himself to release his house from the malediction that hung over it. Possibly he was strengthened in his resolutions by the grief he experienced for the death of his dearly beloved."

"Oh!" cried Ferdinand deeply affected, "how like my friend!"

"He had, however, in the ardour of his enthusiasm, forgotten to guard his sister's sensibility," said the baron.

"How so?" demanded Ferdinand.

"It is in consequence of this," answered the baron, "that I now address myself to you, and reveal to you the secret. I have told you that Ditmar demonstrated a paternal affection to the daughter of his enemy, had given her a handsome portion, and had married her to a valiant knight. Learn then, that this knight was Adelbert de Meltheim, from whom the counts of this name descended in a direct line."

"Is it possible?" exclaimed Ferdinand, "the author of my race!"

"The same," answered the baron; "and according to appearances, Ditmar designed that the family of Meltheim should succeed him on the extinction of his own. Haste, then, in order to establish your probable right to the—"

"Never—" said Ferdinand, "—so long as Emily—"

"This is no more than I expected from you," replied the baron; "but remember, that in Ditmar's time the girls were not thought of in deeds of this kind. Your inconsiderate generosity would be prejudicial to Emily. For the next of kin who lay claim to the fief, do not probably possess very gallant ideas."

"As a relation, though only on the female side, I have taken the necessary measures; and I think it right you should be present at the castle of Wartbourg when the seals are broken, that you may be immediately recognised as the only immediate descendant of Adelbert, and that you may take instant possession of the inheritance."

"And Emily?" demanded Ferdinand.

"As for what is to be done for her," replied the baron, "I leave to you; and feel certain of her being provided for suitably, since her destiny will be in the hands of a man whose birth equals her own, who knows how to appreciate the rank in which she is placed, and who will evince his claims to merit and esteem."

"Have I a right, then," said Ferdinand, "to flatter myself with the hope that Emily will permit me to surrender her the property to which she is actually entitled?"

"Consult Emily on the subject," said the baron.—And here finished the conference.

Ferdinand, delighted, ran to Emily. She answered with the same frankness he had manifested; and they were neither of them slow to confess their mutual passion.

Several days passed in this amiable delirium. The inhabitants of the château participated in the joy of the young lovers; and Ferdinand at length wrote to his mother, to announce the choice he had made.

They were occupied in preparations for removing to the castle of Wartbourg, when a letter arrived, which at once destroyed Ferdinand's happiness. His mother's refusal to consent to his marriage with Emily: her husband having, she said, on his death-bed, insisted on his wedding the baron of Hainthal's daughter, and that she should refuse her consent to any other marriage. He had discovered a family secret, which forced him peremptorily to press this point, on which depended his son's welfare, and the happiness of his family; she had given her promise, and was obliged to maintain it, although much afflicted at being compelled to act contrary to her son's inclinations.

In vain did Ferdinand conjure his mother to change her determination; he declared to her that he would be the last of his race, rather than renounce Emily. She was not displeased with his entreaties, but remained inflexible.

The baron plainly perceived, from Ferdinand's uneasiness and agitation, that his happiness had fled; and as he possessed his entire confidence, he soon became acquainted with the cause of his grief. He wrote in consequence to the countess Meltheim, and expressed his astonishment at the singular disposition the count had made on his death-bed: but all he could obtain from her, was a promise to come to the castle of Wartbourg, to see the female whom she destined for her son, and the one whom he had himself chosen; and probably to elucidate by her arrival so singular and complicated an affair.

Spring was beginning to enliven all nature, when Ferdinand, accompanied by Emily, the baron, and his daughter, arrived at the castle of Wartbourg. The preparations which the principal cause of their journey required, occupied some days. Ferdinand and Emily consoled themselves in the hope that the countess of Meltheim's presence would remove every obstacle which opposed their love, and that at sight of the two lovers she would overcome her scruples.

A few days afterwards she arrived, embraced Emily in the most affectionate manner, and called her, her dear daughter, at the same time expressing great regret that she could not really consider her such, being obliged to fulfill a promise made to her dying husband.

The baron at length persuaded her to reveal the motive for this singular determination: and after deliberating a short time, she thus expressed herself:—

"The secret you are anxious I should reveal to you, concerns your family, Monsieur le Baron: consequently, if you release me from the necessity of longer silence, I am very willing to abandon my scruples. A fatal picture has, you know, robbed me of my daughter; and my husband, after this melancholy accident, determined on entirely removing this unfortunate portrait: he accordingly gave orders for it to be put in a heap of old furniture, where no one would think of looking for it; and in order to discover the best place to conceal it, he was present when it was taken there. In the removal, he perceived a piece of parchment behind the canvass which the fall had a little damaged: having removed it, he discovered it to be an old document, of a singular nature. The original of this portrait, (said the deed,) was called Bertha de Hainthal; she fixes her looks on her female descendants, in order that if any one of them should receive its death by this portrait, it may prove an expiatory sacrifice which will reconcile her to God. She will then see the families of Hainthal and Meltheim united by the bonds of love; and finding herself released, she will have cause to rejoice in the birth of her after-born descendants.

"This then is the motive which made my husband anxious to fulfill, by the projected marriage, the vows of Bertha; for the death of his daughter, caused by Bertha, had rendered her very name formidable to him. You see, therefore, I have the same reasons for adhering to the promise made my dying husband."

"Did not the count," demanded the baron, "allege any more positive reason for this command?"

"Nothing more, most assuredly," replied the countess.

"Well then," answered the baron, "in case the writing of which you speak should admit of an explanation wholly differing from, but equally clear with, the one attached thereto by the deceased, would you sooner follow the sense than the letter of the writing?"

"There is no doubt on that subject," answered the countess; "for no one is more anxious than myself to see that unfortunate promise set aside."

"Know then," said the baron, "that the corpse of that Bertha, who occasioned the death of your daughter, reposes here at Wartbourg; and that, on this subject, as well as all the other mysteries of the castle, we shall have our doubts satisfied."

The baron would not at this time explain himself further; but said to the countess, that the documents contained in the archives of the castle would afford the necessary information; and recommended that Ferdinand should, with all possible dispatch, hasten every thing relative to the succession. Comfortable to the baron's wish, it was requisite that, previous to any other research, the secret deeds contained in the archives should be opened. The law commissioners, and the next of kin who were present, who, most likely, promised themselves an ample compensation for their curiosity in the contents of the other parts of the records, were anxious to raise objections; but the baron represented to them, that the secrets off the family appertained to the unknown heir alone, and that consequently no one had a right to become acquainted with them, unless permitted by him.

These reasons produced the proper effect. They followed the baron into the immense vault in which were deposited the family records. They therein discovered an iron chest, which had not been opened for nearly a thousand years. A massive chain, which several times wound round it, was strongly fixed to the floor and to the wall; but the emperor's grand seal was a greater security for this sacred deposit, than all the chains and bolts which guarded it. It was instantly recognised and removed: the strong bolts yielded; and from the chest was taken the old parchment which had resisted the effects of time. This piece contained, as the baron expected, the disposition which confirmed the right of inheritance to the house of Meltheim, in case of the extinction of the house of Wartbourg: and Ferdinand, according to the baron's advice, having in readiness the deeds justifying and acknowledging him as the lawful heir to the house of Meltheim, the next of kin with regret permitted what they could not oppose; and he took possession of the inheritance. The baron having made him a signal, he immediately sealed the chest with his seal. He afterwards entertained the strangers in a splendid manner; and at night found himself in possession of his castle, with only his mother, Emily, the baron, and his daughter.

"It will be but just," said the baron, "to devote this night, which introduces a new name into this castle, to the memory of those who have hitherto possessed it. And we shall acquit ourselves most suitably in this duty, by reading in the council-chamber the documents which, without doubt, are destined to explain, as supplementary deeds, the will of Ditmar."

This arrangement was instantly adopted. The hearts of Emily and Ferdinand were divided between hope and fear; for they impatiently, yet doubtingly, awaited the denouement of Bertha's history, which, after so many successive generations, had in so incomprehensible a manner interfered with their attachment.

The chamber was lighted: Ferdinand opened the iron case; and the baron examined the old parchments .

"This," cried he, after having searched some short time, "will inform us." So saying, he drew from the chest some sheets of parchment. On the one which enveloped the rest was the portrait of a knight of an agreeable figure, and habited in the costume of the tenth century: and the inscription at the bottom called him Ditmar; but they could scarcely discover the slightest resemblance in it to the frightful portrait in the state-chamber.

The baron offered to translate, in reading to them the document written in Latin, provided they would make allowances for the errors which were likely to arise from so hasty a translation. The curiosity of his auditors was so greatly excited, that they readily consented; and he then read as follows:

"I the undersigned Tutilon, monk of St. Gall,* have, with the lord Ditmar's consent, written the following narrative: I have omitted nothing, nor written aught of my own accord.

"Being sent for to Metz, to carve in stone the image of the Virgin Mary; and that mother of our blessed Saviour having opened my eyes and directed my hands, so that I could contemplate her celestial countenance, and represent it on stone to be worshipped by true believers, the lord Ditmar discovered me, and engaged me to follow him to his castle, in order that I might execute his portrait for his descendants. I began painting it in the state-chamber of his castle; and on returning the following day to resume my task, I found that a strange hand had been at work, and had given to the portrait quite a different countenance, which was horrible to look at, for it resembled one who had risen from the dead. I trembled with terror: however, I effaced these hideous features and I painted anew the count Ditmar's figure, according to my recollection; but the following day I again discovered the nocturnal labour of the stranger hand. I was seized with still greater fear, but resolved to watch during the night; and I recommenced painting the knight's figure, such as it really was. At midnight I took a torch, and advancing softly into the chamber to examine the portrait, I perceived a spectre resembling the skeleton of a child; it held a pencil, and was endeavouring to give Ditmar's image the hideous features of death.

"On my entering, the spectre slowly turned its head towards me, that I might see its frightful visage. My terror became extreme: I advanced no

---

* Tutilon—or, as he is more commonly known, Tutilo—was a real monk in the tenth century who was an accomplished painter, sculptor, and composer. He was canonized and is now known as Saint Tutilo (or Saint Tuotilo), and his feast day in the Catholic calendar is celebrated on March 28.

further, but retired to my room, where I remained in prayer till morning; for I was unwilling to interrupt the work executed in the dead of night.[*] In the morning, discovering the same strange features in Ditmar's portrait as that of the two preceding mornings, I did not again risk effacing the work of the nightly painter; but went in search of the knight, and related to him what I had seen. I shewed him the picture. He trembled with horror, and confessed his crimes to me, for which he required absolution. Having for three successive days invoked all the saints to my assistance, I imposed on him as a penance for the murder of his enemy, which he had avowed to me, to submit to the most rigid mortifications in a dungeon during the rest of his life. But I told him, that as he had murdered an innocent child, his spirit would never be at rest till it had witnessed the extermination of his race; for the Almighty would punish the death of that child by the death of the children of Ditmar, who, with the exception of one in each generation, would all be carried off in early life; and as for him, his spirit would wander during the night, resembling the portrait painted by the hand of the skeleton child; and that he would condemn to death, by a kiss, the children who were the sacrifices to his crimes, in the same manner as he had given one to his enemy's child before he killed it: and that, in fine, his race should not become extinct so long as stone remained on stone in the tower where he had permitted his enemy to die of hunger. I then gave him absolution. He immediately made over his seigniory to his son; and married the daughter of his enemy, who had been brought up by him, to the brave knight Sir Adelbert. He bequeathed all his property, in case of his race becoming extinct, to this knight's descendants, and caused this will to be ratified by the emperor Otho. After having done so, he retired to a cave near the tower, where his corpse is interred; for he died like a pious recluse, and expiated his crimes by extreme penance. As soon as he was laid in his coffin, he resembled the portrait in the state-chamber; but during his life he was like the portrait depicted on this parchment, which I was able to paint without interruption, after having given him absolution: and by his

---

[*] Ghost stories surrounding priests and monks were numerous in the Middle Ages. The eleventh-century bishop Thietmar of Merseburg recorded many, including one in which dead spirits gathered in a reconstructed church and burned the local priest on the altar, so this monk has good reason to be seized with fear.

command I have written and signed this document since his death; and I deposit it, with the emperor's letters patent, in an iron chest, which I have caused to be sealed. I pray God speedily to deliver his soul, and to cause his body to rise from the dead to everlasting felicity!"

"He is delivered," cried Emily, greatly affected; "and his image will no longer spread terror around. But I confess that the sight of that figure, and even that of the frightful portrait itself, would never have led me to dream of such horrible crimes as the monk Tutilon relates. Certain I am, his enemy must have mortally wounded his happiness, or he undoubtedly would have been incapable of committing such frightful crimes."

"Possibly," said the baron, continuing his researches, "we shall discover some explanation on that point."

"We must also find some respecting Bertha," replied Ferdinand in a low tone, and casting a timid look on Emily and his mother.

"This night," answered the baron, "is consecrated to the memory of the dead; let us therefore forget our own concerns, since those of the past call our attention."

"Assuredly," exclaimed Emily, "the unfortunate person who secured these sheets in the chest, ardently looked forward to the hope of their coming to light; let us therefore delay it no longer."

The baron, after having examined several, read aloud these words:

"The confession of Ditmar." And he continued thus:—"Peace and health. When this sheet is drawn from the obscurity in which it is now buried, my soul will, I hope firmly in God and the saints, be at eternal rest and peace. But for your good I have ordered to be committed to paper the cause of my chastisement, in order that you may learn that vengeance belongs to God alone, and not to men; for the most just amongst them knows not how to judge: and again, that you may not in your heart condemn me, but rather that you may pity me; for my misery has nearly equalled my crimes; and my spirit would never have dreamt of evil, if man had not rent my heart."

"How justly," exclaimed Ferdinand, "has Emily's good sense divined this much!"

The baron continued: "My name is Ditmar; they surnamed me The Rich, though I was then only a poor knight, and my only possession was a very small castle. When the emperor Otho departed for Italy, whither he was called by the beautiful Adelaide to receive her hand, I followed him; and I gained the affection of the most charming woman in Pavia, whom I conducted as my intended spouse to the castle of my forefathers. Already the day appointed for the celebration of my nuptials was at hand: the emperor sent for me. His favourite, the count Bruno de Hainthal had seen Bertha—"

"Bertha!" exclaimed every one present. But the baron, without permitting them to interrupt him, continued his translation.

"One day, when the emperor had promised to grant him any recompense that he thought his services merited, he asked of him my intended bride. Otho was mute with astonishment;—but his imperial word was given. I presented myself before the emperor, who offered me riches, lands, honours, if I would but consent to yield Bertha to the count: but she was dearer to me than every worldly good. The emperor yielded to a torrent of anger: he carried off my intended bride by force, ordered my castle to be pulled down, and caused me to be thrown into prison.

"I cursed his power and my destiny. The amiable figure of Bertha, however, appeared to me in a dream; and I consoled myself during the day by the sweet illusions of the night. At length my keeper said to me: 'I pity you, Ditmar; you suffer in a prison for your fidelity, while Bertha abandons you. To-morrow she weds the count: accede then to the emperor's wish, ere it be too late; and ask of him what you think fit, as a recompense for the loss of the faithless fair.' These words froze my heart. The following night, instead of the gracious image of Bertha, the frightful spirit of vengeance presented itself to me. The following morning I said to my keeper: Go and tell the emperor I yield Bertha to his Bruno; but as a recompense, I demand this tower, and as much land as will be requisite to build me a new castle.' The emperor was satisfied; for he frequently repented his violent passions, but he could not alter what he had already decided. He therefore gave me the tower in which I had been confined, and all the lands around it for the space of four leagues. He also gave me more gold and silver than was sufficient to build a castle much more magnificent than the one he had caused to be pulled down. I took unto myself a wife, in order to perpetuate my race; but Bertha still reigned sole mistress of my heart. I also built myself a castle, from which I made a communication, by subterranean and secret passages, with my former prison the tower, and with the castle of Bruno, the residence of my mortal enemy. As soon as the edifice was completed, I entered the fortress by the secret passage, and appeared as the spirit of one of his ancestors before the bed of his son, the heir with which Bertha had presented him. The women who lay beside him were seized with fear: I leaned over the child, who was the precise image of its mother, and kissed its forehead; but—it was the kiss of death; it carried with it a secret poison.

"Bruno and Bertha acknowledged the vengeance of Heaven: they received it as a punishment for the wrongs they had occasioned me; and they devoted their first child to the service of God. As it was a girl, I spared it: but Bertha had no more children; and Bruno, irritated to find his race so nearly annihilated, repudiated his wife, as if he repented the injustice of which he had been guilty in taking her, and married another. The unfortunate Bertha took refuge in a monastery, and consecrated herself to Heaven: but her reason fled; and one night she quitted her retreat, came to the tower in which I had been confined in consequence of her perfidy, there bewailed her crime, and there grief terminated her existence; which circumstance gave rise to that tower being called the Nun's Rock. I heard, during the night, her sobs; and on going to the tower found Bertha extended motionless; the dews of night had seized her:—she was dead. I then resolved to avenge her loss. I placed her corpse in a deep vault beneath the tower; and having by means of my subterranean passage discovered all the count's movements, I attacked him when unguarded; and dragging him to the vault which contained his wife's corpse, I there abandoned him. The emperor, irritated against him for having divorced Bertha, gave me all his possessions, as a remuneration for the injustice I had heretofore experienced.

"I caused all the subterranean passages to be closed. I took under my care his daughter Hildegarde, and brought her up as my child: she loved the count Adelbert de Meltheim. But one night her mother's ghost appeared to her, and reminded her that she was consecrated to the Almighty: this vision, however, could not deter her from marrying Adelbert. The night of her marriage the phantom appeared again before her bed, and thus addressed her:

"'Since you have infringed the vow I made, my spirit can never be at rest, till one of your female descendants receives its death from me.'

"This discourse occasioned me to send for the venerable Tutilon, monk of St. Gall, who was very celebrated, in order that he might paint a portrait of Bertha, as she had painted herself in the monastery during her insanity; and I gave it to her daughter.

"Tutilon concealed behind that portrait a writing on parchment, the contents of which were as follows:

"'I am Bertha; and I look at my daughters, to see whether one of them will not die for me, in expiation of my crimes, and thus reconcile me to God. Then shall I see the two families of Meltheim and Hainthal reunited by love, and in the birth of their descendants I shall enjoy happiness.'"

"This then," exclaimed Ferdinand, "is the fatal writing that is to separate me from Emily; but which, in fact, only unites me to her more firmly! and Bertha, delivered from her penance blesses the alliance; for by my marriage with Emily, the descendants of Bertha and Ditmar will be reunited."

"Do you think," demanded the baron of the countess, "that this explanation can admit of the slightest doubt?"

The only answer the countess made, was by embracing Emily, and placing her hand in that of her son.

The joy was universal. Clotilde in particular had an air of extreme delight; and her father several times, in a jocular manner, scolded her for expressing her joy so vehemently. The following morning they removed the seals from the state-chamber, in order to contemplate the horrible portrait with somewhat less of sadness than heretofore: but they found that it had faded in a singular manner, and the colours, which formerly appeared so harsh, had blended and become softened.

Shortly after arrived the young man who was anxious to enter into an argument with Ferdinand on the explication of the mysteries relative to the portraits. Clotilde did not conceal that he was far from indifferent to her; and they discovered the joy she had evinced, in discovering the favourable turn Emily's attachment had taken, was not altogether disinterested, but occasioned by the prospect it afforded of happiness to herself. Her father, in fact, would never have approved her choice, had not the countess Meltheim removed all pretensions to Clotilde.

"But," asked Ferdinand of Clotilde's intended, "do you not forgive our having searched into certain mysteries which concerned us?"

"Completely," he answered; "but not less disinterestedly than formerly, when I maintained a contrary opinion. I ought now to confess to you, that I was present at the fatal accident which caused your sister's death, and that I then discovered the writing concealed behind the portrait. I naturally explained it as your father did afterwards; but I held my peace; for the consequences have brought to light what the discovery of that writing had caused me to apprehend or my love."

"Unsatisfactory explanations are bad," replied Ferdinand, laughing.

The happy issues of these discoveries spread universal joy amongst the inhabitants of the castle, which was in some degree heightened by the beauty of the season. The lovers were anxious to celebrate their marriage ere the fall of the leaf. And when next the primrose's return announced the approach of spring, Emily gave birth to a charming boy.

Ferdinand's mother, Clotilde and her husband, and all the friends of the family, among whom were the pastor who was so fond of music, and his pretty little wife, assembled at the fête given in honour of the christening. When the priest who was performing the ceremony asked what name he was to give the child, that of Ditmar was uttered by every mouth, as if they had previously agreed on it. The christening over, Ferdinand, elated with joy, accompanied by his relations and guests, carried his son to the state-chamber, before his forefather's portrait; but it was no longer perceptible; the colours, figure—all had disappeared; not the slightest trace remained.

* [note for page 5] Apel's story first appeared in German in 1805 and was reprinted in his anthology *Cicaden* (1810). It was subsequently included (without crediting Apel) in *Fantasmagoriana; ou Recueil d'Histoires, d'Apparitions, de Spectres, Revenans, Fantomes, etc., traduit de l'allemand, par un amateur* (1812), translated into French anonymously by Jean-Baptiste Benoît Eyriès (1767–1846). The book was subsequently translated into English by Sarah Elizabeth Utterson and published in 1813 as *Tales of the Dead* (note that we have used Utterson's translation, in which she adds an opening quote from Shakespeare's *The Winter's Tale* not found in the original).

Mary Shelley, her husband Percy Shelley, her half-sister Claire Clairmont, Lord Byron, and his companion John Polidori spent several evenings in the summer of 1816 reading aloud tales (it is unknown whether they read them in French or English) from *Fantasmagoriana*, with the result that Byron challenged them all to write their own ghost stories. In the introduction to the 1831 revised edition of Mary Shelley's 1818 novel *Frankenstein* (the seed of which was sown in that storytelling contest), she recounted her recollection of the book: "There was the tale of the sinful founder of his race, whose miserable doom it was to bestow the kiss of death on all the younger sons of his fated house, just when they reached the age of promise. His gigantic, shadowy form, clothed like the ghost in Hamlet, in complete armour, but with the beaver up, was seen at midnight, by the moon's fitful beams, to advance slowly along the gloomy avenue. The shape was lost beneath the shadow of the castle walls; but soon a gate swung back, a step was heard, the door of the chamber opened, and he advanced to the couch of the blooming youths, cradled in healthy sleep. Eternal sorrow sat upon his face as he bent down and kissed the forehead of the boys, who from that hour withered like flowers snapt upon the stalk. I have not seen these stories since then; but their incidents are as fresh in my mind as if I had read them yesterday." Note that her summary makes no mention of the "family portraits"!

The Tapestried Chamber, or The Lady in the Square

by SIR WALTER SCOTT

Sir Walter Scott (1771–1832) is best remembered today for his classic Scottish/English novels, Waverly *(1814), hailed as the first historical novel,* Rob Roy *(1817),* The Bride of Lammermoor *(1819), and* Ivanhoe *(1820). His first great successes were his epic poems* The Lay of the Last Minstrel *(1805) and* Marmion *(1808). He was a prolific poet, essayist, dramatist, and novelist, with more than twenty novels to his credit. Scott was an early champion of* Frankenstein, *reviewing it when it first appeared in 1818, though he—like many others—assumed that its anonymous author was Percy Shelley. The following story is one of three that first appeared in* The Keepsake *for 1829, published in December 1828. Though many of his longer works reference folklore and legends of ghosts, this is Scott's only pure ghost story, and many scholars consider it to be the first important short ghost story.*

About the end of the American war, when the officers of Lord Cornwallis's army which surrendered at Yorktown, and others, who had been made prisoners during the impolitic and ill-fated controversy* were returning to their own country, to relate their adventures and repose themselves after their fatigues, there was amongst them a general officer, to whom Miss S. gave the name of Browne, but merely, as I understood, to save the inconvenience of introducing a nameless agent in the narrative. He was an officer of merit, as well as a gentleman of high consideration for family and attainments.

Some business had carried General Browne upon a tour through the western counties,† when, in the conclusion of a morning stage, he found himself in the vicinity of a small country town, which presented a scene of uncommon beauty and of a character peculiarly English.

The little town, with its stately old church whose tower bore testimony to the devotion of ages long past, lay amidst pasture and corn-fields of small extent, but bounded and divided with hedgerow timber of great age and size. There were few marks of modern improvement. The environs of the place intimated neither the solitude of decay, nor the bustle of novelty; the houses were old, but in good repair; and the beautiful little river murmured freely on its way to the left of the town, neither restrained by a dam, nor bordered by a towing-path.

Upon a gentle eminence, nearly a mile to the southward of the town, were seen amongst many venerable oaks and tangled thickets the turrets of a castle, as old as the wars of York and Lancaster,‡ but which seemed to have received important alterations during the age of Elizabeth and her successors. It had not been a place of great size; but whatever accommodation it formerly afforded, was, it must be supposed, still to be obtained within its walls; at least, such was the inference which General Browne drew from observing the smoke arise merrily from several of the ancient wreathed and carved chimney-stalks.

The wall of the park ran alongside of the highway for two or three hundred yards, and, through the different points by which the eye found glimpses into the woodland scenery, it seemed to be well stocked. Other

---

* This refers to the American Revolutionary War.

† The western counties of England, that is; General Browne was an English officer.

‡ The English civil wars known as the Wars of the Roses, in the mid-fifteenth century.

points of view opened in succession; now a full one, of the front of the old castle, and now a side glimpse at its particular towers; the former rich in all the bizarrerie of the Elizabethan school, while the simple and solid strength of other parts of the building seemed to show that they had been raised more for defence than ostentation.

Delighted with the partial glimpses which he obtained of the castle through the woods and glades by which this ancient feudal fortress was surrounded, our military traveller was determined to inquire whether it might not deserve a nearer view, and whether it contained family pictures or other objects of curiosity worthy of a stranger's visit, when, leaving the vicinity of the park, he rolled through a clean and well-paved street, and stopped at the door of a well-frequented inn.

Before ordering horses to proceed on his journey, General Browne made inquiries concerning the proprietor of the château which had so attracted his admiration, and was equally surprised and pleased at hearing in reply a nobleman named whom we shall call Lord Woodville. How fortunate! Much of Browne's early recollections, both at school and at college, had been connected with young Woodville, whom, by a few questions, he now ascertained to be the same with the owner of this fair domain. He had been raised to the peerage by the decease of his father a few months before, and, as the General learned from the landlord, the term of mourning being ended, was now taking possession of his paternal estate in the jovial season of merry autumn, accompanied by a select party of friends to enjoy the sports of a country famous for game.

This was delightful news to our traveller. Frank Woodville had been Richard Browne's fag at Eton,* and his chosen intimate at Christ Church; their pleasures and their tasks had been the same; and the honest soldier's heart warmed to find his early friend in possession of so delightful a residence, and of an estate, as the landlord assured him with a nod and a wink, fully adequate to maintain and add to his dignity. Nothing was more natural than that the traveller should suspend a journey, which there was nothing to render hurried, to pay a visit to an old friend under such agreeable circumstances.

---

* A fag was a younger school-boy who served an older student.

The fresh horses, therefore, had only the brief task of conveying the General's travelling-carriage to Woodville Castle. A porter admitted them at a modern Gothic lodge, built in that style to correspond with the castle itself, and at the same time rang a bell to give warning of the approach of visitors. Apparently the sound of the bell had suspended the separation of the company, bent on the various amusements of the morning; for, on entering the court of the château, several young men were lounging about in their sporting-dresses, looking at, and criticizing, the dogs which the keepers held in readiness to attend their pastime.

As General Browne alighted, the young lord came to the gate of the hall, and for an instant gazed, as at a stranger, upon the countenance of his friend, on which war, with its fatigues and its wounds, had made a great alteration. But the uncertainty lasted no longer than till the visitor had spoken, and the hearty greeting which followed was such as can only be exchanged betwixt those who have passed together merry days of careless boyhood or early youth.

"If I could have formed a wish, my dear Browne," said Lord Woodville, "it would have been to have you here, of all men, upon this occasion, which my friends are good enough to hold as a sort of holiday. Do not think you have been unwatched during the years you have been absent from us. I have traced you through your dangers, your triumphs, your misfortunes, and was delighted to see that, whether in victory or defeat, the name of my old friend was always distinguished with applause."

The General made a suitable reply, and congratulated his friend on his new dignities, and the possession of a place and domain so beautiful.

"Nay, you have seen nothing of it as yet," said Lord Woodville, "and I trust you do not mean to leave us till you are better acquainted with it. It is true, I confess, that my present party is pretty large, and the old house, like other places of the kind, does not possess so much accommodation as the extent of the outward walls appears to promise. But we can give you a comfortable old-fashioned room, and I venture to suppose that your campaigns have taught you to be glad of worse quarters."

The General shrugged his shoulders, and laughed. "I presume," he said, "the worst apartment in your château is considerably superior to the old tobacco-cask,* in which I was fain to take up my night's lodging when I was in the Bush, as the Virginians call it, with the light corps. There I lay, like Diogenes himself,† so delighted with my covering from the elements, that I made a vain attempt to have it rolled on to my next quarters; but my commander for the time would give way to no such luxurious provision, and I took farewell of my beloved cask with tears in my eyes."

"Well, then, since you do not fear your quarters," said Lord Woodville "you will stay with me a week at least. Of guns, dogs, fishing-rods, flies, and means of sport by sea and land, we have enough and to spare: you cannot pitch on an amusement, but we will pitch on the means of pursuing it. But if you prefer the gun and pointers,‡ I will go with you myself, and see whether you have mended your shooting since you have been amongst the Indians of the back settlements."

The General gladly accepted his friendly host's proposal in all its points. After a morning of manly exercise, the company met at dinner, where it was the delight of Lord Woodville to conduce to the display of the high properties of his recovered friend, so as to recommend him to his guests, most of whom were persons of distinction. He led General Browne to speak of the scenes he had witnessed; and as every word marked alike the brave officer and the sensible man, who retained possession of his cool judgement under the most imminent dangers, the company looked upon the soldier with general respect, as on one who had proved himself possessed of an uncommon portion of personal courage—that attribute, of all others, of which everybody desires to be thought possessed.

The day at Woodville Castle ended as usual in such mansions. The hospitality stopped within the limits of good order; music, in which the young lord was a proficient, succeeded to the circulation of the bottle; cards and billiards, for those who preferred such amusements, were in readiness; but

---

* Tobacco-casks, or hogsheads, were large in colonial times—48 inches long and 30 inches in diameter.

† Diogenes was a fourth-century-B.C. Greek philosopher who believed in the virtue of poverty and often slept in a large ceramic jar.

‡ General Browne is here being invited to a fox-hunt.

the exercise of the morning required early hours, and not long after eleven o'clock the guests began to retire to their several apartments.

The young lord himself conducted his friend, General Browne, to the chamber destined for him, which answered the description he had given of it, being comfortable, but old-fashioned. The bed was of the massive form used in the end of the seventeenth century, and the curtains of faded silk, heavily trimmed with tarnished gold. But then the sheets, pillows, and blankets looked delightful to the campaigner, when he thought of his "mansion, the cask."

There was an air of gloom in the tapestry hangings which, with their worn-out graces, curtained the walls of the little chamber, and gently undulated as the autumnal breeze found its way through the ancient lattice-window, which pattered and whistled as the air gained entrance. The toilet too, with its mirror, turbaned, after the manner of the beginning of the century, with a coiffure of murrey-coloured* silk, and its hundred strange-shaped boxes, providing for arrangements which had been obsolete for more than fifty years, had an antique, and in so far a melancholy, aspect. But nothing could blaze more brightly and cheerfully than the two large wax candles; or if aught could rival them, it was the flaming bickering fagots in the chimney, that sent at once their gleam and their warmth through the snug apartment; which, notwithstanding the general antiquity of its appearance, was not wanting in the least convenience that modern habits rendered either necessary or desirable.

"This is an old-fashioned sleeping apartment, General," said the young lord; "but I hope you will find nothing that makes you envy your old tobacco-cask."

"I am not particular respecting my lodgings," replied the General; "yet were I to make any choice, I would prefer this chamber by many degrees, to the gayer and more modern rooms of your family mansion. Believe me that when I unite its modern air of comfort with its venerable antiquity, and recollect that it is your lordship's property, I shall feel in better quarters here, than if I were in the best hotel London could afford."

"I trust—I have no doubt—that you will find yourself as comfort-able as I wish you, my dear General," said the young nobleman; and

---

* Dark red or purple

once more bidding his guest good night, he shook him by the hand and withdrew.

The General once more looked round him, and internally congratulating himself on his return to peaceful life, the comforts of which were endeared by the recollection of the hardships and dangers he had lately sustained, undressed himself, and prepared himself for a luxurious night's rest.

Here, contrary to the custom of this species of tale, we leave the General in possession of his apartment until the next morning.

The company assembled for breakfast at an early hour, but without the appearance of General Browne, who seemed the guest that Lord Woodville was desirous of honouring above all whom his hospitality had assembled around him. He more than once expressed surprise at the General's absence, and at length sent a servant to make inquiry after him. The man brought back information that General Browne had been walking abroad since an early hour of the morning, in defiance of the weather, which was misty and ungenial.

"The custom of a soldier," said the young nobleman to his friends: "many of them acquire habitual vigilance, and cannot sleep after the early hour at which their duty usually commands them to be alert."

Yet the explanation which Lord Woodville thus offered to the company seemed hardly satisfactory to his own mind, and it was in a fit of silence and abstraction that he awaited the return of the General. It took place near an hour after the breakfast-bell had rung. He looked fatigued and feverish. His hair, the powdering and arrangement of which was at this time one of the most important occupations of a man's whole day, and marked his fashion as much as, in the present time, the tying of a cravat or the want of one, was dishevelled, uncurled, void of powder, and dank with dew. His clothes were huddled on with a careless negligence, remarkable in a military man, whose real or supposed duties are usually held to include some attention to the toilet; and his looks were haggard and ghastly in a peculiar degree.

"So you have stolen a march upon us this morning, my dear General," said Lord Woodville; "or you have not found your bed so much to your mind as I had hoped and you seemed to expect. How did you rest last night?"

"Oh, excellently well—remarkably well—never better in my life!" said General Browne rapidly, and yet with an air of embarrassment which was obvious to his friend. He then hastily swallowed a cup of tea, and, neglecting or refusing whatever else was offered, seemed to fall into a fit of abstraction.

"You will take the gun to-day, General?" said his friend and host, but had to repeat the question twice ere he received the abrupt answer, "No, my Lord; I am sorry I cannot have the honour of spending another day with your lordship; my post horses are ordered, and will be here directly."

All who were present showed surprise, and Lord Woodville immediately replied, "Post horses, my good friend! What can you possibly want with them, when you promised to stay with me quietly for at least a week?"

"I believe," said the General, obviously much embarrassed, "that I might, in the pleasure of my first meeting with your lordship, have said something about stopping here a few days; but I have since found it altogether impossible."

"That is very extraordinary," answered the young nobleman. "You seemed quite disengaged yesterday, and you cannot have had a summons to-day; for our post has not come up from the town, and therefore you cannot have received any letters."

General Browne, without giving any further explanation, muttered something of indispensable business, and insisted on the absolute necessity of his departure in a manner which silenced all opposition on the part of his host, who saw that his resolution was taken, and forbore further importunity.

"At least, however," he said, "permit me, my dear Browne, since go you will or must, to show you the view from the terrace, which the mist that is now rising, will soon display."

He threw open a sash-window, and stepped down upon the terrace as he spoke. The General followed him mechanically, but seemed little to attend to what his host was saying, as, looking across an extended and rich prospect, he pointed out the different objects worthy of observation. Thus they moved on till Lord Woodville had attained his purpose of drawing his guest entirely apart from the rest of the company, when, turning round upon him with an air of great solemnity, he addressed him thus:

"Richard Browne, my old and very dear friend, we are now alone. Let me conjure you to answer me upon the word of a friend, and the honour of a soldier. How did you in reality rest during last night?"

"Most wretchedly indeed, my lord," answered the General, in the same tone of solemnity; "so miserably, that I would not run the risk of such a second night, not only for all the lands belonging to this castle, but for all the country which I see from this elevated point of view."

"This is most extraordinary," said the young lord, as if speaking to himself; "then there must be something in the reports concerning that apartment." Again turning to the General, he said, "For God's sake, my dear friend, be candid with me, and let me know the disagreeable particulars which have befallen you under a roof where, with consent of the owner, you should have met nothing save comfort."

The General seemed distressed by this appeal, and paused a moment before he replied. "My dear lord," he at length said, "what happened to me last night is of nature so peculiar and so unpleasant, that I could hardly bring myself to detail it even to your lordship, were it not that, independent of my wish to gratify any request of yours, I think that sincerity on my part may lead to some explanation about a circumstance equally painful and mysterious. To others, the communications I am about to make, might place me in the light of a weak-minded, superstitious fool who suffered his own imagination to delude and bewilder him; but you have known me in childhood and youth, and will not suspect me of having adopted in manhood the feelings and frailties from which my early years were free." Here he paused, and his friend replied:

"Do not doubt my perfect confidence in the truth of your communication, however strange it may be," replied Lord Woodville. "I know your firmness of disposition too well, to suspect you could be made the object of imposition, and am aware that your honour and your friendship will equally deter you from exaggerating whatever you may have witnessed."

"Well then," said the General, "I will proceed with my story as well as I can, relying upon your candour; and yet distinctly feeling that I would rather face a battery than recall to my mind the odious recollections of last night."

He paused a second time, and then perceiving that Lord Woodville remained silent and in an attitude of attention, he commenced, though not without obvious reluctance, the history of his night's adventures in the Tapestried Chamber.

"I undressed and went to bed, so soon as your lordship left me yesterday evening; but the wood in the chimney, which nearly fronted my bed, blazed brightly and cheerfully, and, aided by a hundred exciting recollections of my childhood and youth, which had been recalled by the unexpected pleasure of meeting your lordship, prevented me from falling immediately asleep. I ought, however, to say that these reflections were all of a pleasant and agreeable kind, grounded on a sense of having for a time exchanged the labour, fatigues, and dangers of my profession, for the enjoyments of a peaceful life, and the reunion of those friendly and affectionate ties which I had torn asunder at the rude summons of war.

"While such pleasing reflections were stealing over my mind, and gradually lulling me to slumber, I was suddenly aroused by a sound like that of the rustling of a silken gown, and the tapping of a pair of high-heeled shoes, as if a woman were walking in the apartment. Ere I could draw the curtain to see what the matter was, the figure of a little woman passed between the bed and the fire. The back of this form was turned to me, and I could observe, from the shoulders and neck, it was that of an old woman, whose dress was an old-fashioned gown, which, I think, ladies call a sacque—that is, a sort of robe, completely loose in the body, but gathered into broad plaits upon the neck and shoulders, which fall down to the ground, and terminate in a species of train.

"I thought the intrusion singular enough, but never harboured for a moment the idea that what I saw was anything more than the mortal form of some old woman about the establishment, who had a fancy to dress like her grandmother, and who, having perhaps (as your lordship mentioned that you were rather straitened for room) been dislodged from her chamber for my accommodation, had forgotten the circumstance, and returned by twelve to her old haunt. Under this persuasion I moved myself in bed and coughed a little, to make the intruder sensible of my being in possession of the premises. She turned slowly round, but gracious Heaven! My lord, what a countenance did she display to me!

"There was no longer any question what she was, or any thought of her being a living being. Upon a face which wore the fixed features of a corpse, were imprinted the traces of the vilest and most hideous passions which had animated her while she lived. The body of some atrocious criminal seemed to have been given up from the grave, and the soul restored from the penal fire, in order to form, for a space, a union with the ancient accomplice of its guilt. I started up in bed, and sat upright, supporting myself on my palms, as I gazed on this horrible spectre. The hag made, as it seemed, a single and swift stride to the bed where I lay, and squatted herself down upon it, in precisely the same attitude which I had assumed in the extremity of horror, advancing her diabolical countenance within half a yard of mine, with a grin which seemed to intimate the malice and the derision of an incarnate fiend."

Here General Browne stopped, and wiped from his brow the cold perspiration with which the recollection of his horrible vision had covered it.

"My lord," he said, "I am no coward. I have been in all the mortal dangers incidental to my profession, and I may truly boast that no man ever knew Richard Browne dishonour the sword he wears; but in these horrible circumstances, under the eyes, and as it seemed, almost in the grasp of an incarnation of an evil spirit, all firmness forsook me, all manhood melted from me like wax in the furnace, and I felt my hair individually bristle. The current of my life-blood ceased to flow, and I sank back in a swoon, as very a victim to panic terror as ever was a village girl or a child of ten years old. How long I lay in this condition I cannot pretend to guess.

"But I was roused by the castle clock striking one, so loud that it seemed as if it were in the very room. It was some time before I dared open my eyes, lest they should again encounter the horrible spectacle. When, however, I summoned courage to look up, she was no longer visible. My first idea was to pull my bell, wake the servants, and remove to a garret or a hay-loft, to be ensured against a second visitation. Nay, I will confess the truth, that my resolution was altered, not by the shame of exposing myself, but by the very fear that, as the bell-cord hung by the chimney, I might, in making my way to it, be again crossed by the fiendish hag, who, I figured to myself, might be still lurking about some corner of the apartment.

"I will not pretend to describe what hot and cold fever-fits tormented me for the rest of the night, through broken sleep, weary vigils, and that dubious state which forms the neutral ground between them. An hundred terrible objects appeared to haunt me; but there was the great difference betwixt the vision which I have described, and those which followed, that I knew the last to be deceptions of my own fancy and overexcited nerves.

"Day at last appeared, and I rose from my bed ill in health, and humiliated in mind. I was ashamed of myself as a man and a soldier, and still more so, at feeling my own extreme desire to escape from the haunted apartment, which, however, conquered all other considerations; so that, huddling on my clothes with the most careless haste, I made my escape from your lordship's mansion, to seek in the open air some relief to my nervous system, shaken as it was by this horrible rencountre* with a visitant, for such I must believe her, from the other world. Your lordship has now heard the cause of my discomposure, and of my sudden desire to leave your hospitable castle. In other places I trust we may often meet; but God protect me from ever spending a second night under that roof!"

Strange as the General's tale was, he spoke with such a deep air of conviction, that it cut short all the usual commentaries which are made on such stories. Lord Woodville never once asked him if he was sure he did not dream of the apparition, or suggested any of the possibilities by which it is fashionable to explain supernatural appearances, as wild vagaries of the fancy or deceptions of the optic nerves. On the contrary, he seemed deeply impressed with the truth and reality of what he had heard; and, after a considerable pause, regretted, with much appearance of sincerity, that his early friend should in his house have suffered so severely.

"I am the more sorry for your pain, my dear Browne," he continued, "that it is the unhappy, though most unexpected, result of an experiment of my own. You must know that, for my father and grandfather's time, at least, the apartment which was assigned to you last night had been shut on account of reports that it was disturbed by supernatural sights and noises. When I came, a few weeks since, into possession of the estate, I thought the accommodation which the castle afforded for my friends was not extensive enough to permit the inhabitants of the invisible world to retain possession of a comfortable sleeping-apartment. I therefore caused the Tapestried Chamber, as we call it, to be opened; and without destroying its air of antiquity, I had such new articles of furniture placed in it as became the modern times.

"Yet, as the opinion that the room was haunted very strongly prevailed among the domestics, and was also known in the neighbourhood and to

---

* An archaic word, meaning an unexpected meeting.

many of my friends, I feared some prejudice might be entertained by the first occupant of the Tapestried Chamber, which might tend to revive the evil report which it had laboured under, and so disappoint my purpose of rendering it a useful part of the house. I must confess, my dear Browne, that your arrival yesterday, agreeable to me for a thousand reasons besides, seemed the most favourable opportunity of removing the unpleasant rumours which attached to the room, since your courage was indubitable, and your mind free of any preoccupation on the subject. I could not, there-fore, have chosen a more fitting subject for my experiment."

"Upon my life," said General Browne, somewhat hastily, "I am infinitely obliged to your lordship—very particularly indebted indeed. I am likely to remember for some time the consequences of the experiment, as your lordship is pleased to call it."

"Nay, now you are unjust, my dear friend," said Lord Woodville. "You have only to reflect for a single moment, in order to be convinced that I could not augur the possibility of the pain to which you have been so unhappily exposed. I was yesterday morning a complete sceptic on the subject of supernatural appearances. Nay, I am sure that, had I told you what was said about that room, those very reports would have induced you, by your own choice, to select it for your accommodation. It was my misfortune, perhaps my error, but really cannot be termed my fault, that you have been afflicted so strangely."

"Strangely indeed!" said the General, resuming his good temper; "and I acknowledge that I have no right to be offended with your lordship for treating me like what I used to think myself, a man of some firmness and courage. But I see my post-horses are arrived, and I must not detain your lordship from your amusement."

"Nay, my old friend," said Lord Woodville, "since you cannot stay with us another day, which, indeed, I can no longer urge, give me at least half an hour more. You used to love pictures, and I have a gallery of portraits, some of them by Vandyke,* representing ancestry to whom this property

---

* The seventeenth-century Flemish painter Anthony van Dyck was a leading court painter in England whose portraits of Charles I were considered to be influential in English portrait painting.

and castle formerly belonged. I think that several of them will strike you as possessing merit."

General Browne accepted the invitation, though somewhat unwillingly. It was evident he was not to breathe freely or at ease until he left Woodville Castle far behind him. He could not refuse his friend's invitation, however; and the less so, that he was a little ashamed of the peevishness which he had displayed towards his well-meaning entertainer.

The general, therefore, followed Lord Woodville through several rooms, into a long gallery hung with pictures, which the latter pointed out to his guest, telling the names, and giving some account, of the personages whose portraits presented themselves in progression. General Browne was but little interested in the details which these accounts conveyed to him. They were, indeed, of the kind which are usually found in an old family gallery. Here was a cavalier who had ruined the estate in the royal cause; there, a fine lady who had reinstated it by contracting a match with a wealthy Roundhead. There hung a gallant who had been in danger for cor-responding with the exiled court at St. Germain's; here, one who had taken arms for William at the Revolution; and there, a third that had thrown his weight alternately into the scale of Whig and Tory.

While Lord Woodville was cramming these words into his guest's ear, "against the stomach of his sense," they gained the middle of the gallery, when he beheld General Browne suddenly start, and assume an attitude of the utmost surprise, not unmixed with fear, as his eyes were caught and suddenly riveted by a portrait of an old lady in a sacque, the fashionable dress of the end of the 17th century.

"There she is!" he exclaimed—"there she is, in form and features, though inferior in demoniac expression to the accursed hag who visited me last night!"

"If that be the case," said the young nobleman, "there can remain no longer any doubt of the horrible reality of your apparition. That is the picture of a wretched ancestress of mine, of whose crimes a black and fearful catalogue is recorded in a family history in my charter-chest. The recital of them would be too horrible; it is enough to say, that in yon fatal apartment incest and unnatural murder were committed. I will restore it to the solitude to which the better judgement of those who preceded me had consigned it; and never shall any one, so long as I can prevent it, be exposed to a repetition of the supernatural horrors which could shake such courage as yours."

Thus the friends, who had met with such glee, parted in a very different mood—Lord Woodville to command the Tapestried Chamber to be unmantled and the door built up; and General Browne to seek in some less beautiful country, and with some less dignified friend, forgetfulness of the painful night which he had passed in Woodville Castle.*

---

* Browne's experience combines the ghost story with the popular folklore belief in the "night-hag," often thought to be a demon or witch rather than a ghost, described as sitting on the chest of the unfortunate victim. The night-hag probably derives from the experience of sleep paralysis.

The Gray Champion

by NATHANIEL HAWTHORNE

Nathaniel Hawthorne (1804–1864) was an American writer of novels and short fiction. Best remembered for his novels The Scarlet Letter *(1850) and* The House of Seven Gables *(1851), his stories were generally set in New England and had a dark Romantic tone, in many cases expressing sentiments in opposition to the Puritan spirit of his homeland. He was a prolific writer of short stories in his younger years, many with supernatural themes (including the Halloween-set witch classic "Young Goodman Brown"). This fine tale first appeared in* New England Magazine, *in January 1835.*

There was once a time, when New-England groaned under the actual pressure of heavier wrongs, than those threatened ones which brought on the Revolution. James II,* the bigoted successor of Charles the Voluptuous, had annulled the charters of all the colonies, and sent a harsh and unprincipled soldier to take away our liberties

---

* James II ruled from 1685 to 1688.

and endanger our religion. The administration of Sir Edmund Andros lacked scarcely a single characteristic of tyranny: a Governor and Council, holding office from the King, and wholly independent of the country; laws made and taxes levied without concurrence of the people, immediate or by their representatives; the rights of private citizens violated, and the titles of all landed property declared void; the voice of complaint stifled by restrictions on the press; and, finally, disaffection overawed by the first band of mercenary troops that ever marched on our free soil. For two years, our ancestors were kept in sullen submission, by that filial love which had invariably secured their allegiance to the mother country, whether its head chanced to be a Parliament, Protector, or popish Monarch. Till these evil times, however, such allegiance had been merely nominal, and the colonists had ruled themselves, enjoying far more freedom, than is even yet the privilege of the native subjects of Great Britain.

At length, a rumor reached our shores, that the Prince of Orange had ventured on an enterprise, the success of which would be the triumph of civil and religious rights and the salvation of New-England. It was but a doubtful whisper; it might be false, or the attempt might fail; and, in either case, the man, that stirred against King James, would lose his head. Still the intelligence produced a marked effect. The people smiled mysteriously in the streets, and threw bold glances at their oppressors; while, far and wide, there was a subdued and silent agitation, as if the slightest signal would rouse the whole land from its sluggish despondency. Aware of their danger, the rulers resolved to avert it by an imposing display of strength, and perhaps to confirm their despotism by yet harsher measures. One afternoon in April, 1689, Sir Edmund Andros and his favorite councillors, being warm with wine, assembled the red-coats of the Governor's Guard, and made their appearance in the streets of Boston. The sun was near setting when the march commenced.

The roll of the drum, at that unquiet crisis, seemed to go through the streets, less as the martial music of the soldiers, than as a muster-call to the inhabitants themselves. A multitude, by various avenues, assembled in King-street, which was destined to be the scene, nearly a century afterwards, of another encounter between the troops of Britain, and a people struggling against her tyranny. Though more than sixty years had elapsed, since the Pilgrims came, this crowd of their descendants still showed the strong and sombre features of their character, perhaps more strikingly in such a stern emergency than on happier occasions. There was the sober garb, the general severity of mien, the gloomy but undismayed expression, the scriptural forms of speech, and the confidence in Heaven's blessing on a righteous cause, which would have marked a band of the original Puritans, when threatened by some peril of the wilderness. Indeed, it was not yet time for the old spirit to be extinct; since there were men in the street, that day, who had worshipped there beneath the trees, before a house was reared to the God, for whom they had become exiles. Old soldiers of the Parliament were here too, smiling grimly at the thought, that their aged arms might strike another blow against the house of Stuart. Here also, were the veterans of King Philip's war, who had burnt villages and slaughtered young and old, with pious fierceness, while the godly souls throughout the land were helping them with prayer. Several ministers were scattered among the crowd, which, unlike all other mobs, regarded them with such reverence, as if there were sanctity in their very garments. These holy men exerted their influence to quiet the people, but not to disperse them. Meantime, the purpose of the Governor, in disturbing the peace of the town, at a period when the slightest commotion might throw the country into a ferment, was almost the universal subject of inquiry, and variously explained.

"Satan will strike his master-stroke presently," cried some, "because he knoweth that his time is short. All our godly pastors are to be dragged to prison! We shall see them at a Smithfield fire in King-street!"

Hereupon, the people of each parish gathered closer round their minister, who looked calmly upwards and assumed a more apostolic dignity, as well befitted a candidate for the highest honor of his profession, the crown of martyrdom. It was actually fancied, at that period, that New-England might have a John Rogers* of her own, to take the place of that worthy in the Primer.

---

* John Rogers, a supporter of William Tyndale, was burned at the stake at Smithfield, England on February 4, 1555, the first of many Protestant martyrs under the reign of Queen Mary.

"The Pope of Rome has given orders for a new St. Bartholomew!" cried others. "We are to be massacred, man and male child!"

Neither was this rumor wholly discredited, although the wiser class believed the Governor's object somewhat less atrocious. His predecessor under the old charter, Bradstreet, a venerable companion of the first settlers, was known to be in town. There were grounds for conjecturing, that Sir Edmund Andros intended, at once, to strike terror, by a parade of military force, and to confound the opposite faction, by possessing himself of their chief.

"Stand firm for the old charter Governor!" shouted the crowd, seizing upon the idea. "The good old Governor Bradstreet!"

While this cry was at the loudest, the people were surprised by the well known figure of Governor Bradstreet himself, a patriarch of nearly ninety, who appeared on the elevated steps of a door, and, with characteristic mildness, besought them to submit to the constituted authorities.

"My children," concluded this venerable person, "do nothing rashly. Cry not aloud, but pray for the welfare of New-England, and expect patiently what the Lord will do in this matter!"

The event was soon to be decided. All this time, the roll of the drum had been approaching through Cornhill, louder and deeper, till, with reverberations from house to house, and the regular tramp of martial footsteps, it burst into the street. A double rank of soldiers made their appearance, occupying the whole breadth of the passage, with shouldered matchlocks, and matches burning, so as to present a row of fires in the dusk. Their steady march was like the progress of a machine, that would roll irresistibly over every thing in its way. Next, moving slowly, with a confused clatter of hoofs on the pavement, rode a party of mounted gentlemen, the central figure being Sir Edmund Andros, elderly, but erect and soldier-like. Those around him were his favorite councillors, and the bitterest foes of New-England. At his right hand rode Edward Randolph, our arch enemy, that "blasted wretch," as Cotton Mather calls him, who achieved the downfall of our ancient government, and was followed with a sensible curse, through life and to his grave. On the other side was Bullivant, scattering jests and mockery as he rode along. Dudley came behind, with a downcast look, dreading, as well he might, to meet the indignant gaze of the people, who beheld him, their only countryman by birth, among the oppressors of his native land. The captain of a frigate in the harbor, and two or three civil officers under the Crown, were also there. But the figure which most attracted the public eye, and stirred up the deepest feeling, was the Episcopal clergyman of King's Chapel, riding haughtily among the magistrates in his priestly vestments, the fitting representative of prelacy and persecution, the union of church and state, and all those abominations which had driven the Puritans to the wilderness. Another guard of soldiers, in double rank, brought up the rear.

The whole scene was a picture of the condition of New-England, and its moral, the deformity of any government that does not grow out of the nature of things and the character of the people. On one side the religious multitude, with their sad visages and dark attire, and on the other, the group of despotic rulers, with the high churchman in the midst, and here and there a crucifix at their bosoms, all magnificently clad, flushed with wine, proud of unjust authority, and scoffing at the universal groan. And the mercenary soldiers, waiting but the word to deluge the street with blood, shewed the only means by which obedience could be secured.

"Oh! Lord of Hosts," cried a voice among the crowd, "provide a Champion for thy people!"

This ejaculation was loudly uttered, and served as a herald's cry, to introduce a remarkable personage. The crowd had rolled back, and were now huddled together nearly at the extremity of the street, while the soldiers had advanced no more than a third of its length. The intervening space was empty—a paved solitude, between lofty edifices, which threw almost a twilight shadow over it. Suddenly, there was seen the figure of an ancient man, who seemed to have emerged from among the people, and was walking by himself along the centre of the street, to confront the armed band. He wore the old Puritan dress, a dark cloak and a steeple-crowned hat, in the fashion of at least fifty years before, with a heavy sword upon his thigh, but a staff in his hand, to assist the tremulous gait of age.

When at some distance from the multitude, the old man turned slowly round, displaying a face of antique majesty, rendered doubly venerable by the hoary beard that descended on his breast. He made a gesture at once of encouragement and warning, then turned again, and resumed his way.

"Who is this gray patriarch?" asked the young men of their sires.

"Who is this venerable brother?" asked the old men among themselves.

But none could make reply. The fathers of the people, those of four-score years and upwards, were disturbed, deeming it strange that they should forget one of such evident authority, whom they must have known in their early days, the associate of Winthrop and all the old Councillors, giving laws, and making prayers, and leading them against the savage. The elderly men ought to have remembered him, too, with locks as gray in their youth, as their own were now. And the young! How could he have passed so utterly from their memories—that hoary sire, the relic of long departed times, whose awful benediction had surely been bestowed on their uncovered heads, in childhood?

"Whence did he come? What is his purpose? Who can this old man be?" whispered the wondering crowd.

Meanwhile, the venerable stranger, staff in hand, was pursuing his solitary walk along the centre of the street. As he drew near the advancing soldiers, and as the roll of their drum came full upon his ear, the old man raised himself to a loftier mien, while the decrepitude of age seemed to fall from his shoulders, leaving him in gray, but unbroken dignity. Now, he marched onward with a warrior's step, keeping time to the military music. Thus the aged form advanced on one side, and the whole parade of soldiers and magistrates on the other, till, when scarcely twenty yards remained between, the old man grasped his staff by the middle, and held it before him like a leader's truncheon.

"Stand!" cried he.

The eye, the face, and attitude of command; the solemn, yet warlike peal of that voice, fit either to rule a host in the battle-field or be raised to God in prayer, were irresistible. At the old man's word and outstretched arm, the roll of the drum was hushed at once, and the advancing line stood still. A tremulous enthusiasm seized upon the multitude. That stately form, combining the leader and the saint, so gray, so dimly seen, in such an ancient garb, could only belong to some old champion of the righteous cause, whom the oppressor's drum had summoned from his grave. They raised a shout of awe and exultation, and looked for the deliverance of New-England.

The Governor, and the gentlemen of his party, perceiving themselves brought to an unexpected stand, rode hastily forward, as if they would have pressed their snorting and affrighted horses right against the hoary apparition. He, however, blenched not a step, but glancing his severe eye round the group, which half encompassed him, at last bent it sternly on Sir Edmund Andros. One would have thought that the dark old man was chief ruler there, and that the Governor and Council, with soldiers at their back, representing the whole power and authority of the Crown, had no alternative but obedience.

"What does this old fellow here?" cried Edward Randolph, fiercely. "On, Sir Edmund! Bid the soldiers forward, and give the dotard the same choice that you give all his countrymen—to stand aside or be trampled on!"

"Nay, nay, let us show respect to the good grandsire," said Bullivant, laughing. "See you not, he is some old roundheaded dignitary, who hath lain asleep these thirty years, and knows nothing of the change of times? Doubtless, he thinks to put us down with a proclamation in Old Noll's name!"*

"Are you mad, old man?" demanded Sir Edmund Andros, in loud and harsh tones. "How dare you stay the march of King James's Governor?"

"I have staid the march of a King himself, ere now," replied the gray figure, with stern composure. "I am here, Sir Governor, because the cry of an oppressed people hath disturbed me in my secret place; and beseeching this favor earnestly of the Lord, it was vouchsafed me to appear once again on earth, in the good old cause of his Saints. And what speak ye of James? There is no longer a popish tyrant on the throne of England, and by to-morrow noon, his name shall be a by-word in this very street, where ye would make it a word of terror.† Back, thou that wast a Governor, back! With this night, thy power is ended—to-morrow, the prison!—back, lest I foretell the scaffold!"

---

* A slang expression for Oliver Cromwell (1599–1658), the Lord-Protector of the commonwealth of England.

† James II, the last Roman Catholic (or "popish") monarch of England, Scotland, and Ireland, abdicated in December 1688 and was replaced by his Protestant elder daughter and her husband William III.

The people had been drawing nearer and nearer, and drinking in the words of their champion, who spoke in accents long disused, like one unaccustomed to converse, except with the dead of many years ago. But his voice stirred their souls. They confronted the soldiers, not wholly without arms, and ready to convert the very stones of the street into deadly weapons. Sir Edmund Andros looked at the old man; then he cast his hard and cruel eye over the multitude, and beheld them burning with that lurid wrath, so difficult to kindle or to quench; and again he fixed his gaze on the aged form, which stood obscurely in an open space, where neither friend nor foe had thrust himself. What were his thoughts, he uttered no word which might discover. But whether the oppressor were overawed by the Gray Champion's look, or perceived his peril in the threatening attitude of the people, it is certain that he gave back, and ordered his soldiers to commence a slow and guarded retreat. Before another sunset, the Governor, and all that rode so proudly with him, were prisoners, and long ere it was known that James had abdicated, King William was proclaimed throughout New-England.

But where was the Gray Champion? Some reported, that when the troops had gone from King-street, and the people were thronging tumultuously in their rear, Bradstreet, the aged Governor, was seen to embrace a form more aged than his own. Others soberly affirmed, that while they marvelled at the venerable grandeur of his aspect, the old man had faded from their eyes, melting slowly into the hues of twilight, till, where he stood, there was an empty space. But all agreed, that the hoary shape was gone. The men of that generation watched for his re-appearance, in sunshine and in twilight, but never saw him more, nor knew when his funeral passed, nor where his grave-stone was.

And who was the Gray Champion? Perhaps his name might be found in the records of that stern Court of Justice, which passed a sentence, too mighty for the age, but glorious in all after times, for its humbling lesson to the monarch and its high example to the subject. I have heard, that, whenever the descendants of the Puritans are to show the spirit of their sires, the old man appears again. When eighty years had passed, he walked once more in King-street. Five years later, in the twilight of an April morning, he stood on the green, beside the meeting-house, at Lexington, where now the obelisk of granite, with a slab of slate inlaid, commemorates the first fallen of the Revolution. And when our fathers were toiling at the breast-work on Bunker's Hill, all through that night, the old warrior walked his rounds. Long, long may it be, ere he comes again! His hour is one of dark-ness, and adversity, and peril. But should domestic tyranny oppress us, or the invader's step pollute our soil, still may the Gray Champion come; for he is the type of New-England's hereditary spirit; and his shadowy march, on the eve of danger, must ever be the pledge, that New-England's sons will vindicate their ancestry.

Ligeia

by EDGAR ALLAN POE

There is little that need be said about the great American short-story writer and poet Edgar Allan Poe (1809–1849) except perhaps to mourn that he wrote only just over sixty tales and had so little fame during his lifetime in his native land. Best known for brilliant gems of mystery and horror, Poe is now hailed as the father of detective fiction and the greatest writer of horror of the nineteenth century. The following is possibly the closest to a traditional ghost story that Poe ever wrote. It first appeared in 1838 in the Baltimore American Museum *and was Poe's personal favorite among his short stories.*

And the will therein lieth, which dieth not. Who knoweth the mysteries of the will, with its vigor? For God is but a great will pervading all things by nature of its intentness. Man doth not yield himself to the angels, nor unto death utterly, save only through the weakness of his feeble will.

—Joseph Glanvill.*

---

* Although the sentiment is certainly Glanvillian, these lines were not written by Joseph Glanvill (1636–1680). They were likely written by Poe himself.

I cannot, for my soul, remember how, when, or even precisely where, I first became acquainted with the lady Ligeia.* Long years have since elapsed, and my memory is feeble through much suffering. Or, perhaps, I cannot now bring these points to mind, because, in truth, the character of my beloved, her rare learning, her singular yet placid cast of beauty, and the thrilling and enthralling eloquence of her low musical language, made their way into my heart by paces so steadily and stealthily progressive that they have been unnoticed and unknown. Yet I believe that I met her first and most frequently in some large, old, decaying city near the Rhine. Of her family—I have surely heard her speak. That it is of a remotely ancient date cannot be doubted. Ligeia! Ligeia! Buried in studies of a nature more than all else adapted to deaden impressions of the outward world, it is by that sweet word alone—by Ligeia—that I bring before mine eyes in fancy the image of her who is no more. And now, while I write, a recollection flashes upon me that I have never known the paternal name of her who was my friend and my betrothed, and who became the partner of my studies, and finally the wife of my bosom. Was it a playful charge on the part of my Ligeia? or was it a test of my strength of affection, that I should institute no inquiries upon this point? or was it rather a caprice of my own—a wildly romantic offering on the shrine of the most passionate devotion? I but indistinctly recall the fact itself—what wonder that I have utterly forgotten the circumstances which originated or attended it? And, indeed, if ever that spirit which is entitled Romance—if ever she, the wan and the misty-winged Ashtophet of idolatrous Egypt,† presided, as they tell, over marriages ill-omened, then most surely she presided over mine.

There is one dear topic, however, on which my memory fails me not. It is the person of Ligeia. In stature she was tall, somewhat slender, and, in her latter days, even emaciated. I would in vain attempt to portray the majesty, the quiet ease, of her demeanor, or the incomprehensible lightness and elasticity of her footfall. She came and departed as a shadow. I was never made aware of her entrance into my closed study save by the dear music

---

* The name "Ligeia" comes from Greek mythology, where it refers to one of the Sirens and means "clear-toned."

† Ishtar, or Ashtoreh, or Astarte—the ancient Mediterranean goddess of love.

of her low sweet voice, as she placed her marble hand upon my shoulder. In beauty of face no maiden ever equalled her. It was the radiance of an opium-dream—an airy and spirit-lifting vision more wildly divine than the phantasies which hovered about the slumbering souls of the daughters of Delos.* Yet her features were not of that regular mould which we have been falsely taught to worship in the classical labors of the heathen. "There is no exquisite beauty," says Bacon, Lord Verulam, speaking truly of all the forms and genera of beauty, "without some strangeness in the proportion."† Yet, although I saw that the features of Ligeia were not of a classic regularity—although I perceived that her loveliness was indeed "exquisite," and felt that there was much of "strangeness" pervading it, yet I have tried in vain to detect the irregularity and to trace home my own perception of "the strange." I examined the contour of the lofty and pale forehead—it was faultless—how cold indeed that word when applied to a majesty so divine!—the skin rivalling the purest ivory, the commanding extent and repose, the gentle prominence of the regions above the temples; and then the raven-black, the glossy, the luxuriant and naturally-curling tresses, setting forth the full force of the Homeric epithet, "hyacinthine!"‡ I looked at the delicate outlines of the nose—and nowhere but in the graceful medallions of the Hebrews had I beheld a similar perfection. There were the same luxurious smoothness of surface, the same scarcely perceptible tendency to the aquiline, the same harmoniously curved nostrils speaking the free spirit. I regarded the sweet mouth. Here was indeed the triumph of all things heavenly—the magnificent turn of the short upper lip—the soft, voluptuous slumber of the under—the dimples which sported, and the color which spoke—the teeth glancing back, with a brilliancy almost startling, every ray of the holy light which fell upon them in her serene and placid,

---

* These were the maidens of the mythological birthplace of Apollo and his twin sister Artemis, who waited upon the lady.

† Poe has slightly misquoted this; the original, from Bacon's essay "Of Beauty" (which appeared in Bacon's 1625 collection *Essays*), actually reads, "There is no excellent beauty that hath not some strangeness in the proportion."

‡ Homer, in the *Odyssey*, refers to locks "like the hyacinthine flower," referring not to the color but the texture and shape of the petals.

yet most exultingly radiant of all smiles. I scrutinized the formation of the chin—and here, too, I found the gentleness of breadth, the softness and the majesty, the fullness and the spirituality, of the Greek—the contour which the god Apollo revealed but in a dream, to Cleomenes, the son of the Athenian.˙ And then I peered into the large eyes of Ligeia.

For eyes we have no models in the remotely antique. It might have been, too, that in these eyes of my beloved lay the secret to which Lord Verulam alludes. They were, I must believe, far larger than the ordinary eyes of our own race. They were even fuller than the fullest of the gazelle eyes of the tribe of the valley of Nourjahad.† Yet it was only at intervals—in moments of intense excitement—that this peculiarity became more than slightly noticeable in Ligeia. And at such moments was her beauty—in my heated fancy thus it appeared perhaps—the beauty of beings either above or apart from the earth—the beauty of the fabulous Houri of the Turk.‡ The hue of the orbs was the most brilliant of black, and, far over them, hung jetty lashes of great length. The brows, slightly irregular in outline, had the same tint. The "strangeness," however, which I found in the eyes, was of a nature distinct from the formation, or the color, or the brilliancy of the features, and must, after all, be referred to the expression. Ah, word of no meaning! behind whose vast latitude of mere sound we intrench our ignorance of so much of the spiritual. The expression of the eyes of Ligeia! How for long hours have I pondered upon it! How have I, through the whole of a midsummer night, struggled to fathom it! What was it—that something more profound than the well of Democritus§—which lay far within the pupils

---

* Poe is likely referring here to the famous Venus de' Medici sculpture from the first century B.C., which bears an inscription at its base reading "Cleomenes Son of Apollodorus of Athens."

† *The History of Nourjahad* was an Oriental romance written by Frances Sheridan in 1767. Nourjahad was a person, not a place.

‡ Houri are found in the Quran, which describes them as companions to true believers who arrive in Paradise; mention is made of their large, beautiful eyes.

§ Poe opened his story "A Descent Into the Maelstrom" with a quote from Glanvill—correctly attributed this time—that includes the phrase "well of Democritus." Democritus was a Greek philosopher who theorized the existence of atoms, and his "well" is an allusion to knowledge.

of my beloved? What was it? I was possessed with a passion to discover. Those eyes! those large, those shining, those divine orbs! they became to me twin stars of Leda,⁎ and I to them devoutest of astrologers.

There is no point, among the many incomprehensible anomalies of the science of mind, more thrillingly exciting than the fact—never, I believe, noticed in the schools—that, in our endeavors to recall to memory something long forgotten, we often find ourselves upon the very verge of remembrance, without being able, in the end, to remember. And thus how frequently, in my intense scrutiny of Ligeia's eyes, have I felt approaching the full knowledge of their expression—felt it approaching—yet not quite be mine—and so at length entirely depart! And (strange, oh strangest mystery of all!) I found, in the commonest objects of the universe, a circle of analogies to that expression. I mean to say that, subsequently to the period when Ligeia's beauty passed into my spirit, there dwelling as in a shrine, I derived, from many existences in the material world, a sentiment such as I felt always around aroused within me by her large and luminous orbs. Yet not the more could I define that sentiment, or analyze, or even steadily view it. I recognized it, let me repeat, sometimes in the survey of a rapidly-growing vine—in the contemplation of a moth, a butterfly, a chrysalis, a stream of running water. I have felt it in the ocean; in the falling of a meteor. I have felt it in the glances of unusually aged people. And there are one or two stars in heaven—(one especially, a star of the sixth magnitude, double and changeable, to be found near the large star in Lyra)† in a telescopic scrutiny of which I have been made aware of the feeling. I have been filled with it by certain sounds from stringed instruments, and not unfrequently by passages from books. Among innumerable other instances, I well remember something in a volume of Joseph Glanvill, which (perhaps merely from its quaintness—who shall say?) never failed to inspire me with the sentiment;—"And the will therein lieth, which dieth not. Who knoweth the mysteries of the will, with its vigor? For God is but a great will pervading all things by nature of its intentness. Man doth

---

⁎ Castor and Pollux, bright stars of the constellation *Gemini*, are the twins born to Leda and Zeus.

† This refers to *Epsilon Lyrae*, a star of varying intensity near Vega (*Alpha Lyrae*).

not yield him to the angels, nor unto death utterly, save only through the weakness of his feeble will."

Length of years, and subsequent reflection, have enabled me to trace, indeed, some remote connection between this passage in the English moralist and a portion of the character of Ligeia. An intensity in thought, action, or speech, was possibly, in her, a result, or at least an index, of that gigantic volition which, during our long intercourse, failed to give other and more immediate evidence of its existence. Of all the women whom I have ever known, she, the outwardly calm, the ever-placid Ligeia, was the most violently a prey to the tumultuous vultures of stern passion. And of such passion I could form no estimate, save by the miraculous expansion of those eyes which at once so delighted and appalled me—by the almost magical melody, modulation, distinctness and placidity of her very low voice—and by the fierce energy (rendered doubly effective by contrast with her manner of utterance) of the wild words which she habitually uttered.

I have spoken of the learning of Ligeia: it was immense—such as I have never known in woman. In the classical tongues was she deeply proficient, and as far as my own acquaintance extended in regard to the modern dialects of Europe, I have never known her at fault. Indeed upon any theme of the most admired, because simply the most abstruse of the boasted erudition of the academy, have I ever found Ligeia at fault? How singularly—how thrillingly, this one point in the nature of my wife has forced itself, at this late period only, upon my attention! I said her knowledge was such as I have never known in woman—but where breathes the man who has traversed, and successfully, all the wide areas of moral, physical, and mathematical science? I saw not then what I now clearly perceive, that the acquisitions of Ligeia were gigantic, were astounding; yet I was sufficiently aware of her infinite supremacy to resign myself, with a child-like confidence, to her guidance through the chaotic world of metaphysical investigation at which I was most busily occupied during the earlier years of our marriage. With how vast a triumph—with how vivid a delight—with how much of all that is ethereal in hope—did I feel, as she bent over me in studies but little sought—but less known—that delicious vista by slow degrees expanding before me, down whose long, gorgeous, and all untrodden path, I might at length pass onward to the goal of a wisdom too divinely precious not to be forbidden!

How poignant, then, must have been the grief with which, after some years, I beheld my well-grounded expectations take wings to themselves and fly away! Without Ligeia I was but as a child groping benighted. Her presence, her readings alone, rendered vividly luminous the many mysteries of the transcendentalism in which we were immersed. Wanting the radiant lustre of her eyes, letters, lambent and golden, grew duller than Saturnian lead.* And now those eyes shone less and less frequently upon the pages over which I pored. Ligeia grew ill. The wild eyes blazed with a too—too glorious effulgence; the pale fingers became of the transparent waxen hue of the grave; and the blue veins upon the lofty forehead swelled and sank impetuously with the tides of the most gentle emotion. I saw that she must die—and I struggled desperately in spirit with the grim Azrael.† And the struggles of the passionate wife were, to my astonishment, even more energetic than my own. There had been much in her stern nature to impress me with the belief that, to her, death would have come without its terrors;—but not so. Words are impotent to convey any just idea of the fierceness of resistance with which she wrestled with the Shadow. I groaned in anguish at the pitiable spectacle. I would have soothed—I would have reasoned; but, in the intensity of her wild desire for life,—for life—but for life—solace and reason were alike the uttermost of folly. Yet not until the last instance, amid the most convulsive writhings of her fierce spirit, was shaken the external placidity of her demeanor. Her voice grew more gentle—grew more low—yet I would not wish to dwell upon the wild meaning of the quietly uttered words. My brain reeled as I hearkened, entranced, to a melody more than mortal—to assumptions and aspirations which mortality had never before known.

That she loved me I should not have doubted; and I might have been easily aware that, in a bosom such as hers, love would have reigned no ordinary passion. But in death only, was I fully impressed with the

---

* In alchemy, lead—which can be transformed into gold via alchemical practices—is aligned with the planet Saturn.

† The Hebrew angel of death.

strength of her affection. For long hours, detaining my hand, would she pour out before me the overflowing of a heart whose more than passionate devotion amounted to idolatry. How had I deserved to be so blessed by such confessions?—how had I deserved to be so cursed with the removal of my beloved in the hour of her making them? But upon this subject I cannot bear to dilate. Let me say only, that in Ligeia's more than womanly abandonment to a love, alas! all unmerited, all unworthily bestowed, I at length recognized the principle of her longing with so wildly earnest a desire for the life which was now fleeing so rapidly away. It is this wild longing—it is this eager vehemence of desire for life—but for life—that I have no power to portray—no utterance capable of expressing.

At high noon of the night in which she departed, beckoning me, peremptorily, to her side, she bade me repeat certain verses composed by herself not many days before. I obeyed her.—They were these:

> Lo! 'tis a gala night
> Within the lonesome latter years!
> An angel throng, bewinged, bedight
> In veils, and drowned in tears,
> Sit in a theatre, to see
> A play of hopes and fears,
> While the orchestra breathes fitfully
> The music of the spheres.
>
> Mimes, in the form of God on high,
> Mutter and mumble low,
> And hither and thither fly—
> Mere puppets they, who come and go
> At bidding of vast formless things
> That shift the scenery to and fro,
> Flapping from out their Condor wings
> Invisible Wo!
>
> That motley drama!—oh, be sure
> It shall not be forgot!

With its Phantom chased forever more,
By a crowd that seize it not,
Through a circle that ever returneth in
To the self-same spot,
And much of Madness and more of Sin
And Horror the soul of the plot.

But see, amid the mimic rout,
A crawling shape intrude!
A blood-red thing that writhes from out
The scenic solitude!
It writhes!—it writhes!—with mortal pangs
The mimes become its food,
And the seraphs sob at vermin fangs
In human gore imbued.

Out—out are the lights—out all!
And over each quivering form,
The curtain, a funeral pall,
Comes down with the rush of a storm,
And the angels, all pallid and wan,
Uprising, unveiling, affirm
That the play is the tragedy, "Man,"
And its hero the Conqueror Worm.*

"O God!" half shrieked Ligeia, leaping to her feet and extending her
arms aloft with a spasmodic movement, as I made an end of these lines—"O
God! O Divine Father!—shall these things be undeviatingly so?—shall this
Conqueror be not once conquered? Are we not part and parcel in Thee?
Who—who knoweth the mysteries of the will with its vigor? Man doth
not yield him to the angels, nor unto death utterly, save only through the
weakness of his feeble will."

---

* The poem first appeared in *Graham's Gentleman's Magazine*, January, 1843 issue, before
Poe incorporated it into this story.

And now, as if exhausted with emotion, she suffered her white arms to fall, and returned solemnly to her bed of death. And as she breathed her last sighs, there came mingled with them a low murmur from her lips. I bent to them my ear and distinguished, again, the concluding words of the passage in Glanvill—"Man doth not yield him to the angels, nor unto death utterly, save only through the weakness of his feeble will."

She died;—and I, crushed into the very dust with sorrow, could no longer endure the lonely desolation of my dwelling in the dim and decaying city by the Rhine. I had no lack of what the world calls wealth. Ligeia had brought me far more, very far more than ordinarily falls to the lot of mortals. After a few months, therefore, of weary and aimless wandering, I purchased, and put in some repair, an abbey, which I shall not name, in one of the wildest and least frequented portions of fair England. The gloomy and dreary grandeur of the building, the almost savage aspect of the domain, the many melancholy and time-honored memories connected with both, had much in unison with the feelings of utter abandonment which had driven me into that remote and unsocial region of the country. Yet although the external abbey, with its verdant decay hanging about it, suffered but little alteration, I gave way, with a child-like perversity, and perchance with a faint hope of alleviating my sorrows, to a display of more than regal magnificence within. For such follies, even in childhood, I had imbibed a taste and now they came back to me as if in the dotage of grief. Alas, I feel how much even of incipient madness might have been discovered in the gorgeous and fantastic draperies, in the solemn carvings of Egypt, in the wild cornices and furniture, in the Bedlam patterns of the carpets of tufted gold! I had become a bounden slave in the trammels of opium, and my labors and my orders had taken a coloring from my dreams. But these absurdities I must not pause to detail. Let me speak only of that one chamber, ever accursed, whither in a moment of mental alienation, I led from the altar as my bride—as the successor of the unforgotten Ligeia—the fair-haired and blue-eyed Lady Rowena Trevanion, of Tremaine.

There is no individual portion of the architecture and decoration of that bridal chamber which is not now visibly before me. Where were the souls of the haughty family of the bride, when, through thirst of gold, they permitted to pass the threshold of an apartment so bedecked, a maiden and a daughter so beloved? I have said that I minutely remember the details of the chamber—yet I am sadly forgetful on topics of deep moment—and here there was no system, no keeping, in the fantastic display, to take hold upon the memory. The room lay in a high turret of the castellated abbey, was pentagonal in shape, and of capacious size. Occupying the whole southern face of the pentagon was the sole window—an immense sheet of unbroken glass from Venice—a single pane, and tinted of a leaden hue, so that the rays of either the sun or moon, passing through it, fell with a ghastly lustre on the objects within. Over the upper portion of this huge window, extended the trellice-work of an aged vine, which clambered up the massy walls of the turret. The ceiling, of gloomy-looking oak, was excessively lofty, vaulted, and elaborately fretted with the wildest and most grotesque specimens of a semi-Gothic, semi-Druidical device. From out the most central recess of this melancholy vaulting, depended, by a single chain of gold with long links, a huge censer of the same metal, Saracenic in pattern, and with many perforations so contrived that there writhed in and out of them, as if endued with a serpent vitality, a continual succession of parti-colored fires.

Some few ottomans and golden candelabra, of Eastern figure, were in various stations about—and there was the couch, too—the bridal couch—of an Indian model, and low, and sculptured of solid ebony, with a pall-like canopy above. In each of the angles of the chamber stood on end a gigantic sarcophagus of black granite, from the tombs of the kings over against Luxor, with their aged lids full of immemorial sculpture. But in the draping of the apartment lay, alas! the chief phantasy of all. The lofty walls, gigantic in height—even unproportionably so—were hung from summit to foot, in vast folds, with a heavy and massive-looking tapestry—tapestry of a material which was found alike as a carpet on the floor, as a covering for the ottomans and the ebony bed, as a canopy for the bed, and as the gorgeous volutes of the curtains which partially shaded the window. The material was the richest cloth of gold. It was spotted all over, at irregular intervals, with arabesque figures, about a foot in diameter, and wrought upon the cloth in patterns of the most jetty black. But these figures partook of the true character of the arabesque only when regarded from a single point of view. By a contrivance now common, and indeed traceable to a very remote period of antiquity, they were made changeable in aspect. To one entering the room, they bore the appearance of simple monstrosities; but upon a farther advance, this appearance gradually departed; and step by step, as the visiter moved his station in the chamber, he saw himself surrounded by an endless succession of the ghastly forms which belong to the superstition of the Norman, or arise in the guilty slumbers of the monk. The phantasmagoric effect was vastly heightened by the artificial introduction of a strong continual current of wind behind the draperies—giving a hideous and uneasy animation to the whole.

In halls such as these—in a bridal chamber such as this—I passed, with the Lady of Tremaine, the unhallowed hours of the first month of our marriage—passed them with but little disquietude. That my wife dreaded the fierce moodiness of my temper—that she shunned me and loved me but little—I could not help perceiving; but it gave me rather pleasure than otherwise. I loathed her with a hatred belonging more to demon than to man. My memory flew back, (oh, with what intensity of regret!) to Ligeia, the beloved, the august, the beautiful, the entombed. I revelled in recollections of her purity, of her wisdom, of her lofty, her ethereal nature, of her passionate, her idolatrous love. Now, then, did my spirit fully and freely burn with more than all the fires of her own. In the excitement of my opium dreams (for I was habitually fettered in the shackles of the drug,) I would call aloud upon her name, during the silence of the night, or among the sheltered recesses of the glens by day, as if, through the wild eagerness, the solemn passion, the consuming ardor of my longing for the departed, I could restore her to the pathway she had abandoned—ah, could it be forever?—upon the earth.

About the commencement of the second month of the marriage, the Lady Rowena was attacked with sudden illness, from which her recovery was slow. The fever which consumed her rendered her nights uneasy; and in her perturbed state of half-slumber, she spoke of sounds, and of motions, in and about the chamber of the turret, which I concluded had no origin save in the distemper of her fancy, or perhaps in the phantasmagoric influences of the chamber itself. She became at length convalescent—finally well. Yet but a brief period elapsed, ere a second more violent disorder again threw her upon a bed of suffering; and from this attack her frame, at all times feeble, never altogether recovered. Her illnesses were, after this epoch, of alarming character, and of more alarming recurrence, defying alike the knowledge and the great exertions of her physicians. With the increase of the chronic disease which had thus, apparently, taken too sure hold upon her constitution to be eradicated by human means, I could not fail to observe a similar increase in the nervous irritation of her temperament, and in her excitability by trivial causes of fear. She spoke again, and now more frequently and pertinaciously, of the sounds—of the slight sounds—and of the unusual motions among the tapestries, to which she had formerly alluded.

One night, near the closing in of September, she pressed this distressing subject with more than usual emphasis upon my attention. She had just awakened from an unquiet slumber, and I had been watching, with feelings half of anxiety, half of vague terror, the workings of her emaciated countenance. I sat by the side of her ebony bed, upon one of the ottomans of India. She partly arose, and spoke, in an earnest low whisper, of sounds which she then heard, but which I could not hear—of motions which she then saw, but which I could not perceive. The wind was rushing hurriedly behind the tapestries, and I wished to show her (what, let me confess it, I could not all believe) that those almost inarticulate breathings, and those very gentle variations of the figures upon the wall, were but the natural effects of that customary rushing of the wind. But a deadly pallor, overspreading her face, had proved to me that my exertions to reassure her would be fruitless. She appeared to be fainting, and no attendants were within call. I remembered where was deposited a decanter of light wine which had been ordered by her physicians, and hastened across the chamber to procure it. But, as I stepped beneath the light of the censer, two circumstances of a startling nature attracted my attention. I had felt that some palpable although invisible object had passed lightly by my person; and I saw that there lay upon the golden carpet, in the very middle of the rich lustre thrown from the censer, a shadow—a faint, indefinite shadow of angelic aspect—such as might be fancied for the shadow of a shade. But I was wild with the excitement of an immoderate dose of opium, and heeded these things but little, nor spoke of them to Rowena. Having found the wine, I recrossed the chamber, and poured out a goblet-ful, which I held to the lips of the fainting lady. She had now partially recovered, however, and took the vessel herself, while I sank upon an ottoman near me, with my eyes fastened upon her person. It was then that I became distinctly aware of a gentle foot-fall upon the carpet, and near the couch; and in a second thereafter, as Rowena was in the act of raising the wine to her lips, I saw, or may have dreamed that I saw, fall within the goblet, as if from some invisible spring in the atmosphere of the room, three or four large drops of a brilliant and ruby colored fluid. If this I saw—not so Rowena. She swallowed the wine unhesitatingly, and I forbore to speak to her of a circumstance which must, after all, I considered, have been but the suggestion of a vivid imagination, rendered morbidly active by the terror of the lady, by the opium, and by the hour.

Yet I cannot conceal it from my own perception that, immediately subsequent to the fall of the ruby-drops, a rapid change for the worse took place in the disorder of my wife; so that, on the third subsequent night, the hands of her menials prepared her for the tomb, and on the fourth, I sat alone, with her shrouded body, in that fantastic chamber which had received her as my bride.—Wild visions, opium-engendered, flitted, shadow-like, before me. I gazed with unquiet eye upon the sarcophagi in the angles of the room, upon the varying figures of the drapery, and upon the writhing of the parti-colored fires in the censer overhead. My eyes then fell, as I called to mind the circumstances of a former night, to the spot beneath the glare of the censer where I had seen the faint traces of the shadow. It was there, however, no longer; and breathing with greater freedom, I turned my glances to the pallid and rigid figure upon the bed. Then rushed upon me a thousand memories of Ligeia—and then came back upon my heart, with the turbulent violence of a flood, the whole of that unutterable wo with which I had regarded her thus enshrouded. The night waned; and still, with a bosom full of bitter thoughts of the one only and supremely beloved, I remained gazing upon the body of Rowena.

It might have been midnight, or perhaps earlier, or later, for I had taken no note of time, when a sob, low, gentle, but very distinct, startled me from my revery. I felt that it came from the bed of ebony—the bed of death. I listened in an agony of superstitious terror—but there was no repetition of the sound. I strained my vision to detect any motion in the corpse—but there was not the slightest perceptible. Yet I could not have been deceived. I had heard the noise, however faint, and my soul was awakened within me. I resolutely and perseveringly kept my attention riveted upon the body. Many minutes elapsed before any circumstance occurred tending to throw light upon the mystery. At length it became evident that a slight, a very feeble, and barely noticeable tinge of color had flushed up within the cheeks, and along the sunken small veins of the eyelids. Through a species of unutterable horror and awe, for which the language of mortality has no sufficiently energetic expression, I felt my heart cease to beat, my limbs grow rigid where I sat. Yet a sense of duty finally operated to restore my self-possession. I could no longer doubt that we had been precipitate in our preparations—that Rowena still lived. It was necessary that some immediate exertion be made; yet the turret was altogether apart from the portion of the abbey tenanted by the servants—there were none within call—I had no means of summoning them to my aid without leaving the room for many minutes—and this I could not venture to do. I therefore struggled alone in my endeavors to call back the spirit still hovering. In a short period it was certain, however, that a relapse had taken place; the color disappeared from both eyelid and cheek, leaving a wanness even more than that of marble; the lips became doubly shrivelled and pinched up in the ghastly expression of death; a repulsive clamminess and coldness overspread rapidly the surface of the body; and all the usual rigorous stiffness immediately supervened. I fell back with a shudder upon the couch from which I had been so startlingly aroused, and again gave myself up to passionate waking visions of Ligeia.

An hour thus elapsed when (could it be possible?) I was a second time aware of some vague sound issuing from the region of the bed. I listened—in extremity of horror. The sound came again—it was a sigh. Rushing to the corpse, I saw—distinctly saw—a tremor upon the lips. In a minute afterward they relaxed, disclosing a bright line of the pearly teeth. Amazement now struggled in my bosom with the profound awe which had hitherto reigned there alone. I felt that my vision grew dim, that my reason wandered; and it was only by a violent effort that I at length succeeded in nerving myself to the task which duty thus once more had pointed out. There was now a partial glow upon the forehead and upon the cheek and throat; a perceptible warmth pervaded the whole frame; there was even a slight pulsation at the heart. The lady lived; and with redoubled ardor I betook myself to the task of restoration. I chafed and bathed the temples and the hands, and used every exertion which experience, and no little medical reading, could suggest. But in vain. Suddenly, the color fled, the pulsation ceased, the lips resumed the expression of the dead, and, in an instant afterward, the whole body took upon itself the icy chilliness, the livid hue, the intense rigidity, the sunken outline, and all the loathsome peculiarities of that which has been, for many days, a tenant of the tomb.

And again I sunk into visions of Ligeia—and again, (what marvel that I shudder while I write?) again there reached my ears a low sob from the region of the ebony bed. But why shall I minutely detail the unspeakable horrors of that night? Why shall I pause to relate how, time after time, until near the period of the gray dawn, this hideous drama of revivication was repeated; how each terrific relapse was only into a sterner and apparently more irredeemable death; how each agony wore the aspect of a struggle with some invisible foe; and how each struggle was succeeded by I know not what of wild change in the personal appearance of the corpse? Let me hurry to a conclusion.

The greater part of the fearful night had worn away, and she who had been dead, once again stirred—and now more vigorously than hitherto, although arousing from a dissolution more appalling in its utter hopelessness than any. I had long ceased to struggle or to move, and remained sitting rigidly upon the ottoman, a helpless prey to a whirl of violent emotions, of which extreme awe was perhaps the least terrible, the least consuming. The corpse, I repeat, stirred, and now more vigorously than before. The hues of life flushed up with unwonted energy into the countenance—the limbs relaxed—and, save that the eyelids were yet pressed heavily together, and that the bandages and draperies of the grave still imparted their charnel character to the figure, I might have dreamed that Rowena had indeed shaken off, utterly, the fetters of Death. But if this idea was not, even then, altogether adopted, I could at least doubt no longer, when, arising from the bed, tottering, with feeble steps, with closed eyes, and with the manner of one bewildered in a dream, the thing that was enshrouded advanced boldly and palpably into the middle of the apartment.

I trembled not—I stirred not—for a crowd of unutterable fancies connected with the air, the stature, the demeanor of the figure, rushing hurriedly through my brain, had paralyzed—had chilled me into stone. I stirred not—but gazed upon the apparition. There was a mad disorder in my thoughts—a tumult unappeasable. Could it, indeed, be the living Rowena who confronted me? Could it indeed be Rowena at all—the fair-haired, the blue-eyed Lady Rowena Trevanion of Tremaine? Why, why should I doubt it? The bandage lay heavily about the mouth—but then might it not be the mouth of the breathing Lady of Tremaine? And the cheeks—there were the roses as in her noon of life—yes, these might indeed be the fair cheeks of the living Lady of Tremaine. And the chin, with its dimples, as in health, might it not be hers?—but had she then grown taller since her malady? What inexpressible madness seized me with that thought? One bound, and I had reached her feet! Shrinking from my touch, she let fall from her head, unloosened, the ghastly cerements which had confined it, and there streamed forth, into the rushing atmosphere of the chamber, huge masses of long and dishevelled hair; it was blacker than the raven wings of the midnight! And now slowly opened the eyes of the figure which stood before me. "Here then, at least," I shrieked aloud, "can I never—can I never be mistaken—these are the full, and the black, and the wild eyes—of my lost love—of the lady—of the LADY LIGEIA."

No. 1 Branch Line: The Signalman

by CHARLES DICKENS

*Charles Dickens (1812–1870) may be credited with single-handedly reviving the
ghost story in England (or at least making such stories respectable). Hailed as a
"literary colossus" by historians, Dickens "had something of a hankering" after
ghosts, recalled his friend and biographer John Forster. Dickens penned over two
dozen ghost stories in the span of his forty-year career, including the now-immortal*
A Christmas Carol *(1843) and* The Haunted Man and the Ghost's Bargain
*(1848), some embedded in his novels, many appearing separately. The following
story first appeared late in Dickens's life, in* All the Year Round *(Christmas 1866).*

"Halloa! Below there!"

When he heard a voice thus calling to him, he was standing
at the door of his box, with a flag in his hand, furled round its
short pole. One would have thought, considering the nature of the ground,
that he could not have doubted from what quarter the voice came; but

instead of looking up to where I stood on the top of the steep cutting nearly over his head, he turned himself about, and looked down the Line.* There was something remarkable in his manner of doing so, though I could not have said for my life what. But I know it was remarkable enough to attract my notice, even though his figure was foreshortened and shadowed, down in the deep trench, and mine was high above him, so steeped in the glow of an angry sunset, that I had shaded my eyes with my hand before I saw him at all.

"Halloa! Below!"

From looking down the Line, he turned himself about again, and, raising his eyes, saw my figure high above him.

"Is there any path by which I can come down and speak to you?"

He looked up at me without replying, and I looked down at him without pressing him too soon with a repetition of my idle question. Just then there came a vague vibration in the earth and air, quickly changing into a violent pulsation, and an oncoming rush that caused me to start back, as though it had force to draw me down. When such vapour as rose to my height from this rapid train had passed me, and was skimming away over the landscape, I looked down again, and saw him refurling the flag he had shown while the train went by.

I repeated my inquiry. After a pause, during which he seemed to regard me with fixed attention, he motioned with his rolled-up flag towards a point on my level, some two or three hundred yards distant. I called down to him, "All right!" and made for that point. There, by dint of looking closely about me, I found a rough zigzag descending path notched out, which I followed.

The cutting was extremely deep, and unusually precipitate. It was made through a clammy stone, that became oozier and wetter as I went down. For these reasons, I found the way long enough to give me time to recall a singular air of reluctance or compulsion with which he had pointed out the path.

When I came down low enough upon the zigzag descent to see him again, I saw that he was standing between the rails on the way by which

---

* The railroad line, that is. The person in question is a railway signalman, whose job it was to occupy a signal box along the tracks and (at the time of the story) by use of flags indicate to the engineer of a passing train the rail conditions ahead, lines to use, etc.

the train had lately passed, in an attitude as if he were waiting for me to appear. He had his left hand at his chin, and that left elbow rested on his right hand, crossed over his breast. His attitude was one of such expectation and watchfulness that I stopped a moment, wondering at it.

I resumed my downward way, and stepping out upon the level of the railroad, and drawing nearer to him, saw that he was a dark sallow man, with a dark beard and rather heavy eyebrows. His post was in as solitary and dismal a place as ever I saw. On either side, a dripping-wet wall of jagged stone, excluding all view but a strip of sky; the perspective one way only a crooked prolongation of this great dungeon; the shorter perspective in the other direction terminating in a gloomy red light, and the gloomier entrance to a black tunnel, in whose massive architecture there was a barbarous, depressing, and forbidding air. So little sunlight ever found its way to this spot, that it had an earthy, deadly smell; and so much cold wind rushed through it, that it struck chill to me, as if I had left the natural world.

Before he stirred, I was near enough to him to have touched him. Not even then removing his eyes from mine, he stepped back one step, and lifted his hand.

This was a lonesome post to occupy (I said), and it had riveted my attention when I looked down from up yonder. A visitor was a rarity, I should suppose; not an unwelcome rarity, I hoped? In me, he merely saw a man who had been shut up within narrow limits all his life, and who, being at last set free, had a newly-awakened interest in these great works. To such purpose I spoke to him; but I am far from sure of the terms I used; for, besides that I am not happy in opening any conversation, there was something in the man that daunted me.

He directed a most curious look towards the red light near the tunnel's mouth, and looked all about it, as if something were missing from it, and then looked it me.

That light was part of his charge? Was it not?

He answered in a low voice,—"Don't you know it is?"

The monstrous thought came into my mind, as I perused the fixed eyes and the saturnine face, that this was a spirit, not a man. I have speculated since, whether there may have been infection in his mind.

In my turn, I stepped back. But in making the action, I detected in his eyes some latent fear of me. This put the monstrous thought to flight.

"You look at me," I said, forcing a smile, "as if you had a dread of me."

"I was doubtful," he returned, "whether I had seen you before."

"Where?"

He pointed to the red light he had looked at.

"There?" I said.

Intently watchful of me, he replied (but without sound), "Yes."

"My good fellow, what should I do there? However, be that as it may, I never was there, you may swear."

"I think I may," he rejoined. "Yes; I am sure I may."

His manner cleared, like my own. He replied to my remarks with readiness, and in well-chosen words. Had he much to do there? Yes; that was to say, he had enough responsibility to bear; but exactness and watchfulness were what was required of him, and of actual work—manual labour—he had next to none. To change that signal, to trim those lights, and to turn this iron handle now and then, was all he had to do under that head. Regarding those many long and lonely hours of which I seemed to make so much, he could only say that the routine of his life had shaped itself into that form, and he had grown used to it. He had taught himself a language down here,—if only to know it by sight, and to have formed his own crude ideas of its pronunciation, could be called learning it. He had also worked at fractions and decimals, and tried a little algebra; but he was, and had been as a boy, a poor hand at figures. Was it necessary for him when on duty always to remain in that channel of damp air, and could he never rise into the sunshine from between those high stone walls? Why, that depended upon times and circumstances. Under some conditions there would be less upon the Line than under others, and the same held good as to certain hours of the day and night. In bright weather, he did choose occasions for getting a little above these lower shadows; but, being at all times liable to be called by his electric bell, and at such times listening for it with redoubled anxiety, the relief was less than I would suppose.

He took me into his box, where there was a fire, a desk for an official book in which he had to make certain entries, a telegraphic instrument with its dial, face, and needles, and the little bell of which he had spoken.

On my trusting that he would excuse the remark that he had been well educated, and (I hoped I might say without offence) perhaps educated above that station, he observed that instances of slight incongruity in such wise would rarely be found wanting among large bodies of men; that he had heard it was so in workhouses, in the police force, even in that last desperate resource, the army; and that he knew it was so, more or less, in any great railway staff. He had been, when young (if I could believe it, sitting in that hut,—he scarcely could), a student of natural philosophy, and had attended lectures; but he had run wild, misused his opportunities, gone down, and never risen again. He had no complaint to offer about that. He had made his bed, and he lay upon it. It was far too late to make another.

All that I have here condensed he said in a quiet manner, with his grave dark regards divided between me and the fire. He threw in the word, "Sir," from time to time, and especially when he referred to his youth,—as though to request me to understand that he claimed to be nothing but what I found him. He was several times interrupted by the little bell, and had to read off messages, and send replies. Once he had to stand without the door, and display a flag as a train passed, and make some verbal communication to the driver. In the discharge of his duties, I observed him to be remarkably exact and vigilant, breaking off his discourse at a syllable, and remaining silent until what he had to do was done.

In a word, I should have set this man down as one of the safest of men to be employed in that capacity, but for the circumstance that while he was speaking to me he twice broke off with a fallen colour, turned his face towards the little bell when it did not ring, opened the door of the hut (which was kept shut to exclude the unhealthy damp), and looked out towards the red light near the mouth of the tunnel. On both of those occasions, he came back to the fire with the inexplicable air upon him which I had remarked, without being able to define, when we were so far asunder.

Said I, when I rose to leave him, "You almost make me think that I have met with a contented man."

(I am afraid I must acknowledge that I said it to lead him on.)

"I believe I used to be so," he rejoined, in the low voice in which he had first spoken; "but I am troubled, sir, I am troubled."

He would have recalled the words if he could. He had said them, however, and I took them up quickly.

"With what? What is your trouble?"

"It is very difficult to impart, sir. It is very, very difficult to speak of. If ever you make me another visit, I will try to tell you."

"But I expressly intend to make you another visit. Say, when shall it be?"

"I go off early in the morning, and I shall be on again at ten to-morrow night, sir."

"I will come at eleven."

He thanked me, and went out at the door with me. "I'll show my white light, sir," he said, in his peculiar low voice, "till you have found the way up. When you have found it, don't call out! And when you are at the top, don't call out!"

His manner seemed to make the place strike colder to me, but I said no more than, "Very well."

"And when you come down to-morrow night, don't call out! Let me ask you a parting question. What made you cry, 'Halloa! Below there!' to-night?"

"Heaven knows," said I. "I cried something to that effect—"

"Not to that effect, sir. Those were the very words. I know them well."

"Admit those were the very words. I said them, no doubt, because I saw you below."

"For no other reason?"

"What other reason could I possibly have?"

"You had no feeling that they were conveyed to you in any supernatural way?"

"No."

He wished me good-night, and held up his light. I walked by the side of the down Line of rails (with a very disagreeable sensation of a train coming behind me) until I found the path. It was easier to mount than to descend, and I got back to my inn without any adventure.

Punctual to my appointment, I placed my foot on the first notch of the zigzag next night, as the distant clocks were striking eleven. He was waiting for me at the bottom, with his white light on. "I have not called out," I said, when we came close together; "may I speak now?"

"By all means, sir."

"Good-night, then, and here's my hand."

"Good-night, sir, and here's mine." With that we walked side by side to his box, entered it, closed the door, and sat down by the fire.

"I have made up my mind, sir," he began, bending forward as soon as we were seated, and speaking in a tone but a little above a whisper, "that you shall not have to ask me twice what troubles me. I took you for some one else yesterday evening. That troubles me."

"That mistake?"

"No. That some one else."

"Who is it?"

"I don't know."

"Like me?"

"I don't know. I never saw the face. The left arm is across the face, and the right arm is waved,—violently waved. This way."

I followed his action with my eyes, and it was the action of an arm gesticulating, with the utmost passion and vehemence, "For God's sake, clear the way!"

"One moonlight night," said the man, "I was sitting here, when I heard a voice cry, 'Halloa! Below there!' I started up, looked from that door, and saw this Some one else standing by the red light near the tunnel, waving as I just now showed you. The voice seemed hoarse with shouting, and it cried, 'Look out! Look out!' And then again, 'Halloa! Below there! Look out!' I caught up my lamp, turned it on red, and ran towards the figure, calling, 'What's wrong? What has happened? Where?' It stood just outside the blackness of the tunnel. I advanced so close upon it that I wondered at its keeping the sleeve across its eyes. I ran right up at it, and had my hand stretched out to pull the sleeve away, when it was gone."

"Into the tunnel?" said I.

"No. I ran on into the tunnel, five hundred yards. I stopped, and held my lamp above my head, and saw the figures of the measured distance, and saw the wet stains stealing down the walls and trickling through the arch. I ran out again faster than I had run in (for I had a mortal abhorrence of the place upon me), and I looked all round the red light with my own red light, and I went up the iron ladder to the gallery atop of it, and I came down again, and ran back here. I telegraphed both ways, 'An alarm has been given. Is anything wrong?' The answer came back, both ways, 'All well.'"

Resisting the slow touch of a frozen finger tracing out my spine, I showed him how that this figure must be a deception of his sense of sight; and how that figures, originating in disease of the delicate nerves that minister to the functions of the eye, were known to have often troubled patients, some of whom had become conscious of the nature of their affliction, and had even proved it by experiments upon themselves. "As to an imaginary cry," said I, "do but listen for a moment to the wind in this unnatural valley while we speak so low, and to the wild harp it makes of the telegraph wires."

That was all very well, he returned, after we had sat listening for a while, and he ought to know something of the wind and the wires,—he who so often passed long winter nights there, alone and watching. But he would beg to remark that he had not finished.

I asked his pardon, and he slowly added these words, touching my arm,—

"Within six hours after the Appearance, the memorable accident on this Line happened, and within ten hours the dead and wounded were brought along through the tunnel over the spot where the figure had stood."

A disagreeable shudder crept over me, but I did my best against it. It was not to be denied, I rejoined, that this was a remarkable coincidence, calculated deeply to impress his mind. But it was unquestionable that remarkable coincidences did continually occur, and they must be taken into account in dealing with such a subject. Though to be sure I must admit, I added (for I thought I saw that he was going to bring the objection to bear upon me), men of common sense did not allow much for coincidences in making the ordinary calculations of life.

He again begged to remark that he had not finished.

I again begged his pardon for being betrayed into interruptions.

"This," he said, again laying his hand upon my arm, and glancing over his shoulder with hollow eyes, "was just a year ago. Six or seven months passed, and I had recovered from the surprise and shock, when one morning, as the day was breaking, I, standing at the door, looked towards the red light, and saw the spectre again." He stopped, with a fixed look at me.

"Did it cry out?"

"No. It was silent."

"Did it wave its arm?"

"No. It leaned against the shaft of the light, with both hands before the face. Like this."

Once more I followed his action with my eyes. It was an action of mourning. I have seen such an attitude in stone figures on tombs.

"Did you go up to it?"

"I came in and sat down, partly to collect my thoughts, partly because it had turned me faint. When I went to the door again, daylight was above me, and the ghost was gone."

"But nothing followed? Nothing came of this?"

He touched me on the arm with his forefinger twice or thrice giving a ghastly nod each time:—

"That very day, as a train came out of the tunnel, I noticed, at a carriage window on my side, what looked like a confusion of hands and heads, and something waved. I saw it just in time to signal the driver, Stop! He shut off, and put his brake on, but the train drifted past here a hundred and fifty yards or more. I ran after it, and, as I went along, heard terrible screams and cries. A beautiful young lady had died instantaneously in one of the compartments, and was brought in here, and laid down on this floor between us."

Involuntarily I pushed my chair back, as I looked from the boards at which he pointed to himself.

"True, sir. True. Precisely as it happened, so I tell it you."

I could think of nothing to say, to any purpose, and my mouth was very dry. The wind and the wires took up the story with a long lamenting wail.

He resumed. "Now, sir, mark this, and judge how my mind is troubled. The spectre came back a week ago. Ever since, it has been there, now and again, by fits and starts."

"At the light?"

"At the Danger-light."

"What does it seem to do?"

He repeated, if possible with increased passion and vehemence, that former gesticulation of, "For God's sake, clear the way!"

Then he went on. "I have no peace or rest for it. It calls to me, for many minutes together, in an agonised manner, 'Below there! Look out! Look out!' It stands waving to me. It rings my little bell—"

I caught at that. "Did it ring your bell yesterday evening when I was here, and you went to the door?"

"Twice."

"Why, see," said I, "how your imagination misleads you. My eyes were on the bell, and my ears were open to the bell, and if I am a living man, it did not ring at those times. No, nor at any other time, except when it was rung in the natural course of physical things by the station communicating with you."

He shook his head. "I have never made a mistake as to that yet, sir. I have never confused the spectre's ring with the man's. The ghost's ring is a strange vibration in the bell that it derives from nothing else, and I have not asserted that the bell stirs to the eye. I don't wonder that you failed to hear it. But I heard it."

"And did the spectre seem to be there, when you looked out?"

"It was there."

"Both times?"

He repeated firmly: "Both times."

"Will you come to the door with me, and look for it now?"

He bit his under lip as though he were somewhat unwilling, but arose. I opened the door, and stood on the step, while he stood in the doorway. There was the Danger-light. There was the dismal mouth of the tunnel. There were the high, wet stone walls of the cutting. There were the stars above them.

"Do you see it?" I asked him, taking particular note of his face. His eyes were prominent and strained, but not very much more so, perhaps, than my own had been when I had directed them earnestly towards the same spot.

"No," he answered. "It is not there."

"Agreed," said I.

We went in again, shut the door, and resumed our seats. I was thinking how best to improve this advantage, if it might be called one, when he took up the conversation in such a matter-of-course way, so assuming that there could be no serious question of fact between us, that I felt myself placed in the weakest of positions.

"By this time you will fully understand, sir," he said, "that what troubles me so dreadfully is the question, What does the spectre mean?"

I was not sure, I told him, that I did fully understand.

"What is its warning against?" he said, ruminating, with his eyes on the fire, and only by times turning them on me. "What is the danger? Where is the danger? There is danger overhanging somewhere on the Line. Some dreadful calamity will happen. It is not to be doubted this third time, after what has gone before. But surely this is a cruel haunting of me. What can I do?"

He pulled out his handkerchief, and wiped the drops from his heated forehead.

"If I telegraph Danger, on either side of me, or on both, I can give no reason for it," he went on, wiping the palms of his hands. "I should get into trouble, and do no good. They would think I was mad. This is the way it would work,—Message: 'Danger! Take care!' Answer: 'What Danger? Where?' Message: 'Don't know. But, for God's sake, take care!' They would displace me. What else could they do?"

His pain of mind was most pitiable to see. It was the mental torture of a conscientious man, oppressed beyond endurance by an unintelligible responsibility involving life.

"When it first stood under the Danger-light," he went on, putting his dark hair back from his head, and drawing his hands outward across and across his temples in an extremity of feverish distress, "why not tell me where that accident was to happen,—if it must happen? Why not tell me how it could be averted,—if it could have been averted? When on its second coming it hid its face, why not tell me, instead, 'She is going to die. Let them keep her at home'? If it came, on those two occasions, only to show me that its warnings were true, and so to prepare me for the third, why not warn me plainly now? And I, Lord help me! A mere poor signal-man on this solitary station! Why not go to somebody with credit to be believed, and power to act?"

When I saw him in this state, I saw that for the poor man's sake, as well as for the public safety, what I had to do for the time was to compose his mind. Therefore, setting aside all question of reality or unreality between us, I represented to him that whoever thoroughly discharged his duty must do well, and that at least it was his comfort that he understood his duty, though he did not understand these confounding Appearances. In this effort I succeeded far better than in the attempt to reason him out of his conviction. He became calm; the occupations incidental to his post as the night advanced began to make larger demands on his attention: and I left him at two in the morning. I had offered to stay through the night, but he would not hear of it.

That I more than once looked back at the red light as I ascended the pathway, that I did not like the red light, and that I should have slept but poorly if my bed had been under it, I see no reason to conceal. Nor did I like the two sequences of the accident and the dead girl. I see no reason to conceal that either.

But what ran most in my thoughts was the consideration how ought I to act, having become the recipient of this disclosure? I had proved the man to be intelligent, vigilant, painstaking, and exact; but how long might he remain so, in his state of mind? Though in a subordinate position, still he held a most important trust, and would I (for instance) like to stake my own life on the chances of his continuing to execute it with precision?

Unable to overcome a feeling that there would be something treacherous in my communicating what he had told me to his superiors in the Company, without first being plain with himself and proposing a middle course to him, I ultimately resolved to offer to accompany him (otherwise keeping his secret for the present) to the wisest medical practitioner we could hear of in those parts, and to take his opinion. A change in his time of duty would come round next night, he had apprised me, and he would be off an hour or two after sunrise, and on again soon after sunset. I had appointed to return accordingly.

Next evening was a lovely evening, and I walked out early to enjoy it. The sun was not yet quite down when I traversed the field-path near the top of the deep cutting. I would extend my walk for an hour, I said to myself, half an hour on and half an hour back, and it would then be time to go to my signal-man's box.

Before pursuing my stroll, I stepped to the brink, and mechanically looked down, from the point from which I had first seen him. I cannot describe the thrill that seized upon me, when, close at the mouth of the tunnel, I saw the appearance of a man, with his left sleeve across his eyes, passionately waving his right arm.

The nameless horror that oppressed me passed in a moment, for in a moment I saw that this appearance of a man was a man indeed, and that there was a little group of other men, standing at a short distance, to whom he seemed to be rehearsing the gesture he made. The Danger-light was not yet lighted. Against its shaft, a little low hut, entirely new to me, had been made of some wooden supports and tarpaulin. It looked no bigger than a bed.

With an irresistible sense that something was wrong,—with a flashing self-reproachful fear that fatal mischief had come of my leaving the man there, and causing no one to be sent to overlook or correct what he did,—I descended the notched path with all the speed I could make.

"What is the matter?" I asked the men.

"Signal-man killed this morning, sir."

"Not the man belonging to that box?"

"Yes, sir."

"Not the man I know?"

"You will recognise him, sir, if you knew him," said the man who spoke for the others, solemnly uncovering his own head, and raising an end of the tarpaulin, "for his face is quite composed."

"O, how did this happen, how did this happen?" I asked, turning from one to another as the hut closed in again.

"He was cut down by an engine, sir. No man in England knew his work better. But somehow he was not clear of the outer rail. It was just at broad day. He had struck the light, and had the lamp in his hand. As the engine came out of the tunnel, his back was towards her, and she cut him down. That man drove her, and was showing how it happened. Show the gentleman, Tom."

The man, who wore a rough dark dress, stepped back to his former place at the mouth of the tunnel.

"Coming round the curve in the tunnel, sir," he said, "I saw him at the end, like as if I saw him down a perspective-glass. There was no time to check speed, and I knew him to be very careful. As he didn't seem to take heed of the whistle, I shut it off when we were running down upon him, and called to him as loud as I could call."

"What did you say?"

"I said, 'Below there! Look out! Look out! For God's sake, clear the way!'"

I started.

"Ah! it was a dreadful time, sir. I never left off calling to him. I put this arm before my eyes not to see, and I waved this arm to the last; but it was no use."

Without prolonging the narrative to dwell on any one of its curious circumstances more than on any other, I may, in closing it, point out the coincidence that the warning of the Engine-Driver included, not only the words which the unfortunate Signal-man had repeated to me as haunting him, but also the words which I myself—not he—had attached, and that only in my own mind, to the gesticulation he had imitated.

Since I Died

by ELIZABETH STUART PHELPS

Elizabeth Stuart Phelps (1844–1911) was an American feminist writer, whose writing challenged the traditional role of women in marriage. The author of fifty-seven volumes of fiction, poetry, and essays, she argued vehemently that women had a proper place outside the home and should be free to pursue careers as doctors, ministers, artists, and the like. Like Arthur Conan Doyle a generation later, Phelps espoused nontraditional, Spiritualist views of the afterlife. These were very popular in reaction to more than 400,000 deaths caused by the American Civil War (just as Conan Doyle's Spiritualist causes were embraced by those affected by the millions of deaths during World War I). Phelps wrote three novels considering the afterlife, including The Gates Ajar *(1868), and the following story, which first appeared in* Scribner's Monthly *(Feb. 1873).*

How very still you sit!

If the shadow of an eyelash stirred upon your cheek; if that gray line about your mouth should snap its tension at this quivering end; if the pallor of your profile warmed a little; if that tiny muscle on your forehead, just at the left eyebrow's curve, should start and twitch; if you would but grow a trifle restless, sitting there beneath my steady gaze; if you moved a finger of your folded hands; if you should turn and look behind your chair, or lift your face, half lingering and half longing, half loving and half loth, to ponder on the annoyed and thwarted cry which the wind is making, where I stand between it and yourself, against the half-closed window.—Ah, there! You sigh and stir, I think. You lift your head. The little muscle is a captive still; the line about your mouth is tense and hard; the deepening hollow in your cheek has no warmer tint, I see, than the great Doric column which the moonlight builds against the wall. I lean against it; I hold out my arms.

You lift your head and look me in the eye.

If a shudder crept across your figure; if your arms, laid out upon the table, leaped but once above your head; if you named my name; if you held your breath with terror, or sobbed aloud for love, or sprang, or cried—.

But you only lift your head and look me in the eye.

If I dared step near, or nearer; if it were permitted that I should cross the current of your living breath; if it were willed that I should feel the leap of human blood within your veins; if I should touch your hands, your cheeks, your lips; if I dropped an arm as lightly as a snowflake round your shoulder—

The fear which no heart has fathomed, the fate which no fancy has faced, the riddle which no soul has read, steps between your substance and my soul.

I drop my arms. I sink into the heart of the pillared light upon the wall. I will not wonder what would happen if my outlines defined upon it to your view. I will not think of that which could be, would be, if I struck across your still-set vision, face to face.

Ah me, how still she sits! With what a fixed, incurious stare she looks me in the eye!

The wind, now that I stand no longer between it and yourself, comes enviously in. It lifts the curtain, and whirls about the room. It bruises the surface of the great pearled pillar where I lean. I am caught within it. Speech and language struggle over me. Mute articulations fill the air.

Tears and laughter, and the sounding of soft lips, and the falling of low cries, possess me. Will she listen? Will she bend her head? Will her lips part in recognition? Is there an alphabet between us? Or have the winds of night a vocabulary to lift before her holden* eyes?

We sat many times together, and talked of this. Do you remember, dear? You held my hand. Tears that I could not see fell on it; we sat by the great hall-window upstairs, where the maple shadow goes to sleep, face down, across the floor upon a lighted night; the old green curtain waved its hands upon us like a mesmerist, I thought; like a priest, you said.

"When we are parted, you shall go," you said; and when I shook my head you smiled—you always smiled when you said that, but you said it always quite the same.

I think I hardly understood you then. Now that I hold your eyes in mine, and you see me not; now when I stretch my hand and you touch me not; now that I cry your name, and you hear it not,—I comprehend you, tender one! A wisdom not of earth was in your words. "To live, is dying; I will die. To die is life, and you shall live."

Now when the fever turned, I thought of this.

That must have been—ah! how long ago? I miss the conception of that for which how long stands index.

Yet I perfectly remember that I perfectly understood it to be at three o'clock on a rainy Sunday morning that I died. Your little watch stood in its case of olive-wood upon the table, and drops were on the window. I noticed both, though you did not know it. I see the watch now, in your pocket; I cannot tell if the hands move, or only pulsate like a heart-throb, to and fro; they stand and point, mute golden fingers, paralyzed and pleading, forever at the hour of three. At this I wonder.

When first you said I "was sinking fast," the words sounded as old and familiar as a nursery tale. I heard you in the hall. The doctor had just left, and you went to mother and took her face in your two arms, and laid your hand across her mouth, as if it were she who had spoken. She cried out and threw up her thin old hands; but you stood as still as Eternity. Then I thought again: "It is she who dies; I shall live."

So often and so anxiously we have talked of this thing called death, that now that it is all over between us, I cannot understand why we found in

_____
* Held.

it such a source of distress. It bewilders me. I am often bewildered here. Things and the fancies of things possess a relation which as yet is new and strange to me. Here is a mystery.

Now, in truth, it seems a simple matter for me to tell you how it has been with me since your lips last touched me, and your arms held me to the vanishing air.

Oh, drawn, pale lips! Nerveless, dropping arms! I told you I would come. Did ever promise fail I spoke to you? "Come and show me Death," you said. I have come to show you Death. I could show you the fairest sight and sweetest that ever blessed your eyes. Why, look! Is it not fair? Am I terrible? Do you shrink or shiver? Would you turn from me, or hide your strained, expectant face?

Would she? Does she? Will she? . . .

Ah, how the room widened! I could tell you that. It grew great and luminous day by day. At night the walls throbbed; lights of rose ran round them, and blue fire, and a tracery as of the shadows of little leaves. As the walls expanded, the air fled. But I tried to tell you how little pain I knew or feared. Your haggard face bent over me. I could not speak; when I would I struggled, and you said "She suffers!" Dear, it was so very little!

Listen, till I tell you how that night came on. The sun fell and the dew slid down. It seemed to me that it slid into my heart, but still I felt no pain. Where the walls pulsed and receded, the hills came in. Where the old bureau stood, above the glass, I saw a single mountain with a face of fire, and purple hair. I tried to tell you this, but you said: "She wanders." I laughed in my heart at that, for it was such a blessed wandering! As the night locked the sun below the mountain's solemn watching face, the Gates of Space were lifted up before me; the ever lasting doors of Matter swung for me upon their rusty hinges, and the King of Glories entered in and out. All the kingdoms of the earth, and the power of them, beckoned to me, across the mist my failing senses made,—ruins and roses, and the brows of Jura* and the singing of the Rhine; a shaft of red light on the Sphinx's smile, and caravans in sand-storms, and an icy wind at sea, and gold adream

---

* The Jura are a European mountain range that separates the Rhine and Rhone river basins.

in mines that no man knew, and mothers sitting at their doors in valleys singing babes to sleep, and women in dank cellars selling souls for bread, and the whir of wheels in giant factories, and a single prayer somewhere in a den of death,—I could not find it, though I searched,—and the smoke of battle, and broken music, and a sense of lilies alone beside a stream at the rising of the sun—and, at last, your face, dear, all alone.

I discovered then, that the walls and roof of the room had vanished quite. The night-wind blew in. The maple in the yard almost brushed my cheek. Stars were about me, and I thought the rain had stopped, yet seemed to hear it, up on the seeming of a window which I could not find.

One thing only hung between me and immensity. It was your single, awful, haggard face. I looked my last into your eyes. Stronger than death, they held and claimed my soul. I feebly raised my hand to find your own. More cruel than the grave, your wild grasp chained me. Then I struggled, and you cried out, and your face slipped, and I stood free.

I stood upon the floor, beside the bed. That which had been I lay there at rest, but terrible, before me. You hid your face, and I saw you slide upon your knees. I laid my hand upon your head; you did not stir; I spoke to you: "Dear, look around a minute!" but you knelt quite still. I walked to and fro about the room, and meeting my mother, touched her on the elbow; she only said, "She's gone!" and sobbed aloud. "I have not gone!" I cried; but she sat sobbing on.

The walls of the room had settled now, and the ceiling stood in its solid place. The window was shut, but the door stood open. Suddenly I was restless, and I ran.

I brushed you in hurrying by, and hit the little light-stand where the tumblers stood; I looked to see if it would fall, but it only shivered as if a breath of wind had struck it once.

But I was restless, and I ran. In the hall I met the Doctor. This amused me, and I stopped to think it over. "Ah, Doctor," said I, "you need not trouble yourself to go up. I'm quite well to-night, you see." But he made me no answer; he gave me no glance; he hung up his hat, and laid his hand upon the banister against which I leaned, and went ponderously up.

It was not until he had nearly reached the landing that it occurred to me, still leaning on the banisters, that his heavy arm must have swept against and through me, where I stood against the oaken mouldings which he grasped.

I saw his feet fall on the stairs above me; but they made no sound which reached my ear. "You'll not disturb me now with your big boots, sir," said I, nodding; "never fear!"

But he disappeared from sight above me, and still I heard no sound.

Now the Doctor had left the front door unlatched.

As I touched it, it blew open wide, and solemnly. I passed out and down steps. I could see that it was chilly, yet I felt no chill. Frost was on the grass, and in the east a pallid streak, like the cheek of one who had watched all night. The flowers in the little square plots hung their heads and drew their shoulders up; there was a lonely, late lily which I broke and gathered to my heart, where I breathed upon it, and it warmed and looked me kindly in the eye. This, I remember, gave me pleasure. I wandered in and out about the garden in the scattering rain; my feet left no trace upon the dripping grass, and I saw with interest that the garment which I wore gathered no moisture and no cold. I sat musing for a while upon the piazza, in the garden-chair, not caring to go in. It was so many months since I had felt able to sit upon the piazza in the open air. "By and by," I thought, I would go in and upstairs to see you once again. The curtains were drawn from the parlor windows and I passed and repassed, looking in.

All this while, the cheek of the east was waning, and the air gathering faint heats and lights about me. I remembered, presently, the old arbor at the garden-foot, where before I was sick, we sat so much together; and thinking, "She will be surprised to know that I have been down alone," I was restless, and I ran again.

I meant to come back and see you, dear, once more. I saw the lights in the room where I had lain sick, overhead; and your shadow on the curtain; and I blessed it, with all the love of life and death, as I bounded by.

The air was thick with sweetness from the dying flowers. The birds woke, and the zenith lighted, and the leap of health was in my limbs. The old arbor held out its soft arms to me—but I was restless, and I ran.

The field opened before me, and meadows with broad bosoms, and a river flashed before me like a scimitar, and woods interlocked their hands to stay me—but being restless, on I ran.

The house dwindled behind me; and the light in my sick-room, and your shadow on the curtain. But yet I was restless, and I ran.

In the twinkling of an eye I fell into a solitary place. Sand and rocks were in it, and a falling wind. I paused, and knelt upon the sand, and mused a little in this place. I mused of you, and life and death, and love and agony;—but these had departed from me, as dim and distant as the fainting wind. A sense of solemn expectation filled the air. A tremor and a trouble wrapped my soul.

"I must be dead!" I said aloud. I had no sooner spoken than I learned that I was not alone.

The sun had risen, and on a ledge of ancient rock, weather-stained and red, there had fallen over against me the outline of a Presence lifted up against the sky, and turning suddenly, I saw. . . .

Lawful to utter, but utterance has fled! Lawful to utter, but a greater than Law restrains me! Am I blotted from your desolate fixed eyes? Lips that my mortal lips have pressed, can you not quiver when I cry? Soul that my eternal soul has loved, can you stand enveloped in my presence, and not spring like a fountain to me? Would you not know how it has been with me since your perishable eyes beheld my perished face? What my eyes have seen or my ears have heard, or my heart conceived without you? If I have missed or mourned for you? If I have watched or longed for you? Marked your solitary days and sleepless nights, and tearless eyes, and monotonous slow echo of my unanswered name? Would you not know?

Alas! would she? Would she not? My soul misgives me with a matchless, solitary fear. I am called, and I slip from her. I am beckoned, and lose her.

Her face dims, and her folded, lonely hands fade from my sight.

Time to tell her a guarded thing! Time to whisper a treasured word! A moment to tell her that *Death is dumb, for Life is deaf!* A moment to tell her.—

Mrs. Zant and the Ghost

by WILKIE COLLINS

Wilkie Collins (1824–1889) was a very successful mid-Victorian English novelist, short-story writer, and playwright. Author of more than a dozen novels, his work, called "sensational fiction" in its day, was an important precursor of modern detective and suspense fiction. The Moonstone (1868) in particular was an important stepping-stone to the success of the Sherlock Holmes stories and the rise of the mystery genre. Both The Moonstone and his earlier great success, The Woman in White (1859) had mysterious figures initially explained as supernatural. Collins was a lifelong friend of Charles Dickens and may well have absorbed Dickens's interest in ghosts. The following was originally published as "The Ghost's Touch" in The Irish Fireside (Sep. 30–Oct. 14, 1885).

I

The course of this narrative describes the return of a disembodied spirit to earth, and leads the reader on new and strange ground. Not in the obscurity of midnight, but in the searching light of day, did the supernatural influence assert itself. Neither revealed by a vision, nor announced by a voice, it reached mortal knowledge through the sense which is least easily self-deceived: the sense that feels.

The record of this event will of necessity produce conflicting impressions. It will raise, in some minds, the doubt which reason asserts; it will invigorate, in other minds, the hope which faith justifies; and it will leave the terrible question of the destinies of man, where centuries of vain investigation have left it–in the dark.

Having only undertaken in the present narrative to lead the way along a succession of events, the writer declines to follow modern examples by thrusting himself and his opinions on the public view. He returns to the shadow from which he has emerged, and leaves the opposing forces of incredulity and belief to fight the old battle over again, on the old ground.

II

The events happened soon after the first thirty years of the present century had come to an end.

On a fine morning, early in the month of April, a gentleman of middle age (named Rayburn) took his little daughter Lucy out for a walk in the woodland pleasure-ground of Western London, called Kensington Gardens.

The few friends whom he possessed reported of Mr. Rayburn (not unkindly) that he was a reserved and solitary man. He might have been more accurately described as a widower devoted to his only surviving child. Although he was not more than forty years of age, the one pleasure which made life enjoyable to Lucy's father was offered by Lucy herself.

Playing with her ball, the child ran on to the southern limit of the Gardens, at that part of it which still remains nearest to the old Palace of Kensington. Observing close at hand one of those spacious covered seats, called in England "alcoves," Mr. Rayburn was reminded that he had the morning's newspaper in his pocket, and that he might do well to rest and read. At that early hour the place was a solitude.

"Go on playing, my dear," he said; "but take care to keep where I can see you."

Lucy tossed up her ball; and Lucy's father opened his newspaper. He had not been reading for more than ten minutes, when he felt a familiar little hand laid on his knee.

"Tired of playing?" he inquired—with his eyes still on the newspaper.

"I'm frightened, papa."

He looked up directly. The child's pale face startled him. He took her on his knee and kissed her.

"You oughtn't to be frightened, Lucy, when I am with you," he said, gently. "What is it?" He looked out of the alcove as he spoke, and saw a little dog among the trees. "Is it the dog?" he asked.

Lucy answered:

"It's not the dog—it's the lady."

The lady was not visible from the alcove.

"Has she said anything to you?" Mr. Rayburn inquired.

"No."

"What has she done to frighten you?"

The child put her arms round her father's neck.

"Whisper, papa," she said; "I'm afraid of her hearing us. I think she's mad."

"Why do you think so, Lucy?"

"She came near to me. I thought she was going to say something. She seemed to be ill."

"Well? And what then?"

"She looked at me."

There, Lucy found herself at a loss how to express what she had to say next—and took refuge in silence.

"Nothing very wonderful, so far," her father suggested.

"Yes, papa—but she didn't seem to see me when she looked."

"Well, and what happened then?"

"The lady was frightened—and that frightened me. I think," the child repeated positively, "she's mad."

It occurred to Mr. Rayburn that the lady might be blind. He rose at once to set the doubt at rest.

"Wait here," he said, "and I'll come back to you."

But Lucy clung to him with both hands; Lucy declared that she was afraid to be by herself. They left the alcove together.

The new point of view at once revealed the stranger, leaning against the trunk of a tree. She was dressed in the deep mourning of a widow. The pallor of her face, the glassy stare in her eyes, more than accounted for the child's terror—it excused the alarming conclusion at which she had arrived.

"Go nearer to her," Lucy whispered.

They advanced a few steps. It was now easy to see that the lady was young, and wasted by illness—but (arriving at a doubtful conclusion perhaps under the present circumstances) apparently possessed of rare personal attractions in happier days. As the father and daughter advanced a little, she discovered them. After some hesitation, she left the tree; approached with an evident intention of speaking; and suddenly paused. A change to astonishment and fear animated her vacant eyes. If it had not been plain before, it was now beyond all doubt that she was not a poor blind creature, deserted and helpless. At the same time, the expression of her face was not easy to understand. She could hardly have looked more amazed and bewildered, if the two strangers who were observing her had suddenly vanished from the place in which they stood.

Mr. Rayburn spoke to her with the utmost kindness of voice and manner.

"I am afraid you are not well," he said. "Is there anything that I can do—"

The next words were suspended on his lips. It was impossible to realize such a state of things; but the strange impression that she had already produced on him was now confirmed. If he could believe his senses, her face did certainly tell him that he was invisible and inaudible to the woman whom he had just addressed! She moved slowly away with a heavy sigh, like a person disappointed and distressed. Following her with his eyes, he saw the dog once more—a little smooth-coated terrier of the ordinary English breed. The dog showed none of the restless activity of his race. With his head down and his tail depressed, he crouched like a creature paralyzed by fear. His mistress roused him by a call. He followed her listlessly as she turned away.

After walking a few paces only, she suddenly stood still.

Mr. Rayburn heard her talking to herself.

"Did I feel it again?" she said, as if perplexed by some doubt that awed or grieved her. After a while her arms rose slowly, and opened with a gentle caressing action—an embrace strangely offered to the empty air! "No," she said to herself, sadly, after waiting a moment. "More perhaps when to-morrow comes—no more to-day." She looked up at the clear blue sky. "The beautiful sunlight! the merciful sunlight!" she murmured. "I should have died if it had happened in the dark."

Once more she called to the dog; and once more she walked slowly away.

"Is she going home, papa?' the child asked.

"We will try and find out," the father answered.

He was by this time convinced that the poor creature was in no condition to be permitted to go out without some one to take care of her. From motives of humanity, he was resolved on making the attempt to communicate with her friends.

III

The lady left the Gardens by the nearest gate; stopping to lower her veil before she turned into the busy thoroughfare which leads to Kensington. Advancing a little way along the High Street, she entered a house of respectable appearance, with a card in one of the windows which announced that apartments were to let.

Mr. Rayburn waited a minute—then knocked at the door, and asked if he could see the mistress of the house. The servant showed him into a room on the ground floor, neatly but scantily furnished. One little white object varied the grim brown monotony of the empty table. It was a visiting-card.

With a child's unceremonious curiosity Lucy pounced on the card, and spelled the name, letter by letter: "Z, A, N, T," she repeated. "What does that mean ?"

Her father looked at the card, as he took it away from her, and put it back on the table. The name was printed, and the address was added in pencil: "Mr. John Zant, Purley's Hotel."

The mistress made her appearance. Mr. Rayburn heartily wished himself out of the house again, the moment he saw her. The ways in which it is possible to cultivate the social virtues are more numerous and more varied than is generally supposed. This lady's way had apparently accustomed her to meet her fellow-creatures on the hard ground of justice without mercy.

Something in her eyes, when she looked at Lucy, said: "I wonder whether that child gets punished when she deserves it?"

"Do you wish to see the rooms which I have to let?" she began.

Mr. Rayburn at once stated the object of his visit—as clearly, as civilly, and as concisely as a man could do it. He was conscious (he added) that he had been guilty perhaps of an act of intrusion.

The manner of the mistress of the house showed that she entirely agreed with him. He suggested, however, that his motive might excuse him. The mistress's manner changed, and asserted a difference of opinion.

"I only know the lady whom you mention," she said, "as a person of the highest respectability, in delicate health. She has taken my first-floor apartments, with excellent references; and she gives remarkably little trouble. I have no claim to interfere with her proceedings, and no reason to doubt that she is capable of taking care of herself."

Mr. Rayburn unwisely attempted to say a word in his own defense.

"Allow me to remind you—" he began.

"Of what, sir?"

"Of what I observed, when I happened to see the lady in Kensington Gardens."

"I am not responsible for what you observed in Kensington Gardens. If your time is of any value, pray don't let me detain you."

Dismissed in those terms, Mr. Rayburn took Lucy's hand and withdrew. He had just reached the door, when it was opened from the outer side. The Lady of Kensington Gardens stood before him. In the position which he and his daughter now occupied, their backs were toward the window. Would she remember having seen them for a moment in the Gardens?

"Excuse me for intruding on you," she said to the landlady. "Your servant tells me my brother-in-law called while I was out. He sometimes leaves a message on his card."

She looked for the message, and appeared to be disappointed: there was no writing on the card.

Mr. Rayburn lingered a little in the doorway on the chance of hearing something more. The landlady's vigilant eyes discovered him.

"Do you know this gentleman?" she said maliciously to her lodger.

"Not that I remember."

Replying in those words, the lady looked at Mr. Rayburn for the first time; and suddenly drew back from him.

"Yes," she said, correcting herself; "I think we met—"

Her embarrassment overpowered her; she could say no more.

Mr. Rayburn compassionately finished the sentence for her.

"We met accidentally in Kensington Gardens," he said.

She seemed to be incapable of appreciating the kindness of his motive. After hesitating a little she addressed a proposal to him, which seemed to show distrust of the landlady.

"Will you let me speak to you upstairs in my own rooms?" she asked.

Without waiting for a reply, she led the way to the stairs. Mr. Rayburn and Lucy followed. They were just beginning the ascent to the first floor, when the spiteful landlady left the lower room, and called to her lodger over their heads: "Take care what you say to this man, Mrs. Zant! He thinks you're mad."

Mrs. Zant turned round on the landing, and looked at him. Not a word fell from her lips. She suffered, she feared, in silence. Something in the sad submission of her face touched the springs of innocent pity in Lucy's heart. The child burst out crying.

That artless expression of sympathy drew Mrs. Zant down the few stairs which separated her from Lucy.

"May I kiss your dear little girl?" she said to Mr. Rayburn. The landlady, standing on the mat below, expressed her opinion of the value of caresses, as compared with a sounder method of treating young persons in tears: "If that child was mine," she remarked, "I would give her something to cry for."

In the meantime, Mrs. Zant led the way to her rooms.

The first words she spoke showed that the landlady had succeeded but too well in prejudicing her against Mr. Rayburn.

"Will you let me ask your child," she said to him, "why you think me mad?"

He met this strange request with a firm answer.

"You don't know yet what I really do think. Will you give me a minute's attention?"

"No," she said positively. "The child pities me, I want to speak to the child. What did you see me do in the Gardens, my dear, that surprised you?" Lucy turned uneasily to her father; Mrs. Zant persisted. "I first saw you by yourself, and then I saw you with your father," she went on. "When I came nearer to you, did I look very oddly—as if I didn't see you at all?"

Lucy hesitated again; and Mr. Rayburn interfered.

"You are confusing my little girl," he said. "Allow me to answer your questions—or excuse me if I leave you."

There was something in his look, or in his tone, that mastered her. She put her hand to her head.

"I don't think I'm fit for it," she answered vacantly. "My courage has been sorely tried already. If I can get a little rest and sleep, you may find me a different person. I am left a great deal by myself; and I have reasons for trying to compose my mind. Can I see you tomorrow? Or write to you? Where do you live?"

Mr. Rayburn laid his card on the table in silence. She had strongly excited his interest. He honestly desired to be of some service to this forlorn creature—abandoned so cruelly, as it seemed, to her own guidance. But he had no authority to exercise, no sort of claim to direct her actions, even if she consented to accept his advice. As a last resource he ventured on an allusion to the relative of whom she had spoken downstairs.

"When do you expect to see your brother-in-law again?" he said.

"I don't know," she answered. "I should like to see him—he is so kind to me."

She turned aside to take leave of Lucy.

"Good-by, my little friend. If you live to grow up, I hope you will never be such a miserable woman as I am." She suddenly looked round at Mr. Rayburn. "Have you got a wife at home?" she asked.

"My wife is dead."

"And you have a child to comfort you! Please leave me; you harden my heart. Oh, sir, don't you understand? You make me envy you!"

Mr. Rayburn was silent when he and his daughter were out in the street again. Lucy, as became a dutiful child, was silent, too. But there are limits to human endurance—and Lucy's capacity for self-control gave way at last.

"Are you thinking of the lady, papa?" she said.

He only answered by nodding his head. His daughter had interrupted him at that critical moment in a man's reflections, when he is on the point of making up his mind. Before they were at home again Mr. Rayburn had arrived at a decision. Mrs. Zant's brother-in-law was evidently ignorant of any serious necessity for his interference—or he would have made arrangements for immediately repeating his visit. In this state of things, if any evil happened to Mrs. Zant, silence on Mr. Rayburn's part might be indirectly to blame for a serious misfortune. Arriving at that conclusion, he decided upon running the risk of being rudely received, for the second time, by another stranger.

Leaving Lucy under the care of her governess, he went at once to the address that had been written on the visiting-card left at the lodging-house, and sent in his name. A courteous message was returned. Mr. John Zant was at home, and would be happy to see him.

IV

Mr. Rayburn was shown into one of the private sitting-rooms of the hotel.

He observed that the customary position of the furniture in a room had been, in some respects, altered. An armchair, a side-table, and a footstool had all been removed to one of the windows, and had been placed as close as possible to the light. On the table lay a large open roll of morocco leather, containing rows of elegant little instruments in steel and ivory. Waiting by the table, stood Mr. John Zant. He said "Good-morning" in a bass voice, so profound and so melodious that those two commonplace words assumed a new importance, coming from his lips. His personal appearance was in harmony with his magnificent voice—he was a tall, finely-made man of dark complexion; with big brilliant black eyes, and a noble curling beard, which hid the whole lower part of his face. Having bowed with a happy mingling of dignity and politeness, the conventional side of this gentleman's character suddenly vanished; and a crazy side, to all appearance, took its place. He dropped on his knees in front of the footstool. Had he forgotten to say his prayers that morning, and was he in such a hurry to remedy the fault that he had no time to spare for consulting appearances? The doubt had hardly suggested itself, before it was set at rest in a most unexpected manner. Mr. Zant looked at his visitor with a bland smile, and said:

"Please let me see your feet."

For the moment, Mr. Rayburn lost his presence of mind. He looked at the instruments on the side-table.

"Are you a corn-cutter?" was all he could say.

"Excuse me, sir," returned the polite operator, "the term you use is quite obsolete in our profession." He rose from his knees, and added modestly: "I am a Chiropodist."

"I beg your pardon."

"Don't mention it! You are not, I imagine, in want of my professional services. To what motive may I attribute the honor of your visit?"

By this time Mr. Rayburn had recovered himself.

"I have come here," he answered, "under circumstances which require apology as well as explanation."

Mr. Zant's highly polished manner betrayed signs of alarm; his suspicions pointed to a formidable conclusion—a conclusion that shook him to the innermost recesses of the pocket in which he kept his money.

"The numerous demands on me—" he began.

Mr. Rayburn smiled.

"Make your mind easy," he replied. "I don't want money. My object is to speak with you on the subject of a lady who is a relation of yours."

"My sister-in-law!" Mr. Zant exclaimed. "Pray take a seat."

Doubting if he had chosen a convenient time for his visit, Mr. Rayburn hesitated.

"Am I likely to be in the way of persons who wish to consult you?" he asked.

"Certainly not. My morning hours of attendance on my clients are from eleven to one." The clock on the mantelpiece struck the quarter-past one as he spoke. "I hope you don't bring me bad news?" he said, very earnestly. "When I called on Mrs. Zant this morning, I heard that she had gone out for a walk. Is it indiscreet to ask how you became acquainted with her?"

Mr. Rayburn at once mentioned what he had seen and heard in Kensington Gardens; not forgetting to add a few words, which described his interview afterward with Mrs. Zant.

The lady's brother-in-law listened with an interest and sympathy, which offered the strongest possible contrast to the unprovoked rudeness of the mistress of the lodging-house. He declared that he could only do justice to his sense of obligation by following Mr. Rayburn's example, and expressing himself as frankly as if he had been speaking to an old friend.

"The sad story of my sister-in-law's life," he said, "will, I think, explain certain things which must have naturally perplexed you. My brother was introduced to her at the house of an Australian gentleman, on a visit to England. She was then employed as governess to his daughters. So sincere was the regard felt for her by the family that the parents had, at the entreaty of their children, asked her to accompany them when they returned to the Colony. The governess thankfully accepted the proposal."

"Had she no relations in England?" Mr. Rayburn asked.

"She was literally alone in the world, sir. When I tell you that she had been brought up in the Foundling Hospital, you will understand what I mean. Oh, there is no romance in my sister-in-law's story! She never has known, or will know, who her parents were or why they deserted her. The happiest moment in her life was the moment when she and my brother first met. It was an instance, on both sides, of love at first sight. Though not a rich man, my brother had earned a sufficient income in mercantile pursuits. His character spoke for itself. In a word, he altered all the poor girl's prospects, as we then hoped and believed, for the better. Her employers deferred their return to Australia, so that she might be married from their house. After a happy life of a few weeks only—"

His voice failed him; he paused, and turned his face from the light.

"Pardon me," he said; "I am not able, even yet, to speak composedly of my brother's death. Let me only say that the poor young wife was a widow, before the happy days of the honeymoon were over. That dreadful calamity struck her down. Before my brother had been committed to the grave, her life was in danger from brain-fever."

Those words placed in a new light Mr. Rayburn's first fear that her intellect might be deranged. Looking at him attentively, Mr. Zant seemed to understand what was passing in the mind of his guest.

"No!" he said. "If the opinions of the medical men are to be trusted, the result of the illness is injury to her physical strength—not injury to her mind. I have observed in her, no doubt, a certain waywardness of temper since her illness; but that is a trifle. As an example of what I mean, I may tell you that I invited her, on her recovery, to pay me a visit. My house is not in London—the air doesn't agree with me—my place of residence is at St. Sallins-on-Sea.* I am not myself a married man; but my excellent housekeeper would have received Mrs. Zant with the utmost kindness. She was resolved—obstinately resolved, poor thing—to remain in London. It is needless to say that, in her melancholy position, I am attentive to her slightest wishes. I took a lodging for her; and, at her special request, I chose a house which was near Kensington Gardens.

"Is there any association with the Gardens which led Mrs. Zant to make that request?"

"Some association, I believe, with the memory of her husband. By the way, I wish to be sure of finding her at home, when I call to-morrow. Did you say (in the course of your interesting statement) that she intended—as you supposed—to return to Kensington Gardens to-morrow? Or has my memory deceived me?"

"Your memory is perfectly accurate."

"Thank you. I confess I am not only distressed by what you have told me of Mrs. Zant—I am at a loss to know how to act for the best. My only idea, at present, is to try a change of air and scene. What do you think yourself?"

"I think you are right."

Mr. Zant still hesitated.

"It would not be easy for me, just now," he said, "to leave my patients and take her abroad."

The obvious reply to this occurred to Mr. Rayburn. A man of larger worldly experience might have felt certain suspicions, and might have remained silent. Mr. Rayburn spoke.

"Why not renew your invitation and take her to your house at the seaside?" he said.

In the perplexed state of Mr. Zant's mind, this plain course of action had apparently failed to present itself. His gloomy face brightened directly.

"The very thing!" he said. "I will certainly take your advice. If the air of St. Sallins does nothing else, it will improve her health and help her to

---

* Not only is this location fictitious, but there is no "St. Sallins" in the Catholic Church.

recover her good looks. Did she strike you as having been (in happier days) a pretty woman?"

This was a strangely familiar question to ask—almost an indelicate question, under the circumstances A certain furtive expression in Mr. Zant's fine dark eyes seemed to imply that it had been put with a purpose. Was it possible that he suspected Mr. Rayburn's interest in his sister-in-law to be inspired by any motive which was not perfectly unselfish and perfectly pure? To arrive at such a conclusion as this might be to judge hastily and cruelly of a man who was perhaps only guilty of a want of delicacy of feeling. Mr. Rayburn honestly did his best to assume the charitable point of view. At the same time, it is not to be denied that his words, when he answered, were carefully guarded, and that he rose to take his leave.

Mr. John Zant hospitably protested.

"Why are you in such a hurry? Must you really go? I shall have the honor of returning your visit to-morrow, when I have made arrangements to profit by that excellent suggestion of yours. Good-by. God bless you."

He held out his hand: a hand with a smooth surface and a tawny color, that fervently squeezed the fingers of a departing friend. "Is that man a scoundrel?" was Mr. Rayburn's first thought, after he had left the hotel. His moral sense set all hesitation at rest—and answered: "You're a fool if you doubt it."

V

Disturbed by presentiments, Mr. Rayburn returned to his house on foot, by way of trying what exercise would do toward composing his mind.

The experiment failed. He went upstairs and played with Lucy; he drank an extra glass of wine at dinner; he took the child and her governess to a circus in the evening; he ate a little supper, fortified by another glass of wine, before he went to bed—and still those vague forebodings of evil persisted in torturing him. Looking back through his past life, he asked himself if any woman (his late wife of course excepted!) had ever taken the predominant place in his thoughts which Mrs. Zant had assumed—without any discernible reason to account for it? If he had ventured to answer his own question, the reply would have been: Never!

All the next day he waited at home, in expectation of Mr. John Zant's promised visit, and waited in vain.

Toward evening the parlor-maid appeared at the family tea-table, and presented to her master an unusually large envelope sealed with black wax, and addressed in a strange handwriting. The absence of stamp and postmark showed that it had been left at the house by a messenger.

"Who brought this?" Mr. Rayburn asked.

"A lady, sir—in deep mourning."

"Did she leave any message?"

"No, sir."

Having drawn the inevitable conclusion, Mr. Rayburn shut himself up in his library. He was afraid of Lucy's curiosity and Lucy's questions, if he read Mrs. Zant's letter in his daughter's presence.

Looking at the open envelope after he had taken out the leaves of writing which it contained, he noticed these lines traced inside the cover:

"My one excuse for troubling you, when I might have consulted my brother-in-law, will be found in the pages which I inclose. To speak plainly, you have been led to fear that I am not in my right senses. For this very reason, I now appeal to you. Your dreadful doubt of me, sir, is my doubt too. Read what I have written about myself—and then tell me, I entreat you, which I am: A person who has been the object of a supernatural revelation? or an unfortunate creature who is only fit for imprisonment in a mad-house?"

Mr. Rayburn opened the manuscript. With steady attention, which soon quickened to breathless interest, he read what follows:

VI: THE LADY'S MANUSCRIPT

Yesterday morning the sun shone in a clear blue sky—after a succession of cloudy days, counting from the first of the month.

The radiant light had its animating effect on my poor spirits. I had passed the night more peacefully than usual; undisturbed by the dream, so cruelly familiar to me, that my lost husband is still living—the dream from which I always wake in tears. Never, since the dark days of my sorrow, have I been so little troubled by the self-tormenting fancies and fears which beset miserable women, as when I left the house, and turned my steps toward Kensington Gardens—for the first time since my husband's death.

Attended by my only companion, the little dog who had been his favorite as well as mine, I went to the quiet corner of the Gardens which is nearest to Kensington.

On that soft grass, under the shade of those grand trees, we had loitered together in the days of our betrothal. It was his favorite walk; and he had taken me to see it in the early days of our acquaintance. There, he had first asked me to be his wife. There, we had felt the rapture of our first kiss. It was surely natural that I should wish to see once more a place sacred to such memories as these? I am only twenty-three years old; I have no child to comfort me, no companion of my own age, nothing to love but the dumb creature who is so faithfully fond of me.

I went to the tree under which we stood, when my dear one's eyes told his love before he could utter it in words. The sun of that vanished day shone on me again; it was the same noontide hour; the same solitude was around me. I had feared the first effect of the dreadful contrast between past and present. No! I was quiet and resigned. My thoughts, rising higher than earth, dwelt on the better life beyond the grave. Some tears came into my eyes. But I was not unhappy. My memory of all that happened may be trusted, even in trifles which relate only to myself—I was not unhappy.

The first object that I saw, when my eyes were clear again, was the dog. He crouched a few paces away from me, trembling pitiably, but uttering no cry. What had caused the fear that overpowered him?

I was soon to know.

I called to the dog; he remained immovable—conscious of some mysterious coming thing that held him spellbound. I tried to go to the poor creature, and fondle and comfort him.

At the first step forward that I took, something stopped me.

It was not to be seen, and not to be heard. It stopped me.

The still figure of the dog disappeared from my view: the lonely scene round me disappeared—excepting the light from heaven, the tree that sheltered me, and the grass in front of me. A sense of unutterable expectation kept my eyes riveted on the grass. Suddenly, I saw its myriad blades rise erect and shivering. The fear came to me of something passing over them with the invisible swiftness of the wind. The shivering advanced. It was all round me. It crept into the leaves of the tree over my head; they shuddered, without a sound to tell of their agitation; their pleasant natural rustling was struck dumb. The song of the birds had ceased. The cries of the water-fowl on the pond were heard no more. There was a dreadful silence.

But the lovely sunshine poured down on me, as brightly as ever.

In that dazzling light, in that fearful silence, I felt an Invisible Presence near me. It touched me gently.

At the touch, my heart throbbed with an overwhelming joy. Exquisite pleasure thrilled through every nerve in my body. I knew him! From the unseen world—himself unseen—he had returned to me. Oh, I knew him!

And yet, my helpless mortality longed for a sign that might give me assurance of the truth. The yearning in me shaped itself into words. I tried to utter the words. I would have said, if I could have spoken: "Oh, my angel, give me a token that it is You!" But I was like a person struck dumb—I could only think it.

The Invisible Presence read my thought. I felt my lips touched, as my husband's lips used to touch them when he kissed me. And that was my answer. A thought came to me again. I would have said, if I could have spoken: "Are you here to take me to the better world?"

I waited. Nothing that I could feel touched me.

I was conscious of thinking once more. I would have said, if I could have spoken: "Are you here to protect me?"

I felt myself held in a gentle embrace, as my husband's arms used to hold me when he pressed me to his breast. And that was my answer.

The touch that was like the touch of his lips, lingered and was lost; the clasp that was like the clasp of his arms, pressed me and fell away. The garden-scene resumed its natural aspect. I saw a human creature near, a lovely little girl looking at me.

At that moment, when I was my own lonely self again, the sight of the child soothed and attracted me. I advanced, intending to speak to her. To my horror I suddenly ceased to see her. She disappeared as if I had been stricken blind.

And yet I could see the landscape round me; I could see the heaven above me. A time passed—only a few minutes, as I thought—and the child became visible to me again; walking hand-in-hand with her father. I approached them; I was close enough to see that they were looking at me with pity and surprise. My impulse was to ask if they saw anything strange in my face or my manner. Before I could speak, the horrible wonder happened again. They vanished from my view.

Was the Invisible Presence still near? Was it passing between me and my fellow-mortals; forbidding communication, in that place and at that time?

It must have been so. When I turned away in my ignorance, with a heavy heart, the dreadful blankness which had twice shut out from me the beings of my own race, was not between me and my dog. The poor little creature filled me with pity; I called him to me. He moved at the sound of my voice, and followed me languidly; not quite awakened yet from the trance of terror that had possessed him.

Before I had retired by more than a few steps, I thought I was conscious of the Presence again. I held out my longing arms to it. I waited in the hope of a touch to tell me that I might return. Perhaps I was answered by indirect means? I only know that a resolution to return to the same place, at the same hour, came to me, and quieted my mind.

The morning of the next day was dull and cloudy; but the rain held off. I set forth again to the Gardens.

My dog ran on before me into the street—and stopped: waiting to see in which direction I might lead the way. When I turned toward the Gardens, he dropped behind me. In a little while I looked back. He was following me no longer; he stood irresolute. I called to him. He advanced a few steps—hesitated—and ran back to the house.

I went on by myself. Shall I confess my superstition? I thought the dog's desertion of me a bad omen.

Arrived at the tree, I placed myself under it. The minutes followed each other uneventfully. The cloudy sky darkened. The dull surface of the grass showed no shuddering consciousness of an unearthly creature passing over it.

I still waited, with an obstinacy which was fast becoming the obstinacy of despair. How long an interval elapsed, while I kept watch on the ground before me, I am not able to say. I only know that a change came.

Under the dull gray light I saw the grass move—but not as it had moved, on the day before. It shriveled as if a flame had scorched it. No flame appeared. The brown underlying earth showed itself winding onward in a thin strip—which might have been a footpath traced in fire. It frightened me. I longed for the protection of the Invisible Presence. I prayed for a warning of it, if danger was near.

A touch answered me. It was as if a hand unseen had taken my hand—had raised it, little by little—had left it, pointing to the thin brown path that wound toward me under the shriveled blades of grass.

I looked to the far end of the path.

The unseen hand closed on my hand with a warning pressure: the revelation of the coming danger was near me—I waited for it. I saw it.

The figure of a man appeared, advancing toward me along the thin brown path. I looked in his face as he came nearer. It showed me dimly the face of my husband's brother—John Zant.

The consciousness of myself as a living creature left me. I knew nothing; I felt nothing. I was dead.

When the torture of revival made me open my eyes, I found myself on the grass. Gentle hands raised my head, at the moment when I recovered my senses. Who had brought me to life again? Who was taking care of me?

I looked upward, and saw—bending over me—John Zant.

VII

There, the manuscript ended.

Some lines had been added on the last page; but they had been so carefully erased as to be illegible. These words of explanation appeared below the canceled sentences:

"I had begun to write the little that remains to be told, when it struck me that I might, unintentionally, be exercising an unfair influence on your opinion. Let me only remind you that I believe absolutely in the supernatural revelation which I have endeavored to describe. Remember this—and decide for me what I dare not decide for myself."

There was no serious obstacle in the way of compliance with this request.

Judged from the point of view of the materialist, Mrs. Zant might no doubt be the victim of illusions (produced by a diseased state of the nervous system), which have been known to exist—as in the celebrated case of the book-seller, Nicolai, of Berlin*—without being accompanied by derangement of the intellectual powers. But Mr. Rayburn was not asked to solve any such intricate problem as this. He had been merely instructed to read the manuscript, and to say what impression it had left on him of the mental condition of the writer; whose doubt of herself had been, in all probability, first suggested by remembrance of the illness from which she had suffered—brain-fever.

Under these circumstances, there could be little difficulty in forming an opinion. The memory which had recalled, and the judgment which had arranged, the succession of events related in the narrative, revealed a mind in full possession of its resources.

Having satisfied himself so far, Mr. Rayburn abstained from considering the more serious question suggested by what he had read.

At any time his habits of life and his ways of thinking would have rendered him unfit to weigh the arguments, which assert or deny supernatural revelation among the creatures of earth. But his mind was now so disturbed by the startling record of experience which he had just read, that he was only conscious of feeling certain impressions—without possessing the capacity to reflect on them. That his anxiety on Mrs. Zant's account had been increased, and that his doubts of Mr. John Zant had been encouraged, were the only practical results of the confidence placed in him of which he was thus far aware. In the ordinary exigencies of life a man of hesitating

---

* Friedrich Nicolai (1733–1811) was a famed German writer and publisher who suffered from a disorder in 1791 that caused him to hallucinate the presence of ghosts for eight weeks. Nicolai believed his delusions were the result of high blood pressure, and he cured himself by applying leeches to his buttocks (a common medical practice at the time). His literary rival Goethe parodied this episode in his classic *Faust*, by creating a character called the "Proktophantasmist" who Faust encounters during the wild revels of Walpurgisnacht (April 30).

disposition, his interest in Mrs. Zant's welfare, and his desire to discover what had passed between her brother-in-law and herself, after their meeting in the Gardens, urged him into instant action. In half an hour more, he had arrived at her lodgings. He was at once admitted.

VIII

Mrs. Zant was alone, in an imperfectly lighted room.

"I hope you will excuse the bad light," she said; "my head has been burning as if the fever had come back again. Oh, don't go away! After what I have suffered, you don't know how dreadful it is to be alone."

The tone of her voice told him that she had been crying. He at once tried the best means of setting the poor lady at ease, by telling her of the conclusion at which he had arrived, after reading her manuscript. The happy result showed itself instantly: her face brightened, her manner changed; she was eager to hear more.

"Have I produced any other impression on you?" she asked.

He understood the allusion. Expressing sincere respect for her own convictions, he told her honestly that he was not prepared to enter on the obscure and terrible question of supernatural interposition. Grateful for the tone in which he had answered her, she wisely and delicately changed the subject.

"I must speak to you of my brother-in-law," she said. "He has told me of your visit; and I am anxious to know what you think of him. Do you like Mr. John Zant?"

Mr. Rayburn hesitated.

The careworn look appeared again in her face. "If you had felt as kindly toward him as he feels toward you," she said, "I might have gone to St. Sallins with a lighter heart."

Mr. Rayburn thought of the supernatural appearances, described at the close of her narrative. "You believe in that terrible warning," he remonstrated; "and yet, you go to your brother-in-law's house!"

"I believe," she answered, "in the spirit of the man who loved me in the days of his earthly bondage. I am under his protection. What have I to do but to cast away my fears, and to wait in faith and hope? It might have helped my resolution if a friend had been near to encourage me." She paused and smiled sadly. "I must remember," she resumed, "that your way of understanding my position is not my way. I ought to have told you that Mr. John Zant feels needless anxiety about my health. He declares that he will not lose sight of me until his mind is at ease. It is useless to attempt to alter his opinion. He says my nerves are shattered—and who that sees me can doubt it? He tells me that my only chance of getting better is to try a change of air and perfect repose—how can I contradict him? He reminds me that I have no relation but himself, and no house open to me but his own—and God knows he is right!"

She said those last words in accents of melancholy resignation, which grieved the good man whose one merciful purpose was to serve and console her. He spoke impulsively with the freedom of an old friend

"I want to know more of you and Mr. John Zant than I know now," he said. "My motive is a better one than mere curiosity. Do you believe that I feel a sincere interest in you?"

"With my whole heart."

That reply encouraged him to proceed with what he had to say. "When you recovered from your fainting-fit," he began, "Mr. John Zant asked questions, of course?"

"He asked what could possibly have happened, in such a quiet place as Kensington Gardens, to make me faint."

"And how did you answer?"

"Answer? I couldn't even look at him!"

"You said nothing?"

"Nothing. I don't know what he thought of me; he might have been surprised, or he might have been offended."

"Is he easily offended?" Mr. Rayburn asked.

"Not in my experience of him."

"Do you mean your experience of him before your illness?"

"Yes. Since my recovery, his engagements with country patients have kept him away from London. I have not seen him since he took these lodgings for me. But he is always considerate. He has written more than once to beg that I will not think him neglectful, and to tell me (what I knew already through my poor husband) that he has no money of his own, and must live by his profession."

"In your husband's lifetime, were the two brothers on good terms?"

"Always. The one complaint I ever heard my husband make of John Zant was that he didn't come to see us often enough, after our marriage. Is there some wickedness in him which we have never suspected? It may be—but how can it be? I have every reason to be grateful to the man against whom I have been supernaturally warned! His conduct to me has been always perfect. I can't tell you what I owe to his influence in quieting my mind, when a dreadful doubt arose about my husband's death."

"Do you mean doubt if he died a natural death?"

"Oh, no! no! He was dying of rapid consumption—but his sudden death took the doctors by surprise. One of them thought that he might have taken an overdose of his sleeping drops, by mistake. The other disputed this conclusion, or there might have been an inquest in the house. Oh, don't speak of it any more! Let us talk of something else. Tell me when I shall see you again."

"I hardly know. When do you and your brother-in-law leave London?"

"To-morrow." She looked at Mr. Rayburn with a piteous entreaty in her eyes; she said, timidly: "Do you ever go to the seaside, and take your dear little girl with you?"

The request, at which she had only dared to hint, touched on the idea which was at that moment in Mr. Rayburn's mind.

Interpreted by his strong prejudice against John Zant, what she had said of her brother-in-law filled him with forebodings of peril to herself; all the more powerful in their influence, for this reason—that he shrank from distinctly realizing them. If another person had been present at the interview, and had said to him afterward: "That man's reluctance to visit his sister-in-law, while her husband was living, is associated with a secret sense of guilt which her innocence cannot even imagine: he, and he alone, knows the cause of her husband's sudden death: his feigned anxiety about her health is adopted as the safest means of enticing her into his house—if those formidable conclusions had been urged on Mr. Rayburn, he would have felt it his duty to reject them, as unjustifiable aspersions on an absent man. And yet, when he took leave that evening of Mrs. Zant, he had pledged himself to give Lucy a holiday at the seaside: and he had said, without blushing, that the child really deserved it, as a reward for general good conduct and attention to her lessons!

IX

Three days later, the father and daughter arrived toward evening at St. Sallins-on-Sea. They found Mrs. Zant at the station.

The poor woman's joy, on seeing them, expressed itself like the joy of a child. "Oh, I am so glad! So glad!" was all she could say when they met. Lucy was half-smothered with kisses, and was made supremely happy by a present of the finest doll she had ever possessed. Mrs. Zant accompanied her friends to the rooms which had been secured at the hotel. She was able to speak confidentially to Mr. Rayburn, while Lucy was in the balcony hugging her doll, and looking at the sea.

The one event that had happened during Mrs. Zant's short residence at St. Sallins was the departure of her brother-in-law that morning, for London. He had been called away to operate on the feet of a wealthy patient who knew the value of his time: his housekeeper expected that he would return to dinner.

As to his conduct toward Mrs. Zant, he was not only as attentive as ever—he was almost oppressively affectionate in his language and manner. There was no service that a man could render which he had not eagerly offered to her. He declared that he already perceived an improvement in her health; he congratulated her on having decided to stay in his house; and (as a proof, perhaps, of his sincerity) he had repeatedly pressed her hand. "Have you any idea what all this means?" she said, simply.

Mr. Rayburn kept his idea to himself. He professed ignorance; and asked next what sort of person the housekeeper was.

Mrs. Zant shook her head ominously.

"Such a strange creature," she said, "and in the habit of taking such liberties that I begin to be afraid she is a little crazy."

"Is she an old woman?"

"No—only middle-aged. This morning, after her master had left the house, she actually asked me what I thought of my brother-in-law! I told her, as coldly as possible, that I thought he was very kind. She was quite insensible to the tone in which I had spoken; she went on from bad to worse. "Do you call him the sort of man who would take the fancy of a young woman?" was her next question. She actually looked at me (I might have been wrong; and I hope I was) as if the "young woman" she had in her mind was myself! I said: "I don't think of such things, and I don't talk about them." Still, she was not in the least discouraged; she made a personal remark next: "Excuse me—but you do look wretchedly pale." I thought she seemed to enjoy the defect in my complexion; I really believe it raised me in her estimation. "We shall get on better in time," she said; "I am beginning to like you." She walked out humming a tune. Don't you agree with me? Don't you think she's crazy?"

"I can hardly give an opinion until I have seen her. Does she look as if she might have been a pretty woman at one time of her life?"

"Not the sort of pretty woman whom I admire!"

Mr. Rayburn smiled. "I was thinking," he resumed, "that this person's odd conduct may perhaps be accounted for. She is probably jealous of any young lady who is invited to her master's house—and (till she noticed your complexion) she began by being jealous of you."

Innocently at a loss to understand how she could become an object of the housekeeper's jealousy, Mrs. Zant looked at Mr. Rayburn in astonishment. Before she could give expression to her feeling of surprise, there was an interruption—a welcome interruption. A waiter entered the room, and announced a visitor; described as "a gentleman."

Mrs. Zant at once rose to retire.

"Who is the gentleman?" Mr. Rayburn asked—detaining Mrs. Zant as he spoke.

A voice which they both recognized answered gayly, from the outer side of the door:

"A friend from London."

X

"Welcome to St. Sallins!" cried Mr. John Zant. "I knew that you were expected, my dear sir, and I took my chance at finding you at the hotel."

He turned to his sister-in-law, and kissed her hand with an elaborate gallantry worthy of Sir Charles Grandison himself.* "When I reached home, my dear, and heard that you had gone out, I guessed that your object was to receive our excellent friend. You have not felt lonely while I have been away? That's right! that's right!" he looked toward the balcony, and discovered Lucy at the open window, staring at the magnificent stranger. "Your little daughter, Mr. Rayburn? Dear child! Come and kiss me."

Lucy answered in one positive word: "No."

Mr. John Zant was not easily discouraged.

"Show me your doll, darling," he said. "Sit on my knee."

Lucy answered in two positive words—"I won't."

Her father approached the window to administer the necessary reproof. Mr. John Zant interfered in the cause of mercy with his best grace. He held up his hands in cordial entreaty. "Dear Mr. Rayburn! The fairies are sometimes shy; and this little fairy doesn't take to strangers at first sight. Dear child! All in good time. And what stay do you make at St. Sallins? May we hope that our poor attractions will tempt you to prolong your visit?"

He put his flattering little question with an ease of manner which was rather too plainly assumed; and he looked at Mr. Rayburn with a watchfulness which appeared to attach undue importance to the reply. When he said: "What stay do you make at St. Sallins?" did he really mean: "How soon do you leave us?" Inclining to adopt this conclusion, Mr. Rayburn answered cautiously that his stay at the seaside would depend on circumstances. Mr. John Zant looked at his sister-in-law, sitting silent in a corner with Lucy on her lap. "Exert your attractions," he said; "make the circumstances agreeable to our good friend. Will you dine with us to-day, my dear sir, and bring your little fairy with you?"

Lucy was far from receiving this complimentary allusion in the spirit in which it had been offered. "I'm not a fairy," she declared. "I'm a child."

"And a naughty child," her father added, with all the severity that he could assume.

"I can't help it, papa; the man with the big beard puts me out."

---

* Sir Charles Grandison is the hero of Samuel Richardson's novel *The History of Sir Charles Grandison* (1753), also known as *Sir Charles Grandison*.

The man with the big beard was amused—amiably, paternally amused—by Lucy's plain speaking. He repeated his invitation to dinner; and he did his best to look disappointed when Mr. Rayburn made the necessary excuses.

"Another day," he said (without, however, fixing the day). "I think you will find my house comfortable. My housekeeper may perhaps be eccentric—but in all essentials a woman in a thousand. Do you feel the change from London already? Our air at St. Sallins is really worthy of its reputation. Invalids who come here are cured as if by magic. What do you think of Mrs. Zant? How does she look?"

Mr. Rayburn was evidently expected to say that she looked better. He said it. Mr. John Zant seemed to have anticipated a stronger expression of opinion.

"Surprisingly better!" he pronounced. "Infinitely better! We ought both to be grateful. Pray believe that we are grateful."

"If you mean grateful to me," Mr. Rayburn remarked, "I don't quite understand—"

"You don't quite understand? Is it possible that you have forgotten our conversation when I first had the honor of receiving you? Look at Mrs. Zant again."

Mr. Rayburn looked; and Mrs. Zant's brother-in-law explained himself.

"You notice the return of her color, the healthy brightness of her eyes. (No, my dear, I am not paying you idle compliments; I am stating plain facts.) For that happy result, Mr. Rayburn, we are indebted to you."

"Surely not?"

"Surely yes! It was at your valuable suggestion that I thought of inviting my sister-in-law to visit me at St. Sallins. Ah, you remember it now. Forgive me if I look at my watch; the dinner hour is on my mind. Not, as your dear little daughter there seems to think, because I am greedy, but because I am always punctual, in justice to the cook. Shall we see you to-morrow? Call early, and you will find us at home."

He gave Mrs. Zant his arm, and bowed and smiled, and kissed his hand to Lucy, and left the room. Recalling their interview at the hotel in London, Mr. Rayburn now understood John Zant's object (on that occasion) in assuming the character of a helpless man in need of a sensible suggestion. If Mrs. Zant's residence under his roof became associated with evil consequences, he could declare that she would never have entered the house but for Mr. Rayburn's advice.

With the next day came the hateful necessity of returning this man's visit. Mr. Rayburn was placed between two alternatives. In Mrs. Zant's interests he must remain, no matter at what sacrifice of his own inclinations, on good terms with her brother-in-law—or he must return to London, and leave the poor woman to her fate. His choice, it is needless to say, was never a matter of doubt. He called at the house, and did his innocent best—without in the least deceiving Mr. John Zant—to make himself agreeable during the short duration of his visit. Descending the stairs on his way out, accompanied by Mrs. Zant, he was surprised to see a middle-aged woman in the hall, who looked as if she was waiting there expressly to attract notice.

"The housekeeper," Mrs. Zant whispered. "She is impudent enough to try to make acquaintance with you."

This was exactly what the housekeeper was waiting in the hall to do.

"I hope you like our watering-place, sir," she began. "If I can be of service to you, pray command me. Any friend of this lady's has a claim on me—and you are an old friend, no doubt. I am only the housekeeper; but I presume to take a sincere interest in Mrs. Zant; and I am indeed glad to see you here. We none of us know—do we?—how soon we may want a friend. No offense, I hope? Thank you, sir. Good-morning."

There was nothing in the woman's eyes which indicated an unsettled mind; nothing in the appearance of her lips which suggested habits of intoxication. That her strange outburst of familiarity proceeded from some strong motive seemed to be more than probable. Putting together what Mrs. Zant had already told him, and what he had himself observed, Mr. Rayburn suspected that the motive might be found in the housekeeper's jealousy of her master.

XI

Reflecting in the solitude of his own room, Mr. Rayburn felt that the one prudent course to take would be to persuade Mrs. Zant to leave St. Sallins.

He tried to prepare her for this strong proceeding, when she came the next day to take Lucy out for a walk.

"If you still regret having forced yourself to accept your brother-in-law's invitation," was all he ventured to say, "don't forget that you are perfect mistress of your own actions. You have only to come to me at the hotel, and I will take you back to London by the next train."

She positively refused to entertain the idea.

"I should be a thankless creature, indeed," she said, "if I accepted your proposal. Do you think I am ungrateful enough to involve you in a personal quarrel with John Zant? No! If I find myself forced to leave the house, I will go away alone."

There was no moving her from this resolution. When she and Lucy had gone out together, Mr. Rayburn remained at the hotel, with a mind ill at ease. A man of readier mental resources might have felt at a loss how to act for the best, in the emergency that now confronted him. While he was still as far as ever from arriving at a decision, some person knocked at the door.

Had Mrs. Zant returned? He looked up as the door was opened, and saw to his astonishment—Mr. John Zant's housekeeper.

"Don't let me alarm you, sir," the woman said. "Mrs. Zant has been taken a little faint, at the door of our house. My master is attending to her."

"Where is the child?" Mr. Rayburn asked.

"I was bringing her back to you, sir, when we met a lady and her little girl at the door of the hotel. They were on their way to the beach—and Miss Lucy begged hard to be allowed to go with them. The lady said the two children were playfellows, and she was sure you would not object."

"The lady is quite right. Mrs. Zant's illness is not serious, I hope?"

"I think not, sir. But I should like to say something in her interests. May I? Thank you." She advanced a step nearer to him, and spoke her next words in a whisper. "Take Mrs. Zant away from this place, and lose no time in doing it."

Mr. Rayburn was on his guard. He merely asked: "Why?"

The housekeeper answered in a curiously indirect manner—partly in jest, as it seemed, and partly in earnest.

"When a man has lost his wife," she said, "there's some difference of opinion in Parliament, as I hear, whether he does right or wrong, if he marries his wife's sister. Wait a bit! I'm coming to the point. My master is one who has a long head on his shoulders; he sees consequences which escape the notice of people like me. In his way of thinking, if one man may marry his wife's sister, and no harm done, where's the objection if another man pays a compliment to the family, and marries his brother's widow? My master, if you please, is that other man. Take the widow away before she marries him."

This was beyond endurance.

"You insult Mrs. Zant," Mr. Rayburn answered, "if you suppose that such a thing is possible!"

"Oh! I insult her, do I? Listen to me. One of three things will happen. She will be entrapped into consenting to it—or frightened into consenting to it—or drugged into consenting to it—"

Mr. Rayburn was too indignant to let her go on.

"You are talking nonsense," he said. "There can be no marriage; the law forbids it."

"Are you one of the people who see no further than their noses?" she asked insolently. "Won't the law take his money? Is he obliged to mention that he is related to her by marriage, when he buys the license?" She paused; her humor changed; she stamped furiously on the floor. The true motive that animated her showed itself in her next words, and warned Mr. Rayburn to grant a more favorable hearing than he had accorded to her yet. "If you won't stop it," she burst out, "I will! If he marries anybody, he is bound to marry ME. Will you take her away? I ask you, for the last time—will you take her away?"

The tone in which she made that final appeal to him had its effect.

"I will go back with you to John Zant's house," he said, "and judge for myself."

She laid her hand on his arm:

"I must go first—or you may not be let in. Follow me in five minutes; and don't knock at the street door."

On the point of leaving him, she abruptly returned.

"We have forgotten something," she said. "Suppose my master refuses to see you. His temper might get the better of him; he might make it so unpleasant for you that you would be obliged to go."

"My temper might get the better of me," Mr. Rayburn replied; "and—if I thought it was in Mrs. Zant's interests—I might refuse to leave the house unless she accompanied me."

"That will never do, sir."

"Why not?"

"Because I should be the person to suffer."

"In what way?"

"In this way. If you picked a quarrel with my master, I should be blamed for it because I showed you upstairs. Besides, think of the lady. You might frighten her out of her senses, if it came to a struggle between you two men."

The language was exaggerated; but there was a force in this last objection which Mr. Rayburn was obliged to acknowledge.

"And, after all," the housekeeper continued, "he has more right over her than you have. He is related to her, and you are only her friend."

Mr. Rayburn declined to let himself be influenced by this consideration, "Mr. John Zant is only related to her by marriage," he said. "If she prefers trusting in me—come what may of it, I will be worthy of her confidence."

The housekeeper shook her head.

"That only means another quarrel," she answered. "The wise way, with a man like my master, is the peaceable way. We must manage to deceive him."

"I don't like deceit."

"In that case, sir, I'll wish you good-by. We will leave Mrs. Zant to do the best she can for herself."

Mr. Rayburn was unreasonable. He positively refused to adopt this alternative.

"Will you hear what I have got to say?" the housekeeper asked.

"There can be no harm in that," he admitted. "Go on."

She took him at his word.

"When you called at our house," she began, "did you notice the doors in the passage, on the first floor? Very well. One of them is the door of the drawing-room, and the other is the door of the library. Do you remember the drawing-room, sir?"

"I thought it a large well-lighted room," Mr. Rayburn answered. "And I noticed a doorway in the wall, with a handsome curtain hanging over it."

"That's enough for our purpose," the housekeeper resumed. "On the other side of the curtain, if you had looked in, you would have found the library. Suppose my master is as polite as usual, and begs to be excused for not receiving you, because it is an inconvenient time. And suppose you are polite on your side and take yourself off by the drawing-room door. You will find me waiting downstairs, on the first landing. Do you see it now?"

"I can't say I do."

"You surprise me, sir. What is to prevent us from getting back softly into the library, by the door in the passage? And why shouldn't we use that second way into the library as a means of discovering what may be going on in the drawing-room? Safe behind the curtain, you will see him if he behaves uncivilly to Mrs. Zant, or you will hear her if she calls for help. In either case, you may be as rough and ready with my master as you find needful; it will be he who has frightened her, and not you. And who can blame the poor housekeeper because Mr. Rayburn did his duty, and protected a helpless woman? There is my plan, sir. Is it worth trying?"

He answered, sharply enough: "I don't like it."

The housekeeper opened the door again, and wished him good-by.

If Mr. Rayburn had felt no more than an ordinary interest in Mrs. Zant, he would have let the woman go. As it was, he stopped her; and, after some further protest (which proved to be useless), he ended in giving way.

"You promise to follow my directions?" she stipulated.

He gave the promise. She smiled, nodded, and left him. True to his instructions, Mr. Rayburn reckoned five minutes by his watch, before he followed her.

XII

The housekeeper was waiting for him, with the street-door ajar.

"They are both in the drawing-room," she whispered, leading the way upstairs. "Step softly, and take him by surprise."

A table of oblong shape stood midway between the drawing-room walls. At the end of it which was nearest to the window, Mrs. Zant was pacing to and fro across the breadth of the room. At the opposite end of the table,

John Zant was seated. Taken completely by surprise, he showed himself in his true character. He started to his feet, and protested with an oath against the intrusion which had been committed on him.

Heedless of his action and his language, Mr. Rayburn could look at nothing, could think of nothing, but Mrs. Zant. She was still walking slowly to and fro, unconscious of the words of sympathy which he addressed to her, insensible even as it seemed to the presence of other persons in the room.

John Zant's voice broke the silence. His temper was under control again: he had his reasons for still remaining on friendly terms with Mr. Rayburn.

"I am sorry I forgot myself just now," he said.

Mr. Rayburn's interest was concentrated on Mrs. Zant; he took no notice of the apology.

"When did this happen?" he asked.

"About a quarter of an hour ago. I was fortunately at home. Without speaking to me, without noticing me, she walked upstairs like a person in a dream."

Mr. Rayburn suddenly pointed to Mrs. Zant.

"Look at her!" he said. "There's a change!"

All restlessness in her movements had come to an end. She was standing at the further end of the table, which was nearest to the window, in the full flow of sunlight pouring at that moment over her face. Her eyes looked out straight before her—void of all expression. Her lips were a little parted: her head drooped slightly toward her shoulder, in an attitude which suggested listening for something or waiting for something. In the warm brilliant light, she stood before the two men, a living creature self-isolated in a stillness like the stillness of death.

John Zant was ready with the expression of his opinion.

"A nervous seizure," he said. "Something resembling catalepsy, as you see."

"Have you sent for a doctor?"

"A doctor is not wanted."

"I beg your pardon. It seems to me that medical help is absolutely necessary."

"Be so good as to remember," Mr. John Zant answered, "that the decision rests with me, as the lady's relative. I am sensible of the honor which your visit confers on me. But the time has been unhappily chosen. Forgive me if I suggest that you will do well to retire."

Mr. Rayburn had not forgotten the housekeeper's advice, or the promise which she had exacted from him. But the expression in John Zant's face was a serious trial to his self-control. He hesitated, and looked back at Mrs. Zant.

If he provoked a quarrel by remaining in the room, the one alternative would be the removal of her by force. Fear of the consequences to herself, if she was suddenly and roughly roused from her trance, was the one consideration which reconciled him to submission. He withdrew.

The housekeeper was waiting for him below, on the first landing. When the door of the drawing-room had been closed again, she signed to him to follow her, and returned up the stairs. After another struggle with himself, he obeyed. They entered the library from the corridor—and placed themselves behind the closed curtain which hung over the doorway. It was easy so to arrange the edge of the drapery as to observe, without exciting suspicion, whatever was going on in the next room.

Mrs. Zant's brother-in-law was approaching her at the time when Mr. Rayburn saw him again.

In the instant afterward, she moved—before he had completely passed over the space between them. Her still figure began to tremble. She lifted her drooping head. For a moment there was a shrinking in her—as if she had been touched by something. She seemed to recognize the touch: she was still again.

John Zant watched the change. It suggested to him that she was beginning to recover her senses. He tried the experiment of speaking to her.

"My love, my sweet angel, come to the heart that adores you!"

He advanced again; he passed into the flood of sunlight pouring over her. "Rouse yourself!" he said.

She still remained in the same position; apparently at his mercy, neither hearing him nor seeing him.

"Rouse yourself!" he repeated. "My darling, come to me!"

At the instant when he attempted to embrace her—at the instant when Mr. Rayburn rushed into the room—John Zant's arms, suddenly turning rigid, remained outstretched. With a shriek of horror, he struggled to draw them back—struggled, in the empty brightness of the sunshine, as if some invisible grip had seized him.

"What has got me?" the wretch screamed. "Who is holding my hands? Oh, the cold of it! the cold of it!"

His features became convulsed; his eyes turned upward until only the white eyeballs were visible. He fell prostrate with a crash that shook the room.

The housekeeper ran in. She knelt by her master's body. With one hand she loosened his cravat. With the other she pointed to the end of the table.

Mrs. Zant still kept her place; but there was another change. Little by little, her eyes recovered their natural living expression—then slowly closed. She tottered backward from the table, and lifted her hands wildly, as if to grasp at something which might support her. Mr. Rayburn hurried to her before she fell—lifted her in his arms—and carried her out of the room.

One of the servants met them in the hall. He sent her for a carriage. In a quarter of an hour more, Mrs. Zant was safe under his care at the hotel.

XIII

That night a note, written by the housekeeper, was delivered to Mrs. Zant.

"The doctors give little hope. The paralytic stroke is spreading upward to his face. If death spares him, he will live a helpless man. I shall take care of him to the last. As for you—forget him."

Mrs. Zant gave the note to Mr. Rayburn.

"Read it, and destroy it," she said. "It is written in ignorance of the terrible truth."

He obeyed—and looked at her in silence, waiting to hear more. She hid her face. The few words she had addressed to him, after a struggle with herself, fell slowly and reluctantly from her lips.

She said: "No mortal hand held the hands of John Zant. The guardian spirit was with me. The promised protection was with me. I know it. I wish to know no more."

Having spoken, she rose to retire. He opened the door for her, seeing that she needed rest in her own room.

Left by himself, he began to consider the prospect that was before him in the future. How was he to regard the woman who had just left him? As a poor creature weakened by disease, the victim of her own nervous delusion? or as the chosen object of a supernatural revelation—unparalleled by any similar revelation that he had heard of, or had found recorded in books? His first discovery of the place that she really held in his estimation dawned on his mind, when he felt himself recoiling from the conclusion which presented her to his pity, and yielding to the nobler conviction which felt with her faith, and raised her to a place apart among other women.

XIV

They left St. Sallins the next day.

Arrived at the end of the journey, Lucy held fast by Mrs. Zant's hand. Tears were rising in the child's eyes.

"Are we to bid her good-by?" she said sadly to her father.

He seemed to be unwilling to trust himself to speak; he only said: "My dear, ask her yourself."

But the result justified him. Lucy was happy again.

An Inhabitant of Carcosa

by AMBROSE BIERCE

Ambrose Bierce (1842–1914?) was an American journalist and short-story writer. Critic Michael Dirda ranked Bierce's horror writing as on a par with that of Edgar Allan Poe and H. P. Lovecraft, and Lovecraft himself greatly admired Bierce's work, calling his stories "grim and savage." Bierce's most famous short story, "An Occurrence at Owl Creek Bridge," makes use of Bierce's Civil War experiences and is one of the most anthologized American stories. In December 1913, he travelled to Mexico to embed himself in the Mexican Revolution and disappeared from sight, presumed dead. Because of his lively wit and immense talent and the mystery of his death, Bierce has appeared as a character in more than fifty novels. The following story, beloved by aficionados of weird fiction, was first published in the San Francisco Newsletter *of December 25, 1886.*

F or there be divers sorts of death—some wherein the body remaineth; and in some it vanisheth quite away with the spirit. This commonly occurreth only in solitude (such is God's will) and, none seeing the end, we say the man is lost, or gone on a long journey—which indeed he hath; but sometimes it hath happened in sight of many, as abundant testimony showeth. In one kind of death the spirit also dieth, and this it hath been known to do while yet the body was in vigor for many years. Sometimes, as is veritably attested, it dieth with the body, but after a season is raised up again in that place where the body did decay.

Pondering these words of Hali* (whom God rest) and questioning their full meaning, as one who, having an intimation, yet doubts if there be not something behind, other than that which he has discerned, I noted not whither I had strayed until a sudden chill wind striking my face revived in me a sense of my surroundings. I observed with astonishment that everything seemed unfamiliar. On every side of me stretched a bleak and desolate expanse of plain, covered with a tall overgrowth of sere grass, which rustled and whistled in the autumn wind with heaven knows what mysterious and disquieting suggestion. Protruded at long intervals above it, stood strangely shaped and somber-colored rocks, which seemed to have an understanding with one another and to exchange looks of uncomfortable significance, as if they had reared their heads to watch the issue of some foreseen event. A few blasted trees here and there appeared as leaders in this malevolent conspiracy of silent expectation.

The day, I thought, must be far advanced, though the sun was invisible; and although sensible that the air was raw and chill my consciousness of that fact was rather mental than physical—I had no feeling of discomfort. Over all the dismal landscape a canopy of low, lead-colored clouds hung like a visible curse. In all this there were a menace and a portent—a hint of evil, an intimation of doom. Bird, beast, or insect there was none. The wind sighed in the bare branches of the dead trees and the gray grass bent to whisper its dread secret to the earth; but no other sound nor motion broke the awful repose of that dismal place.

---

* According to Marco Frenschkowski ("Hali," *Crypt of Cthulhu* 92 [Eastertide, 1966], 8–11), Hali is the name attributed to several Arabian scholars, mystics, and alchemists, including Khalid ibn Yazid ibn Mu'awiyah. It is also a town southeast of Mecca. Robert W. Chambers, in his seminal book *The King in Yellow* (1895), transmutes it into a lake near the (fictional) city of Hastur, and H. P. Lovecraft references the lake in his story "The Whisperer in Darkness."

I observed in the herbage a number of weather-worn stones, evidently shaped with tools. They were broken, covered with moss and half sunken in the earth. Some lay prostrate, some leaned at various angles, none was vertical. They were obviously headstones of graves, though the graves themselves no longer existed as either mounds or depressions; the years had leveled all. Scattered here and there, more massive blocks showed where some pompous tomb or ambitious monument had once flung its feeble defiance at oblivion. So old seemed these relics, these vestiges of vanity and memorials of affection and piety, so battered and worn and stained—so neglected, deserted, forgotten the place, that I could not help thinking myself the discoverer of the burial-ground of a prehistoric race of men whose very name was long extinct.

Filled with these reflections, I was for some time heedless of the sequence of my own experiences, but soon I thought, "How came I hither?" A moment's reflection seemed to make this all clear and explain at the same time, though in a disquieting way, the singular character with which my fancy had invested all that I saw or heard. I was ill. I remembered now that I had been prostrated by a sudden fever, and that my family had told me that in my periods of delirium I had constantly cried out for liberty and air, and had been held in bed to prevent my escape out-of-doors. Now I had eluded the vigilance of my attendants and had wandered hither to—to where? I could not conjecture. Clearly I was at a considerable distance from the city where I dwelt—the ancient and famous city of Carcosa.*

No signs of human life were anywhere visible nor audible; no rising smoke, no watch-dog's bark, no lowing of cattle, no shouts of children at play—nothing but that dismal burial-place, with its air of mystery and dread, due to my own disordered brain. Was I not becoming again delirious, there beyond human aid? Was it not indeed ALL an illusion of my madness? I called aloud the names of my wives and sons, reached out

---

* A fictional city, perhaps derived from the medieval town of Carcassonne, called Carcaso in Roman times. The city was under Arab rule from 720 to 759 c.e. Robert W. Chambers borrowed the name for his story "The King in Yellow" and placed Carcosa on the banks of Lake Hali. These fictional place-names have been subsequently adopted by other admiring writers.

my hands in search of theirs, even as I walked among the crumbling stones and in the withered grass.

A noise behind me caused me to turn about. A wild animal—a lynx—was approaching. The thought came to me: If I break down here in the desert—if the fever return and I fail, this beast will be at my throat. I sprang toward it, shouting. It trotted tranquilly by within a hand's breadth of me and disappeared behind a rock.

A moment later a man's head appeared to rise out of the ground a short distance away. He was ascending the farther slope of a low hill whose crest was hardly to be distinguished from the general level. His whole figure soon came into view against the background of gray cloud. He was half naked, half clad in skins. His hair was unkempt, his beard long and ragged. In one hand he carried a bow and arrow; the other held a blazing torch with a long trail of black smoke. He walked slowly and with caution, as if he feared falling into some open grave concealed by the tall grass. This strange apparition surprised but did not alarm, and taking such a course as to intercept him I met him almost face to face, accosting him with the familiar salutation, "God keep you."

He gave no heed, nor did he arrest his pace.

"Good stranger," I continued, "I am ill and lost. Direct me, I beseech you, to Carcosa."

The man broke into a barbarous chant in an unknown tongue, passing on and away.

An owl on the branch of a decayed tree hooted dismally and was answered by another in the distance. Looking upward, I saw through a sudden rift in the clouds Aldebaran and the Hyades!* In all this there was a hint of night—the lynx, the man with the torch, the owl. Yet I saw—I saw even the stars in absence of the darkness. I saw, but was apparently not seen nor heard. Under what awful spell did I exist?

---

* The Hyades is a cluster of hundreds of stars, visible in the constellation Taurus. The Hyades were the daughters of Atlas and Aethra and the half-sisters to the Pleiades. Aldebaran (the "follower") is an orange giant star, also known as Alpha Tauri, in the same constellation and near the Hyades. The name "Aldebaran" was originally given to the entire group of the Hyades, though Aldebaran is much closer than the Hyades and simply lies in the line of sight of the latter.

I seated myself at the root of a great tree, seriously to consider what it were best to do. That I was mad I could no longer doubt, yet recognized a ground of doubt in the conviction. Of fever I had no trace. I had, withal, a sense of exhilaration and vigor altogether unknown to me—a feeling of mental and physical exaltation. My senses seemed all alert; I could feel the air as a ponderous substance; I could hear the silence.

A great root of the giant tree against whose trunk I leaned as I sat held inclosed in its grasp a slab of stone, a part of which protruded into a recess formed by another root. The stone was thus partly protected from the weather, though greatly decomposed. Its edges were worn round, its corners eaten away, its surface deeply furrowed and scaled. Glittering particles of mica were visible in the earth about it—vestiges of its decomposition. This stone had apparently marked the grave out of which the tree had sprung ages ago. The tree's exacting roots had robbed the grave and made the stone a prisoner.

A sudden wind pushed some dry leaves and twigs from the uppermost face of the stone; I saw the low-relief letters of an inscription and bent to read it. God in Heaven! MY name in full!—the date of MY birth!—the date of MY death!

A level shaft of light illuminated the whole side of the tree as I sprang to my feet in terror. The sun was rising in the rosy east. I stood between the tree and his broad red disk—no shadow darkened the trunk!

A chorus of howling wolves saluted the dawn. I saw them sitting on their haunches, singly and in groups, on the summits of irregular mounds and tumuli filling a half of my desert prospect and extending to the horizon. And then I knew that these were ruins of the ancient and famous city of Carcosa.

Such are the facts imparted to the medium Bayrolles* by the spirit Hoseib Alar Robardin.†

---

* The medium Bayrolles also appears in Bierce's story "The Moonlit Road."

† This is not a valid Arabic name.

The Last of Squire Ennismore

by CHARLOTTE (MRS. J. H.) RIDDELL

Charlotte Riddell (1832–1906) was a prolific Irish-born writer of novels and short stories. She was also co-owner of St. James's Magazine, *an influential London-based literary journal. Though she wrote more than fifty books, supernatural phenomena appeared in some of her more noteworthy novels—in particular,* Fairy Water, The Uninhabited House, The Haunted River, The Disappearance of Mr. Jeremiah Redworth, *and* The Nun's Curse—*Riddell also wrote a number of shorter ghost stories, such as "The Open Door" and "Nut Bush Farm." The following first appeared in her collection* Idle Tales *in 1887.*

D id I see it myself? No, sir; I did not see it; and my father before me did not see it; nor his father before him, and he was Phil Regan, just the same as myself. But it is true, for all that; just as true as that you are looking at the very place where the whole thing happened. My great-grandfather (and he did not die till he was ninety-eight) used to tell, many and many's the time, how he met the stranger, night after night, walking lonesome-hike about the sands where most of the wreckage came ashore."

"And the old house, then, stood behind that belt of Scotch firs?"

"Yes; and a fine house it was, too. Hearing so much talk about it when a boy, my father said, made him often feel as if he knew every room in the building, though it had all fallen to ruin before he was born. None of the family ever lived in it after the squire went away. Nobody else could be got to stop in the place. There used to be awful noises, as if something was being pitched from the top of the great staircase down in to the hall; and then there would be a sound as if a hundred people were clinking glasses and talking all together at once. And then it seemed as if barrels were rolling in the cellars;* and there would be screeches, and howls, and laughing, fit to make your blood run cold. They say there is gold hid away in the cellars; but not one has ever ventured to find it. The very children won't come here to play; and when the men are plowing the field behind, nothing will make them stay in it, once the day begins to change. When the night is coming on, and the tide creeps in on the sand, more than one thinks he has seen mighty queer things on the shore."

"But what is it really they think they see? When I asked my landlord to tell me the story from beginning to end, he said he could not remember it; and, at any rate, the whole rigmarole was nonsense, put together to please strangers."

"And what is he but a stranger himself? And how should he know the doings of real quality like the Ennismores? For they were gentry, every one of them—good old stock; and as for wickedness, you might have searched Ireland through and not found their match. It is a sure thing, though, that if Riley can't tell you the story, I can; for, as I said, my own people were in it, of a manner of speaking. So, if your honour will rest yourself off your feet, on that bit of a bank, I'll set down my creel and give you the whole pedigree of how Squire Ennismore went away from Ardwinsagh."†

---

* Mrs. Riddell may be referring here to a well-known story from about 1864 in which the wine cellar of a wealthy man's estate in Blackheath was said to be haunted. When the merchant finally organized a search party, they discovered, behind the barrels, a snoring servant who had imbibed another kind of spirit from the barrels.

† All of the locations used in this story are fictitious.

It was a lovely day, in the early part of June; and, as the Englishman cast himself on a low ridge of sand, he looked over Ardwinsagh Bay with a feeling of ineffable content. To his left lay the Purple Headland; to his right, a long range of breakers, that went straight out into the Atlantic till they were lost from sight; in front lay the Bay of Ardwinsagh, with its bluish-green water sparkling in the summer sunlight, and here and there breaking over some sunken rock, against which the waves spent themselves in foam.

"You see how the current's set, Sir? That is what makes it dangerous for them as doesn't know the coast, to bathe here at any time, or walk when the tide is flowing. Look how the sea is creeping in now, like a race-horse at the finish. It leaves that tongue of sand bars to the last, and then, before you could look round, it has you up to the middle. That is why I made bold to speak to you; for it is not alone on the account of Squire Ennismore the bay has a bad name. But it is about him and the old house you want to hear. The last mortal being that tried to live in it, my great-grandfather said, was a creature, by name Molly Leary; and she had neither kith nor kin, and begged for her bite and sup, sheltering herself at night in a turf cabin she had built at the back of a ditch. You may be sure she thought herself a made woman when the agent said, 'Yes: she might try if she could stop in the house; there was peat and bog-wood,' he told her, 'and half-a-crown a week for the winter, and a golden guinea once Easter came,' when the house was to be put in order for the family; and his wife gave Molly some warm clothes and a blanket or two; and she was well set up.

"You may be sure she didn't choose the worst room to sleep in; and for a while all went quiet, till one night she was wakened by feeling the bedstead lifted by the four corners and shaken like a carpet. It was a heavy four-post bedstead, with a solid top: and her life seemed to go out of her with the fear. If it had been a ship in a storm off the Headland, it couldn't have pitched worse and then, all of a sudden, it was dropped with such a bang as nearly drove the heart into her mouth.

"But that, she said, was nothing to the screaming and laughing, and hustling and rushing that filled the house. If a hundred people had been running hard along the passages and tumbling downstairs, they could not have made greater noise.

"Molly never was able to tell how she got clear of the place; but a man coming late home from Ballycloyne Fair found the creature crouched under the old thorn there, with very little on her—saving your honour's presence. She had a bad fever, and talked about strange things, and never was the same woman after."

"But what was the beginning of all this? When did the house first get the name of being haunted?"

"After the old Squire went away: that was what I purposed telling you. He did not come here to live regularly till he had got well on in years. He was near seventy at the time I am talking about; but he held himself as upright as ever, and rode as hard as the youngest; and could have drunk a whole roomful under the table, and walked up to bed as unconcerned as you please at the dead of the night.

"He was a terrible man. You couldn't lay your tongue to a wickedness he had not been in the forefront of—drinking, duelling, gambling,—all manner of sins had been meat and drink to him since he was a boy almost. But at last he did something in London so bad, so beyond the beyonds, that he thought he had best come home and live among people who did not know so much about his goings on as the English. It was said that he wanted to try and stay in this world for ever; and that he had got some secret drops that kept him well and hearty. There was something wonderful queer about him, anyhow.

"He could hold foot with the youngest; and he was strong, and had a fine fresh colour in his face; and his eyes were like a hawk's; and there was not a break in his voice—and him near upon threescore and ten!

"At last and at long last it came to be the March before he was seventy—the worst March ever known in all these parts—such blowing, sheeting, snowing, had not been experienced in the memory of man; when one blusterous night some foreign vessel went to bits on the Purple Headland. They say it was an awful sound to hear the death-cry that went up high above the noise of the wind; and it was as bad a sight to see the shore there strewed with corpses of all sorts and sizes, from the little cabin-boy to the grizzled seaman.

"They never knew who they were or where they came from, but some of the men had crosses, and beads, and such like, so the priest said they belonged to him, and they were all buried deeply and decently in the chapel graveyard.

"There was not much wreckage of value drifted on shore. Most of what is lost about the Head stays there; but one thing did come into the bay—a puncheon* of brandy.

"The Squire claimed it; it was his right to have all that came on his land, and he owned this sea-shore from the Head to the breakers—every foot—so, in course, he had the brandy; and there was sore illwill because he gave his men nothing, not even a glass of whiskey.

"Well, to make a long story short, that was the most wonderful liquor anybody ever tasted. The gentry came from far and near to take share, and it was cards and dice, and drinking and story-telling night after night—week in, week out. Even on Sundays, God forgive them! The officers would drive over from Ballyclone, and sit emptying tumbler after tumbler till Monday morning came, for it made beautiful punch.

"But all at once people quit coming—a word went round that the liquor was not all it ought to be. Nobody could say what ailed it, but it got about that in some way men found it did not suit them.

"For one thing, they were losing money very fast.

"They could not make head against the Squire's luck, and a hint was dropped the puncheon ought to have been towed out to sea, and sunk in fifty fathoms of water.

"It was getting to the end of April, and fine, warm weather for the time of year, when first one and then another, and then another still, began to take notice of a stranger who walked the shore alone at night. He was a dark man, the same colour as the drowned crew lying in the chapel graveyard, and had rings in his ears, and wore a strange kind of hat, and cut wonderful antics as he walked, and had an ambling sort of gait, curious to look at. Many tried to talk to him, but he only shook his head; so, as nobody could make out where he came from or what he wanted, they made sure he was the spirit of some poor wretch who was tossing about the Head, longing for a snug corner in holy ground.

"The priest went and tried to get some sense out of him.

---

* A puncheon was a cask that held about eighty gallons.

"'Is it Christian burial you're wanting?' asked his reverence; but the creature only shook his head.

"'Is it word sent to the wives and daughters you've left orphans and widows, you'd like?' But no; it wasn't that.

"'Is it for sin committed you're doomed to walk this way? Would masses comfort ye? There's a heathen,' said his reverence; 'Did you ever hear tell of a Christian that shook his head when masses were mentioned?'

"'Perhaps he doesn't understand English, Father,' says one of the officers who was there; 'Try him with Latin.'

"No sooner said than done. The priest started off with such a string of ayes and paters that the stranger fairly took to his heels and ran.

"'He is an evil spirit,' explained the priest, when he stopped, tired out, 'and I have exorcised him.'"

"But next night my gentleman was back again, as unconcerned as ever.

"'And he'll just have to stay,' said his reverence, 'For I've got lumbago in the small of my back, and pains in all my joints—never to speak of a hoarseness with standing there shouting; and I don't believe he understood a sentence I said.'

"Well, this went on for a while, and people got that frightened of the man, or appearance of a man, they would not go near the sand; till in the end, Squire Ennismore, who had always scoffed at the talk, took it into his head he would go down one night, and see into the rights of the matter.

"He, maybe, was feeling lonesome, because, as I told your honour before, people had left off coming to the house, and there was nobody for him to drink with.

"Out he goes, then, bold as brass; and there were a few followed him. The man came forward at sight of the Squire and took off his hat with a foreign flourish. Not to be behind in civility, the Squire lifted his.

"'I have come, sir,' he said, speaking very loud, to try to make him understand, 'to know if you are looking for anything, and whether I can assist you to find it.'

"The man looked at the Squire as if he had taken the greatest liking to him, and took off his hat again.

"'Is it the vessel that was wrecked you are distressed about?'

"There came no answer, only a mournful shake of the head.

"'Well, I haven't your ship, you know; it went all to bits months ago; and, as for the sailors, they are snug and sound enough in consecrated ground.'

"The man stood and looked at the Squire with a queer sort of smile on his face."

"'What do you want?' asked Mr. Ennismore in a bit of a passion. 'If anything belonging to you went down with the vessel, it's about the Head you ought to be looking for it, not here—unless, indeed, it's after the brandy you're fretting!'

"Now, the Squire had tried him in English and French, and was now speaking a language you'd have thought nobody could understand; but, faith, it seemed natural as kissing to the stranger.

"'Oh! That's where you are from, is it?' said the Squire. 'Why couldn't you have told me so at once? I can't give you the brandy, because it mostly is drunk; but come along, and you shall have as stiff a glass of punch as ever crossed your lips.' And without more to-do off they went, as sociable as you please, jabbering together in some outlandish tongue that made moderate folks' jaws ache to hear it.

"That was the first night they conversed together, but it wasn't the last. The stranger must have been the height of good company, for the Squire never tired of him. Every evening, regularly, he came up to the house, always dressed the same, always smiling and polite, and then the Squire called for brandy and hot water, and they drank and played cards till cock-crow, talking and laughing into the small hours.

"This went on for weeks and weeks, nobody knowing where the man came from, or where he went; only two things the old housekeeper did know—that the puncheon was nearly empty, and that the Squire's flesh was wasting off him; and she felt so uneasy she went to the priest, but he could give her no manner of comfort.

"She got so concerned at last that she felt bound to listen at the dining-room door; but they always talked in that foreign gibberish, and whether it was blessing or cursing they were at she couldn't tell.

"Well, the upshot of it came one night in July—on the eve of the Squire's birthday—there wasn't a drop of spirit left in the puncheon—no, not as much as would drown a fly. They had drunk the whole lot clean up—and the old woman stood trembling, expecting every minute to hear the bell ring for more brandy, for where was she to get more if they wanted any?"

"All at once the Squire and the stranger came out into the hall. It was a full moon, and light as day."

"'I'll go home with you to-night by way of a change,' says the Squire.

"'Will you so?' asked the other.

"'That I will,' answered the Squire. "'It is your own choice, you know.'

"'Yes; it is my own choice; let us go.'

"So they went. And the housekeeper ran up to the window on the great staircase and watched the way they took. Her niece lived there as housemaid, and she came and watched, too; and, after a while, the butler as well. They all turned their faces this way, and looked after their master walking beside the strange man along these very sands. Well, they saw them walk on, and on, and on, and on, till the water took them to their knees, and then to their waists, and then to their arm-pits, and then to their throats and their heads; but long before that the women and the butler were running out on the shore as fast as they could, shouting for help.

"Well?" said the Englishman.

"Living or dead, Squire Ennismore never came back again. Next morning, when the tides ebbed again, one walking over the sand saw the print of a cloven foot—that he tracked to the water's edge. Then everybody knew where the Squire had gone, and with whom."

"And no more search was made?"

"Where would have been the use searching?"

"Not much, I suppose. It's a strange story, anyhow."

"But true, your honour—every word of it."

"Oh! I have no doubt of that," was the satisfactory reply.

The Philosophy of Relative Existences

by FRANK STOCKTON

Remembered today perhaps solely for his story "The Lady, or the Tiger?" (1882), widely anthologized and read wherever fine writing is taught, Frank R. Stockton (1834–1902) was a prolific American writer and humorist. He wrote many children's tales popular in the late Victorian era—some subsequently illustrated by Maurice Sendak—as well as early speculative fiction. The following first appeared in The Century Magazine *(Aug. 1892).*

I n a certain summer, not long gone, my friend Bentley and I found ourselves in a little hamlet which overlooked a placid valley, through which a river gently moved, winding its way through green stretches until it turned the end of a line of low hills and was lost to view. Beyond this river, far away, but visible from the door of the cottage where we dwelt, there lay a city. Through the mists which floated over the valley we could see the outlines of steeples and tall roofs; and buildings of a character which indicated thrift and business stretched themselves down to the opposite edge of the river. The more distant parts of the city, evidently a small one, lost themselves in the hazy summer atmosphere.

Bentley was young, fair-haired, and a poet; I was a philosopher, or trying to be one. We were good friends, and had come down into this peaceful region to work together. Although we had fled from the bustle and distractions of the town, the appearance in this rural region of a city, which, so far as we could observe, exerted no influence on the quiet character of the valley in which it lay, aroused our interest. No craft plied up and down the river; there were no bridges from shore to shore; there were none of those scattered and half-squalid habitations which generally are found on the outskirts of a city; there came to us no distant sound of bells; and not the smallest wreath of smoke rose from any of the buildings.

In answer to our inquiries our landlord told us that the city over the river had been built by one man, who was a visionary, and who had a great deal more money than common sense. "It is not as big a town as you would think, sirs," he said, "because the general mistiness of things in this valley makes them look larger than they are. Those hills, for instance, when you get to them are not as high as they look to be from here. But the town is big enough, and a good deal too big; for it ruined its builder and owner, who when he came to die had not money enough left to put up a decent tombstone at the head of his grave. He had a queer idea that he would like to have his town all finished before anybody lived in it, and so he kept on working and spending money year after year and year after year until the city was done and he had not a cent left. During all the time that the place was building hundreds of people came to him to buy houses, or to hire them, but he would not listen to anything of the kind. No one must live in his town until it was all done. Even his workmen were obliged to go away at night to lodge. It is a town, sirs, I am told, in which nobody has slept for even a night. There are streets there, and places of business, and churches, and public halls, and everything that a town full of inhabitants could need; but it is all empty and deserted, and has been so as far back as I can remember, and I came to this region when I was a little boy."

"And is there no one to guard the place?" we asked; "no one to protect it from wandering vagrants who might choose to take possession of the buildings?"

"There are not many vagrants in this part of the country," he said, "and if there were they would not go over to that city. It is haunted."

"By what?" we asked.

"Well, sirs, I scarcely can tell you; queer beings that are not flesh and blood, and that is all I know about it. A good many people living hereabouts have visited that place once in their lives, but I know of no one who has gone there a second time."

"And travellers," I said, "are they not excited by curiosity to explore that strange uninhabited city?"

"Oh yes," our host replied; "almost all visitors to the valley go over to that queer city—generally in small parties, for it is not a place in which one wishes to walk about alone. Sometimes they see things and sometimes they don't. But I never knew any man or woman to show a fancy for living there, although it is a very good town."

This was said at supper-time, and, as it was the period of full moon, Bentley and I decided that we would visit the haunted city that evening. Our host endeavored to dissuade us, saying that no one ever went over there at night; but as we were not to be deterred he told us where we would find his small boat tied to a stake on the river-bank. We soon crossed the river, and landed at a broad but low stone pier, at the land end of which a line of tall grasses waved in the gentle night wind as if they were sentinels warning us from entering the silent city. We pushed through these, and walked up a street fairly wide, and so well paved that we noticed none of the weeds and other growths which generally denote desertion or little use. By the bright light of the moon we could see that the architecture was simple, and of a character highly gratifying to the eye. All the buildings were of stone, and of good size. We were greatly excited and interested, and proposed to continue our walks until the moon should set, and to return on the following morning—"to live here, perhaps," said Bentley. "What could be so romantic and yet so real? What could conduce better to the marriage of verse and philosophy?" But as he said this we saw around the corner of a cross-street some forms as of people hurrying away.

"The spectres," said my companion, laying his hand on my arm.

"Vagrants, more likely," I answered, "who have taken advantage of the superstition of the region to appropriate this comfort and beauty to themselves."

"If that be so," said Bentley, "we must have a care for our lives."

We proceeded cautiously, and soon saw other forms fleeing before us and disappearing, as we supposed, around corners and into houses. And now suddenly finding ourselves upon the edge of a wide, open public square, we saw in the dim light—for a tall steeple obscured the moon—the forms of vehicles, horses, and men moving here and there. But before, in our astonishment, we could say a word one to the other, the moon moved past the steeple, and in its bright light we could see none of the signs of life and traffic which had just astonished us.

Timidly, with hearts beating fast, but with not one thought of turning back, nor any fear of vagrants—for we were now sure that what we had seen was not flesh and blood, and therefore harmless—we crossed the open space and entered a street down which the moon shone clearly. Here and there we saw dim figures, which quickly disappeared; but, approaching a low stone balcony in front of one of the houses, we were surprised to see, sitting thereon and leaning over a book which lay open upon the top of the carved parapet, the figure of a woman who did not appear to notice us.

"That is a real person," whispered Bentley, "and she does not see us."

"No," I replied; "it is like the others. Let us go near it."

We drew near to the balcony and stood before it. At this the figure raised its head and looked at us. It was beautiful, it was young; but its substance seemed to be of an ethereal quality which we had never seen or known of. With its full, soft eyes fixed upon us, it spoke.

"Why are you here?" it asked. "I have said to myself that the next time I saw any of you I would ask you why you come to trouble us. Cannot you live content in your own realms and spheres, knowing, as you must know, how timid we are, and how you frighten us and make us unhappy? In all this city there is, I believe, not one of us except myself who does not flee and hide from you whenever you cruelly come here. Even I would do that, had not I declared to myself that I would see you and speak to you, and endeavor to prevail upon you to leave us in peace."

The clear, frank tones of the speaker gave me courage. "We are two men," I answered, "strangers in this region, and living for the time in the beautiful country on the other side of the river. Having heard of this quiet city, we have come to see it for ourselves. We had supposed it to be uninhabited, but now that we find that this is not the case, we would assure you from our hearts that we do not wish to disturb or annoy any one who lives here. We simply came as honest travellers to view the city."

The figure now seated herself again, and as her countenance was nearer to us, we could see that it was filled with pensive thought. For a moment she looked at us without speaking. "Men!" she said. "And so I have been right. For a long time I have believed that the beings who sometimes come here, filling us with dread and awe, are men."

"And you," I exclaimed—"who are you, and who are these forms that we have seen, these strange inhabitants of this city?"

She gently smiled as she answered, "We are the ghosts of the future. We are the people who are to live in this city generations hence. But all of us do not know that, principally because we do not think about it and study about it enough to know it. And it is generally believed that the men and women who sometimes come here are ghosts who haunt the place."

"And that is why you are terrified and flee from us?" I exclaimed. "You think we are ghosts from another world?"

"Yes," she replied; "that is what is thought, and what I used to think."

"And you," I asked, "are spirits of human beings yet to be?"

"Yes," she answered; "but not for a long time. Generations of men—I know not how many—must pass away before we are men and women."

"Heavens!" exclaimed Bentley, clasping his hands and raising his eyes to the sky, "I shall be a spirit before you are a woman."

"Perhaps," she said again, with a sweet smile upon her face, "you may live to be very, very old."

But Bentley shook his head. This did not console him. For some minutes I stood in contemplation, gazing upon the stone pavement beneath my feet. "And this," I ejaculated, "is a city inhabited by the ghosts of the future, who believe men and women to be phantoms and spectres?"

She bowed her head.

"But how is it," I asked, "that you discovered that you are spirits and we mortal men?"

"There are so few of us who think of such things," she answered, "so few who study, ponder, and reflect. I am fond of study, and I love philosophy; and from the reading of many books I have learned much. From the book which I have here I have learned most; and from its teachings I have gradually come to the belief, which you tell me is the true one, that we are spirits and you men."

"And what book is that?" I asked.

"It is 'The Philosophy of Relative Existences,' by Rupert Vance."

"Ye gods!" I exclaimed, springing upon the balcony, "that is my book, and I am Rupert Vance." I stepped toward the volume to seize it, but she raised her hand.

"You cannot touch it," she said. "It is the ghost of a book. And did you write it?"

"Write it? No," I said; "I am writing it. It is not yet finished."

"But here it is," she said, turning over the last pages. "As a spirit book it is finished. It is very successful; it is held in high estimation by intelligent thinkers; it is a standard work."

I stood trembling with emotion. "High estimation!" I said. "A standard work!"

"Oh yes," she replied, with animation; "and it well deserves its great success, especially in its conclusion. I have read it twice."

"But let me see these concluding pages," I exclaimed. "Let me look upon what I am to write."

She smiled, and shook her head, and closed the book. "I would like to do that," she said, "but if you are really a man you must not know what you are going to do."

"Oh, tell me, tell me," cried Bentley from below, "do you know a book called 'Stellar Studies,' by Arthur Bentley? It is a book of poems."

The figure gazed at him. "No," it said, presently, "I never heard of it."

I stood trembling. Had the youthful figure before me been flesh and blood, had the book been a real one, I would have torn it from her.

"O wise and lovely being!" I exclaimed, falling on my knees before her, "be also benign and generous. Let me but see the last page of my book. If I have been of benefit to your world; more than all, if I have been of benefit to you, let me see, I implore you—let me see how it is that I have done it."

She rose with the book in her hand. "You have only to wait until you have done it," she said, "and then you will know all that you could see here." I started to my feet and stood alone upon the balcony.

"I am sorry," said Bentley, as we walked toward the pier where we had left our boat, "that we talked only to that ghost girl, and that the other spirits were all afraid of us. Persons whose souls are choked up with philosophy are not apt to care much for poetry; and even if my book is to be widely known, it is easy to see that she may not have heard of it."

I walked triumphant. The moon, almost touching the horizon, beamed like red gold. "My dear friend," said I, "I have always told you that you should put more philosophy into your poetry. That would make it live."

"And I have always told you," said he, "that you should not put so much poetry into your philosophy. It misleads people."

"It didn't mislead that ghost girl," said I.

"How do you know?" said Bentley. "Perhaps she is wrong, and the other inhabitants of the city are right, and we may be the ghosts after all. Such things, you know, are only relative. Anyway," he continued, after a little pause, "I wish I knew that those ghosts were now reading the poem which I am going to begin to-morrow."

The Real Right Thing

by HENRY JAMES

Henry James (1843–1916) is primarily regarded as a modern novelist, many of his books exploring the marital relationship. His novels also drew heavily on his own experiences as an American transplanted to Europe. James was also a prolific writer of short stories, many of which explored psychological themes. His most famous—and many forget that it is a ghost story—is probably "The Turn of the Screw" (1898) but his fascination with the psychological aspects of the supernatural goes back to one of his earliest works, "The Romance of Certain Old Clothes" (1868). The following powerful tale first appeared in Black and White: A Weekly Illustrated Record and Review *(Apr. 16, 1892).*

I

W hen, after the death of Ashton Doyne—but three months after—George Withermore was approached, as the phrase is, on the subject of a "volume," the communication came straight from his publishers, who had been, and indeed much more, Doyne's own; but he was not surprised to learn, on the occurrence of the interview they next suggested, that a certain pressure as to the early issue of a Life had been brought to bear upon them by their late client's widow. Doyne's relations with his wife had been, to Withermore's knowledge, a very special chapter—which would present itself, by the way, as a delicate one for the biographer; but a sense of what she had lost, and even of what she had lacked, had betrayed itself, on the poor woman's part, from the first days of her bereavement, sufficiently to prepare an observer at all initiated for some attitude of reparation, some espousal even exaggerated of the interests of a distinguished name. George Withermore was, as he felt, initiated; yet what he had not expected was to hear that she had mentioned him as the person in whose hands she would most promptly place the materials for a book.

These materials—diaries, letters, memoranda, notes, documents of many sorts—were her property, and wholly in her control, no conditions at all attaching to any portion of her heritage; so that she was free at present to do as she liked—free, in particular, to do nothing. What Doyne would have arranged had he had time to arrange could be but supposition and guess. Death had taken him too soon and too suddenly, and there was all the pity that the only wishes he was known to have expressed were wishes that put it positively out of account. He had broken short off—that was the way of it; and the end was ragged and needed trimming. Withermore was conscious, abundantly, how close he had stood to him, but he was not less aware of his comparative obscurity. He was young, a journalist, a critic, a hand-to-mouth character, with little, as yet, as was vulgarly said, to show. His writings were few and small, his relations scant and vague. Doyne, on the other hand, had lived long enough—above all had had talent enough—to become great, and among his many friends gilded also with greatness were several to whom his wife would have struck those who knew her as much more likely to appeal.

The preference she had, at all events, uttered—and uttered in a roundabout, considerate way that left him a measure of freedom—made our young man feel that he must at least see her and that there would be in any case a good deal to talk about. He immediately wrote to her, she as promptly named an hour, and they had it out. But he came away with his particular idea immensely strengthened. She was a strange woman, and he had never thought her an agreeable one; only there was something that touched him now in her bustling, blundering impatience. She wanted the book to make up, and the individual whom, of her husband's set, she probably believed she might most manipulate was in every way to help it to make up. She had not taken Doyne seriously enough in life, but the biography should be a solid reply to every imputation on herself. She had scantly known how such books were constructed, but she had been looking and had learned something. It alarmed Withermore a little from the first to see that she would wish to go in for quantity. She talked of "volumes"—but he had his notion of that.

"My thought went straight to you, as his own would have done," she had said almost as soon as she rose before him there in her large array of mourning—with her big black eyes, her big black wig, her big black fan and gloves, her general gaunt, ugly, tragic, but striking and, as might have been thought from a certain point of view, "elegant" presence. "You're the one he liked most; oh, *much!*"—and it had been quite enough to turn Withermore's head. It little mattered that he could afterward wonder if she had known Doyne enough, when it came to that, to be sure. He would have said for himself indeed that her testimony on such a point would scarcely have counted. Still, there was no smoke without fire; she knew at least what she meant, and he was not a person she could have an interest in flattering. They went up together, without delay, to the great man's vacant study, which was at the back of the house and looked over the large green garden—a beautiful and inspiring scene, to poor Withermore's view—common to the expensive row.

"You can perfectly work here, you know," said Mrs. Doyne: "you shall have the place quite to yourself—I'll give it all up to you; so that in the evenings, in particular, don't you see? for quiet and privacy, it will be perfection."

Perfection indeed, the young man felt as he looked about—having explained that, as his actual occupation was an evening paper and his earlier hours, for a long time yet, regularly taken up, he would have to come always at night. The place was full of their lost friend; everything in it had belonged to him; everything they touched had been part of his life. It was for the moment too much for Withermore—too great an honour and even too great a care; memories still recent came back to him, and, while his heart beat faster and his eyes filled with tears, the pressure of his loyalty seemed almost more than he could carry. At the sight of his tears Mrs. Doyne's own rose to her lids, and the two, for a minute, only looked at each other. He half expected her to break out: 'Oh, help me to feel as I know you know I want to feel!' And after a little one of them said, with the other's deep assent—it didn't matter which: "It's here that we're *with* him." But it was definitely the young man who put it, before they left the room, that it was there he was with *them*.

The young man began to come as soon as he could arrange it, and then it was, on the spot, in the charmed stillness, between the lamp and the fire and with the curtains drawn, that a certain intenser consciousness crept over him. He turned in out of the black London November; he passed through the large, hushed house and up the red-carpeted staircase where he only found in his path the whisk of a soundless, trained maid, or the reach, out of a doorway, of Mrs. Doyne's queenly weeds* and approving tragic face; and then, by a mere touch of the well-made door that gave so sharp and pleasant a click, shut himself in for three or four warm hours with the spirit—as he had always distinctly declared it—of his master. He was not a little frightened when, even the first night, it came over him that he had really been most affected, in the whole matter, by the prospect, the privilege and the luxury, of this sensation. He had not, he could now reflect, definitely considered the question of the book—as to which there was here, even already, much to consider: he had simply let his affection and admiration—to say nothing of his gratified pride—meet, to the full, the temptation Mrs. Doyne had offered them.

How did he know, without more thought, he might begin to ask himself, that the book was, on the whole, to be desired? What warrant had he ever received from Ashton Doyne himself for so direct and, as it were, so familiar an approach? Great was the art of biography, but there were lives and lives, there were subjects and subjects. He confusedly recalled, so far as that went, old words dropped by Doyne over contemporary compilations, suggestions of how he himself discriminated as to other heroes and other panoramas. He even remembered how his friend, at moments, would have seemed to show himself as holding that the 'literary' career might—save

---

* Garments.

in the case of a Johnson and a Scott, with a Boswell and a Lockhart* to help—best content itself to be represented. The artist was what he *did*—he was nothing else. Yet how, on the other hand, was not he, George Withermore, poor devil, to have jumped at the chance of spending his winter in an intimacy so rich? It had been simply dazzling—that was the fact. It hadn't been the 'terms,' from the publishers—though these were, as they said at the office, all right; it had been Doyne himself, his company and contact and presence—it had been just what it was turning out, the possibility of an intercourse closer than that of life. Strange that death, of the two things, should have the fewer mysteries and secrets! The first night our young man was alone in the room it seemed to him that his master and he were really for the first time together.

II

Mrs. Doyne had for the most part let him expressively alone, but she had on two or three occasions looked in to see if his needs had been met, and he had had the opportunity of thanking her on the spot for the judgment and zeal with which she had smoothed his way. She had to some extent herself been looking things over and had been able already to muster several groups of letters; all the keys of drawers and cabinets she had, moreover, from the first placed in his hands, with helpful information as to the apparent whereabouts of different matters. She had put him, in a word, in the fullest possible possession, and whether or no her husband had trusted her, she at least, it was clear, trusted her husband's friend. There grew upon Withermore, nevertheless, the impression that, in spite of all these offices, she was not yet at peace, and that a certain unappeasable anxiety continued even to keep step with her confidence. Though she was full of consideration, she was at the same time perceptibly *there*: he felt her, through a supersubtle sixth sense that the whole connection had already brought into play, hover, in the still hours, at the top of landings and on

---

* Samuel Johnson, whose biographer was James Boswell, and Sir Walter Scott, whose biographer was his son-in-law John Gibson Lockhart.

the other side of doors, gathered from the soundless brush of her skirts the hint of her watchings and waitings. One evening when, at his friend's table, he had lost himself in the depths of correspondence, he was made to start and turn by the suggestion that some one was behind him. Mrs. Doyne had come in without his hearing the door, and she gave a strained smile as he sprang to his feet. "I hope," she said, "I haven't frightened you."

"Just a little—I was so absorbed. It was as if, for the instant," the young man explained, "it had been himself."

The oddity of her face increased in her wonder. "Ashton?"

"He does seem so near," said Withermore.

"To you too?"

This naturally struck him. "He does then to you?"

She hesitated, not moving from the spot where she had first stood, but looking round the room as if to penetrate its duskier angles. She had a way of raising to the level of her nose the big black fan which she apparently never laid aside and with which she thus covered the lower half of her face, her rather hard eyes, above it, becoming the more ambiguous. "Sometimes."

"Here," Withermore went on, "it's as if he might at any moment come in. That's why I jumped just now. The time is so short since he really used to—it only *was* yesterday. I sit in his chair, I turn his books, I use his pens, I stir his fire, exactly as if, learning he would presently be back from a walk, I had come up here contentedly to wait. It's delightful—but it's strange."

Mrs. Doyne, still with her fan up, listened with interest. "Does it worry you?"

"No—I like it."

She hesitated again. "Do you ever feel as if he were—a—quite—a—personally in the room?"

"Well, as I said just now," her companion laughed, "on hearing you behind me I seemed to take it so. What do we want, after all," he asked, "but that he shall be with us?"

"Yes, as you said he would be—that first time." She stared in full assent. "He *is* with us."

She was rather portentous, but Withermore took it smiling. "Then we must keep him. We must do only what he would like."

"Oh, only that, of course—only. But if he *is* here—?" And her sombre eyes seemed to throw it out, in vague distress, over her fan.

"It shows that he's pleased and wants only to help? Yes, surely; it must show that."

She gave a light gasp and looked again round the room. "Well," she said as she took leave of him, "remember that I too want only to help." On which, when she had gone, he felt sufficiently—that she had come in simply to see he was all right.

He was all right more and more, it struck him after this, for as he began to get into his work he moved, as it appeared to him, but the closer to the idea of Doyne's personal presence. When once this fancy had begun to hang about him he welcomed it, persuaded it, encouraged it, quite cherished it, looking forward all day to feeling it renew itself in the evening, and waiting for the evening very much as one of a pair of lovers might wait for the hour of their appointment. The smallest accidents humoured and confirmed it, and by the end of three or four weeks he had come quite to regard it as the consecration of his enterprise. Wasn't it what settled the question of what Doyne would have thought of what they were doing? What they were doing was what he wanted done, and they could go on, from step to step, without scruple or doubt. Withermore rejoiced indeed at moments to feel this certitude: there were times of dipping deep into some of Doyne's secrets when it was particularly pleasant to be able to hold that Doyne desired him, as it were, to know them. He was learning many things that he had not suspected, drawing many curtains, forcing many doors, reading many riddles, going, in general, as they said, behind almost everything. It was at an occasional sharp turn of some of the duskier of these wanderings "behind" that he really, of a sudden, most felt himself, in the intimate, sensible way, face to face with his friend; so that he could scarcely have told, for the instant, if their meeting occurred in the narrow passage and tight squeeze of the past, or at the hour and in the place that actually held him. Was it '67, or was it but the other side of the table?

Happily, at any rate, even in the vulgarest light publicity could ever shed, there would be the great fact of the way Doyne was "coming out." He was coming out too beautifully—better yet than such a partisan as Withermore could have supposed. Yet, all the while, as well, how would this partisan have represented to any one else the special state of his own consciousness? It wasn't a thing to talk about—it was only a thing to feel. There were moments, for instance, when, as he bent over his papers, the light breath of his dead host was as distinctly in his hair as his own elbows were on the table before him. There were moments when, had he been able to look up, the other side of the table would have shown him this companion as vividly as the shaded lamplight showed him his page. That he couldn't at such a juncture look up was his own affair, for the situation was ruled—that was but natural—by deep delicacies and fine timidities, the dread of too sudden or too rude an advance. What was intensely in the air was that if Doyne was there it was not nearly so much for himself as for the young priest of his altar. He hovered and lingered, he came and went, he might almost have been, among the books and the papers, a hushed, discreet librarian, doing the particular things, rendering the quiet aid, liked by men of letters.

Withermore himself, meanwhile, came and went, changed his place, wandered on quests either definite or vague; and more than once, when, taking a book down from a shelf and finding in it marks of Doyne's pencil, he got drawn on and lost, he had heard documents on the table behind him gently shifted and stirred, had literally, on his return, found some letter he had mislaid pushed again into view, some wilderness cleared by the opening of an old journal at the very date he wanted. How should he have gone so, on occasion, to the special box or drawer, out of fifty receptacles, that would help him, had not his mystic assistant happened, in fine prevision, to tilt its lid, or to pull it half open, in just the manner that would catch his eye?—in spite, after all, of the fact of lapses and intervals in which, could one have really looked, one would have seen somebody standing before the fire a trifle detached and over-erect—somebody fixing one the least bit harder than in life.

III

That this auspicious relation had in fact existed, had continued, for two or three weeks, was sufficiently proved by the dawn of the distress with which our young man found himself aware that he had, for some reason, from a certain evening, begun to miss it. The sign of that was an abrupt, surprised sense—on the occasion of his mislaying a marvellous unpublished page which, hunt where he would, remained stupidly, irrecoverably lost—that his protected state was, after all, exposed to some confusion and even to some depression. If, for the joy of the business, Doyne and he had, from the start, been together, the situation had, within a few days of his first new suspicion of it, suffered the odd change of their ceasing to be so. That was what was the matter, he said to himself, from the moment an impression of mere mass and quantity struck him as taking, in his happy outlook at his material, the place of his pleasant assumption of a clear course and a lively pace. For five nights he struggled; then, never at his table, wandering about the room, taking up his references only to lay them down, looking out of the window, poking the fire, thinking strange thoughts and listening for signs and sounds not as he suspected or imagined, but as he vainly desired and invoked them, he made up his mind that he was, for the time at least, forsaken.

The extraordinary thing thus became that it made him not only sad not to feel Doyne's presence, but in a high degree uneasy. It was stranger, somehow, that he shouldn't be there than it had ever been that he was—so strange indeed at last that Withermore's nerves found themselves quite inconsequently affected. They had taken kindly enough to what was of an order impossible to explain, perversely reserving their sharpest state for the return to the normal, the supersession of the false. They were remarkably beyond control when, finally, one night, after resisting an hour or two, he simply edged out of the room. It had only now, for the first time, become impossible to him to remain there. Without design, but panting a little and positively as a man scared, he passed along his usual corridor and reached the top of the staircase. From this point he saw Mrs. Doyne looking up at him from the bottom quite as if she had known he would come; and the most singular thing of all was that, though he had been conscious of no notion to resort to her, had only been prompted to relieve himself by escape, the sight of her position made him recognize it as just, quickly feel it as a part of some monstrous oppression that was closing over both of them. It was wonderful how, in the mere modern London hall, between the Tottenham Court Road rugs and the electric light, it came up to him from the tall black lady, and went again from him down to her, that he knew what she meant by looking as if he would know. He descended straight, she turned into her own little lower room, and there, the next thing, with the door shut, they were, still in silence and with queer faces, confronted over confessions that had taken sudden life from these two or three movements. Withermore gasped as it came to him why he had lost his friend. "He has been with *you*?"

With this it was all out—out so far that neither had to explain and that, when "What do you suppose is the matter?" quickly passed between them, one appeared to have said it as much as the other. Withermore looked about at the small, bright room in which, night after night, she had been living her life as he had been living his own upstairs. It was pretty, cosy, rosy; but she had by turns felt in it what he had felt and heard in it what he had heard. Her effect there—fantastic black, plumed and extravagant, upon deep pink—was that of some "decadent" coloured print, some poster of the newest school. "You understood he had left me?" he asked.

She markedly wished to make it clear. "This evening—yes. I've made things out."

"You knew—before—that he was with me?"

She hesitated again. "I felt he wasn't with *me*. But on the stairs—"

"Yes?"

"Well—he passed, more than once. He was in the house. And at your door—"

"Well?" he went on as she once more faltered.

"If I stopped I could sometimes tell. And from your face," she added, "to-night, at any rate, I knew your state."

"And that was why you came out?"

"I thought you'd come to me."

He put out to her, on this, his hand, and they thus, for a minute, in silence, held each other clasped. There was no peculiar presence for either, now—nothing more peculiar than that of each for the other. But the place had suddenly become as if consecrated, and Withermore turned over it again his anxiety. "What is then the matter?"

"I only want to do the real right thing," she replied after a moment.

"And are we not doing it?"

"I wonder. Are *you* not?"

He wondered too. "To the best of my belief. But we must think."

"We must think," she echoed. And they did think—thought, with intensity, the rest of that evening together, and thought, independently—Withermore at least could answer for himself—during many days that followed. He intermitted for a little his visits and his work, trying, in meditation, to catch himself in the act of some mistake that might have accounted for their disturbance. Had he taken, on some important point—or looked as if he might take—some wrong line or wrong view? had he somewhere benight-edly falsified or inadequately insisted? He went back at last with the idea of having guessed two or three questions he might have been on the way to muddle; after which he had, above stairs, another period of agitation, presently followed by another interview, below, with Mrs. Doyne, who was still troubled and flushed.

"He's there?"

"He's there."

"I knew it!" she returned in an odd gloom of triumph. Then as to make it clear: "He has not been again with me."

"Nor with me again to help," said Withermore.

She considered. "Not to help?"

"I can't make it out—I'm at sea. Do what I will, I feel I'm wrong."

She covered him a moment with her pompous pain. "How do you feel it?"

"Why, by things that happen. The strangest things. I can't describe them—and you wouldn't believe them."

"Oh yes, I would!" Mrs. Doyne murmured.

"Well, he intervenes." Withermore tried to explain. "However I turn, I find him."

She earnestly followed. "'Find' him?"

"I meet him. He seems to rise there before me."

Mrs. Doyne, staring, waited a little. "Do you mean you see him?"

"I feel as if at any moment I may. I'm baffled. I'm checked." Then he added: "I'm afraid."

"Of *him*?" asked Mrs. Doyne.

He thought. "Well—of what I'm doing."

"Then what, that's so awful, *are* you doing?"

"What you proposed to me. Going into his life."

She showed, in her gravity, now, a new alarm. "And don't you *like* that?"

"Doesn't *he*? That's the question. We lay him bare. We serve him up. What is it called? We give him to the world."

Poor Mrs. Doyne, as if on a menace to her hard atonement, glared at this for an instant in deeper gloom. "And why shouldn't we?"

"Because we don't know. There are natures, there are lives, that shrink. He mayn't wish it," said Withermore. "We never asked him."

"How *could* we?"

He was silent a little. "Well, we ask him now. That's, after all, what our start has, so far, represented. We've put it to him."

"Then—if he has been with us—we've had his answer."

Withermore spoke now as if he knew what to believe. "He hasn't been 'with' us—he has been against us."

"Then why did you think—"

"What I *did* think, at first—that what he wishes to make us feel is his sympathy? Because, in my original simplicity, I was mistaken. I was—I don't know what to call it—so excited and charmed that I didn't understand. But I understand at last. He only wanted to communicate. He strains forward out of his darkness; he reaches toward us out of his mystery; he makes us dim signs out of his horror."

"'Horror'?" Mrs. Doyne gasped with her fan up to her mouth.

"At what we're doing." He could by this time piece it all together. "I see now that at first—"

"Well, what?"

"One had simply to feel he was there, and therefore not indifferent. And the beauty of that misled me. But he's there as a protest."

"Against *my* Life?" Mrs. Doyne wailed.

"Against *any* Life. He's there to *save* his Life. He's there to be let alone."

"So you give up?" she almost shrieked.

He could only meet her. "He's there as a warning."

For a moment, on this, they looked at each other deep. "You are afraid!" she at last brought out.

It affected him, but he insisted. "He's there as a curse!"

With that they parted, but only for two or three days; her last word to him continuing to sound so in his ears that, between his need really to satisfy her and another need presently to be noted, he felt that he might not yet take up his stake. He finally went back at his usual hour and found her in her usual place. "Yes, I am afraid," he announced as if he had turned that well over and knew now all it meant. "But I gather that you're not."

She faltered, reserving her word. "What is it you fear?"

"Well, that if I go on I *shall* see him."

"And then—?"

"Oh, then," said George Withermore, "I *should* give up!"

She weighed it with her lofty but earnest air. "I think, you know, we must have a clear sign."

"You wish me to try again?"

She hesitated. "You see what it means—for me—to give up."

"Ah, but you needn't," Withermore said.

She seemed to wonder, but in a moment she went on. "It would mean that he won't take from me—" But she dropped for despair.

"Well, what?"

"Anything," said poor Mrs. Doyne.

He faced her a moment more. "I've thought myself of the clear sign. I'll try again."

As he was leaving her, however, she remembered. "I'm only afraid that to-night there's nothing ready—no lamp and no fire."

"Never mind," he said from the foot of the stairs; "I'll find things."

To which she answered that the door of the room would probably, at any rate, be open; and retired again as if to wait for him. She had not long to wait; though, with her own door wide and her attention fixed, she may not have taken the time quite as it appeared to her visitor. She heard him, after an interval, on the stair, and he presently stood at her entrance, where, if he had not been precipitate, but rather, as to step and sound, backward and vague, he showed at least as livid and blank.

"I give up."

"Then you've seen him?"

"On the threshold—guarding it."

"Guarding it?" She glowed over her fan. "Distinct?"

"Immense. But dim. Dark. Dreadful," said poor George Withermore.
She continued to wonder. "You didn't go in?"

The young man turned away. "He forbids!"

"You say *I* needn't," she went on after a moment. "Well then, need I?"

"See him?" George Withermore asked.

She waited an instant. "Give up."

"You must decide." For himself he could at last but drop upon the sofa with his bent face in his hands. He was not quite to know afterwards how long he had sat so; it was enough that what he did next know was that he was alone among her favourite objects. Just as he gained his feet, however, with this sense and that of the door standing open to the hall, he found himself afresh confronted, in the light, the warmth, the rosy space, with her big black perfumed presence. He saw at a glance, as she offered him a huger, bleaker stare over the mask of her fan that she had been above; and so it was that, for the last time, they faced together their strange question. "You've seen him?" Withermore asked.

He was to infer later on from the extraordinary way she closed her eyes and, as if to steady herself, held them tight and long, in silence, that beside the unutterable vision of Ashton Doyne's wife his own might rank as an escape. He knew before she spoke that all was over. "I give up."

The Lady's Maid's Bell

by EDITH WHARTON

Edith Wharton (1862–1937) is another American (and a friend of Henry James) who wrote compellingly of life among the upper classes. She is best remembered for her novels and novella, such as Ethan Frome *(1911) and* The Age of Innocence *(1920)—the latter work won the Pulitzer Prize for Literature, making Wharton the first women to win a Pulitzer in any category. However, Wharton was also a prolific author of short stories, with twelve collections published during her lifetime. Her strong interest in ghosts is evident from the titles of two such collections:* Tales of Men and Ghosts *(1910) and* Ghosts *(1937). The following, one of her first ghost stories, appeared in her collection* The Descent of Man and Other Stories *(1904) and has been widely analyzed for its subtle themes of feminism and abortion.*

I

I t was the autumn after I had the typhoid.* I'd been three months in hospital, and when I came out I looked so weak and tottery that the two or three ladies I applied to were afraid to engage me. Most of my

---

* Typhoid fever (caused by *Salmonella typhi* bacteria) was the scourge of the American Civil War and killed millions before the development of antibiotics. Highly contagious, it had a mortality rate of 10% to 20%; today, less than 1% of its victims die.

money was gone, and after I'd boarded for two months, hanging about the employment-agencies, and answering any advertisement that looked any way respectable, I pretty nearly lost heart, for fretting hadn't made me fatter, and I didn't see why my luck should ever turn. It did though—or I thought so at the time. A Mrs. Railton, a friend of the lady that first brought me out to the States, met me one day and stopped to speak to me: she was one that had always a friendly way with her. She asked me what ailed me to look so white, and when I told her, "Why, Hartley," says she, "I believe I've got the very place for you. Come in to-morrow and we'll talk about it."

The next day, when I called, she told me the lady she'd in mind was a niece of hers, a Mrs. Brympton, a youngish lady, but something of an invalid, who lived all the year round at her country-place on the Hudson, owing to not being able to stand the fatigue of town life.

"Now, Hartley," Mrs. Railton said, in that cheery way that always made me feel things must be going to take a turn for the better—"now understand me; it's not a cheerful place I'm sending you to. The house is big and gloomy; my niece is nervous, vaporish; her husband—well, he's generally away; and the two children are dead. A year ago, I would as soon have thought of shutting a rosy active girl like you into a vault; but you're not particularly brisk yourself just now, are you? and a quiet place, with country air and wholesome food and early hours, ought to be the very thing for you. Don't mistake me," she added, for I suppose I looked a trifle downcast; "you may find it dull, but you won't be unhappy. My niece is an angel. Her former maid, who died last spring, had been with her twenty years and worshipped the ground she walked on. She's a kind mistress to all, and where the mistress is kind, as you know, the servants are generally good-humored, so you'll probably get on well enough with the rest of the household. And you're the very woman I want for my niece: quiet, well-mannered, and educated above your station. You read aloud well, I think? That's a good thing; my niece likes to be read to. She wants a maid that can be something of a companion: her last was, and I can't say how she misses her. It's a lonely life . . . Well, have you decided?"

"Why, ma'am," I said, "I'm not afraid of solitude."

"Well, then, go; my niece will take you on my recommendation. I'll telegraph her at once and you can take the afternoon train. She has no one to wait on her at present, and I don't want you to lose any time."

I was ready enough to start, yet something in me hung back; and to gain time I asked, "And the gentleman, ma'am?"

"The gentleman's almost always away, I tell you," said Mrs. Ralston, quick-like—"and when he's there," says she suddenly, "you've only to keep out of his way."

I took the afternoon train and got out at D——station at about four o'clock. A groom in a dog-cart was waiting, and we drove off at a smart pace. It was a dull October day, with rain hanging close overhead, and by the time we turned into the Brympton Place woods the daylight was almost gone. The drive wound through the woods for a mile or two, and came out on a gravel court shut in with thickets of tall black-looking shrubs. There were no lights in the windows, and the house *did* look a bit gloomy.

I had asked no questions of the groom, for I never was one to get my notion of new masters from their other servants: I prefer to wait and see for myself. But I could tell by the look of everything that I had got into the right kind of house, and that things were done handsomely. A pleasant-faced cook met me at the back door and called the house-maid to show me up to my room. "You'll see madam later," she said. "Mrs. Brympton has a visitor."

I hadn't fancied Mrs. Brympton was a lady to have many visitors, and somehow the words cheered me. I followed the house-maid upstairs, and saw, through a door on the upper landing, that the main part of the house seemed well-furnished, with dark panelling and a number of old portraits. Another flight of stairs led us up to the servants' wing. It was almost dark now, and the house-maid excused herself for not having brought a light. "But there's matches in your room," she said, "and if you go careful you'll be all right. Mind the step at the end of the passage. Your room is just beyond."

I looked ahead as she spoke, and half-way down the passage, I saw a woman standing. She drew back into a doorway as we passed, and the house-maid didn't appear to notice her. She was a thin woman with a white face, and a darkish stuff gown and apron. I took her for the housekeeper and thought it odd that she didn't speak, but just gave me a long look as she went by. My room opened into a square hall at the end of the passage. Facing my door was another which stood open: the house-maid exclaimed when she saw it.

"There—Mrs. Blinder's left that door open again!" said she, closing it.

"Is Mrs. Blinder the housekeeper?"

"There's no housekeeper: Mrs. Blinder's the cook."

"And is that her room?"

"Laws, no," said the house-maid, cross-like. "That's nobody's room. It's empty, I mean, and the door hadn't ought to be open. Mrs. Brympton wants it kept locked."

She opened my door and led me into a neat room, nicely furnished, with a picture or two on the walls; and having lit a candle she took leave, telling me that the servants'-hall tea was at six, and that Mrs. Brympton would see me afterward.

I found them a pleasant-spoken set in the servants' hall, and by what they let fall I gathered that, as Mrs. Railton had said, Mrs. Brympton was the kindest of ladies; but I didn't take much notice of their talk, for I was watching to see the pale woman in the dark gown come in. She didn't show herself, however, and I wondered if she ate apart; but if she wasn't the housekeeper, why should she? Suddenly it struck me that she might be a trained nurse, and in that case her meals would of course be served in her room. If Mrs. Brympton was an invalid it was likely enough she had a nurse. The idea annoyed me, I own, for they're not always the easiest to get on with, and if I'd known, I shouldn't have taken the place. But there I was, and there was no use pulling a long face over it; and not being one to ask questions, I waited to see what would turn up.

When tea was over, the house-maid said to the footman: "Has Mr. Ranford gone?" and when he said yes, she told me to come up with her to Mrs. Brympton.

Mrs. Brympton was lying down in her bedroom. Her lounge stood near the fire and beside it was a shaded lamp. She was a delicate-looking lady, but when she smiled I felt there was nothing I wouldn't do for her. She spoke very pleasantly, in a low voice, asking me my name and age and so on, and if I had everything I wanted, and if I wasn't afraid of feeling lonely in the country.

"Not with you I wouldn't be, madam," I said, and the words surprised me when I'd spoken them, for I'm not an impulsive person; but it was just as if I'd thought aloud.

She seemed pleased at that, and said she hoped I'd continue in the same mind; then she gave me a few directions about her toilet, and said Agnes the house-maid would show me next morning where things were kept.

"I am tired to-night, and shall dine upstairs," she said. "Agnes will bring me my tray, that you may have time to unpack and settle yourself; and later you may come and undress me."

"Very well, ma'am," I said. "You'll ring, I suppose?"

I thought she looked odd.

"No—Agnes will fetch you," says she quickly, and took up her book again.

Well—that was certainly strange: a lady's maid having to be fetched by the house-maid whenever her lady wanted her! I wondered if there were no bells in the house; but the next day I satisfied myself that there was one in every room, and a special one ringing from my mistress's room to mine; and after that it did strike me as queer that, whenever Mrs. Brympton wanted anything, she rang for Agnes, who had to walk the whole length of the servants' wing to call me.

But that wasn't the only queer thing in the house. The very next day I found out that Mrs. Brympton had no nurse; and then I asked Agnes about the woman I had seen in the passage the afternoon before. Agnes said she had seen no one, and I saw that she thought I was dreaming. To be sure, it was dusk when we went down the passage, and she had excused herself for not bringing a light; but I had seen the woman plain enough to know her again if we should meet. I decided that she must have been a friend of the cook's, or of one of the other women-servants: perhaps she had come down from town for a night's visit, and the servants wanted it kept secret. Some ladies are very stiff about having their servants' friends in the house overnight. At any rate, I made up my mind to ask no more questions.

In a day or two, another odd thing happened. I was chatting one afternoon with Mrs. Blinder, who was a friendly disposed woman, and had been longer in the house than the other servants, and she asked me if I was quite comfortable and had everything I needed. I said I had no fault to find with my place or with my mistress, but I thought it odd that in so large a house there was no sewing-room for the lady's maid.

"Why," says she, "there *is* one; the room you're in is the old sewing-room."

"Oh," said I, "and where did the other lady's maid sleep?"

At that she grew confused, and said hurriedly that the servants' rooms had all been changed about last year, and she didn't rightly remember.

That struck me as peculiar, but I went on as if I hadn't noticed: "Well, there's a vacant room opposite mine, and I mean to ask Mrs. Brympton if I mayn't use that as a sewing-room."

To my astonishment, Mrs. Blinder went white, and gave my hand a kind of squeeze. "Don't do that, my dear," said she, trembling-like. "To tell you the truth, that was Emma Saxon's room, and my mistress has kept it closed ever since her death."

"And who was Emma Saxon?"

"Mrs. Brympton's former maid."

"The one that was with her so many years?" said I, remembering what Mrs. Railton had told me.

Mrs. Blinder nodded.

"What sort of woman was she?"

"No better walked the earth," said Mrs. Blinder. "My mistress loved her like a sister."

"But I mean—what did she look like?"

Mrs. Blinder got up and gave me a kind of angry stare. "I'm no great hand at describing," she said; "and I believe my pastry's rising." And she walked off into the kitchen and shut the door after her.

II

I had been near a week at Brympton before I saw my master. Word came that he was arriving one afternoon, and a change passed over the whole household. It was plain that nobody loved him below stairs. Mrs. Blinder took uncommon care with the dinner that night, but she snapped at the kitchen-maid in a way quite unusual with her; and Mr. Wace, the butler, a serious, slow-spoken man, went about his duties as if he'd been getting ready for a funeral. He was a great Bible-reader, Mr. Wace was, and had a beautiful assortment of texts at his command; but that day he used such dreadful language that I was about to leave the table, when he assured me it was all out of Isaiah;* and I noticed that whenever the master came Mr. Wace took to the prophets.

About seven, Agnes called me to my mistress's room; and there I found Mr. Brympton. He was standing on the hearth; a big fair bull-necked man, with a red face and little bad-tempered blue eyes: the kind of man a young simpleton might have thought handsome, and would have been like to pay dear for thinking it.

He swung about when I came in, and looked me over in a trice. I knew what the look meant, from having experienced it once or twice in my former places. Then he turned his back on me, and went on talking to his wife; and I knew what *that* meant, too. I was not the kind of morsel he was after. The typhoid had served me well enough in one way: it kept that kind of gentleman at arm's-length.

"This is my new maid, Hartley," says Mrs. Brympton in her kind voice; and he nodded and went on with what he was saying.

In a minute or two he went off, and left my mistress to dress for dinner, and I noticed as I waited on her that she was white, and chill to the touch.

Mr. Brympton took himself off the next morning, and the whole house drew a long breath when he drove away. As for my mistress, she put on her hat and furs (for it was a fine winter morning) and went out for a walk in the gardens, coming back quite fresh and rosy, so that for a minute, before her color faded, I could guess what a pretty young lady she must have been, and not so long ago, either.

She had met Mr. Ranford in the grounds, and the two came back together, I remember, smiling and talking as they walked along the terrace under my window. That was the first time I saw Mr. Ranford, though I had often heard his name mentioned in the hall. He was a neighbor, it appeared, living a mile or two beyond Brympton, at the end of the village;

---

* Isaiah 6:3 recounts that the prophet said, "Then said I, Woe is me! for I am undone; because I am a man of unclean lips, and I dwell in the midst of a people of unclean lips: for mine eyes have seen the King, the LORD of hosts." (King James Version) Although "dreadful language" may be used occasionally in the Bible, it is not approved of.

and as he was in the habit of spending his winters in the country he was almost the only company my mistress had at that season. He was a slight tall gentleman of about thirty, and I thought him rather melancholy-looking till I saw his smile, which had a kind of surprise in it, like the first warm day in spring. He was a great reader, I heard, like my mistress, and the two were forever borrowing books of one another, and sometimes (Mr. Wace told me) he would read aloud to Mrs. Brympton by the hour, in the big dark library where she sat in the winter afternoons. The servants all liked him, and perhaps that's more of a compliment than the masters suspect. He had a friendly word for every one of us, and we were all glad to think that Mrs. Brympton had a pleasant companionable gentleman like that to keep her company when the master was away. Mr. Ranford seemed on excellent terms with Mr. Brympton too; though I couldn't but wonder that two gentlemen so unlike each other should be so friendly. But then I knew how the real quality can keep their feelings to themselves.

As for Mr. Brympton, he came and went, never staying more than a day or two, cursing the dulness and the solitude, grumbling at everything, and (as I soon found out) drinking a deal more than was good for him. After Mrs. Brympton left the table he would sit half the night over the old Brympton port and madeira, and once, as I was leaving my mistress's room rather later than usual, I met him coming up the stairs in such a state that I turned sick to think of what some ladies have to endure and hold their tongues about.

The servants said very little about their master; but from what they let drop I could see it had been an unhappy match from the beginning. Mr. Brympton was coarse, loud and pleasure-loving; my mistress quiet, retiring, and perhaps a trifle cold. Not that she was not always pleasant-spoken to him: I thought her wonderfully forbearing; but to a gentleman as free as Mr. Brympton I daresay she seemed a little offish.

Well, things went on quietly for several weeks. My mistress was kind, my duties were light, and I got on well with the other servants. In short, I had nothing to complain of; yet there was always a weight on me. I can't say why it was so, but I know it was not the loneliness that I felt. I soon got used to that; and being still languid from the fever, I was thankful for the quiet and the good country air. Nevertheless, I was never quite easy in my mind. My mistress, knowing I had been ill, insisted that I should take my walk regular, and often invented errands for me:—a yard of ribbon to be fetched from the village, a letter posted, or a book returned to Mr. Ranford. As soon as I was out of doors my spirits rose, and I looked forward to my walks through the bare moist-smelling woods; but the moment I caught sight of the house again my heart dropped down like a stone in a well. It was not a gloomy house exactly, yet I never entered it but a feeling of gloom came over me.

Mrs. Brympton seldom went out in winter; only on the finest days did she walk an hour at noon on the south terrace. Excepting Mr. Ranford, we had no visitors but the doctor, who drove over from D——about once a week. He sent for me once or twice to give me some trifling direction about my mistress, and though he never told me what her illness was, I thought, from a waxy look she had now and then of a morning, that it might be the heart that ailed her. The season was soft and unwholesome, and in January we had a long spell of rain. That was a sore trial to me, I own, for I couldn't go out, and sitting over my sewing all day, listening to the drip, drip of the eaves, I grew so nervous that the least sound made me jump. Somehow, the thought of that locked room across the passage began to weigh on me. Once or twice, in the long rainy nights, I fancied I heard noises there; but that was nonsense, of course, and the daylight drove such notions out of my head. Well, one morning Mrs. Brympton gave me quite a start of pleasure by telling me she wished me to go to town for some shopping. I hadn't known till then how low my spirits had fallen. I set off in high glee, and my first sight of the crowded streets and the cheerful-looking shops quite took me out of myself. Toward afternoon, however, the noise and confusion began to tire me, and I was actually looking forward to the quiet of Brympton, and thinking how I should enjoy the drive home through the dark woods, when I ran across an old acquaintance, a maid I had once been in service with. We had lost sight of each other for a number of years, and I had to stop and tell her what had happened to me in the interval. When I mentioned where I was living she rolled up her eyes and pulled a long face.

"What! The Mrs. Brympton that lives all the year at her place on the Hudson? My dear, you won't stay there three months."

"Oh, but I don't mind the country," says I, offended somehow at her tone. "Since the fever I'm glad to be quiet."

She shook her head. "It's not the country I'm thinking of. All I know is she's had four maids in the last six months, and the last one, who was a friend of mine, told me nobody could stay in the house."

"Did she say why?" I asked.

"No—she wouldn't give me her reason. But she says to me, *Mrs. Ansey*, she says, *if ever a young woman as you know of thinks of going there, you tell her it's not worthwhile to unpack her boxes.*"

"Is she young and handsome?" said I, thinking of Mr. Brympton.

"Not her! She's the kind that mothers engage when they've gay young gentlemen at college."

Well, though I knew the woman was an idle gossip, the words stuck in my head, and my heart sank lower than ever as I drove up to Brympton in the dusk. There *was* something about the house—I was sure of it now . . .

When I went in to tea I heard that Mr. Brympton had arrived, and I saw at a glance that there had been a disturbance of some kind. Mrs. Blinder's hand shook so that she could hardly pour the tea, and Mr. Wace quoted the most dreadful texts full of brimstone. Nobody said a word to me then, but when I went up to my room Mrs. Blinder followed me.

"Oh, my dear," says she, taking my hand, "I'm so glad and thankful you've come back to us!"

That struck me, as you may imagine. "Why," said I, "did you think I was leaving for good?"

"No, no, to be sure," said she, a little confused, "but I can't a-bear to have madam left alone for a day even." She pressed my hand hard, and, "Oh, Miss Hartley," says she, "be good to your mistress, as you're a Christian woman." And with that she hurried away, and left me staring.

A moment later Agnes called me to Mrs. Brympton. Hearing Mr. Brympton's voice in her room, I went round by the dressing-room, thinking I would lay out her dinner-gown before going in. The dressing-room is a large room with a window over the portico that looks toward the gardens. Mr. Brympton's apartments are beyond. When I went in, the door into the bedroom was ajar, and I heard Mr. Brympton saying angrily:—"One would suppose he was the only person fit for you to talk to."

"I don't have many visitors in winter," Mrs. Brympton answered quietly.

"You have *me!*" he flung at her, sneering.

"You are here so seldom," said she.

"Well—whose fault is that? You make the place about as lively as a family vault—"

With that I rattled the toilet-things, to give my mistress warning and she rose and called me in.

The two dined alone, as usual, and I knew by Mr. Wace's manner at supper that things must be going badly. He quoted the prophets something terrible, and worked on the kitchen-maid so that she declared she wouldn't go down alone to put the cold meat in the ice-box. I felt nervous myself, and after I had put my mistress to bed I was half-tempted to go down again and persuade Mrs. Blinder to sit up awhile over a game of cards. But I heard her door closing for the night, and so I went on to my own room. The rain had begun again, and the drip, drip, drip seemed to be dropping into my brain. I lay awake listening to it, and turning over what my friend in town had said. What puzzled me was that it was always the maids who left . . .

After a while I slept; but suddenly a loud noise wakened me. My bell had rung. I sat up, terrified by the unusual sound, which seemed to go on jangling through the darkness. My hands shook so that I couldn't find the matches. At length I struck a light and jumped out of bed. I began to think I must have been dreaming; but I looked at the bell against the wall, and there was the little hammer still quivering.

I was just beginning to huddle on my clothes when I heard another sound. This time it was the door of the locked room opposite mine softly opening and closing. I heard the sound distinctly, and it frightened me so that I stood stock still. Then I heard a footstep hurrying down the passage toward the main house. The floor being carpeted, the sound was very faint, but I was quite sure it was a woman's step. I turned cold with the thought of it, and for a minute or two I dursn't breathe or move. Then I came to my senses.

"Alice Hartley," says I to myself, "someone left that room just now and ran down the passage ahead of you. The idea isn't pleasant, but you may as well face it. Your mistress has rung for you, and to answer her bell you've got to go the way that other woman has gone."

Well—I did it. I never walked faster in my life, yet I thought I should never get to the end of the passage or reach Mrs. Brympton's room. On the way I heard nothing and saw nothing: all was dark and quiet as the grave. When I reached my mistress's door the silence was so deep that I began to think I must be dreaming, and was half-minded to turn back. Then a panic seized me, and I knocked.

There was no answer, and I knocked again, loudly. To my astonishment the door was opened by Mr. Brympton. He started back when he saw me, and in the light of my candle his face looked red and savage.

"*You!*" he said, in a queer voice. "*How many of you are there, in God's name?*"

At that I felt the ground give under me; but I said to myself that he had been drinking, and answered as steadily as I could: "May I go in, sir? Mrs. Brympton has rung for me."

"You may all go in, for what I care," says he, and, pushing by me, walked down the hall to his own bedroom. I looked after him as he went, and to my surprise I saw that he walked as straight as a sober man.

I found my mistress lying very weak and still, but she forced a smile when she saw me, and signed to me to pour out some drops for her. After that she lay without speaking, her breath coming quick, and her eyes closed. Suddenly she groped out with her hand, and "*Emma,*" says she, faintly.

"It's Hartley, madam," I said. "Do you want anything?"

She opened her eyes wide and gave me a startled look.

"I was dreaming," she said. "You may go, now, Hartley, and thank you kindly. I'm quite well again, you see." And she turned her face away from me.

III

There was no more sleep for me that night, and I was thankful when daylight came.

Soon afterward, Agnes called me to Mrs. Brympton. I was afraid she was ill again, for she seldom sent for me before nine, but I found her sitting up in bed, pale and drawn-looking, but quite herself.

"Hartley," says she quickly, "will you put on your things at once and go down to the village for me? I want this prescription made up—" here she hesitated a minute and blushed—"and I should like you to be back again before Mr. Brympton is up."

"Certainly, madam," I said.

"And—stay a moment—" she called me back as if an idea had just struck her—"while you're waiting for the mixture, you'll have time to go on to Mr. Ranford's with this note."

It was a two-mile walk to the village, and on my way I had time to turn things over in my mind. It struck me as peculiar that my mistress should wish the prescription made up without Mr. Brympton's knowledge; and, putting this together with the scene of the night before, and with much else that I had noticed and suspected, I began to wonder if the poor lady was weary of her life, and had come to the mad resolve of ending it. The idea took such hold on me that I reached the village on a run, and dropped breathless into a chair before the chemist's counter. The good man, who was just taking down his shutters, stared at me so hard that it brought me to myself.

"Mr. Limmel," I says, trying to speak indifferent, "will you run your eye over this, and tell me if it's quite right?"

He put on his spectacles and studied the prescription.

"Why, it's one of Dr. Walton's," says he. "What should be wrong with it?"

"Well—is it dangerous to take?"

"Dangerous—how do you mean?"

I could have shaken the man for his stupidity.

"I mean—if a person was to take too much of it—by mistake of course—" says I, my heart in my throat.

"Lord bless you, no. It's only lime-water.* You might feed it to a baby by the bottleful."

I gave a great sigh of relief, and hurried on to Mr. Ranford's. But on the way another thought struck me. If there was nothing to conceal about my visit to the chemist's, was it my other errand that Mrs. Brympton wished me to keep private? Somehow, that thought frightened me worse than the other. Yet the two gentlemen seemed fast friends, and I would have staked

---

* Lime-water was a diluted solution of calcium hydroxide, occasionally prescribed as a mild antacid or used as an astringent.

my head on my mistress's goodness. I felt ashamed of my suspicions, and concluded that I was still disturbed by the strange events of the night. I left the note at Mr. Ranford's—and, hurrying back to Brympton, slipped in by a side door without being seen, as I thought.

An hour later, however, as I was carrying in my mistress's breakfast, I was stopped in the hall by Mr. Brympton.

"What were you doing out so early?" he says, looking hard at me.

"Early—me, sir?" I said, in a tremble.

"Come, come," he says, an angry red spot coming out on his forehead, "didn't I see you scuttling home through the shrubbery an hour or more ago?"

I'm a truthful woman by nature, but at that a lie popped out ready-made. "No, sir, you didn't," said I, and looked straight back at him.

He shrugged his shoulders and gave a sullen laugh. "I suppose you think I was drunk last night?" he asked suddenly.

"No, sir, I don't," I answered, this time truthfully enough.

He turned away with another shrug. "A pretty notion my servants have of me!" I heard him mutter as he walked off.

Not till I had settled down to my afternoon's sewing did I realize how the events of the night had shaken me. I couldn't pass that locked door without a shiver. I knew I had heard someone come out of it, and walk down the passage ahead of me. I thought of speaking to Mrs. Blinder or to Mr. Wace, the only two in the house who appeared to have an inkling of what was going on, but I had a feeling that if I questioned them they would deny everything, and that I might learn more by holding my tongue and keeping my eyes open. The idea of spending another night opposite the locked room sickened me, and once I was seized with the notion of packing my trunk and taking the first train to town; but it wasn't in me to throw over a kind mistress in that manner, and I tried to go on with my sewing as if nothing had happened.

I hadn't worked ten minutes before the sewing-machine broke down. It was one I had found in the house, a good machine, but a trifle out of order: Mrs. Blinder said it had never been used since Emma Saxon's death. I stopped to see what was wrong, and as I was working at the machine a drawer which I had never been able to open slid forward and a photograph fell out. I picked it up and sat looking at it in a maze. It was a woman's likeness, and I knew I had seen the face somewhere—the eyes had an asking look that I had felt on me before. And suddenly I remembered the pale woman in the passage.

I stood up, cold all over, and ran out of the room. My heart seemed to be thumping in the top of my head, and I felt as if I should never get away from the look in those eyes. I went straight to Mrs. Blinder. She was taking her afternoon nap, and sat up with a jump when I came in.

"Mrs. Blinder," said I, "who is that?" And I held out the photograph.

She rubbed her eyes and stared.

"Why, Emma Saxon," says she. "Where did you find it?"

I looked hard at her for a minute. "Mrs. Blinder," I said, "I've seen that face before."

Mrs. Blinder got up and walked over to the looking-glass. "Dear me! I must have been asleep," she says. "My front is all over one ear.* And now do run along, Miss Hartley, dear, for I hear the clock striking four, and I must go down this very minute and put on the Virginia ham for Mr. Brympton's dinner."

IV

To all appearances, things went on as usual for a week or two. The only difference was that Mr. Brympton stayed on, instead of going off as he usually did, and that Mr. Ranford never showed himself. I heard Mr. Brympton remark on this one afternoon when he was sitting in my mistress's room before dinner.

"Where's Ranford?" says he. "He hasn't been near the house for a week. Does he keep away because I'm here?"

Mrs. Brympton spoke so low that I couldn't catch her answer.

"Well," he went on, "two's company and three's trumpery; I'm sorry to be in Ranford's way, and I suppose I shall have to take myself off again in a day or two and give him a show." And he laughed at his own joke.

---

* "Front" meant forehead in older usage—perhaps Mrs. Brympton is complaining that her bangs are not straight because of the way she slept?

The very next day, as it happened, Mr. Ranford called. The footman said the three were very merry over their tea in the library, and Mr. Brympton strolled down to the gate with Mr. Ranford when he left.

I have said that things went on as usual; and so they did with the rest of the household; but as for myself, I had never been the same since the night my bell had rung. Night after night I used to lie awake, listening for it to ring again, and for the door of the locked room to open stealthily. But the bell never rang, and I heard no sound across the passage. At last the silence began to be more dreadful to me than the most mysterious sounds. I felt that *someone* were cowering there, behind the locked door, watching and listening as I watched and listened, and I could almost have cried out, "Whoever you are, come out and let me see you face to face, but don't lurk there and spy on me in the darkness!"

Feeling as I did, you may wonder I didn't give warning. Once I very nearly did so; but at the last moment something held me back. Whether it was compassion for my mistress, who had grown more and more dependent on me, or unwillingness to try a new place, or some other feeling that I couldn't put a name to, I lingered on as if spell-bound, though every night was dreadful to me, and the days but little better.

For one thing, I didn't like Mrs. Brympton's looks. She had never been the same since that night, no more than I had. I thought she would brighten up after Mr. Brympton left, but though she seemed easier in her mind, her spirits didn't revive, nor her strength either. She had grown attached to me, and seemed to like to have me about; and Agnes told me one day that, since Emma Saxon's death, I was the only maid her mistress had taken to. This gave me a warm feeling for the poor lady, though after all there was little I could do to help her.

After Mr. Brympton's departure, Mr. Ranford took to coming again, though less often than formerly. I met him once or twice in the grounds, or in the village, and I couldn't but think there was a change in him too; but I set it down to my disordered fancy.

The weeks passed, and Mr. Brympton had now been a month absent. We heard he was cruising with a friend in the West Indies, and Mr. Wace said that was a long way off, but though you had the wings of a dove and went to the uttermost parts of the earth, you couldn't get away from the Almighty. Agnes said that as long as he stayed away from Brympton, the Almighty might have him and welcome; and this raised a laugh, though Mrs. Blinder tried to look shocked, and Mr. Wace said the bears would eat us.

We were all glad to hear that the West Indies were a long way off, and I remember that, in spite of Mr. Wace's solemn looks, we had a very merry dinner that day in the hall. I don't know if it was because of my being in better spirits, but I fancied Mrs. Brympton looked better too, and seemed more cheerful in her manner. She had been for a walk in the morning, and after luncheon she lay down in her room, and I read aloud to her. When she dismissed me I went to my own room feeling quite bright and happy, and for the first time in weeks walked past the locked door without thinking of it. As I sat down to my work I looked out and saw a few snow-flakes falling. The sight was pleasanter than the eternal rain, and I pictured to myself how pretty the bare gardens would look in their white mantle. It seemed to me as if the snow would cover up all the dreariness, indoors as well as out.

The fancy had hardly crossed my mind when I heard a step at my side. I looked up, thinking it was Agnes.

"Well, Agnes—" said I, and the words froze on my tongue; for there, in the door, stood Emma Saxon.

I don't know how long she stood there. I only know I couldn't stir or take my eyes from her. Afterward I was terribly frightened, but at the time it wasn't fear I felt, but something deeper and quieter. She looked at me long and long, and her face was just one dumb prayer to me—but how in the world was I to help her? Suddenly she turned, and I heard her walk down the passage. This time I wasn't afraid to follow—I felt that I must know what she wanted. I sprang up and ran out. She was at the other end of the passage, and I expected her to take the turn toward my mistress's room; but instead of that she pushed open the door that led to the backstairs. I followed her down the stairs, and across the passageway to the back door. The kitchen and hall were empty at that hour, the servants being off duty, except for the footman, who was in the pantry. At the door she stood still a moment, with another look at me; then she turned the handle, and stepped out. For a minute I hesitated. Where was she leading me to? The door had closed softly after her, and I opened it and looked out, half-expecting to find that she had disappeared. But I saw her a few yards off, hurrying across the court-yard to the path through the woods. Her figure looked black and lonely in the snow, and for a second my heart failed me and I thought of turning back. But all the while she was drawing me after her; and catching up an old shawl of Mrs. Blinder's I ran out into the open.

Emma Saxon was in the wood-path now. She walked on steadily, and I followed at the same pace, till we passed out of the gates and reached the high-road. Then she struck across the open fields to the village. By this time the ground was white, and as she climbed the slope of a bare hill ahead of me I noticed that she left no foot-prints behind her. At sight of that, my heart shrivelled up within me, and my knees were water. Somehow, it was worse here than indoors. She made the whole countryside seem lonely as the grave, with none but us two in it, and no help in the wide world.

Once I tried to go back; but she turned and looked at me, and it was as if she had dragged me with ropes. After that I followed her like a dog. We came to the village, and she led me through it, past the church and the blacksmith's shop, and down the lane to Mr. Ranford's. Mr. Ranford's house stands close to the road: a plain old-fashioned building, with a flagged path leading to the door between box-borders. The lane was deserted, and as I turned into it, I saw Emma Saxon pause under the old elm by the gate. And now another fear came over me. I saw that we had reached the end of our journey, and that it was my turn to act. All the way from Brympton I had been asking myself what she wanted of me, but I had followed in a trance, as it were, and not till I saw her stop at Mr. Ranford's gate did my brain begin to clear itself. It stood a little way off in the snow, my heart beating fit to strangle me, and my feet frozen to the ground; and she stood under the elm and watched me.

I knew well enough that she hadn't led me there for nothing. I felt there was something I ought to say or do—but how was I to guess what it was? I had never thought harm of my mistress and Mr. Ranford, but I was sure now that, from one cause or another, some dreadful thing hung over them. *She* knew what it was; she would tell me if she could; perhaps she would answer if I questioned her.

It turned me faint to think of speaking to her; but I plucked up heart and dragged myself across the few yards between us. As I did so, I heard the house-door open, and saw Mr. Ranford approaching. He looked handsome and cheerful, as my mistress had looked that morning, and at sight of him the blood began to flow again in my veins.

"Why, Hartley," said he, "what's the matter? I saw you coming down the lane just now, and came out to see if you had taken root in the snow." He stopped and stared at me. "What are you looking at?" he says.

I turned toward the elm as he spoke, and his eyes followed me; but there was no one there. The lane was empty as far as the eye could reach.

A sense of helplessness came over me. She was gone, and I had not been able to guess what she wanted. Her last look had pierced me to the marrow; and yet it had not told me! All at once, I felt more desolate than when she had stood there watching me. It seemed as if she had left me all alone to carry the weight of the secret I couldn't guess. The snow went round me in great circles, and the ground fell away from me. . . .

A drop of brandy and the warmth of Mr. Ranford's fire soon brought me to, and I insisted on being driven back at once to Brympton. It was nearly dark, and I was afraid my mistress might be wanting me. I explained to Mr. Ranford that I had been out for a walk and had been taken with a fit of giddiness as I passed his gate. This was true enough; yet I never felt more like a liar than when I said it.

When I dressed Mrs. Brympton for dinner she remarked on my pale looks and asked what ailed me. I told her I had a headache, and she said she would not require me again that evening, and advised me to go to bed.

It was a fact that I could scarcely keep on my feet; yet I had no fancy to spend a solitary evening in my room. I sat downstairs in the hall as long as I could hold my head up; but by nine I crept upstairs, too weary to care what happened if I could but get my head on a pillow. The rest of the household went to bed soon afterward; they kept early hours when the master was away, and before ten I heard Mrs. Blinder's door close, and Mr. Wace's soon after.

It was a very still night, earth and air all muffled in snow. Once in bed I felt easier, and lay quiet, listening to the strange noises that come out in a house after dark. Once I thought I heard a door open and close again below: it might have been the glass door that led to the gardens. I got up and peered out of the window; but it was in the dark of the moon, and nothing visible outside but the streaking of snow against the panes.

I went back to bed and must have dozed, for I jumped awake to the furious ringing of my bell. Before my head was clear I had sprung out of bed, and was dragging on my clothes. *It is going to happen now*, I heard myself saying; but what I meant I had no notion. My hands seemed to be covered with glue—I thought I should never get into my clothes. At last I opened my door and peered down the passage. As far as my candle-flame carried, I could see nothing unusual ahead of me. I hurried on, breathless; but as I pushed open the baize door leading to the main hall my heart stood still, for there at the head of the stairs was Emma Saxon, peering dreadfully down into the darkness.

For a second I couldn't stir; but my hand slipped from the door, and as it swung shut the figure vanished. At the same instant there came another sound from below stairs—a stealthy mysterious sound, as of a latch-key turning in the house-door. I ran to Mrs. Brympton's room and knocked.

There was no answer, and I knocked again. This time I heard some one moving in the room; the bolt slipped back and my mistress stood before me. To my surprise I saw that she had not undressed for the night. She gave me a startled look.

"What is this, Hartley?" she says in a whisper. "Are you ill? What are you doing here at this hour?"

"I am not ill, madam; but my bell rang."

At that she turned pale, and seemed about to fall.

"You are mistaken," she said harshly; "I didn't ring. You must have been dreaming." I had never heard her speak in such a tone. "Go back to bed," she said, closing the door on me.

But as she spoke I heard sounds again in the hall below: a man's step this time; and the truth leaped out on me.

"Madam," I said, pushing past her, "there is someone in the house—"

"Someone—?"

"Mr. Brympton, I think—I hear his step below—"

A dreadful look came over her, and without a word, she dropped flat at my feet. I fell on my knees and tried to lift her: by the way she breathed I saw it was no common faint. But as I raised her head there came quick steps on the stairs and across the hall: the door was flung open, and there stood

Mr. Brympton, in his travelling-clothes, the snow dripping from him. He drew back with a start as he saw me kneeling by my mistress.

"What the devil is this?" he shouted. He was less high-colored than usual, and the red spot came out on his forehead.

"Mrs. Brympton has fainted, sir," said I.

He laughed unsteadily and pushed by me. "It's a pity she didn't choose a more convenient moment. I'm sorry to disturb her, but—"

I raised myself up, aghast at the man's action.

"Sir," said I, "are you mad? What are you doing?"

"Going to meet a friend," said he, and seemed to make for the dressing-room.

At that my heart turned over. I don't know what I thought or feared; but I sprang up and caught him by the sleeve.

"Sir, sir," said I, "for pity's sake look at your wife!"

He shook me off furiously.

"It seems that's done for me," says he, and caught hold of the dressing-room door.

At that moment I heard a slight noise inside. Slight as it was, he heard it too, and tore the door open; but as he did so he dropped back. On the threshold stood Emma Saxon. All was dark behind her, but I saw her plainly, and so did he. He threw up his hands as if to hide his face from her; and when I looked again she was gone.

He stood motionless, as if the strength had run out of him; and in the stillness my mistress suddenly raised herself, and opening her eyes fixed a look on him. Then she fell back, and I saw the death-flutter pass over her. . . .

We buried her on the third day, in a driving snow-storm. There were few people in the church, for it was bad weather to come from town, and I've a notion my mistress was one that hadn't many near friends. Mr. Ranford was among the last to come, just before they carried her up the aisle. He was in black, of course, being such a friend of the family, and I never saw a gentleman so pale. As he passed me, I noticed that he leaned a trifle on a stick he carried; and I fancy Mr. Brympton noticed it too, for the red spot came out sharp on his forehead, and all through the service he kept staring across the church at Mr. Ranford, instead of following the prayers as a mourner should.

When it was over and we went out to the graveyard, Mr. Ranford had disappeared, and as soon as my poor mistress's body was underground, Mr. Brympton jumped into the carriage nearest the gate and drove off without a word to any of us. I heard him call out, "To the station," and we servants went back alone to the house.

A Ghost Story

by MARK TWAIN

*There is little that need be said about Samuel Clemens (1835–1910), who wrote as Mark Twain. America's greatest humorist and author of what many regard as The Great American Novel (*Adventures of Huckleberry Finn, *1884), Twain had little patience with the irrational and supernatural and what he regarded as "humbug," as is evident from the following (which first appeared in his collection* Sketches New and Old, *1875).*

I took a large room, far up Broadway, in a huge old building whose upper stories had been wholly unoccupied for years; until I came. The place had long been given up to dust and cobwebs, to solitude and silence. I seemed groping among the tombs and invading the privacy of the dead, that first night I climbed up to my quarters. For the first time in my life a superstitious dread came over me; and as I turned a dark angle of the stairway and an invisible cobweb swung its lazy woof in my face and clung there, I shuddered as one who had encountered a phantom.

I was glad enough when I reached my room and locked out the mould and darkness. A cheery fire was burning in the grate, and I sat down before it with a comforting sense of relief. For two hours I sat there, thinking of bygone times; recalling old scenes, and summoning half-forgotten faces out of the mists of the past; listening, in fancy, to voices that long ago grew silent for all time, and to once familiar songs that nobody sings now. And as my reverie softened down to a sadder and sadder pathos, the shrieking of the winds outside softened to a wail, the angry beating of the rain against the panes diminished to a tranquil patter, and one by one the noises in the street subsided, until the hurrying footsteps of the last belated straggler died away in the distance and left no sound behind.

The fire had burned low. A sense of loneliness crept over me. I arose and undressed, moving on tiptoe about the room, doing stealthily what I had to do, as if I were environed by sleeping enemies whose slumbers it would be fatal to break. I covered up in bed, and lay listening to the rain and wind and the faint creaking of distant shutters, till they lulled me to sleep.

I slept profoundly, but how long I do not know. All at once I found myself awake, and filled with a shuddering expectancy. All was still. All but my own heart—I could hear it beat. Presently the bedclothes began to slip away slowly toward the foot of the bed, as if some one were pulling them! I could not stir; I could not speak. Still the blankets slipped deliberately away, till my breast was uncovered. Then with a great effort I seized them and drew them over my head. I waited, listened, waited. Once more that steady pull began, and once more I lay torpid a century of dragging seconds till my breast was naked again. At last I roused my energies and snatched the covers back to their place and held them with a strong grip. I waited. By and by I felt a faint tug, and took a fresh grip. The tug strengthened to a steady strain—it grew stronger and stronger. My hold parted, and for the third time the blankets slid away. I groaned. An answering groan came from the foot of the bed! Beaded drops of sweat stood upon my forehead. I was more dead than alive. Presently I heard a heavy footstep in my room—the step of an elephant it seemed to me—it was not like anything human. But it was moving from me—there was relief in that. I heard it approach the door—pass out without moving bolt or lock—and wander away among the dismal corridors, straining the floors and joists till they creaked again as it passed—and then silence reigned once more.

When my excitement had calmed, I said to myself, "This is a dream—simply a hideous dream." And so I lay thinking it over until I convinced myself that it was a dream, and then a comforting laugh relaxed my lips and I was happy again. I got up and struck a light; and when I found the locks and bolts were just as I had left them, another soothing laugh welled in my heart and rippled from my lips. I took my pipe and lit it, and was just sitting down before the fire, when—down went the pipe out of my nerveless fingers, the blood forsook my cheeks, and my placid breathing was cut short with a gasp! In the ashes on the hearth, side by side with my own bare footprint, was another, so vast that in comparison, mine was but an infant's! Then I had had a visitor, and the elephant tread was explained.

I put out the light and returned to bed, palsied with fear. I lay a long time, peering into the darkness, and listening. Then I heard a grating noise overhead, like the dragging of a heavy body across the floor; then the throwing down of the body, and the shaking of my windows in response to the concussion. In distant parts of the building I heard the muffled slamming of doors. I heard, at intervals, stealthy footsteps creeping in and out among the corridors, and up and down the stairs. Sometimes these noises approached my door, hesitated, and went away again. I heard the clanking of chains faintly, in remote passages, and listened while the clanking grew nearer—while it wearily climbed the stairways, marking each move by the loose surplus of chain that fell with an accented rattle upon each succeeding step as the goblin that bore it advanced. I heard muttered sentences, half-uttered screams that seemed smothered violently; and the swish of invisible garments and the rush of invisible wings. Then I became conscious that my chamber was invaded—that I was not alone. I heard sighs and breathings about my bed, and mysterious whisperings. Three little spheres of phosphorescent light appeared on the ceiling directly over my head, clung and glowed there a moment, and then dropped—two of them upon my face and one upon the pillow. They spattered, liquidly, and felt warm. Intuition told me they had turned to gouts of blood as they fell—I needed no light to satisfy myself of that. Then I saw pallid faces, dimly luminous, and white uplifted hands, floating bodiless in the air—floating a moment and then disappearing. The whispering ceased, and the voices and the sounds, and a solemn stillness followed. I waited and listened. I felt that I must have light or die. I was weak with fear. I slowly raised myself toward a sitting posture, and my face came in contact with a clammy hand! All strength went from me apparently, and I fell back like a stricken invalid. Then I heard the rustle of a garment—it seemed to pass to the door and go out.

When everything was still once more, I crept out of bed, sick and feeble, and lit the gas with a hand that trembled as if it were aged with a hundred years. The light brought some little cheer to my spirits. I sat down and fell into a dreamy contemplation of that great footprint in the ashes. By and by its outlines began to waver and grow dim. I glanced up and the broad gas flame was slowly wilting away. In the same moment I heard that elephantine tread again. I noted its approach, nearer and nearer, along the musty halls, and dimmer and dimmer the light waned. The tread reached my very door and paused—the light had dwindled to a sickly blue, and all things about me were in a spectral twilight. The door did not open, and yet I felt a faint gust of air fan my cheek, and presently was conscious of a huge, cloudy presence before me. I watched it with fascinated eyes. A pale glow stole over the Thing; gradually its cloudy folds took shape—an arm appeared, then legs, then a body, and last a great sad face looked out of the vapour. Stripped of its filmy housings, naked, muscular and comely, the majestic Cardiff Giant* loomed above me!

All my misery vanished—for a child might know that no harm could come with that benignant countenance. My cheerful spirits returned at

---

* The Cardiff Giant was purportedly a "petrified man" uncovered on October 16, 1869, by workers in Cardiff, New York. The "giant" was in fact commissioned by George Hull, who buried it on the farm of his cousin William Newell. Newell exhibited the Cardiff Giant to the public, charging for admission to the farmyard. Later, Newell moved the artifact to Syracuse, New York, where the public exhibition continued. P.T. Barnum offered $50,000 to Newell for the find, and when Newell refused to sell it, he made a copy and displayed it to the public, claiming that his was the genuine Cardiff Giant. Hull had sold his interest to David Hannum, who sued Barnum for disparaging the genuineness of the original discovery. Hannum allegedly said of those taken in by Barnum's copy, "There's a sucker born every minute" (an aphorism later attributed to Barnum). The court ruled in 1870 that Hannum's claim could only be upheld if the Cardiff Giant himself testified and that Barnum's disparagement of Hannum's Giant as a fake was not actionable because *both* were fakes.

once, and in sympathy with them the gas turned up brightly again. Never a lone outcast was so glad to welcome company as I was to greet the friendly giant. I said:

"Why, is it nobody but you? Do you know, I have been scared to death for the last two or three hours? I am most honestly glad to see you. I wish I had a chair—Here, here, don't try to sit down in that thing!"

But it was too late. He was in before I could stop him, and down he went—I never saw a chair shivered so in my life.

"Stop, stop, you'll ruin ev—"

Too late again. There was another crash, and another chair was resolved into its original elements.

"Confound it, haven't you got any judgment at all? Do you want to ruin all the furniture on the place? Here, here, you petrified fool—"

But it was no use. Before I could arrest him he had sat down on the bed, and it was a melancholy ruin.

"Now what sort of a way is that to do? First you come lumbering about the place bringing a legion of vagabond goblins along with you to worry me to death, and then, when I overlook an indelicacy of costume which would not be tolerated anywhere by cultivated people except in a respectable theater, and not even there if the nudity were of your sex, you repay me by wrecking all the furniture you can find to sit down on. And why will you? You damage yourself as much as you do me. You have broken off the end of your spinal column, and littered up the floor with chips of your hands till the place looks like a marble yard. You ought to be ashamed of yourself—you are big enough to know better."

"Well, I will not break any more furniture. But what am I to do? I have not had a chance to sit down for a century." And the tears came into his eyes.

"Poor devil," I said, "I should not have been so harsh with you. And you are an orphan, too, no doubt. But sit down on the floor here—nothing else can stand your weight—and, besides, we cannot be sociable with you away up there above me; I want you down where I can perch on this high counting-house stool and gossip with you face to face."

So he sat down on the floor, and lit a pipe which I gave him, threw one of my red blankets over his shoulders, inverted my sitz-bath on his head, helmet fashion, and made himself picturesque and comfortable. Then he crossed his ankles, while I renewed the fire, and exposed the flat, honey-combed bottoms of his prodigious feet to the grateful warmth.

"What is the matter with the bottom of your feet and the back of your legs, that they are gouged up so?"

"Infernal chilblains—I caught them clear up to the back of my head, roosting out there under Newell's farm. But I love the place; I love it as one loves his old home. There is no peace for me like the peace I feel when I am there."

We talked along for half an hour, and then I noticed that he looked tired, and I spoke of it.

"Tired?" he said. "Well, I should think so. And now I will tell you all about it, since you have treated me so well. I am the spirit of the Petrified Man that lies across the street there in the museum. I am the ghost of the Cardiff Giant. I can have no rest, no peace, till they have given that poor body burial again. Now what was the most natural thing for me to do, to make men satisfy this wish? Terrify them into it!—haunt the place where the body lay! So I haunted the museum night after night. I got the other spirits to help me. But it did no good, for nobody ever came to the museum at midnight. Then it occurred to me to come over the way and haunt this place a little. I felt that if I ever got a hearing I must succeed, for I had the most efficient company that tradition could furnish. Night after night we have shivered around through these mildewed halls, dragging chains, groaning, whispering, tramping up and down stairs, till, to tell you the truth, I am almost worn out. But when I saw a light in your room to-night, I roused my energies again and went at it with a deal of the old freshness. But I am tired out—entirely fagged out. Give me, I beseech you, give me some hope!"

I lit off my perch in a burst of excitement, and exclaimed:

"This transcends everything! Everything that ever did occur—why, you poor blundering old fossil, you have had all your trouble for nothing—you have been haunting a plaster cast of yourself—the real Cardiff Giant is in Albany!

"Confound it, don't you know your own remains?"

I never saw such an eloquent look of shame, of pitiable humiliation, overspread a countenance before.

The Petrified Man rose slowly to his feet, and said: "Honestly, is that true?"

"As true as I am sitting here."

He took the pipe from his mouth and laid it on the mantle, then stood irresolute a moment (unconsciously, from old habit, thrusting his hands where his pantaloon pockets should have been, and meditatively dropping his chin on his breast), and finally said:

"Well—I never felt so absurd before. The Petrified Man has sold everything else and now the mean fraud has ended by selling his own ghost! My son, if there is any charity left in your heart for a poor friendless phantom like me, don't let this get out. Think how you would feel if you had made such an ass of yourself."

I heard his stately tramp die away, step by step down the stairs and out into the deserted street, and felt sorry that he had gone, poor fellow—and sorrier still that he had carried off my red blanket and my bathtub.

Oh, Whistle and I'll Come to You, My Lad

by M. R. JAMES

There is little doubt that Montague Rhodes James (1862–1934) nearly single-handedly restored the nineteenth-century ghost story to its pinnacle, by moving the adventures to a contemporary setting. He wrote dozens of "antiquarian" ghost stories, many featuring a scholar or antiquarian who experiences the supernatural. James wrote that he aimed to "put the reader into the position of saying to himself, 'If I'm not very careful, something of this kind may happen to me!'" It is difficult to choose among James's gems, but the following, which first appeared in his collection Ghost Stories of an Antiquary *(1904), is especially compelling.*

I suppose you will be getting away pretty soon, now Full Term is over, Professor," said a person not in the story to the Professor of Ontography,* soon after they had sat down next to each other at a feast in the hospitable hall of St James's College.

---

* James invented the term of "Ontography," although it has recently been used by philosophers to describe a branch of knowledge dealing with human response to the natural environment.

The Professor was young, neat, and precise in speech.

"Yes," he said; "my friends have been making me take up golf this term, and I mean to go to the East Coast—in point of fact to Burnstow*—(I dare say you know it) for a week or ten days, to improve my game. I hope to get off tomorrow."

"Oh, Parkins," said his neighbour on the other side, "if you are going to Burnstow, I wish you would look at the site of the Templars' preceptory,† and let me know if you think it would be any good to have a dig there in the summer."

It was, as you might suppose, a person of antiquarian pursuits who said this, but, since he merely appears in this prologue, there is no need to give his entitlements.

"Certainly," said Parkins, the Professor: "if you will describe to me whereabouts the site is, I will do my best to give you an idea of the lie of the land when I get back; or I could write to you about it, if you would tell me where you are likely to be."

"Don't trouble to do that, thanks. It's only that I'm thinking of taking my family in that direction in the Long, and it occurred to me that, as very few of the English preceptories have ever been properly planned, I might have an opportunity of doing something useful on off-days."

The Professor rather sniffed at the idea that planning out a preceptory could be described as useful. His neighbour continued:

"The site—I doubt if there is anything showing above ground—must be down quite close to the beach now. The sea has encroached tremendously, as you know, all along that bit of coast. I should think, from the map, that it must be about three-quarters of a mile from the Globe Inn, at the north end of the town. Where are you going to stay?"

"Well, at the Globe Inn, as a matter of fact," said Parkins; "I have engaged a room there. I couldn't get in anywhere else; most of the lodging-houses are shut up in winter, it seems; and, as it is, they tell me that the

---

* Although Burnstow is fictitious, James based it on the coastal Suffolk town of Felixstowe.

† A preceptory is a community of the Knights Templars, a Catholic military order that was active from 1119 to about 1312.

only room of any size I can have is really a double-bedded one, and that they haven't a corner in which to store the other bed, and so on. But I must have a fairly large room, for I am taking some books down, and mean to do a bit of work; and though I don't quite fancy having an empty bed—not to speak of two—in what I may call for the time being my study, I suppose I can manage to rough it for the short time I shall be there."

"Do you call having an extra bed in your room roughing it, Parkins?" said a bluff person opposite. "Look here, I shall come down and occupy it for a bit; it'll be company for you."

The Professor quivered, but managed to laugh in a courteous manner.

"By all means, Rogers; there's nothing I should like better. But I'm afraid you would find it rather dull; you don't play golf, do you?"

"No, thank Heaven!" said rude Mr. Rogers.

"Well, you see, when I'm not writing I shall most likely be out on the links, and that, as I say, would be rather dull for you, I'm afraid."

"Oh, I don't know! There's certain to be somebody I know in the place; but, of course, if you don't want me, speak the word, Parkins; I shan't be offended. Truth, as you always tell us, is never offensive."

Parkins was, indeed, scrupulously polite and strictly truthful. It is to be feared that Mr. Rogers sometimes practised upon his knowledge of these characteristics. In Parkins's breast there was a conflict now raging, which for a moment or two did not allow him to answer. That interval being over, he said:

"Well, if you want the exact truth, Rogers, I was considering whether the room I speak of would really be large enough to accommodate us both comfortably; and also whether (mind, I shouldn't have said this if you hadn't pressed me) you would not constitute something in the nature of a hindrance to my work."

Rogers laughed loudly.

"Well done, Parkins!" he said. "It's all right. I promise not to interrupt your work; don't you disturb yourself about that. No, I won't come if you don't want me; but I thought I should do so nicely to keep the ghosts off." Here he might have been seen to wink and to nudge his next neighbour. Parkins might also have been seen to become pink. "I beg pardon, Parkins," Rogers continued; "I oughtn't to have said that. I forgot you didn't like levity on these topics."

"Well," Parkins said, "as you have mentioned the matter, I freely own that I do not like careless talk about what you call ghosts. A man in my position," he went on, raising his voice a little, "cannot, I find, be too careful about appearing to sanction the current beliefs on such subjects. As you know, Rogers, or as you ought to know; for I think I have never concealed my views—"

"No, you certainly have not, old man," put in Rogers *sotto voce*.

"—I hold that any semblance, any appearance of concession to the view that such things might exist is equivalent to a renunciation of all that I hold most sacred. But I'm afraid I have not succeeded in securing your attention."

"Your undivided attention, was what Dr. Blimber actually said,"* Rogers interrupted, with every appearance of an earnest desire for accuracy. "But I beg your pardon, Parkins: I'm stopping you."

"No, not at all," said Parkins. "I don't remember Blimber; perhaps he was before my time. But I needn't go on. I'm sure you know what I mean."

"Yes, yes," said Rogers, rather hastily—"just so. We'll go into it fully at Burnstow, or somewhere."

In repeating the above dialogue I have tried to give the impression which it made on me, that Parkins was something of an old woman—rather henlike, perhaps, in his little ways; totally destitute, alas! of the sense of humour, but at the same time dauntless and sincere in his convictions, and a man deserving of the greatest respect. Whether or not the reader has gathered so much, that was the character which Parkins had.

On the following day Parkins did, as he had hoped, succeed in getting away from his college, and in arriving at Burnstow. He was made welcome at the Globe Inn, was safely installed in the large double-bedded room of which we have heard, and was able before retiring to rest to arrange his materials for work in apple-pie order upon a commodious table which occupied the outer end of the room, and was surrounded on three sides by windows looking out seaward; that is to say, the central window looked straight out to sea, and those on the left and right commanded prospects along the shore to the north and south respectively. On the south you saw the

---

* [Author's note] Mr. Rogers was wrong, *vide Dombey and Son*, chapter xii.

village of Burnstow. On the north no houses were to be seen, but only the beach and the low cliff backing it. Immediately in front was a strip—not considerable—of rough grass, dotted with old anchors, capstans, and so forth; then a broad path; then the beach. Whatever may have been the original distance between the Globe Inn and the sea, not more than sixty yards now separated them.

The rest of the population of the inn was, of course, a golfing one, and included few elements that call for a special description. The most conspicuous figure was, perhaps, that of an *ancien militaire*, secretary of a London club, and possessed of a voice of incredible strength, and of views of a pronouncedly Protestant type. These were apt to find utterance after his attendance upon the ministrations of the Vicar, an estimable man with inclinations towards a picturesque ritual, which he gallantly kept down as far as he could out of deference to East Anglian tradition.

Professor Parkins, one of whose principal characteristics was pluck, spent the greater part of the day following his arrival at Burnstow in what he had called improving his game, in company with this Colonel Wilson; and during the afternoon—whether the process of improvement were to blame or not, I am not sure—the Colonel's demeanour assumed a colouring so lurid that even Parkins jibbed at the thought of walking home with him from the links. He determined, after a short and furtive look at that bristling moustache and those incarnadined features, that it would be wiser to allow the influences of tea and tobacco to do what they could with the Colonel before the dinner-hour should render a meeting inevitable.

"I might walk home tonight along the beach," he reflected—"yes, and take a look—there will be light enough for that—at the ruins of which Disney was talking. I don't exactly know where they are, by the way; but I expect I can hardly help stumbling on them."

This he accomplished, I may say, in the most literal sense, for in picking his way from the links to the shingle beach his foot caught, partly in a gorse-root and partly in a biggish stone, and over he went. When he got up and surveyed his surroundings, he found himself in a patch of somewhat broken ground covered with small depressions and mounds. These latter, when he came to examine them, proved to be simply masses of flints embedded in mortar and grown over with turf. He must, he quite rightly concluded, be on the site of the preceptory he had promised to look at. It seemed not unlikely to reward the spade of the explorer; enough of the foundations was probably left at no great depth to throw a good deal of light on the general plan. He remembered vaguely that the Templars, to whom this site had belonged, were in the habit of building round churches, and he thought a particular series of the humps or mounds near him did appear to be arranged in something of a circular form. Few people can resist the temptation to try a little amateur research in a department quite outside their own, if only for the satisfaction of showing how successful they would have been had they only taken it up seriously. Our Professor, however, if he felt something of this mean desire, was also truly anxious to oblige Mr. Disney. So he paced with care the circular area he had noticed, and wrote down its rough dimensions in his pocket-book. Then he proceeded to examine an oblong eminence which lay east of the centre of the circle, and seemed to his thinking likely to be the base of a platform or altar. At one end of it, the northern, a patch of the turf was gone—removed by some boy or other creature *ferae naturae*. It might, he thought, be as well to probe the soil here for evidences of masonry, and he took out his knife and began scraping away the earth. And now followed another little discovery: a portion of soil fell inward as he scraped, and disclosed a small cavity. He lighted one match after another to help him to see of what nature the hole was, but the wind was too strong for them all. By tapping and scratching the sides with his knife, however, he was able to make out that it must be an artificial hole in masonry. It was rectangular, and the sides, top, and bottom, if not actually plastered, were smooth and regular. Of course it was empty. No! As he withdrew the knife he heard a metallic clink, and when he introduced his hand it met with a cylindrical object lying on the floor of the hole. Naturally enough, he picked it up, and when he brought it into the light, now fast fading, he could see that it, too, was of man's making—a metal tube about four inches long, and evidently of some considerable age.

By the time Parkins had made sure that there was nothing else in this odd receptacle, it was too late and too dark for him to think of undertaking any further search. What he had done had proved so unexpectedly interesting that he determined to sacrifice a little more of the daylight on the morrow to archaeology. The object which he now had safe in his pocket was bound to be of some slight value at least, he felt sure.

Bleak and solemn was the view on which he took a last look before starting homeward. A faint yellow light in the west showed the links, on which a few figures moving towards the club-house were still visible, the squat martello tower, the lights of Aldsey village, the pale ribbon of sands intersected at intervals by black wooden groynings,* the dim and murmuring sea. The wind was bitter from the north, but was at his back when he set out for the Globe. He quickly rattled and clashed through the shingle and gained the sand, upon which, but for the groynings which had to be got over every few yards, the going was both good and quiet. One last look behind, to measure the distance he had made since leaving the ruined Templars' church, showed him a prospect of company on his walk, in the shape of a rather indistinct personage, who seemed to be making great efforts to catch up with him, but made little, if any, progress. I mean that there was an appearance of running about his movements, but that the distance between him and Parkins did not seem materially to lessen. So, at least, Parkins thought, and decided that he almost certainly did not know him, and that it would be absurd to wait until he came up. For all that, company, he began to think, would really be very welcome on that lonely shore, if only you could choose your companion. In his unenlightened days he had read of meetings in such places which even now would hardly bear thinking of. He went on thinking of them, however, until he reached home, and particularly of one which catches most people's fancy at some time of their childhood. "Now I saw in my dream that Christian had gone but a very little way when he saw a foul fiend coming over the field to meet him."† "What should I do now," he thought, "if I looked back and caught sight of a black figure sharply defined against the yellow sky, and saw that it had horns and wings? I wonder whether I should stand or run for it. Luckily, the gentleman behind is not of that kind, and he seems to be about as far off now as when I saw him first. Well, at this rate, he won't

---

* Protective structures designed to keep a beach from washing away.

† Parkins remembers a line from John Bunyan's *A Pilgrim's Progress* (1678–84).

get his dinner as soon as I shall; and, dear me! it's within a quarter of an hour of the time now. I must run!"

Parkins had, in fact, very little time for dressing. When he met the Colonel at dinner, Peace—or as much of her as that gentleman could manage—reigned once more in the military bosom; nor was she put to flight in the hours of bridge that followed dinner, for Parkins was a more than respectable player. When, therefore, he retired towards twelve o'clock, he felt that he had spent his evening in quite a satisfactory way, and that, even for so long as a fortnight or three weeks, life at the Globe would be supportable under similar conditions—"especially," thought he, "if I go on improving my game."

As he went along the passages he met the boots* of the Globe, who stopped and said:

"Beg your pardon, sir, but as I was abrushing your coat just now there was something fell out of the pocket. I put it on your chest of drawers, sir, in your room, sir—a piece of a pipe or somethink of that, sir. Thank you, sir. You'll find it on your chest of drawers, sir—yes, sir. Good night, sir."

The speech served to remind Parkins of his little discovery of that afternoon. It was with some considerable curiosity that he turned it over by the light of his candles. It was of bronze, he now saw, and was shaped very much after the manner of the modern dog-whistle; in fact it was—yes, certainly it was—actually no more nor less than a whistle. He put it to his lips, but it was quite full of a fine, caked-up sand or earth, which would not yield to knocking, but must be loosened with a knife. Tidy as ever in his habits, Parkins cleared out the earth on to a piece of paper, and took the latter to the window to empty it out. The night was clear and bright, as he saw when he had opened the casement, and he stopped for an instant to look at the sea and note a belated wanderer stationed on the shore in front of the inn. Then he shut the window, a little surprised at the late hours people kept at Burnstow, and took his whistle to the light again. Why, surely there were marks on it, and not merely marks, but letters! A very little rubbing rendered the deeply-cut inscription quite legible, but the Professor had to confess, after some earnest thought, that the meaning of it was as obscure

---

* A hotel employee who cleans boots and carries luggage (in modern parlance, a bellboy).

to him as the writing on the wall to Belshazzar.* There were legends both on the front and on the back of the whistle. The one read thus:

FUR FLA
FLE BIS

The other:

✠QUIS EST ISTE QUI VENIT✠

"I ought to be able to make it out," he thought; "but I suppose I am a little rusty in my Latin. When I come to think of it, I don't believe I even know the word for a whistle. The long one does seem simple enough. It ought to mean: "Who is this who is coming?" Well, the best way to find out is evidently to whistle for him."

He blew tentatively and stopped suddenly, startled and yet pleased at the note he had elicited. It had a quality of infinite distance in it, and, soft as it was, he somehow felt it must be audible for miles round. It was a sound, too, that seemed to have the power (which many scents possess) of forming pictures in the brain. He saw quite clearly for a moment a vision of a wide, dark expanse at night, with a fresh wind blowing, and in the midst a lonely figure—how employed, he could not tell. Perhaps he would have seen more had not the picture been broken by the sudden surge of a gust of wind against his casement, so sudden that it made him look up, just in time to see the white glint of a seabird's wing somewhere outside the dark panes.

The sound of the whistle had so fascinated him that he could not help trying it once more, this time more boldly. The note was little, if at all, louder than before, and repetition broke the illusion—no picture followed, as he had half hoped it might. "But what is this? Goodness! what force the wind can get up in a few minutes! What a tremendous gust! There! I knew

---

* This story appears in the Book of Daniel, and tells of a feast conducted by King Belshazzar that's interrupted when a mysterious hand appears and writes strange words on a wall.

that window-fastening was no use! Ah! I thought so—both candles out. It is enough to tear the room to pieces."

The first thing was to get the window shut. While you might count twenty Parkins was struggling with the small casement, and felt almost as if he were pushing back a sturdy burglar, so strong was the pressure. It slackened all at once, and the window banged to and latched itself. Now to relight the candles and see what damage, if any, had been done. No, nothing seemed amiss; no glass even was broken in the casement. But the noise had evidently roused at least one member of the household: the Colonel was to be heard stumping in his stockinged feet on the floor above, and growling. Quickly as it had risen, the wind did not fall at once. On it went, moaning and rushing past the house, at times rising to a cry so desolate that, as Parkins disinterestedly said, it might have made fanciful people feel quite uncomfortable; even the unimaginative, he thought after a quarter of an hour, might be happier without it.

Whether it was the wind, or the excitement of golf, or of the researches in the preceptory that kept Parkins awake, he was not sure. Awake he remained, in any case, long enough to fancy (as I am afraid I often do myself under such conditions) that he was the victim of all manner of fatal disorders: he would lie counting the beats of his heart, convinced that it was going to stop work every moment, and would entertain grave suspicions of his lungs, brain, liver, etc.—suspicions which he was sure would be dispelled by the return of daylight, but which until then refused to be put aside. He found a little vicarious comfort in the idea that someone else was in the same boat. A near neighbour (in the darkness it was not easy to tell his direction) was tossing and rustling in his bed, too.

The next stage was that Parkins shut his eyes and determined to give sleep every chance. Here again over-excitement asserted itself in another form—that of making pictures. *Experto crede,** pictures do come to the closed eyes of one trying to sleep, and are often so little to his taste that he must open his eyes and disperse them.

Parkins's experience on this occasion was a very distressing one. He found that the picture which presented itself to him was continuous. When

---

* "Trust the expert . . ."

he opened his eyes, of course, it went; but when he shut them once more it framed itself afresh, and acted itself out again, neither quicker nor slower than before. What he saw was this:

A long stretch of shore—shingle edged by sand, and intersected at short intervals with black groynes running down to the water—a scene, in fact, so like that of his afternoon's walk that, in the absence of any landmark, it could not be distinguished therefrom. The light was obscure, conveying an impression of gathering storm, late winter evening, and slight cold rain. On this bleak stage at first no actor was visible. Then, in the distance, a bobbing black object appeared; a moment more, and it was a man running, jumping, clambering over the groynes, and every few seconds looking eagerly back. The nearer he came the more obvious it was that he was not only anxious, but even terribly frightened, though his face was not to be distinguished. He was, moreover, almost at the end of his strength. On he came; each successive obstacle seemed to cause him more difficulty than the last. "Will he get over this next one?" thought Parkins; "it seems a little higher than the others." Yes; half climbing, half throwing himself, he did get over, and fell all in a heap on the other side (the side nearest to the spectator). There, as if really unable to get up again, he remained crouching under the groyne, looking up in an attitude of painful anxiety.

So far no cause whatever for the fear of the runner had been shown; but now there began to be seen, far up the shore, a little flicker of something light-coloured moving to and fro with great swiftness and irregularity. Rapidly growing larger, it, too, declared itself as a figure in pale, fluttering draperies, ill-defined. There was something about its motion which made Parkins very unwilling to see it at close quarters. It would stop, raise arms, bow itself towards the sand, then run stooping across the beach to the water-edge and back again; and then, rising upright, once more continue its course forward at a speed that was startling and terrifying. The moment came when the pursuer was hovering about from left to right only a few yards beyond the groyne where the runner lay in hiding. After two or three ineffectual castings hither and thither it came to a stop, stood upright, with arms raised high, and then darted straight forward towards the groyne.

It was at this point that Parkins always failed in his resolution to keep his eyes shut. With many misgivings as to incipient failure of eyesight, overworked brain, excessive smoking, and so on, he finally resigned himself to light his candle, get out a book, and pass the night waking, rather than be tormented by this persistent panorama, which he saw clearly enough could only be a morbid reflection of his walk and his thoughts on that very day.

The scraping of match on box and the glare of light must have startled some creatures of the night—rats or what not—which he heard scurry across the floor from the side of his bed with much rustling. Dear, dear! the match is out! Fool that it is! But the second one burnt better, and a candle and book were duly procured, over which Parkins pored till sleep of a wholesome kind came upon him, and that in no long space. For about the first time in his orderly and prudent life he forgot to blow out the candle, and when he was called next morning at eight there was still a flicker in the socket and a sad mess of guttered grease on the top of the little table.

After breakfast he was in his room, putting the finishing touches to his golfing costume—fortune had again allotted the Colonel to him for a partner—when one of the maids came in.

"Oh, if you please," she said, "would you like any extra blankets on your bed, sir?"

"Ah! thank you," said Parkins. "Yes, I think I should like one. It seems likely to turn rather colder."

In a very short time the maid was back with the blanket.

"Which bed should I put it on, sir?" she asked.

"What? Why, that one—the one I slept in last night," he said, pointing to it.

"Oh yes! I beg your pardon, sir, but you seemed to have tried both of 'em; leastways, we had to make 'em both up this morning."

"Really? How very absurd!" said Parkins. "I certainly never touched the other, except to lay some things on it. Did it actually seem to have been slept in?"

"Oh yes, sir!" said the maid. "Why, all the things was crumpled and throwed about all ways, if you'll excuse me, sir—quite as if anyone 'adn't passed but a very poor night, sir."

"Dear me," said Parkins. "Well, I may have disordered it more than I thought when I unpacked my things. I'm very sorry to have given you the extra trouble, I'm sure. I expect a friend of mine soon, by the way—a gentleman from Cambridge—to come and occupy it for a night or two. That will be all right, I suppose, won't it?"

"Oh yes, to be sure, sir. Thank you, sir. It's no trouble, I'm sure," said the maid, and departed to giggle with her colleagues.

Parkins set forth, with a stern determination to improve his game.

I am glad to be able to report that he succeeded so far in this enterprise that the Colonel, who had been rather repining at the prospect of a second day's play in his company, became quite chatty as the morning advanced; and his voice boomed out over the flats, as certain also of our own minor poets have said, "like some great bourdon in a minster tower."*

"Extraordinary wind, that, we had last night," he said. "In my old home we should have said someone had been whistling for it."

"Should you, indeed!" said Perkins. "Is there a superstition of that kind still current in your part of the country?"

"I don't know about superstition," said the Colonel. "They believe in it all over Denmark and Norway, as well as on the Yorkshire coast; and my experience is, mind you, that there's generally something at the bottom of what these country-folk hold to, and have held to for generations. But it's your drive" (or whatever it might have been: the golfing reader will have to imagine appropriate digressions at the proper intervals).

When conversation was resumed, Parkins said, with a slight hesitancy:

"*A propos* of what you were saying just now, Colonel, I think I ought to tell you that my own views on such subjects are very strong. I am, in fact, a convinced disbeliever in what is called the 'supernatural.'"

"What!" said the Colonel, "do you mean to tell me you don't believe in second-sight, or ghosts, or anything of that kind?"

"In nothing whatever of that kind," returned Parkins firmly.

"Well," said the Colonel, "but it appears to me at that rate, sir, that you must be little better than a Sadducee."†

Parkins was on the point of answering that, in his opinion, the Sadducees were the most sensible persons he had ever read of in the Old Testament;

---

* A "bourdon" is the deepest-sounding and hence largest bell of a peal.

† The Sadducees were a Jewish sect that didn't believe in an afterlife or resurrection of the dead.

but feeling some doubt as to whether much mention of them was to be found in that work, he preferred to laugh the accusation off.

"Perhaps I am," he said; "but—Here, give me my cleek, boy!—Excuse me one moment, Colonel." A short interval. "Now, as to whistling for the wind, let me give you my theory about it. The laws which govern winds are really not at all perfectly known—to fisherfolk and such, of course, not known at all. A man or woman of eccentric habits, perhaps, or a stranger, is seen repeatedly on the beach at some unusual hour, and is heard whistling. Soon afterwards a violent wind rises; a man who could read the sky perfectly or who possessed a barometer could have foretold that it would. The simple people of a fishing-village have no barometers, and only a few rough rules for prophesying weather. What more natural than that the eccentric personage I postulated should be regarded as having raised the wind, or that he or she should clutch eagerly at the reputation of being able to do so? Now, take last night's wind: as it happens, I myself was whistling. I blew a whistle twice, and the wind seemed to come absolutely in answer to my call. If anyone had seen me—"

The audience had been a little restive under this harangue, and Parkins had, I fear, fallen somewhat into the tone of a lecturer; but at the last sentence the Colonel stopped.

"Whistling, were you?" he said. "And what sort of whistle did you use? Play this stroke first." Interval.

"About that whistle you were asking, Colonel. It's rather a curious one. I have it in my—No; I see I've left it in my room. As a matter of fact, I found it yesterday."

And then Parkins narrated the manner of his discovery of the whistle, upon hearing which the Colonel grunted, and opined that, in Parkins's place, he should himself be careful about using a thing that had belonged to a set of Papists, of whom, speaking generally, it might be affirmed that you never knew what they might not have been up to. From this topic he diverged to the enormities of the Vicar, who had given notice on the previous Sunday that Friday would be the Feast of St. Thomas the Apostle, and that there would be service at eleven o'clock in the church. This and other similar proceedings constituted in the Colonel's view a strong presumption that the Vicar was a concealed Papist, if not a Jesuit; and Parkins, who could not very readily follow the Colonel in this region, did not disagree with him. In fact, they got on so well together in the morning that there was not talk on either side of their separating after lunch.

Both continued to play well during the afternoon, or at least, well enough to make them forget everything else until the light began to fail them. Not until then did Parkins remember that he had meant to do some more investigating at the preceptory; but it was of no great importance, he reflected. One day was as good as another; he might as well go home with the Colonel.

As they turned the corner of the house, the Colonel was almost knocked down by a boy who rushed into him at the very top of his speed, and then, instead of running away, remained hanging on to him and panting. The first words of the warrior were naturally those of reproof and objurgation, but he very quickly discerned that the boy was almost speechless with fright. Inquiries were useless at first. When the boy got his breath he began to howl, and still clung to the Colonel's legs. He was at last detached, but continued to howl.

"What in the world is the matter with you? What have you been up to? What have you seen?" said the two men.

"Ow, I seen it wive at me out of the winder," wailed the boy, "and I don't like it."

"What window?" said the irritated Colonel. "Come pull yourself together, my boy."

"The front winder it was, at the 'otel," said the boy.

At this point Parkins was in favour of sending the boy home, but the Colonel refused; he wanted to get to the bottom of it, he said; it was most dangerous to give a boy such a fright as this one had had, and if it turned out that people had been playing jokes, they should suffer for it in some way. And by a series of questions he made out this story: The boy had been playing about on the grass in front of the Globe with some others; then they had gone home to their teas, and he was just going, when he happened to look up at the front winder and see it a-wiving at him. It seemed to be a figure of some sort, in white as far as he knew—couldn't see its face; but it wived at him, and it warn't a right thing—not to say not a right person. Was there a light in the room? No, he didn't think to look if there was a light. Which was the window? Was it the top one or the second one? The seckind one it was—the big winder what got two little uns at the sides.

"Very well, my boy," said the Colonel, after a few more questions. 'You run away home now. I expect it was some person trying to give you a start. Another time, like a brave English boy, you just throw a stone—well, no, not that exactly, but you go and speak to the waiter, or to Mr. Simpson, the landlord, and—yes—and say that I advised you to do so."

The boy's face expressed some of the doubt he felt as to the likelihood of Mr. Simpson's lending a favourable ear to his complaint, but the Colonel did not appear to perceive this, and went on:

"And here's a sixpence—no, I see it's a shilling—and you be off home, and don't think any more about it."

The youth hurried off with agitated thanks, and the Colonel and Parkins went round to the front of the Globe and reconnoitred. There was only one window answering to the description they had been hearing.

"Well, that's curious," said Parkins; "it's evidently my window the lad was talking about. Will you come up for a moment, Colonel Wilson? We ought to be able to see if anyone has been taking liberties in my room."

They were soon in the passage, and Parkins made as if to open the door. Then he stopped and felt in his pockets.

"This is more serious than I thought," was his next remark. "I remember now that before I started this morning I locked the door. It is locked now, and, what is more, here is the key." And he held it up. "Now," he went on, "if the servants are in the habit of going into one's room during the day when one is away, I can only say that—well, that I don't approve of it at all." Conscious of a somewhat weak climax, he busied himself in opening the door (which was indeed locked) and in lighting candles. "No," he said, "nothing seems disturbed."

"Except your bed," put in the Colonel.

"Excuse me, that isn't my bed," said Parkins. "I don't use that one. But it does look as if someone had been playing tricks with it."

It certainly did: the clothes were bundled up and twisted together in a most tortuous confusion. Parkins pondered.

"That must be it," he said at last. "I disordered the clothes last night in unpacking, and they haven't made it since. Perhaps they came in to make it, and that boy saw them through the window; and then they were called away and locked the door after them. Yes, I think that must be it."

"Well, ring and ask," said the Colonel, and this appealed to Parkins as practical.

The maid appeared, and, to make a long story short, deposed that she had made the bed in the morning when the gentleman was in the room, and hadn't been there since. No, she hadn't no other key. Mr Simpson, he kep' the keys; he'd be able to tell the gentleman if anyone had been up.

This was a puzzle. Investigation showed that nothing of value had been taken, and Parkins remembered the disposition of the small objects on tables and so forth well enough to be pretty sure that no pranks had been played with them. Mr. and Mrs. Simpson furthermore agreed that neither of them had given the duplicate key of the room to any person whatever during the day. Nor could Parkins, fair-minded man as he was, detect anything in the demeanour of master, mistress, or maid that indicated guilt. He was much more inclined to think that the boy had been imposing on the Colonel.

The latter was unwontedly silent and pensive at dinner and throughout the evening. When he bade goodnight to Parkins, he murmured in a gruff undertone:

"You know where I am if you want me during the night."

"Why, yes, thank you, Colonel Wilson, I think I do; but there isn't much prospect of my disturbing you, I hope. By the way," he added, "did I show you that old whistle I spoke of? I think not. Well, here it is."

The Colonel turned it over gingerly in the light of the candle.

"Can you make anything of the inscription?" asked Parkins, as he took it back.

"No, not in this light. What do you mean to do with it?"

"Oh, well, when I get back to Cambridge I shall submit it to some of the archaeologists there, and see what they think of it; and very likely, if they consider it worth having, I may present it to one of the museums."

"M!" said the Colonel. "Well, you may be right. All I know is that, if it were mine, I should chuck it straight into the sea. It's no use talking, I'm well aware, but I expect that with you it's a case of live and learn. I hope so, I'm sure, and I wish you a good night."

He turned away, leaving Parkins in act to speak at the bottom of the stair, and soon each was in his own bedroom.

By some unfortunate accident, there were neither blinds nor curtains to the windows of the Professor's room. The previous night he had thought little of this, but tonight there seemed every prospect of a bright moon rising to shine directly on his bed, and probably wake him later on. When he noticed this he was a good deal annoyed, but, with an ingenuity which I can only envy, he succeeded in rigging up, with the help of a railway-rug, some safety-pins, and a stick and umbrella, a screen which, if it only held together, would completely keep the moonlight off his bed. And shortly afterwards he was comfortably in that bed. When he had read a somewhat solid work long enough to produce a decided wish to sleep, he cast a drowsy glance round the room, blew out the candle, and fell back upon the pillow.

He must have slept soundly for an hour or more, when a sudden clatter shook him up in a most unwelcome manner. In a moment he realized what had happened: his carefully-constructed screen had given way, and a very bright frosty moon was shining directly on his face. This was highly annoying. Could he possibly get up and reconstruct the screen? or could he manage to sleep if he did not?

For some minutes he lay and pondered over all the possibilities; then he turned over sharply, and with his eyes open lay breathlessly listening. There had been a movement, he was sure, in the empty bed on the opposite side of the room. Tomorrow he would have it moved, for there must be rats or something playing about in it. It was quiet now. No! the commotion began again. There was a rustling and shaking: surely more than any rat could cause.

I can figure to myself something of the Professor's bewilderment and horror, for I have in a dream thirty years back seen the same thing happen; but the reader will hardly, perhaps, imagine how dreadful it was to him to see a figure suddenly sit up in what he had known was an empty bed. He was out of his own bed in one bound, and made a dash towards the window, where lay his only weapon, the stick with which he had propped his screen. This was, as it turned out, the worst thing he could have done, because the personage in the empty bed, with a sudden smooth motion, slipped from the bed and took up a position, with outspread arms, between the two beds, and in front of the door. Parkins watched it in a horrid perplexity. Somehow, the idea of getting past it and escaping through the door was intolerable to him; he could not have borne—he didn't know why—to touch it; and as for its touching him, he would sooner dash himself through the window than have that happen. It stood for the moment in a band of dark shadow, and he had not seen what its face was like. Now it began to move, in a stooping posture, and all at once the spectator realized, with some horror and some relief, that it must be blind, for it seemed to feel about it with its muffled arms in a groping and random fashion. Turning half away from him, it became suddenly conscious of the bed he had just left, and darted towards it, and bent and felt over the pillows in a way which made Parkins shudder as he had never in his life thought it possible. In a very few moments it seemed to know that the bed was empty, and then, moving forward into the area of light and facing the window, it showed for the first time what manner of thing it was.

Parkins, who very much dislikes being questioned about it, did once describe something of it in my hearing, and I gathered that what he chiefly remembers about it is a horrible, an intensely horrible, face of crumpled linen. What expression he read upon it he could not or would not tell, but that the fear of it went nigh to maddening him is certain.

But he was not at leisure to watch it for long. With formidable quickness it moved into the middle of the room, and, as it groped and waved, one corner of its draperies swept across Parkins's face. He could not, though he knew how perilous a sound was—he could not keep back a cry of disgust, and this gave the searcher an instant clue. It leapt towards him upon the instant, and the next moment he was half-way through the window backwards, uttering cry upon cry at the utmost pitch of his voice, and the linen face was thrust close into his own. At this, almost the last possible second, deliverance came, as you will have guessed: the Colonel burst the door open, and was just in time to see the dreadful group at the window. When he reached the figures only one was left. Parkins sank forward into the room in a faint, and before him on the floor lay a tumbled heap of bed-clothes.

Colonel Wilson asked no questions, but busied himself in keeping everyone else out of the room and in getting Parkins back to his bed; and himself, wrapped in a rug, occupied the other bed, for the rest of the night.

Early on the next day Rogers arrived, more welcome than he would have been a day before, and the three of them held a very long consultation in the Professor's room. At the end of it the Colonel left the hotel door carrying a small object between his finger and thumb, which he cast as far into the sea as a very brawny arm could send it. Later on the smoke of a burning ascended from the back premises of the Globe.

Exactly what explanation was patched up for the staff and visitors at the hotel I must confess I do not recollect. The Professor was somehow cleared of the ready suspicion of delirium tremens, and the hotel of the reputation of a troubled house.

There is not much question as to what would have happened to Parkins if the Colonel had not intervened when he did. He would either have fallen out of the window or else lost his wits. But it is not so evident what more the creature that came in answer to the whistle could have done than frighten. There seemed to be absolutely nothing material about it save the bedclothes of which it had made itself a body. The Colonel, who remembered a not very dissimilar occurrence in India,* was of the opinion that if Parkins had closed with it it could really have done very little, and that its one power was that of frightening. The whole thing, he said, served to confirm his opinion of the Church of Rome.

There is really nothing more to tell, but, as you may imagine, the Professor's views on certain points are less clear cut than they used to be. His nerves, too, have suffered: he cannot even now see a surplice hanging on a door quite unmoved, and the spectacle of a scarecrow in a field late on a winter afternoon has cost him more than one sleepless night.

---

* The Colonel undoubtedly served in the Raj; however, James may also be alluding here to Rudyard Kipling's "My Own True Ghost Story" (1888), which similarly presents a stay in an inn which is interrupted when a violent wind precedes the appearance of ghosts.

The Shell of Sense

by OLIVIA HOWARD DUNBAR

Olivia Howard Dunbar (1873–1953) was an American journalist and short-story writer, who wrote predominately ghost stories. She was also active in the women's suffrage movement. Dunbar was an early defender of the horror genre, especially in her 1905 essay, "The Decay of the Ghost in Fiction." The following, her best-known work, first appeared in Harpers Magazine *(Dec. 1908).*

I t was intolerably unchanged, the dim, dark-toned room. In an agony of recognition my glance ran from one to another of the comfortable, familiar things that my earthly life had been passed among. Incredibly distant from it all as I essentially was. I noted sharply that the very gaps that I myself had left in my bookshelves still stood unfilled; that the delicate fingers of the ferns that I had tended were still stretched futilely toward the light; that the soft agreeable chuckle of my own little clock, like some elderly woman with whom conversation has become automatic, was undiminished.

Unchanged—or so it seemed at first. But there were certain trivial differences that shortly smote me. The windows were closed too tightly; for I had always kept the house very cool, although I had known that Theresa preferred warm rooms. And my work-basket was in disorder; it was preposterous that so small a thing should hurt me so. Then, for this was my first experience of the shadow-folded transition, the odd alteration of my emotions bewildered me. For at one moment the place seemed so humanly familiar, so distinctly my own proper envelope, that for love of it I could have laid my cheek against the wall; while in the next I was miserably conscious of strange new shrillnesses. How could they be endured—and had I ever endured them?—those harsh influences that I now perceived at the window; light and color so blinding that they obscured the form of the wind, tumult so discordant that one could scarcely hear the roses open in the garden below?

But Theresa did not seem to mind any of these things. Disorder, it is true, the dear child had never minded. She was sitting all this time at my desk—at *my* desk—occupied, I could only too easily surmise how. In the light of my own habits of precision it was plain that that sombre correspondence should have been attended to before; but I believe that I did not really reproach Theresa, for I knew that her notes, when she did write them, were perhaps less perfunctory than mine. She finished the last one as I watched her, and added it to the heap of black-bordered envelopes that lay on the desk. Poor girl! I saw now that they had cost her tears. Yet, living beside her day after day, year after year, I had never discovered what deep tenderness my sister possessed. Toward each other it had been our habit to display only a temperate affection, and I remember having always thought it distinctly fortunate for Theresa, since she was denied my happiness, that she could live so easily and pleasantly without emotions of the devastating sort. . . . And now, for the first time, I was really to behold her. . . . Could it be Theresa, after all, this tangle of subdued turbulences? Let no one suppose that it is an easy thing to bear, the relentlessly lucid understanding that I then first exercised; or that, in its first enfranchisement, the timid vision does not yearn for its old screens and mists.

Suddenly, as Theresa sat there, her head, filled with its tender thoughts of me, held in her gentle hands, I felt Allan's step on the carpeted stair outside. Theresa felt it, too—but how? for it was not audible. She gave a start, swept the black envelopes out of sight, and pretended to be writing in a little book. Then I forgot to watch her any longer in my absorption in Allan's coming. It was he, of course, that I was awaiting. It was for him that I had made this first lonely, frightened effort to return, to recover. . . . It was not that I had supposed he would allow himself to recognize my presence, for I had long been sufficiently familiar with his hard and fast denials of the invisible. He was so reasonable always, so sane—so blindfolded. But I had hoped that because of his very rejection of the ether that now contained me* I could perhaps all the more safely, the more secretly, watch him, linger near him. He was near now, very near—but why did Theresa, sitting there in the room that had never belonged to her, appropriate for herself his coming? It was so manifestly I who had drawn him, I whom he had come to seek.

The door was ajar. He knocked softly at it "Are you there, Theresa?" he called. He expected to find her, then, there in my room? I shrank back, fearing, almost, to stay.

"I shall have finished in a moment," Theresa told him, and he sat down to wait for her.

No spirit still unreleased can understand the pang that I felt with Allan sitting almost within my touch. Almost irresistibly the wish beset me to let him for an instant feel my nearness. Then I checked myself, remembering—oh, absurd, piteous human fears!—that my too unguarded closeness might alarm him. It was not so remote a time that I myself had known them, those blind, uncouth timidities. I came, therefore, somewhat nearer—but I did not touch him. I merely leaned toward him and with incredible softness whispered his name. That much I could not have forborne; the spell of life was still too strong in me.

But it gave him no comfort, no delight. "Theresa!" he called, in a voice dreadful with alarm—and in that instant the last veil fell, and desperately, scarce believingly, I beheld how it stood between them, those two.

She turned to him that gentle look of hers.

---

* A common belief in Spiritualism is that an unseen "ether" fills the blank spaces in the universe and provides a dwelling place for spirits.

"Forgive me," came from him hoarsely. "But I had suddenly the most—unaccountable sensation. Can there be too many windows open? There is such a—chill—about."

"There are no windows open," Theresa assured him. "I took care to shut out the chill. You are not well, Allan!"

"Perhaps not." He embraced the suggestion. "And yet I feel no illness apart from this abominable sensation that persists—persists. . . . Theresa, you must tell me: do I fancy it, or do you, too, feel—something—strange here?"

"Oh, there is something very strange here," she half sobbed. "There always will be."

"Good heavens, child, I didn't mean that!" He rose and stood looking about him. "I know, of course, that you have your beliefs, and I respect them, but you know equally well that I have nothing of the sort! So—don't let us conjure up anything inexplicable."

I stayed impalpably, imponderably near him. Wretched and bereft though I was, I could not have left him while he stood denying me.

"What I mean," he went on, in his low, distinct voice, "is a special, an almost ominous sense of cold. Upon my soul, Theresa,"—he paused—"if I *were* superstitious, if I *were* a woman, I should probably imagine it to seem—a presence!"

He spoke the last word very faintly, but Theresa shrank from it nevertheless.

"*Don't* say that, Allan!" she cried out. "Don't think it, I beg of you! I've tried so hard myself not to think it—and you must help me. You know it is only perturbed, uneasy spirits that wander. With her it is quite different. She has always been so happy—she must still be."

I listened, stunned, to Theresa's sweet dogmatism. From what blind distances came her confident misapprehensions, how dense, both for her and for Allan, was the separating vapor!

Allan frowned. "Don't take me literally, Theresa," he explained; and I, who a moment before had almost touched him, now held myself aloof and heard him with a strange untried pity, new born in me. "I'm not speaking of what you call—spirits. It's something much more terrible." He allowed his head to sink heavily on his chest. "If I did not positively know that I had never done her any harm, I should suppose myself to be suffering from guilt, from remorse. . . . Theresa, you know better than I, perhaps. Was she content, always? Did she believe in me?"

"Believe in you?—when she knew you to be so good!—when you adored her!"

"She thought that? She said it? Then what in Heaven's name ails me?—unless it is all as you believe, Theresa, and she knows now what she didn't know then, poor dear, and minds ——"

"Minds what? What do you mean, Allan?"

I, who with my perhaps illegitimate advantage saw so clear, knew that he had not meant to tell her: I did him that justice, even in my first jealousy. If I had not tortured him so by clinging near him, he would not have told her. But the moment came, and overflowed, and he did tell her—passionate, tumultuous story that it was. During all our life together, Allan's and mine, he had spared me, had kept me wrapped in the white cloak of an unblemished loyalty. But it would have been kinder, I now bitterly thought, if, like many husbands, he had years ago found for the story he now poured forth some clandestine listener; I should not have known. But he was faithful and good, and so he waited till I, mute and chained, was there to hear him. So well did I know him, as I thought, so thoroughly had he once been mine, that I saw it in his eyes, heard it in his voice, before the words came. And yet, when it came, it lashed me with the whips of an unbearable humiliation. For I, his wife, had not known how greatly he could love.

And that Theresa, soft little traitor, should, in her still way, have cared too! Where was the iron in her, I moaned within my stricken spirit, where the steadfastness? From the moment he bade her, she turned her soft little petals up to him—and my last delusion was spent. It was intolerable; and none the less so that in another moment she had, prompted by some belated thought of me, renounced him. Allan was hers, yet she put him from her; and it was my part to watch them both.

Then in the anguish of it all I remembered, awkward, untutored spirit that I was, that I now had the Great Recourse. Whatever human things were unbearable, I had no need to bear. I ceased, therefore, to make the effort that kept me with them. The pitiless poignancy was dulled, the sounds and the light ceased, the lovers faded from me, and again I was mercifully drawn into the dim, infinite spaces.

There followed a period whose length I cannot measure and during which I was able to make no progress in the difficult, dizzying experience of release. "Earth-bound" my jealousy relentlessly kept me. Though my two dear ones had forsworn each other, I could not trust them, for theirs seemed to me an affectation of a more than mortal magnanimity. Without a ghostly sentinel to prick them with sharp fears and recollections, who could believe that they would keep to it? Of the efficacy of my own vigilance, so long as I might choose to exercise it, I could have no doubt, for I had by this time come to have a dreadful exultation in the new power that lived in me. Repeated delicate experiment had taught me how a touch or a breath, a wish or a whisper, could control Allan's acts, could keep him from Theresa. I could manifest myself as palely, as transiently, as a thought. I could produce the merest necessary flicker, like the shadow of a just-opened leaf, on his trembling, tortured consciousness. And these unrealized perceptions of me he interpreted, as I had known that he would, as his soul's inevitable penance. He had come to believe that he had done evil in silently loving Theresa all these years, and it was my vengeance to allow him to believe this, to prod him ever to believe it afresh.

I am conscious that this frame of mind was not continuous in me. For I remember, too, that when Allan and Theresa were safely apart and sufficiently miserable I loved them as dearly as I ever had, more dearly perhaps. For it was impossible that I should not perceive, in my new emancipation, that they were, each of them, something more and greater than the two beings I had once ignorantly pictured them. For years they had practiced a selflessness of which I could once scarcely have conceived, and which even now I could only admire without entering into its mystery. While I had lived solely for myself, these two divine creatures had lived exquisitely for me. They had granted me everything, themselves nothing. For my undeserving sake their lives had been a constant torment of renunciation—a torment they had not sought to alleviate by the exchange of a single glance of understanding. There were even marvelous moments when, from the depths of my newly informed heart, I pitied them—poor creatures, who, withheld from the infinite solaces that I had come to know, were still utterly within that

Shell of sense
So frail, so piteously contrived for pain.*

Within it, yes; yet exercising qualities that so sublimely transcended it. Yet the shy, hesitating compassion that thus had birth in me was far from being able to defeat the earlier, earthlier emotion. The two, I recognized, were in a sort of conflict; and I, regarding it, assumed that the conflict would never end; that for years, as Allan and Theresa reckoned time, I should be obliged to withhold myself from the great spaces and linger suffering, grudging, shamed, where they lingered.

It can never have been explained, I suppose, what, to devitalized perception such as mine, the contact of mortal beings with each other appears to be. Once to have exercised this sense-freed perception is to realize that the gift of prophecy, although the subject of such frequent marvel, is no longer mysterious. The merest glance of our sensitive and uncloyed vision can detect the strength of the relation between two beings, and therefore instantly calculate its duration. If you see a heavy weight suspended from a slender string, you can know, without any wizardry, that in a few moments the string will snap; well, such, if you admit the analogy, is prophecy, is foreknowledge. And it was thus that I saw it with Theresa and Allan. For it was perfectly visible to me that they would very little longer have the strength to preserve, near each other, the denuded impersonal relation that they, and that I, behind them, insisted on; and that they would have to separate. It was my sister, perhaps the more sensitive, who first realized this. It had now become possible for me to observe them almost constantly, the effort necessary to visit them had so greatly diminished; so that I watched her, poor, anguished girl, prepare to leave him. I saw each reluctant movement that she made. I saw her eyes, worn from self-searching; I heard her step grown timid from inexplicable fears; I entered her very heart and heard its pitiful, wild beating. And still I did not interfere.

---

* From William Vaughn Moody's play "The Masque of Judgment" (1900).

For at this time I had a wonderful, almost demoniacal sense of disposing of matters to suit my own selfish will. At any moment I could have checked their miseries, could have restored happiness and peace. Yet it gave me, and I could weep to admit it, a monstrous joy to know that Theresa thought she was leaving Allan of her own free intention, when it was I who was contriving, arranging, insisting. . . . And yet she wretchedly felt my presence near her; I am certain of that.

A few days before the time of her intended departure my sister told Allan that she must speak with him after dinner. Our beautiful old house branched out from a circular hall with great arched doors at either end; and it was through the rear doorway that always in summer, after dinner, we passed out into the garden adjoining. As usual, therefore, when the hour came, Theresa led the way. That dreadful daytime brilliance that in my present state I found so hard to endure was now becoming softer. A delicate, capricious twilight breeze danced inconsequently through languidly whispering leaves. Lovely pale flowers blossomed like little moons in the dusk, and over them the breath of mignonette hung heavily. It was a perfect place—and it had so long been ours, Allan's and mine. It made me restless and a little wicked that those two should be there together now.

For a little they walked about together, speaking of common, daily things. Then suddenly Theresa burst out:

"I am going away, Allan. I have stayed to do everything that needed to be done. Now your mother will be here to care for you, and it is time for me to go."

He stared at her and stood still. Theresa had been there so long, she so definitely, to his mind, belonged there. And she was, as I also had jealously known, so lovely there, the small, dark, dainty creature, in the old hall, on the wide staircases, in the garden. . . . Life there without Theresa, even the intentionally remote, the perpetually renounced Theresa—he had not dreamed of it, he could not, so suddenly, conceive of it.

"Sit here," he said, and drew her down beside him on a bench, "and tell me what it means, why you are going. Is it because of something that I have been—have done?"

She hesitated. I wondered if she would dare tell him. She looked out and away from him, and he waited long for her to speak.

The pale stars were sliding into their places. The whispering of the leaves was almost hushed. All about them it was still and shadowy and sweet. It was that wonderful moment when, for lack of a visible horizon, the not yet darkened world seems infinitely greater—a moment when anything can happen, anything be believed in. To me, watching, listening, hovering, there came a dreadful purpose and a dreadful courage. Suppose for one moment, Theresa should not only feel, but *see* me—would she dare to tell him then?

There came a brief space of terrible effort, all my fluttering, uncertain forces strained to the utmost. The instant of my struggle was endlessly long and the transition seemed to take place outside me—as one sitting in a train, motionless, sees the leagues of earth float by. And then, in a bright, terrible flash I knew I had achieved it—I had *attained visibility*. Shuddering, insubstantial, but luminously apparent, I stood there before them. And for the instant that I maintained the visible state I looked straight into Theresa's soul.

She gave a cry. And then, thing of silly, cruel impulses that I was, I saw what I had done. The very thing that I wished to avert I had precipitated. For Allan, in his sudden terror and pity, had bent and caught her in his arms. For the first time they were together; and it was I who had brought them.

Then, to his whispered urging to tell the reason of her cry, Theresa said:

"Frances was here. You did not see her, standing there, under the lilacs, with no smile on her face?"

"My dear, my dear!" was all that Allan said. I had so long now lived invisibly with them, he knew that she was right.

"I suppose you know what it means?" she asked him, calmly.

"Dear Theresa," Allan said, slowly, "if you and I should go away somewhere, could we not evade all this ghostliness? And will you come with me?"

"Distance would not banish her," my sister confidently asserted. And then she said, softly: "Have you thought what a lonely, awesome thing it must be to be so newly dead? Pity her, Allan. We who are warm and alive should pity her. She loves you still—that is the meaning of it all, you know—and she wants us to understand that for that reason we must keep apart. Oh, it was so plain in her white face as she stood there. And you did not see her?"

"It was your face that I saw," Allan solemnly told her—oh, how different he had grown from the Allan that I had known!—"and yours is the only face that I shall ever see." And again he drew her to him.

She sprang from him. "You are defying her, Allan!" she cried. "And you must not. It is her right to keep us apart, if she wishes. It must be as she insists. I shall go, as I told you. And, Allan, I beg of you, leave me the courage to do as she demands!"

They stood facing each other in the deep dusk, and the wounds that I had dealt them gaped red and accusing. "We must pity her," Theresa had said. And as I remembered that extraordinary speech, and saw the agony in her face, and the greater agony in Allan's, there came the great irreparable cleavage between mortality and me. In a swift, merciful flame the last of my mortal emotions—gross and tenacious they must have been—were consumed. My cold grasp of Allan loosened and a new unearthly love of him bloomed in my heart.

I was now, however, in a difficulty with which my experience in the newer state was scarcely sufficient to deal. How could I make it plain to Allan and Theresa that I wished to bring them together, to heal the wounds that I had made?

Pityingly, remorsefully, I lingered near them all that night and the next day. And by that time had brought myself to the point of a great determination. In the little time that was left, before Theresa should be gone and Allan bereft and desolate, I saw the one way that lay open to me to convince them of my acquiescence in their destiny.

In the deepest darkness and silence of the next night I made a greater effort than it will ever be necessary for me to make again. When they think of me, Allan and Theresa, I pray now that they will recall what I did that night, and that my thousand frustrations and selfishnesses may shrivel and be blown from their indulgent memories.

Yet the following morning, as she had planned, Theresa appeared at breakfast dressed for her journey. Above in her room there were the sounds of departure. They spoke little during the brief meal, but when it was ended Allan said:

"Theresa, there is half an hour before you go. Will you come upstairs with me? I had a dream that I must tell you of."

"Allan!" She looked at him, frightened, but went with him. "It was of Frances you dreamed," she said, quietly, as they entered the library together.

"Did I say it was a dream? But I was awake—thoroughly awake. I had not been sleeping well, and I heard, twice, the striking of the clock. And as I lay there, looking out at the stars, and thinking—thinking of you, Theresa—she came to me, stood there before me, in my room. It was no sheeted specter, you understand; it was Frances, literally she. In some inexplicable fashion I seemed to be aware that she wanted to make me know something, and I waited, watching her face. After a few moments it came. She did not speak, precisely. That is, I am sure I heard no sound. Yet the words that came from her were definite enough. She said: 'Don't let Theresa leave you. Take her and keep her.' Then she went away. Was that a dream?"

"I had not meant to tell you," Theresa eagerly answered, "but now I must. It is too wonderful. What time did your clock strike, Allan?"

"One, the last time."

"Yes; it was then that I awoke. And she had been with me. I had not seen her, but her arm had been about me and her kiss was on my cheek. Oh. I knew; it was unmistakable. And the sound of her voice was with me."

"Then she bade you, too—"

"Yes, to stay with you. I am glad we told each other." She smiled tearfully and began to fasten her wrap.

"But you are not going—*now!*" Allan cried. "You know that you cannot, now that she has asked you to stay."

"Then you believe, as I do, that it was she?" Theresa demanded.

"I can never understand, but I know," he answered her. "And now you will not go?"

I am freed. There will be no further semblance of me in my old home, no sound of my voice, no dimmest echo of my earthly self. They have no further need of me, the two that I have brought together. Theirs is the fullest joy that the dwellers in the shell of sense can know. Mine is the transcendent joy of the unseen spaces.

The Bowmen

by ARTHUR MACHEN

The Welshman Arthur Machen (1863–1947) was an influential writer and mystic. His story "The Great God Pan" (1894) is one of the cornerstones of "weird fiction," and "The White People" (1904) is a frequently-anthologized story of a young girl exploring witchcraft. H. P. Lovecraft wrote of him in 1927: "Of living creators of cosmic fear raised to its most artistic pitch, few if any can hope to equal the versatile Arthur Machen." The following, based on actual news reports, first appeared in The (London) Evening News *(Sep. 29, 1914).*

I

I t was during the Retreat of the Eighty Thousand,* and the authority of the Censorship is sufficient excuse for not being more explicit. But it was on the most awful day of that awful time, on the day when ruin and disaster came so near that their shadow fell over London far away; and, without any certain news, the hearts of men failed within them and

---

* The retreat of the British Expeditionary Forces from Mons to the Marne in August and September 1914.

grew faint; as if the agony of the army in the battlefield had entered into their souls.

On this dreadful day, then, when three hundred thousand men in arms with all their artillery swelled like a flood against the little English company, there was one point above all other points in our battle line that was for a time in awful danger, not merely of defeat, but of utter annihilation. With the permission of the Censorship and of the military expert, this corner may, perhaps, be described as a salient, and if this angle were crushed and broken, then the English force as a whole would be shattered, the Allied left would be turned, and Sedan would inevitably follow.*

All the morning the German guns had thundered and shrieked against this corner, and against the thousand or so of men who held it. The men joked at the shells, and found funny names for them, and had bets about them, and greeted them with scraps of music-hall songs. But the shells came on and burst, and tore good Englishmen limb from limb, and tore brother from brother, and as the heat of the day increased so did the fury of that terrific cannonade. There was no help, it seemed. The English artillery was good, but there was not nearly enough of it; it was being steadily battered into scrap iron.

II

There comes a moment in a storm at sea when people say to one another, "It is at its worst; it can blow no harder," and then there is a blast ten times more fierce than any before it. So it was in these British trenches.

There were no stouter hearts in the whole world than the hearts of these men; but even they were appalled as this seven-times-heated hell of the German cannonade fell upon them and overwhelmed them and destroyed them. And at this very moment they saw from their trenches that a tremendous host was moving against their lines. Five hundred of the thousand

---

* The Battle of Sedan, fought during the Franco-Prussian War on September 1 and 2, 1870, was the decisive battle of the war, a total victory for the Prussian forces; Sedan was also an important site in World War I, figuring prominently in the 1914 Battle of the Ardennes.

remained, and as far as they could see the German infantry was pressing on against them, column upon column, a gray world of men, ten thousand of them, as it appeared afterwards.

There was no hope at all. They shook hands, some of them. One man improvised a new version of the battle-song, "Good-by, good-by to Tipperary," ending with "And we shan't get there."* And they all went on firing steadily. The officer pointed out that such an opportunity for high-class fancy shooting might never occur again; the Tipperary humorist asked, "What price Sidney Street?"† And the few machine guns did their best. But everybody knew it was of no use. The dead gray bodies lay in companies and battalions, as others came on and on and on, and they swarmed and stirred, and advanced from beyond and beyond.

"World without end. Amen," said one of the British soldiers with some irrelevance as he took aim and fired. And then he remembered—he says he cannot think why or wherefore—a queer vegetarian restaurant in London where he had once or twice eaten eccentric dishes of cutlets made of lentils and nuts that pretended to be steak. On all the plates in this restaurant there was printed a figure of St. George in blue, with the motto, "*Adsit Anglis Sanctus Georgius*"—"May St. George be a present help to the English."‡ This soldier happened to know Latin and other useless things, and now, as he fired at his man in the gray advancing mass—three hundred yards away—he uttered the pious vegetarian motto. He went on firing to the end, and at last Bill on his right had to clout him cheerfully over the head to make him stop, pointing out as he did so that the King's ammunition

---

* "It's a Long Way to Tipperary" is a 1912 British music hall song written by Jack Judge and Harry Williams. It became an anthem for British soldiers longing for home. The chorus is, "It's a long way to Tipperary,/It's a long way to go./It's a long way to Tipperary,/To the sweetest girl I know!/Goodbye, Piccadilly, Farewell, Leicester Square!/It's a long long way to Tipperary,/But my heart's right there."

† The Siege of Sidney Street of January 1911, also known as the Battle of Stepney, was a gunfight in the East End of London between a combined police and army force and Latvian revolutionaries, the result of a bank robbery gone wrong. It was the first time in history that the English police required military assistance.

‡ St. George is the patron saint of England.

cost money and was not lightly to be wasted in drilling funny patterns into dead Germans.

III

For as the Latin scholar uttered his invocation he felt something between a shudder and an electric shock pass through his body. The roar of the battle died down in his ears to a gentle murmur; instead of it, he says, he heard a great voice and a shout louder than a thunder-peal crying, "Array, array, array!"

His heart grew hot as a burning coal, it grew cold as ice within him, as it seemed to him that a tumult of voices answered to his summons. He heard, or seemed to hear, thousands shouting: "St. George! St. George!"

"Ha! Messire, ha! sweet Saint, grant us good deliverance!"

"St. George for merry England!"

"Harow! Harow! Monseigneur St. George, succor us!"

"Ha! St. George! Ha! St. George! a long bow and a strong bow."

"Heaven's Knight, aid us!"

And as the soldier heard these voices he saw before him, beyond the trench, a long line of shapes, with a shining about them. They were like men who drew the bow, and with another shout, their cloud of arrows flew singing and tingling through the air towards the German hosts.

The other men in the trench were firing all the while. They had no hope; but they aimed just as if they had been shooting at Bisley.[*]

Suddenly one of them lifted up his voice in the plainest English.

"Gawd help us!" he bellowed to the man next to him, "but we're blooming marvels! Look at those gray . . . gentlemen, look at them! D'ye see them? They're not going down in dozens nor in 'undreds; it's thousands, it is. Look! look! there's a regiment gone while I'm talking to ye."

---

[*] The Bisley Ranges, near the Surrey town of Bisley, are the headquarters of the National Rifle Association of the United Kingdom, founded in 1859; the Ranges were first used for competitions in 1890.

IV

"Shut it!" the other soldier bellowed, taking aim, "what are ye gassing about?"

But he gulped with astonishment even as he spoke, for, indeed, the gray men were falling by the thousands. The English could hear the guttural scream of the German officers, the crackle of their revolvers as they shot the reluctant; and still line after line crashed to the earth.

All the while the Latin-bred soldier heard the cry:

"Harow! Harow! Monseigneur, dear Saint, quick to our aid! St. George help us!"

"High Chevalier, defend us!"

The singing arrows fled so swift and thick that they darkened the air, the heathen horde melted from before them.

"More machine guns!" Bill yelled to Tom.

"Don't hear them," Tom yelled back.

"But, thank God, anyway; they've got it in the neck."

In fact, there were ten thousand dead German soldiers left before that salient of the English army, and consequently there was no Sedan. In Germany, a country ruled by scientific principles, the Great General Staff decided that the contemptible English must have employed shells containing an unknown gas of a poisonous nature, as no wounds were discernible on the bodies of the dead German soldiers. But the man who knew what nuts tasted like when they called themselves steak* knew also that St. George had brought his Agincourt Bowmen† to help the English.

---

* This is a slang phrase, meaning someone who knows truth from falsity.

† The Battle of Agincourt (1415) was one of the most important fought during the Hundred Years War, and it was won by 5,000 English soldiers armed with powerful longbows, who fired 75,000 arrows in one minute.

The Substitute

by GEORGIA WOOD PANGBORN

Georgia Wood Pangborn (1872–1955) was an American novelist and short-story writer whose common themes were the supernatural. Her work clearly influenced her son Edgar Pangborn (1909–1976), a prolific writer himself of science-fiction and mysteries. The following, a haunting tale of the power of a mother's love, first appeared in Harpers Monthly *(Dec. 1914).*

The day's heat, for a time made endurable by a small breeze, had been weighed down toward evening by a thunderous humidity. Only along the line of the beach it was tolerable.

Miss Marston had sat so long over her coffee that the room was now in twilight, but she had intercepted by a fretful gesture the maid who would have turned on the light. Her dining-room windows overlooked the water. Fifty feet below she could see the blurred figures of people on the beach, and could hear their voices at intervals, among them the piping staccato of Mrs. Van Duyne's convalescent children, allowed to stay up and be active in the cool of the evening to atone for the languor of the afternoon. Now and then the fretful cry of an ailing baby overrode the other voices. But the babies that were sent to Mrs. Van Duyne always got well. That was her very wonderful business—making them well.

The heat was like a presence—a thing of definite substance that could be touched. Like a drug, too, making the senses strange, distorting distance and time. Although her eyes were upon the ocean, where the foam appeared and vanished dimly in long lines, lit only a little way out by the lights at the pier-head, it was the dark campus of her college town that Anna Marston's vision beheld, and the unsteady foam-crests of the waves were girls in white dresses, long rows of them coming and going within the obscurity of the trees.

"I am thirty-two," said Miss Marston aloud, and for that reason thought more keenly about when she was twenty-two. The same heavy air had folded in the evening of her Commencement Day, yet the girls had not seemed to mind.

"I suppose we had plenty of other things to think about," said she.

For a while she had gone about the campus with them, singing and laughing, and then, like this, had come to her window-seat to think; to decide, finally, not to marry Willis.

"And Mary Hannaford came in—Mary Hannaford—to show me her ring. I told her she was silly!"

Miss Marston moved restlessly.

Matters long ago forgotten will upon occasion freakishly insist upon remembrance, approaching suddenly, like the surprise of a familiar face in a crowded street. A dream plucks us by the sleeve, and we turn to see a childish countenance which has no more right than our own to inextinguishable youth. Or again, a word or a bar of music causes the barrier of years to fall as though it had never been, and we are in gardens that were dust years and years ago. Having once returned, these revenants keep us company for a while.

"I don't see why I should keep on thinking of Mary Hannaford," said Miss Marston, and went on thinking about Mary Hannaford—that perhaps she had not been silly, after all, but rather sensible to marry instead of keeping sulkily to something she called an "ideal," as Anna Marston had done.

"I wish—" said Miss Marston, vaguely, then frowned as the cry of the sick baby came up from the beach.

"Children—" said she; yet her tone, though troubled, was not exactly that of annoyance. Annoyance does not make the eyes wet.

She struck her clenched hand into her open palm, then lay back, drowsily inert in attitude, except that her underlip was caught between her teeth and her forehead was wrinkled with discontent.

She knew that the maids had slipped out for their walk on the beach. They had passed in their black-and-white, giggling, to the bluff stairs, and their squeals of joy at their release had reached her as soon as they were out of sight. She was alone, therefore. Yet she did not feel as if she were alone; not that there seemed to be another presence in the house, but the house itself had changed. Girls—so many!—went in light-footed haste through the halls. The room in which she sat was no longer a conventional dining-room. The walls, hidden in shadow, were garishly sprinkled with photographs and college pennants; the cushions of the window-seats were bright with college colors, and in a moment more Mary Hannaford would come in, wanting to talk under cover of the darkness about how happy she was, how fortunate above all other girls in the world. Mary Hannaford again!

Some one spoke her name. She sat up quickly and was aware of the indistinct pallor of a face.

It was by the voice, however, rather than by anything she saw that she recognized her visitor.

"Why, Mary Hannaford!" said she. "I haven't seen you for ten years! And I've been thinking of you all day."

The figure came forward swiftly and seated itself at the other end of the window-seat. Anna sank back, her sudden rousing having caused that odd vertigo which is common enough in times of great heat. She could not have said whether for an instant her hand touched that of her guest or not.

When the dizziness had passed, Mary was speaking. She sat with her knees drawn up and her hands clasped about them in the attitude Anna so well remembered.

"It's ever so long since I stopped being Mary Hannaford. I'm Mary Barclay, you know."

"Of course. You were the first of our set to go. How romantic we all felt about it! But you stopped writing after the babies came. All girls do. That's what turns us old maids so sour—at least, partly. But do tell me! Have you a cottage here? And how did you find me?"

Mary Barclay appeared to be looking down at the beach. She did not answer her friend's eager queries.

Anna Marston leaned forward and regarded her anxiously.

"Aren't you feeling fit? You seem so pale."

"Oh, quite!"

Anna reached toward the electric button, but Mary Barclay's hand intervened, protesting.

"We don't want lights, do we: Don't you remember how we always liked to talk in the dark like this?"

"Well," laughed Anna, "I'd just as soon you didn't see my wrinkles yet. *You* look just the same, except that you haven't any color, You had the reddest cheeks in the class,"

"And you didn't marry, after all," said Mary Barclay, slowly.

"No," admitted Anna, rather fretfully, "The right man wouldn't have me."

"That is like you. You'd never make a second choice. Not that I think it's wise of you."

From the beach the baby's cry rose again, weak, fretful, insistent. Anna Marston fidgeted.

"One of Mrs. Van Duyne's patients. Of course I know the children there are all right, but sometimes I wish they weren't quite so near. That's a marasmus baby* that came to-day. Its parents are very rich people. She's keeping the children on the beach late this evening for the coolness. Think," she broke out suddenly—"think what this day has been for the babies in the tenements! If it has been bad here, what must it have been there!"

"Yes," said Mary Barclay, "It is very bad in the city just now." She was looking steadily down toward the beach.

Anna waited for a moment, then asked timidly, "Aren't you going to tell me something about yourself and your family?"

---

* "Marasmus" is severe malnutrition caused by a protein deficiency and is usually the result of severe poverty or climatic conditions resulting in a lack of food. With "very rich parents," the child was either abused or suffered from viral, bacterial, or parasitic infection.

Ten years is a long time in which to know nothing of a friend—time enough for tragedies which will not bear discussing.

"Calvin died three years ago," said Mary Barclay, after a silence,

"I didn't know," said Anna, softly.

"Three years ago. Benny was a year old then. There—wasn't anything. We had been living on his salary. Death—we had forgotten there was such a thing. I found work. You know I had a sort of cleverness about clothes. I found fashion work that paid pretty well, only . . . they weren't very strong babies. They had to have the best, or—or they wouldn't stay, you know. Until now—they've stayed."

"They are well now, then?"

"They are well now."

Anna rose with an exclamation and walked up and down.

"Then I envy you. What a full life! Working—and for your own children. Lucky woman! In spite of your sorrow, lucky, lucky woman! Look at me. What good am I? I started out being my father's companion and secretary. It did very well for a time. Then he married again, and I took my mother's fortune and went my own way—clubs, municipal reform, every galvanic imitation of life I could find. I've been so desperate at times—"

"I know," said Mary Barclay.

"How can you know?"

Anna halted in her pacing to stare at her friend through the obscurity.

"That was partly why I came over here," said Mary Barclay, in an odd, still voice. "I had to come, anyway, to see my babies. I had to do that," she repeated.

"Your babies? At Mrs. Van Duyne's? But you said they were well now."

"Yes," said Mary Barclay, "She knows how to keep them well. The right air and food. There is so much to know. It isn't simple. If I'd tried to keep them in the city—" She shook her head. "Calvin and I always agreed that if we could only bring them safely through the first five years they would be as strong as anybody's children. Their brains are ahead of their bodies. But they aren't weaklings! If they had been—weaklings don't get anything out of life worth staying for. I—shouldn't have been able to come here to-night if they hadn't been worthwhile. But, you see, I know now—better than I did before—what they are."

She broke off with a cry, yet when Anna would have drawn her arms about her she evaded her like a mist.

"Envy me," moaned Mary Barclay, "but pity me, too!"

Recovering herself quickly, she leaned forward and spoke rapidly: "What becomes of children when fathers and mothers die? Sometimes things turn out all right, I know. It isn't always the same as when parent birds are shot and the nestlings starve. But sometimes it's like that. When there are no relatives to take them, and no money has been left for their support—

"What happens when a little girl is left without a mother to tell her about growing up? And then children are always so—themselves. One child is never like another, yet people who don't know try to treat them all alike.

"My little Martha! She never tells when her heart is broken or she has a pain and is really sick. She just gets cross, and you have to guess. She is apt to be rather naughty anyway. I've had to be patient—very. And, oh, such strange big thoughts as she thinks! And she can suffer, too! And then Benny; I suppose it was his sickness that—It was too much. Mrs. Van Duyne saved him. He was dying when I took him there. She saved him, but—I didn't take care of Martha right when Benny was sick, and so she began to be sick, too. What could I do? So I've let her have them. Anything less than the best wouldn't do, you see. I sold things—all I could—and went to work to earn money to pay her. Perhaps I worked a little too hard. I thought, I suppose, that so long as I was doing it for them nothing could beat me. Well, what's done is done. They laugh and have red cheeks. But—"

She rose and looked down at her friend, then out of the window.

"The nurses are bringing them in from the beach to go to bed. They are very sweet when they are going to bed. Shall we meet them?"

They stepped from the window to the porch, Mary Barclay going lightly ahead. Her dress, of some indefinite color which mingled with that of the sand, made her almost invisible.

There was a long flight of steps leading from the bluff down to the beach. From its summit the slow footsteps of the nurses and children and their mingled voices were audible before their heads came into sight.

One rather fat and sleepy voice counted the steps incorrectly: "One, two, free, seventeen, a hundred—I got up first!"

The pioneer appeared abruptly on all-fours—something of a wounded veteran by his bandaged head, but cheerful. Terrible warfare he had been through, coming out of it with flags flying and glory redounding to the surgeon first, but to Mrs. Van Duyne with even honor. He bore the proud title of Double Mastoid.* Death had been close at his heels; Pain unspeakable had held him very tight in her terrible arms for a long time. Silence had threatened, too: no more kind voices, no music—but all those ogres had been sent to the right-about, far away now from a fat little boy. Already he was forgetting that anything had been wrong.

"I got up quicker 'n anybody," he crowed.

Then appeared a white cap, somewhat awry, and strong, kerchiefed shoulders. A young face bent over a tiny sleeping creature on an air-cushion carried steadily and lightly. This was little Marasmus, the latest recruit, and his attendant.

Then came just a plain feeding-case, whose mother didn't dare take him back for fear that she and he would go and do the same wicked things over again just as soon as his Auntie Van Duyne's back was turned. He was sleeping like a cherub. Nothing whatever the matter with *him*! He was one of Mrs. Van Duyne's "Results," said to have been once the duplicate of little Marasmus, but now the kind of person that tired-eyed physicians wag their heads over gloatingly and poke in the ribs—*not* with a stethoscope—and call "Old Top" in a companionable way, as if they respected him for having done something rather fine all on his own responsibility. He had had about a year of it, and Mrs. Van Duyne was going to hang on to him as long as she could, for she had her own opinion of mothers. Often and often they had undone her fine work just as she had everything going nicely. They never knew anything whatever of their children's inwardness; clothes and hair were as far as they could go. She had all that wonderful hidden territory mapped out. She didn't believe in raw milk very much, for one thing, and she did believe in a few other things which—well, she got results, anyway. Look at "Old Top"!

After him came two children, hand-in-hand; and these, Anna knew at once, were Mary's two. She would have known even without the long

---

* Mastoiditis is the result of an uncontrolled middle-ear infection, often resulting in air pockets inside the skull.

trembling sigh that breathed past her ear. The little girl looked so like Mary! She was about six, Anna judged, and her hair was twisted in a little knob on top of her head for coolness' sake—a fashion of hair-dressing for very little girls which, more than another, perhaps, brings a lump into the throat. Is it because of its sweet caricature of maturity, as though both the promise and the menace of the years were revealed in those lines? Or is it that the curve of the back of the neck shown in this way is so lovely that it has a spiritual significance, like the odor of the first grass in spring or the color of evening sky through trees?

She walked with a rather conceited air, her gait indicating a lofty scorn of the Double Mastoid's claim to be a pioneer, She made it very evident that *she* could come up one foot after another, just like all other grown-ups, and she did it with a swagger, to render as obvious as possible her superiority in age, strength, and wisdom over the little boy at her side, who could do no better than one step at a time, and even so had to touch his hand to the tread now and then.

They were thin children, but thin like elves—not with the sadness and languor of sickness. And their faces in the twilight had a lambent quality, their eyes a liquid brightness. One felt that if the whim took them they might easily thrust forth gauzy wings and suddenly sail away with other night creatures.

In their conversation there was a pleasing breadth of impossibility that showed them to be as yet little acquainted with the restrictions of mortal life; "I'm going to be an engineer when I grow up," stated the boy, "but I'm not going to be a man. I'm going to be a mother. My name isn't Benny."

"What is your name?" the girl asked, without surprise,

"I'm Nelly."

"Well, then, I won't be Martha, I'll be Rosie, and you're my little sister." She was in a kindly mood, which might not last. Only so long as the current of her dream flowed smoothly would Martha be good. The interruption came quickly.

"No, I'm your *big* sister. I'm not little at all. Auntie Van Duyne says I'm getting bigger every day."

"All right, then; I sha'n't play with you," quoth Martha, crisply, and stalked ahead; as naughty as her mother had described. And then Anna saw Mary, who had silently left her side, stoop over and apparently whisper softly to the cross little face surmounted by its wisp of topknot. Martha stopped, finger in mouth, to kick the sand with her toe and look with sidelong friendliness at Benny as he arrived, panting. Then they went on, once more in amity, their short arms stretched about each other's waists. And the mother kept beside them, still whispering in their ears and kissing them. Yet—they did not turn to her or answer.

"I hope mother'll bring us some paints," Martha was saying as they passed beyond hearing.

"If she does, I'll make her a picture of an engine," Benny joyfully planned.

"Mary!" called Anna. She was surprised to feel that she was trembling, not that she was in any way afraid. She could not have said what had so shaken her. No longer seeing her friend, she laughed and said aloud, "Oh, she must have gone into the house ahead of them."

A slower step was now coming up the bluff stairs, and there appeared a figure in professional white, strong and purposeful, but for the moment rather weary and thoughtful.

Miss Marston stepped forward.

"Good evening, Mrs. Van Duyne. I was coming over to see the Barclay children."

The troubled face was crossed by a flash of joyful surprise and relief.

"Oh, do you know them? I'm so thankful. I wish I'd known before. I've been nearly frantic. Of course, then, you know—"

She took a twist of yellow paper from her belt and handed it to Anna Marston, who did not open it, but trembled very much as she looked at Mrs. Van Duyne, in whose fine, wise eyes the tears glittered and brimmed over, unheeded.

Tears were something which in Mrs. Van Duyne's code were a matter to be disregarded, like any other physical weakness in a person who never allowed herself to be sick,

"I haven't told them, of course. I shall put it off—as long as I possibly can. She worked herself to death—" She broke off with a burst of that kindly anger to which the very good and just are so easily stirred. "Her heart wasn't strong, and the heat finished her. The telegram came this afternoon.

I can't tell you how glad I am to find out you are her friend. So far as I can make out she had no relatives. I"—she spread out her hands with a sort of desperation—"I do what I can."

Anna had heard tales enough to know that "what I can" meant an amazing amount of work without return in money, that it meant great kindliness, of which advantage was often taken by weak and selfish people. Not that Mrs. Van Duyne ever told. Nevertheless, it had got about that one of the babies had never paid its board since it was a month old, yet you could not have guessed which was the delinquent by any difference between its care and that of "Old Top" or little Marasmus, for example, whose parents came and went in limousines loaded down with all sorts of expensive, foolish toys, whose wardrobes were all silken-fine, and who, when they grew up, would be very high and mighty folk indeed. Old Top, certainly; Marasmus, in all probability—though that was going to be pretty brisk and delicate work for a while.

"Since you are a friend," went on Mrs. Van Duyne, "perhaps you can tell me what to do. I'm not talking about the immediate present. They—well, they are here, and they are dear children, though that little Martha is certainly a handful." She half laughed through her tears. "But there is so much future. . . . What about the years and years?"

Anna Marston was still shaking as though through the heat an icy wind had blown upon her. Once more she was aware of Mary Barclay—vividly aware—but this time it was not with her physical eyes that she seemed to see her. There was no further illusion—if it had been illusion—of that indistinct figure bending above those little, unconscious heads, touching them, kissing them, enveloping them, like a bird hovering over its nest.

Instead there was, as it were, an inward vision. She and Mary Barclay were again face to face, but it was not in any way a pitiful entreaty for charity which she read in her friend's eyes. Rather it was a command.

"Dear Mrs. Van Duyne," said Anna, trying to bring her voice under control, "Mary Barclay knows that I am ready to take her place. She knows I—I want them—both of them—more than anything else in the world."

The first sigh of the coming coolness breathed past them from the sea. It was like the long breath of one who, after great restlessness, turns at last to sleep.

Acknowledgments

From Les: What a joy to rediscover the chills of ghost stories! As usual, this book is the product of many hands. First and foremost, it is a thrill to co-edit a book with my longtime pal Lisa Morton, whose work I have long admired. I hope that this will be but the first of many collaborations! Many thanks to my agent Don Maass, who is always supportive of even my wildest ideas. Claiborne Hancock and the rest of the Pegasus team—Maria Fernandez and Sabrina Plomitallo-González in particular—lavished it with care and attention. I'm always grateful to my writer-friends, Laurie R. King, Neil Gaiman, Nicholas Meyer, Cornelia Funke, and especially Peter Straub, from whom we shamelessly stole the title. Sherlockian pals Mike Whelan, Steve Rothman, Andy Peck, and Jerry Margolin are constant cheerleaders. My family is always understanding of my disappearances as I indulge in research and writing. Finally, without my wife Sharon, none of my writing would ever see the light. She has always been, and remains, "the woman."

From Lisa: It was a long-held dream to work with my friend Les, and I couldn't be happier with or more grateful for the experience. Among those who helped make it possible: Donald Maass; Claiborne Hancock, Maria Fernandez, Sabrina Plomitallo-González and the rest of the wonderful Pegasus crew; the Iliad Bookshop in North Hollywood, CA; and my ever-tolerant and supportive s.o. Ricky Grove. But I must save my ultimate thanks for the authors, all ghosts themselves now, who created the beautiful and chilling work we used for this book.